"What do you think you're doing, shooting without knowing what you're shooting at? You might have killed me."

The man smiled good-naturedly but the smile did not touch the pale green eyes. "No danger of that, Miss O'Brien. I always hit my target. You might say I was in a bit of a rush to catch your attention."

"Well, you certainly did that," I said grimly. "Now do you mind telling me why?"

He stepped around me warily, motioning the dogs back with one wave of his hand. Then, taking a long stick, he brushed aside the matted leaves directly on the ground before me, exposing a shallow, wide hole.

It was not the pit, though, that brought a sharp cry of revulsion to my lips. It was the gleaming saw-tooth metal jaws of a trap that waited, like a gaping, obscene mouth, at the bottom of the pit. Waiting, perhaps, for me. . . .

ABBEY COURT

Marcella Thum

A FAWCETT CREST BOOK

Fawcett Books, Greenwich, Connecticut

To Verna and John

ABBEY COURT

THIS BOOK CONTAINS THE COMPLETE TEXT OF THE
ORIGINAL HARDCOVER EDITION.

A Fawcett Crest Book reprinted by arrangement with
Doubleday and Company, Inc.

Copyright © 1976 by Marcella Thum
ALL RIGHTS RESERVED

ISBN: 0-449-23396-0

Printed in the United States of America

10   9   8   7   6   5   4   3   2   1

1

It snowed the day my mother died, a spring snow which caught unawares the early-blooming forsythia and daffodils in our brick-walled Beacon Hill garden. Standing at the window of my mother's bedroom, I watched the feathery flakes turn graceful arches of gold into mounds of white, daffodils into startled yellow stars embroidered on a white, woolly blanket. But not for long. By tomorrow, I knew, the smoke and soot from Boston's chimney pots would change that lovely pristine whiteness into an ugly, grimy gray, the snowy streets into black slush underfoot.

The heat in the bedroom was oppressive. Leaning my forehead against the cool windowpane, I thought longingly of the winters I had known as a young girl in Colorado. I could close my eyes and see the great blinding snowdrifts, pure enough to be melted for drinking water, I could smell the pine trees and the mountain air, crystal clear, heady as chilled wine if breathed too deeply.

Unbidden the thought flashed bitterly through my mind: if only Mother had listened to Jamie. If only we had never left Denver, perhaps she wouldn't be lying in her bed now, Father McCully patiently trying to understand the garbled sounds that came from her throat as she struggled to make her last confession.

Wearily I set the thought aside. There was no reason to believe that the stroke that had felled Fiona, leaving her virtually speechless, her right arm and side paralyzed, couldn't have happened as easily in Denver as in Boston. In fact, those early hard days in Colorado where she had gone in 1859 with my father, Jamie, one young child in tow, myself on the way, had contributed, no doubt, to her later ill-health. Life in a primitive, brawling mining camp was backbreaking enough for a man, much more so for a woman, even one as strong-willed and iron-spined as Fiona O'Brien.

Behind me, the murmuring voices had ceased. The confession must have ended, I realized, and when I turned I saw that the two young Irish parlormaids and Sara Mulhaven, our cook, had already silently entered the room. Quickly I joined them at the bedside for the remainder of the last rites.

Against the pillows my mother's face, one side jerked upward in a grotesque half grimace, was dreadfully still, the blue-veined eyelids closed. I felt a stab of fear. Had the effort of making the confession been too much for her? Was she already gone?

Suddenly I was remembering Denver again, and that other, terrible time, the day my father's friends had carried him home, Jamie's shirt blackened with gunpowder, soaked red with blood. Just as today a priest had been hastily summoned. Jamie's life, though, had gushed from that terrible, gaping hole in his chest before the priest had arrived. Was it too late for my mother too?

Then Father McCully bent over the still, small figure on the bed, administering the last communion. Thankfully I saw Fiona's lips part to receive the Host. The sacrament of extreme unction began, the sprinkling of the holy water, the prayers, and finally the anointing. As the priest made a cross with the blessed oil at the eyelids, the ears, the nostrils, the mouth, and the hands, he prayed for forgiveness for the sins Fiona O'Brien had committed with the cooperation of each of the senses.

Listening, an unchristian resentment surged through me. Of what terrible sins could my mother have been guilty—left an orphan in Ireland at an early age, fleeing a nightmare of fever and famine as a young woman, married to a man who, despite his adoration, was more a third child than a husband, then spending the rest of her life working and scheming to make sure that Patrick and I had a better life than she had had. Whatever sins Fiona might have committed were for her family's sake, never her own.

I lifted my eyes and saw that Father McCully was watching me sternly and, guiltily, I once again bowed my head. Finally, after a brief litany and another prayer, it was over.

Our Protestant housekeeper, Mrs. Johnson, opened the door, then stepped quietly into the room. Casting a sidelong, uncertain glance at the priest, she whispered, "Dr. Allen is here. May I show him in now?"

I looked at Father McCully, who removed his stole, kissed it before folding it carefully, then stepped back, motioning us to rise. The servants left hastily, Mrs. Mulhaven, who had worked longer for Mother than any of the others, wiping her eyes on her apron. "Tell the doctor to come in, Mrs. Johnson," I said, following the priest out into the hallway.

"Thank you for coming so quickly, Father. Would you like some coffee or perhaps a sherry?"

He shook his head, regarding me somberly. I felt ill at ease beneath his gaze, remembering that neither Mother nor I was the most faithful of worshipers in Father McCully's parish. Fiona, of course, had made sure that her children were baptized in the Catholic faith, but it wasn't until Jamie made his strike and we moved to Denver that we were able to attend mass with any regularity. Then Jamie died and Mother and I moved back east, and although not for anything in the world would my mother have denied her faith, still she did not flaunt it either. Fiona was well aware that to be both Irish *and* Catholic in Boston almost automatically closed off any chance of being accepted into the rigidly controlled society of the city.

"I must be going," Father McCully said. "I promised the Mulligans I'd stop by. Mrs. Mulligan and the children are down with a fever." Then, his voice softening, "Your mother tried to make a good confession, my child. I sensed there was a heavy weight on her mind, a great desire for confession, but the paralysis . . ." He made a helpless gesture. "I could understand very little, I'm afraid, of what she said."

I nodded bleakly. That had been one of the most painful parts of the last weeks, not just to watch Mother lying helpless but to see her eyes constantly following after me imploringly, to hear her fight to form words that came out so much gibberish, to watch time and time again a pen slipping through her lifeless hand. It was as if a desperate need drove Fiona to impart some last words, some final instruction.

" 'Tis a warning to all of us," the priest said, his eyes fastening on me like pincers, as if he were remembering exactly how long it had been since I had been to confession. "In the midst of life, death is but a step behind us. None of us are too young and healthy, but we should . . ."

"Miss Meg, the doctor says come quickly."

The housekeeper's urgent command cut short Father McCully's lecture. Excusing myself, I flew back into the bedroom. Dr. Allen stood at the foot of the bed. "I'm sorry, Miss O'Brien," he said quietly. "It's only a matter of time now." He shook his head, puzzled. "It's a miracle, as small and frail as your mother is, she's lasted this long."

I knelt down beside the bed, gently brushing back a tendril of tawny red hair, still more gold than gray, from my mother's unlined forehead. I thought absently how often people had been fooled by Fiona's delicate beauty. There were few who guessed the rocklike constitution, the will of iron behind the fragile air. How else could Fiona have survived that long, arduous trek west, the years of living like gypsies, moving with my father from mining camp to mining camp, until Jamie finally found for her that mountain of silver? And how else, except through stubborn will power, could she have endured the thousand snubs and barriers flung up before her these last years as she obstinately sought to breach the impenetrable wall of Boston society?

"Mother," I whispered, picking up her hand. As I did so, the lace ruffle at the wrist of her nightgown fell back and I saw the ugly pinched flesh on the inside of her right wrist, an old scar that Fiona never spoke about but aways carefully kept hidden. Gently I replaced the ruffle before I spoke again. "Mother, is there anything you want?"

The eyelids fluttered, opened slowly. The luminous deep blue eyes, the one good feature I had inherited from Fiona, still shone with a burnished glow as if not even approaching death could extinguish that blaze. Her twisted mouth moved, made a tortured request. "Pat . . . rick."

"Patrick's been sent for, Mother," I assured her. "He'll be here soon."

It was a lie, of course. I had wired my brother as soon as we realized this attack was much more serious than the others had been. The message had been sent to Abbey Court in Ireland but, for all I knew, Patrick and his bride might still be honeymooning on the Continent and I had no address for him there. And even if he had returned to Abbeymore and booked passage on the first available ship, it would take him at least a week to reach Boston.

The eyes, blazing, fastened on my face, as if the last of her energy was concentrated in that accusing gaze. I had never been a skillful liar. Jamie had always teased me, saying, "I'll never make a poker player out of you, Maggie, not with everything you feel right there on your face for the whole world to see."

Fiona's eyes closed wearily. Only her lips still moved, forcing out words, although the effort caused perspiration to break out on her forehead. "Pat . . . rick . . . warn . . . watch . . ." Then the words became garbled. She

8

lapsed into Irish, the Gaelic she spoke when she was upset and which I had never learned to speak. I leaned closer. She seemed to be reliving a scene from her past. Her face was flushed, she was agitated, but the only words I could make out were, "Oh . . . kill . . . oh . . . kill . . ."

Mrs. Johnson brought a chair for me. "Sit down, child. You look as if you're ready to drop—no sleep for three days and hardly a bite to eat. Let me get you a cup of tea."

I shook my head, the tears rolling unheeded down my face. "I should have sent for Patrick weeks ago," I reproached myself. "I shouldn't have waited."

"There now, how could you have known?" the housekeeper said soothingly. "Why, when I came into the bedroom and saw your mother on the floor, the letter from young Mr. O'Brien still clutched in her hand, I thought myself it was just a fainting spell from the shock of the news. Some mothers take it hard, the marriage of an only son, and announced that way in a letter so sudden like, with no warning." Hastily she added, as if not wanting to sound disapproving, "No doubt, though, your new sister-in-law is a fine woman. The daughter of a duke, isn't she? That would make her a duchess, wouldn't it?"

"Cousin to Lord Fletcher, the Earl of Abbeymore," I corrected absently. And I had no idea what rank, if any, that made my sister-in-law. But she could have been a duchess and my mother wouldn't have thought her good enough for Patrick. No girl ever was, as far as Fiona was concerned. Still, in a way, it was a stroke of irony that Patrick should marry into the Fletcher family of Abbey Court. The young Fiona had been in service at Abbey Court and, though Mother seldom spoke of her life in Ireland, I had the impression that her years there had not always been easy ones.

Once more the eyelids lifted. That feverish blue gaze seemed to be searching the room for something or someone. It was Mrs. Johnson who understood. She crossed to Mother's dressing table and came back with a small daguerreotype of Patrick in a gold frame. He had sat for the picture when he graduated from Harvard, but the almost too prettily handsome, stiff-faced young gentleman in the photograph with his mouth frozen in a disdainful smile was a far cry from the warm and loving brother I knew.

Mrs. Johnson placed the picture where Mother could see it, and the deep-set eyes fastening upon it were filled with such a longing and despair that it was almost more than I could endure. I had always known that Patrick was my mother's favorite, just as I suppose I would have been Jamie's, if my father, whose love was boundless, had ever chosen a favorite. Yet it had never made any difference between my brother and me. I suppose in my own way I idolized Patrick as much as Mother did. Although he was almost nine years older than I, we were unusually close, partly because, growing up in isolated mining camps, there had been few other children with whom to be friends.

After Jamie had made his big strike and Mother had insisted over Jamie's protest that my brother, then sixteen, be sent back to Boston to school, Patrick and I still kept in constant touch by letter. I was as proud as Mother of his success in school—first at an expensive prep school then at Harvard—and of the friendships he formed, the doors that somehow opened to him which remained forever closed to Mother and me.

"Meg." The word came out surprisingly sharp and clear.

"Yes, Mother, I'm here."

I grasped her hand more firmly. The bones felt as light as the skeleton of a bird. Her eyes burned into my face. "Pat ... rick ... watch ... take care."

I nodded and tried to smile. "You know I've always kept an eye on Patrick. Only you forget, he has a wife to look after him now."

For some reason my answer seemed to agitate her. She half lifted herself from the bed. Each painful word seemed to take an eternity to form; her eyes were frantic, and I had the eerie feeling that she had slipped back into another time. "Hurry ... must ... hide ... kill ... oh, kill ... dear God ... the flames ..."

The doctor came quickly forward and pressed his patient back on the pillow. His hand felt for her pulse, his voice was calming. "You mustn't exert yourself, Mrs. O'Brien. Don't try to talk."

She lay back, her eyes closed. I could see no movement beneath the ruffled bodice of the nightgown. With her eyes shut, Fiona's face already seemed empty, deserted, as if it were only the eyes that were still alive behind the marbled eyelids. My mother seemed already gone somewhere else, out of my reach and the sound of my voice.

Then for the last time the eyelids opened. Surprisingly there was no longer any despair or desperation in their luminous depths. Fiona stared past me joyfully, without seeing me or anyone else, I was sure, in the room. For the briefest moment a smile touched her mouth, the tremulous, heart-catching smile of a young girl gazing at her first love. She murmured what sounded like a man's name. Then she sighed peacefully and seemed to curl up like a child into a deep sleep.

Gently the doctor held her wrist a few moments before he placed her hand beneath the coverlet. "I'm sorry," he said softly. "She's gone."

Mrs. Johnson's arms tightened around me comfortingly. "It was an easy death, child. Be thankful for that. And what a blessing, calling out to your dear, dead father there at the end, as if he were standing here in the room with her."

I shook my head, taking one last, bewildered look at Fiona's now blissfully serene face. No, whatever the man's name my mother had called out at the end, I could swear it had not been Jamie's.

2

Only two carriages followed Mother's funeral cortege to the cemetery. The attendance at the funeral mass had not been much larger. Mr. Cornelius Adams, Mother's lawyer; the servants; some friends of Patrick's; several nuns from the Convent of St. Agnes; and a few curiosity seekers appeared, but not one member of the so-called first families of Boston.

As I stood watching the coffin being slowly lowered into the ground, I told myself it didn't matter who had come. Certainly Mother was past caring. As for myself, over the last years I had schooled myself to endure the humiliation of rejection, the countless subtle snubs that were the more embarrassing because Fiona never seemed to notice, blithely ignoring anything she didn't want to see, stubbornly convinced it was only a matter of time before we would have Boston society at our feet.

I couldn't help thinking bitterly of how the church in Denver would have been crowded with Mother's friends;

how the whole town had turned out for Jamie O'Brien's funeral and the sheriff had had to restrain a mob from lynching the drunken cardsharp who had shot him.

I wished now I had insisted that Mother's body be sent to lie beside my father's in the cemetery outside of Denver, even though Mr. Adams had tactfully pointed out the impracticality. "Your mother made no such request and this time of year in Colorado, the ground must still be frozen and snow covered."

The short service at the cemetery was finished. Mrs. Johnson slipped an arm around my waist, gently pulling me away from the canopy sheltering me from an icy rain that had begun when we reached the cemetery. "Come along, child, before you catch a chill."

But I knew the reason for her haste. She didn't want me to hear the sound of the earth falling on my mother's casket, that terrible, final sound I remembered from my father's funeral. All at once I was shivering, whether from cold or exhaustion or grief I didn't know. My parents were both gone now and my own mortality stared me in the face.

As soon as we reached home, Mrs. Johnson insisted I go straight to bed but first I wanted to write to Patrick. There had been no possibility of his reaching Boston in time for the funeral and the telegram I had sent to Abbey Court, telling him of Mother's death, had had to be cruelly brief. Now I wrote him all I could remember of Fiona's last hours, of the words she had struggled to speak which had made no sense to me but showed that her last thoughts had been filled with concern for him. Then the housekeeper tucked me into bed and prepared a vile concoction for me to drink, guaranteed, she assured me, to ward off a chill.

Unhappily, her elixir didn't work. For the next two weeks I remained in bed, fighting off a congestion of the lungs and a raging fever. In the nightmarish dreams that went along with the fever, I kept reliving those last moments before my mother died. Once I even thought in my delirium that I saw Fiona standing beside my bed, her gold-red hair streaming over her shoulders. She did not speak a word, only her eyes implored me mutely, begging for what I did not know. When I reached out my arms to console her, she vanished like mist.

When the fever finally left me, I was weak as a kitten but at least able to sit up in bed and take the broth Mrs. Johnson fed me. The housekeeper had been unstinting in the time and concern she had lavished on me during my illness and, looking up into the sharp-boned face that I had always thought rather cold and forbidding, I wondered now how I could have overlooked the essential kindness of the woman. Impulsively I reached for her hand. "I'll never be able to thank you. I don't know what I would have done without you these last months."

"Nonsense, child," she said briskly, the tips of her ears reddening. "You've got grit, as we say up home. A person either stands up to life or he doesn't and that's all there is to it." She reached into her apron pocket. "Your brother has wired several times, inquiring as to your health, and yesterday this letter arrived from him. I knew you'd want to read it first thing."

After Mrs. Johnson left the room I simply held the envelope in my hand. My brother's familiar script with all its flourishes and loops reached out like a known beloved hand to comfort me.

At last I took out the several sheets of thick vellum paper, raced through the letter, then settled back and reread it slowly.

Dearest Meg,
    You know too well my sorrow at the news that Mother has left us. I still cannot believe it. And my grief is doubled that I was not able to be with her at the end. Thank God that you, at least, are on the road to full recovery.
    I can imagine how difficult these last weeks have been for you but now you must quickly get better and come join me at Abbey Court as soon as possible. It'll be like old times, our being together again. I want you to feel always that, wherever I may be, my home is your home.
    I would come to Boston myself to help settle Mother's estate—although I'm sure the estimable Mr. Adams will take care of all the bothersome details—but I hesitate to leave Abbey Court at this time. You've heard, no doubt, of the troubles we are having here in Ireland. The rack-renting and the tenants' rebellions against the landlords are causing untold death and suffering on both sides. Fortunately Abbey Court has been reasonably calm, although I am afraid it may only be the calm before the storm.
    The present Earl of Abbeymore is a fine chap, only a a few years younger than I, and we have become close

friends as well as sharing a mutual interest in art. Lord Fletcher is building an excellent collection here at Abbey Court. However, he leaves the management of the estate in the hands of my father-in-law, Cormac Fletcher, and my brother-in-law, Sean Fletcher. As much as I dislike speaking ill of my new in-laws, it is distressing to see them behave as if this were the Middle Ages and they were feudal lords, with the tenants having few rights or safeguards over their life and property.

I have done what I can to alleviate matters but it is slow going. With men such as my father-in-law in the position of power here in Ireland, it is no wonder the land is in a turmoil and the tenants are in rebellion. I can well understand now why Mother fled Ireland, no matter the ridiculous stories that have been spread as to the real reason for her leave-taking.

Nevertheless, with all the troubles, I know you will love Ireland at first sight, Meg, the same way I did. It's a beautiful country and the people, despite the hardships they endure, are warm and friendly. I am convinced that this is where my real roots are, and here is where I belong.

There is so much more I have to tell you but it will have to wait until I see you, very soon, I hope. I miss my little sister more than I thought possible and even more now that we have lost our dear mother. . . .

After I had reread the letter for a third time, I settled back against my pillows, frowning. What did Patrick mean . . . the ridiculous stories about Mother's leaving Ireland? It was famine that drove her away, of course, as it had thousands of other Irish emigrants to America. Something else, less tangible, about the letter bothered me, too. Not once had Patrick mentioned his wife, Regan, and the other letter had been filled with her.

Opening the drawer of the small table beside the bed, I took out the letter Mother had received from Patrick, the letter still clutched in her hand when Mrs. Johnson found her, unconscious on the floor.

Patrick's fulsome script sprawled happily across the page of this letter as if it could not contain itself.

Dearest Mother,

Please forgive my dropping my bombshell with so little warning. I am married—to the most beautiful, dearest girl in the world. Her name is Regan Marie Louise Fletcher and she is cousin to Lord Kevin Michael Fletcher, the Earl of Abbeymore. I know I didn't mention that I was going to visit Ireland when I came abroad, but you remember how curious I've always been about your childhood home. I had only intended visiting the village of Abbeymore, since I had no letter of introduction to the present earl. However, while staying in the village, by chance I met Regan and her brother Sean, and they very kindly invited me to stay with them at Abbey Court.

From the first moment I met Regan I was bewitched. And by a blessed miracle, she felt the same. Neither of us wanted to wait for a long engagement and we were married by the parish priest yesterday. Tomorrow we leave on our honeymoon in France and Italy, and as soon as we return to Abbey Court you and Meg must come for a long visit. Regan is looking forward to meeting you both.

You cannot know the present earl but you undoubtedly remember his father, Lord Michael Fletcher, who was at Abbey Court while you were here. Although Lord Michael died some years ago, his wife, the Dowager Countess Margaret, is still living at Abbey Court, as is Cormac Fletcher, Regan's father, and the present Lord Fletcher's great-uncle, whom you may also remember. However, because of a hunting accident, my father-in-law is confined to his bed and seldom receives visitors.

I know this letter must come as a great shock to you, dearest Mother, but please be happy for me. I am sure when you and Meg meet Regan you will love her almost as much as I do.

Devotedly . . . Patrick

No doubt, I thought, the letter had been a shock to Mother. I had been surprised myself. Not that Patrick hadn't had several young women interested in him—he was far too attractive not to be sought after—but he had never shown any serious interest in any of them. Yet I had heard that was how it often happened. The bachelors who were the most marriage-shy fell the hardest when the right girl came along.

Thoughtfully I slipped Patrick's letter back into the envelope, wondering if Regan were as eager as Patrick to invite an unknown sister-in-law to share her home permanently. Still, Abbey Court must be a large place. It wouldn't be as if I were constantly underfoot. Perhaps Regan and I might even become good friends. After all, we both loved Patrick.

Mrs. Johnson knocked softly, then opened the door. "It's Mr. Adams to see you," she said, her face aggrieved. "I told him you're not well enough for visitors but he insisted I should inform you he was here; that he'd only take a few minutes of your time. Shall I tell him to come back next week?"

I reached for my robe. "No, I'll see him, Mrs. Johnson."

Stopping at my dressing-table mirror, I ran a brush over my hair, securing as many flyaway tendrils as possible in a chignon at the nape of my neck, smoothing the fringe of bangs across my forehead. I noticed that my illness had left my face with a pallor that made the freckles sprinkled across my nose stand out as bold as confetti and made my hair appear even more garishly red, if possible. "Carrottop," Patrick had always called me, until I was big enough to pummel him into silence.

Tying the sash of my robe more tightly around my waist, I saw, pleased, that there had been some advantages to being ill. I had managed to lose a few pounds. Fiona had always groaned when she watched me eat. "Ladies nibble their food, Meg. They don't eat as if each meal is their last. If you're not careful, you'll be fat as Paddy's pig." But then, I thought ruefully, smoothing the robe over my more than ample hips, Fiona had never had to worry about gaining weight. No matter what she ate, she had kept the slim figure of a young girl until the day she died.

Going down the steps to the front parlor, I found my legs were not quite as steady as I thought, and I held tightly to the banister rail. In the parlor, Mr. Adams hastily held out a chair for me. "I do apologize, intruding upon you this way, Miss O'Brien, but there are some matters that must be attended to . . ."

"I'm feeling much better, thank you," I said crisply. Fiona had always had the highest respect for Mr. Adams, mostly, I suspected, because through his marriage he was distantly connected to the Cabot family, but I could not forget that Mrs. Adams had never once asked Mother to tea at their home, much less dinner. Nor had Mrs. Adams shown up at Mother's funeral.

Mr. Adams' salt and pepper mustache wiggled as he adjusted his eyeglasses carefully on his thin nose. "One hates to bring up legal matters at a time like this and especially with a young woman like yourself who, naturally, has no experience . . ."

"I am twenty-three years old, Mr. Adams," I interrupted curtly. "I'm hardly a child. I assume this visit has to do with Mother's will."

"You are aware, then, of the contents of the will?"

"Yes, of course. After my father's death, Mother gave outright to Patrick half of the money from the sale of the Silver Lady Mine. The rest she kept in shares of the mine and cash which she told me would come to me at her death."

Mr. Adams cleared his throat and pulled up a chair. "That's more or less correct. Still, as you are one of the main beneficiaries, I am required to read the terms of the will to you." He drew out the document and read aloud Mother's will, which was much as Fiona had told me, except for one unusually large bequest to the Sisters of the Convent of St. Agnes which I didn't recall her mentioning; and several smaller bequests to the household staff.

When he had finished, Mr. Adams folded the document and said, "The bequest to the convent was larger than I felt wise; however, I suppose Mrs. O'Brien had her reasons."

I said quietly, "The nuns took care of my mother when Patrick was born, and afterward. Mother always said that many Irish immigrants besides herself and Patrick would have died of starvation and disease if it hadn't been for the good sisters. My father, of course, did what he could but, as you know, there were few jobs or any welcome at all for Irishmen in Boston in the 1850s."

"Yes, yes, indeed." Mr. Adams shifted uncomfortably in his chair, not looking directly at me. "A most unfortunate time, so many destitute and ill foreigners pouring into the city, spreading disease and poverty, fine neighborhoods ruined, a terrible burden to the taxpayer. Yet one did what one could." Then, as if anxious to change an unpleasant subject, "By any chance, did your mother speak to you lately about the Silver Lady Mine shares?"

"No," I said, then added, "however, I do read the newspapers, Mr. Adams. I am aware that, with the government threatening to suspend the coinage of silver and turn to the gold standard, the price of silver shares has dropped. There's still the money, though, that Mother brought with her from Denver. I had the impression it was a considerable amount. Wasn't your firm in charge of the investment of those funds for my mother?"

"Indeed we have been, and the funds would have been completely safe today, even with your silver shares being practically worthless," Mr. Adams assured me. "Our firm has a well-deserved reputation for investing money soundly and safely. However, your mother, I'm afraid, withdrew the money as quickly as we invested it for her. She had a good many expenses, of course, buying this house and furnishings, the horses and livery, the servants, the charities she gave to so liberally . . ." He hesitated. "And then there were other costs, too."

Meaning my expensive governess, and finishing school, dancing and riding lessons, and fashionable gowns from Paris, I thought grimly. Not to mention my distastrous coming-out party, which must have cost Fiona a pretty packet. And all for nothing. My brother, bless him, had coerced as many of his friends as he could to attend the ball, but there had been a noticeable lack of fashionably young ladies or their parents present. Poor Mother. Despite all her money and enthusiasm, she had done everything wrong. She hadn't realized that in Boston the right people brought out their daughters at a dull, small party overseen by some grim grandmother dowager, not at a vulgar, lavish ball. Any more than she had ever understood that giving huge sums of money to the symphony and other favorite Boston charities, or having the flashiest jewels or the most expensively decorated home on Beacon Hill, meant that she would be socially acceptable. The more she spent her money, the more the newspapers played up Fiona O'Brien as the beautiful but eccentric Silver Queen, the more Boston society frowned and withdrew in icy disapproval.

"It isn't as if you should consider yourself without any funds," Mr. Adams assured me. "There are your mother's jewels and this house, which should bring a tidy amount." He paused. "Unless you plan to continue living here."

"I have no intention of remaining in Boston, Mr. Adams," I said firmly. "I'd appreciate your putting this house and Mother's jewels up for sale as quickly as it can be arranged. My brother has asked me to come live with him and his wife and I'd like to leave as soon as possible."

"Yes, of course." Mr. Adams frowned, then asked slowly, "Your brother, then, is making a success of his investments in Ireland? I'm glad to hear of it. I've been quite concerned."

"Investments?" Now it was my turn to look startled. "What investments?"

"I thought, naturally, you knew," Mr. Adams said, his face settling into somber, pompous lines. "Our firm has been handling your brother's financial affairs for several years. Three days before his marriage he withdrew the major portion of his funds and made a sizable loan to the estate of the Earl of Abbeymore at Abbey Court."

3

"I don't understand." I stared at Mr. Adams, bewildered. "Surely Lord Fletcher must be a very wealthy man. Why should Patrick loan him money?"

Mr. Adams' long nose twitched shrewdly. "Land proud and penny poor," he sniffed. "That's all you'll find behind many a fancy title, that and a houseful of bad debts. I warned your mother when she turned one half of her estate over to Patrick with no strings attached that it was a mistake. Not that your brother isn't a fine young man," he added hastily, "but he's hardly a businessman. A spendthrift trust, I told Mrs. O'Brien, that's how the money should have been handled."

I had heard vaguely of spendthrift trusts, a practice that had helped preserve the fortune of many an old Boston family, generation after generation, no matter how indolent or extravagant the inheritors became. Unfortunately, I suspected the lawyer was right. Patrick was too kindhearted, too trusting, to be a good businessman. Nevertheless, I would not allow my brother to be criticized in my presence and I bristled, annoyed. "I'm sure Patrick had a good reason for making the loan, Mr. Adams."

"Perhaps," he agreed grudgingly. "The opinion of our business advisers was not asked in the matter or we would have told your brother that this was a very bad time to be investing in a country as politically and economically unstable as Ireland. Every other year, it seems, the Irish are plotting revolution. I recall the speech one of Ireland's leaders, a Mr. Charles Parnell, gave here in Boston a few years back, trying to raise money for the Irish cause. His words were pure rabble rousing, actually telling Irish tenant farmers not to pay rent to their landlords and boycott any farmer who did." His voice sputtered indignantly. "And I understand he managed to raise thousands of dollars, good American cash that's the same as poured down a drainhole, used to support anarchy and revolution against England."

"Mother and I heard Mr. Parnell's speech," I said. "We thought his talk very impressive and Mr. Parnell himself an intelligent, courageous man." I remembered Mother's exact words had been: "Oh, he's a grand, handsome lad, Maggie. He's the leader Ireland has been praying for. He'll get England's heel off Ireland's neck once and for all."

"As a matter of fact," I continued, "I believe Mother gave a large check to Mr. Parnell herself. As for plotting revolution against the British, wasn't it your ancestors here in Boston, Mr. Adams, not many years ago who did much the same thing?"

The man gave me a sharp glance, then began to gather his papers, his voice stiff. "One shouldn't expect a young woman to understand the difference between politics and business, Miss O'Brien. I felt it only my duty to tell your mother at the time she gave that check to Mr. Parnell that she was simply throwing her money away." He frowned uncomfortably in memory. "However, she was quite . . . quite insistent. Mrs. O'Brien was in many ways a most unusual woman."

I ducked my head, hiding a smile. I was sure that Fiona had told Mr. Adams in no uncertain terms to mind his own business. Living in mining camps, Fiona had picked up a colorful vocabulary that she didn't hesitate to use when necessary.

For the first time I felt a little sorry for the attorney, having felt the rough edge of my mother's tongue a few times myself. It couldn't have been easy for a man of Mr. Adams' prudent temperament to try to protect Fiona O'Brien from her own generosity and extravagance. To Fiona, money was simply a means to an end, not something to be enshrined in a vault and worshiped.

"I'm sure Mother appreciated all you did for her, Mr.

Adams," I said, and couldn't help thinking that perhaps it was a blessing that Mother hadn't lived to see the day when what must have seemed a never ending stream of wealth from the Silver Lady Mine had trickled to an end. "If you'll have the necessary legal papers drawn up for the sale of the house, I'll begin tomorrow to go through Mother's jewels and decide which pieces should be sold." I rose unsteadily to my feet. "Now if you'll excuse me, I am feeling a little tired."

I was surprised, myself, at how suddenly weak I felt. Or perhaps it was only the delayed shock at the realization of the change in my financial condition. It was one thing to go live with my brother when I had sufficient private income to come and go as I pleased, and another thing to arrive as a dependent spinster relative with nowhere else to turn. Mother, I'm afraid, wasn't the only one who had confidently relied upon the unending bounty from the Silver Lady.

A day's rest in bed, however, restored my spirits. I reminded myself that I wasn't, after all, poverty-stricken. I would have the money from the sale of the house and furniture and there were still Mother's jewels. I asked Mrs. Johnson to fetch me Mother's velvet jewel case and she watched, disapprovingly, as I tumbled jeweled pins and combs, necklaces, bracelets, earrings, rings, and even a diamond tiara upon the bed in a sunburst of diamonds, sapphires, rubies, and emeralds.

"Lucky we weren't all murdered in our beds, keeping valuables like that in the house," Mrs. Johnson complained, drawing the blinds and carefully closing the bedroom door behind her when she left.

Although I knew that most Boston matrons kept their jewels in bank vaults and wore paste imitations, Mother was proud of her jewelry and childishly loved to show it off. I could still see her in black velvet, diamonds flashing at her throat and wrists and tucked into her tawny hair, not caring or seeing the disapproving glances cast her way at such a deliberate flaunting of wealth.

Each piece was a gift from Jamie, most of them in celebration of birthdays or anniversaries, but some, I recalled wryly, had been gifts given in penitence. The week Jamie disappeared on a tear with some old cronies he had returned meekly with a terrible hangover and the ruby and diamond necklace for Fiona. I remembered the disastrous two-day poker game at which Jamie had almost lost the Silver Lady to an inside straight. That was the day Fiona had received the ring with a diamond large enough to act as a doorstop. And the tiara . . . I frowned, remembering that particular incident.

There had been a bitter quarrel about sending Patrick back east to school. Mother had won, as usual, and Father had stormed out of the house. He returned early the next morning. I could hear him walking softly past my door and into Mother's room. The mansion my parents had built in Denver—for all its elaborate wooden scrollwork, cast-iron trim, and stone statuary on the lawn—had thin walls.

I could hear Mother's furious whisper. "Don't you dare come near me, Jamie O'Brien, with the smell of that harlot from Market Street on you."

Jamie mumbled something too low for me to hear. Then the bedsprings creaked and finally his voice rose angrily: "Damn you, woman, you think I like sharing my bed with a ghost? If a man can't find warmth in his own bed, he'll go where it doesn't matter if he isn't a fine gentleman."

"Be still." Fiona's voice was an anguished cry. "Maggie will hear you."

But she needn't have worried. I had pulled the pillow over my head and could hear nothing more. And the next day, I remembered, the diamond tiara had arrived, so spectacularly beautiful that not even Fiona could remain angry.

On an impulse I shoved the jewelry back into the case. I would sell everything, I thought. The jewels brought back too many memories, happy and unhappy. All except one, I thought, reaching for a brooch that seemed oddly out of place among the other glittering gems.

The brooch, in the shape of an open circle, was made of filigreed gold wire and studs of blue and red enamel. Tiny human heads carved of amethyst, and birds, fish, and animals intricately formed of amber and other semiprecious stones ornamented the front and back of the pin. Although less showy than her other jewels, it was the piece my mother had worn most often.

Once, while we were still living in Denver and she had let me go through her jewel case, I had asked her about the pin. "Is it very valuable?"

"It has a value beyond price," Mother had replied softly. "It's a relic of holy Ireland, perhaps from the days of the blessed St. Patrick himself. You know, in those early centuries when Ireland was her own land, the Irish monasteries had the most accomplished goldsmiths in all of Europe."

I gazed at the brooch—which had struck me as rather

strange-looking—with a little more respect, then said doubtfully, "It doesn't look that old."

"Well, of course, this is only a copy of the Abbeymore brooch," Fiona explained. "I had it made at Tiffany's in New York. It took more than a year for their jewelers to get it right from the drawings I sent them. I saw the brooch the first time when I was just a lass, not much older than you."

I felt a childish jealousy at this part of my mother's life which didn't include Jamie, Patrick, or me—but I felt an even greater itch of curiosity. "Isn't that where you lived as a young girl, at Abbey Court near Abbeymore? Was it as grand as our home?"

"Much grander," Mother assured me, a lilt in her voice I had not heard before. "The grandest sight in all Ireland, saving that of the Holy Rock of Cashel. The house is built of Connemara stone, white and glistening against the green park, with the Ballyhouras in the distance. On a clear day, from the ballroom on the top floor you can see the Irish Sea. And nearby stand the ruins of the old Abbey and Kilcallen Castle where the O'Neills—your ancestors, Maggie, never be forgetting that—lived for generations. The O'Neills were descendants of kings with rich lands, until the curse of Cromwell came upon them."

I was startled at the bitterness in Mother's voice, as if Cromwell's invasion of Ireland had happened only yesterday, instead of more than two centuries before. "Was it Cromwell who destroyed the castle?"

"Not the old devil himself but blackhearted Daniel Fletcher with a company of Cromwell's men put a torch to the castle. They killed every O'Neill they could find, save for Rosaleen O'Neill, the youngest daughter, that old Daniel dragged off and finally married. He was given every inch of the O'Neill demesne by Cromwell as a reward for services rendered."

"Then it was Daniel Fletcher who built Abbey Court?"

"He began it, a wedding present, they say, for the fair Rosaleen, but it was his son Brian who finished the house. Afterward Brian became a Catholic and went off to fight for King James II and was killed himself at the Battle of the Boyne. Before he died, though, he had been given an earldom by James II and he became the first Earl of Abbeymore."

"Was it very splendid, living at Abbey Court?" I asked

wistfully. Few members of the nobility ever appeared in Denver society.

But I had gone too far. Mother's mouth tightened, her voice was suddenly sharp. "I didn't live at Abbey Court. I worked there, as a maid for Lady Caroline Fletcher, and I was glad of the job to keep food in my stomach." Her hand had touched, almost unconsciously, the scar at her wrist. Then she shrugged and gave me a hug, as if to make up for her crossness. "All this talk of the past . . ." She smiled. "You're as bad as Patrick with your questions. It's the future you should be thinking of." She drew me to her dressing table, her arm around my shoulders. "Wait till we move back to Boston. We'll have our own Abbey Court and you'll be a grand young lady with all the young men from the finest families coming to call."

I gazed uncertainly at my reflection. Although I don't suppose I was more than fourteen at the time, I had already accepted the fact that I wasn't going to wake up some morning and miraculously discover that overnight I had grown as beautiful as Fiona. Unfairly, it was Patrick who had inherited Mother's creamy skin, long dark lashes, and tawny gold hair. My face was Jamie's: the same full cheeks, short nose, too firm chin, and bright red hair, like the map of Ireland written plain to see. I was tall and raw-boned like Jamie, too, though lately, thankfully, I had noticed that on my own I was developing some interesting curves. Nevertheless, I had grave doubts that I would ever be hotly pursued by men callers in Denver or in Boston.

"Father said we'd never go back east," I reminded Mother. "He told me the people in Boston had hearts as black and cold as Castle Keep."

"Ah, Jamie," Fiona said, shrugging indifferently. "He'll change his mind. And you'll see, the Bostonians will be as friendly as can be when they see the color of our money."

Well, Mother had certainly been wrong about that, I thought now as I put the case away, carefully placing the engraved brooch to one side. No matter the size of Fiona's fortune, it was still first-generation money. The newspapers might love her flamboyant gowns and entertaining, the sometimes earthy way she had of expressing herself, but to the people who mattered Fiona O'Brien would always remain that upstart Irish Catholic girl who had taken in washing for a living and then, after an eccentric and no doubt unladylike life in mining towns in the West, had

had the colossal gall to return and try to breach the bastions of Boston society.

My thoughts were interrupted by Mrs. Johnson's knocking. She opened the door at once, her usually calm voice flustered. "There are two nuns to see you. I'm sure I didn't know where to put them."

"The front parlor will be fine, Mrs. Johnson," I assured her. "And would you have tea prepared for us?"

Changing quickly from my morning robe into a black bombazine mourning gown, I hurried down the stairs. The two black-coifed nuns with pleated white ruching around their faces were seated like twin statues on Mother's plum velvet sofa.

They rose when I entered. The youngest one—at least her face was unlined—spoke first. "I am Sister Marie Theresa, Miss O'Brien, and this"—she indicated her companion—"is Sister Cecelia. We are from the Convent of St. Agnes. Mother Superior would have come herself but she is confined to her room with the rheumatism."

"Please be seated," I said quickly. "Would you care for tea?"

Sister Marie Theresa hesitated but Sister Cecelia, her face as wrinkled as a raisin, but her faded eyes still merry, nodded happily. "Oh yes, that would be nice."

"Were you soliciting donations for the convent, Sister?" I asked, regretting that I hadn't thought to bring my reticule downstairs with me.

"Oh no." She looked shocked. "Your mother's bequest was more than generous. The sisters say novenas for her daily. You can't imagine how much good the money will do. We are not a rich order, you know."

Just then Mrs. Johnson had the parlormaid serve the tea while she hovered in the hallway, as if loath to come into the room herself.

Sister Marie Thereas smiled. "Your housekeeper seems upset by our visit."

"I'm afraid she hasn't met many nuns," I explained, embarrassed. I busied myself pouring the tea into Mother's Meissen cups. Fiona had chosen the tea set to match the plum and rose décor of the parlor and had loved to sit behind the ornately engraved silver service to pour afternoon tea. I blinked back sudden tears. Now I supposed the Meissen and the tea service would be sold along with the other household furnishings.

Sister Marie Theresa said gently, "It must be a great loss for you, your mother's death."

"Did you know her?" I asked eagerly.

The younger sister shook her head. "I saw her, of course, at mass. However, Sister Cecelia knew her. I believe she attended your mother when your brother was born."

Sister Cecelia stopped in the midst of nibbling a cinnamon cookie and nodded, pleased. "Oh, to be sure, I knew Fiona O'Brien. She had been in labor a whole day when your father came to the convent and begged a sister to come with him. I've never seen a man so crazed with fear. He took me to a hovel in a basement that housed at least twenty other poor Irish souls, no water or heat, and your mother there on a shawl on the floor. The child had turned in the womb and become entangled in the cord. It was God's mercy the poor mite wasn't born strangled. On St. Stephen's Day, it was." She smiled in memory. "The blessed saint must have been watching over your mother. Such a beautiful baby, too, as beautiful as its mother, and your father as proud as a peacock of both of them. They had met aboard the ship bringing them to America, you know, and the captain married them."

I had heard about the marriage ceremony aboard the overcrowded ship that had brought my parents, as well as many other Irish emigrants, packed like cattle, to America. Coffin ships, they were called, because at least one fourth of the passengers died on the way.

"Mother spoke often of your kindness during the years they spent here in Boston, before they moved west."

"Och, those were sad times," Sister Cecelia said. "No jobs at all for a strong-backed Irishman like your father, no matter how hard he looked. And your mother taking in washing, till her hands were cracked and raw. There were many like your family who decided finally to go west and seek their fortunes. I remember the day before they left, your mother came by the convent, with little Patrick. He was a fine, brave boy. You must be looking forward to seeing him."

I glanced at Sister Cecelia, startled. How did she know I was going to Ireland to join Patrick? Sister Marie Theresa inserted quickly, "There now, we've not mentioned the real reason for our visit. Mr. Cornelius Adams sent a message to the convent that you were planning to visit Ireland and did we know of a possible chaperone for you on the trip."

So that was it, I thought, amused. Trust Mr. Adams not

to overlook the fact that no proper young unmarried lady would ever travel unaccompanied.

"It so happened that Sister Cecelia here is returning to our mother house near Dublin and Mother Superior thought, if you are willing, the two of you could travel together."

I looked through lowered lashes at Sister Cecelia, who was still happily stuffing herself like a chipmunk with the cinnamon cookies. I decided that, in spite of her age, I could look hard for a more cheerful companion.

"It's very kind of Mother Superior. Please thank her for me," I said, and then anxiously, "You do realize that I am planning on leaving as soon as possible?"

I was assured that would present no problem; Sister Cecelia would be ready whenever I was.

As it turned out, however, I couldn't leave Boston as soon as I had hoped. Weeks dragged by while Mr. Adams put in motion the necessary legal machinery for settling Mother's estate. "The wheels of probate grind slowly, my dear," he protested when I chafed with impatience at the numerous delays.

It was the middle of May when I received still another letter from Patrick, the fourth since Mother's death. As in his other letters, he made no reference to his wife but asked again how soon I would be arriving at Abbey Court. "You haven't changed your mind, Maggie? I am counting on you. Even when we were children you were the one person upon whom I could always depend. I need your common sense, your loyalty, now more than ever. I blunder along the best I can but I'm afraid I'm making more enemies than friends here at Abbey Court. Lord Fletcher is very kind but he is away a good deal and does not fully appreciate the unfortunate situation among his tenants, or even the problems in his own household. I long for someone I can talk to, someone I can trust. Please don't disappoint me."

It was after I received this strangely disquieting letter that I made up my mind. I sent word to Mr. Adams informing him that, whether he approved or not, I intended leaving for Ireland on the first available ship.

4

Discovering that I could dig in my heels as stubbornly as my mother when I wished, Mr. Adams used his influence to secure passage for Sister Cecelia and myself on a Cunard liner leaving New York the following week. Sister Cecelia turned out to be a poor sailor and I spent a great deal of time tending her in her cabin, but she was so patient and good-natured, despite her discomfort, that I didn't mind at all acting as nursemaid.

Occasionally, when my patient was sleeping, I would take a turn on deck, along with the other passengers who were enjoying their constitutional. One young couple in particular caught my eye. The deck steward had told me they were on their honeymoon but it would have been obvious in any case that they were deeply in love. Even when the deck was perfectly steady, his arm would stay around her tiny waist and they constantly clung to one another, oblivious of all others around them.

Once, on an evening stroll, I saw them in a deep embrace at a far corner of the deck, half hidden in the shadow of a lifeboat. I turned away abruptly, loneliness like a weight in my chest. Not that I hadn't had one or two serious suitors in Boston after my coming-out party, but Mother had pegged them at once as the fortune hunters they were, attracted, I suppose, by visions of marrying the heiress to a silver mine. Under Fiona's withering gaze, their attentions had never progressed beyond a surreptitious damp hand-squeezing and a murmured endearment.

Returning to Sister Cecelia's cabin to make sure she didn't want anything before I retired, I reflected that even such second-best suitors might not be available to me, now that I was no longer an heiress. What was it Patrick had said I possessed—common sense, loyalty? Those were not the qualities that I noticed young men looked for in wives.

As I ministered to Sister Cecelia, she thanked me and said drowsily, "You have a sweet, giving nature, my child. Have you ever thought of entering the holy orders?"

I caught a glimpse of my reflection in the night-blackened porthole as she spoke, my hair in wild disarray about my round, plain face. Did Sister Cecelia think, too, that I would never receive a marriage proposal from a mortal man, and that marriage to God was the only answer for such as myself?

Perhaps guessing my thoughts, the nun said quickly, "It is a grand honor and blessing to give oneself to the Lord. Marriage is not for every woman and not every marriage is a bed of roses."

How well I knew that. I nodded, remembering the friction between Fiona and Jamie that was like a constant crackling of lightning, often exploding into violent storms. But I also remembered the way Jamie's eyes lit up whenever Fiona came into the room, and how the first thing he asked whenever he entered the house was a booming "And where's your mother?"

As for Fiona, why would she have endured all the hard years, that would have destroyed a lesser woman, if not for her deep love of Jamie. Except—I frowned, the memory of those last moments in my mother's bedroom suddenly returning to torment me. I saw again that tender, girlish smile on Fiona's lips, I heard her voice calling out eagerly at the end—to whom? Of course, it must have been Jamie, I decided, annoyed with myself for thinking anything else.

My heart lightened at the thought that within a few days I would be seeing Patrick again. Tomorrow the ship would dock at Portsmouth and we would take the train across England to the port of Holyhead in Wales. Even Sister Cecelia became excited as a child as we drew closer to Ireland.

On the Irish Mail train from London to Holyhead, she regaled me with stories of her childhood in Ireland and with tales of the leprechauns, the little people who had inhabited the country long before the arrival of the early Celts, the raiding Vikings, and the conquering Normans.

"Not that I've ever seen the little creatures myself," she said wistfully. "But my mother, bless her sainted soul"— she crossed herself without breaking the lilting rhythm of her speech—"once throwing out her dirty dishwater after dark, accidentally doused one of the fairy creatures. And after that, nothing went right in the house, the milk soured, the fire wouldn't burn. And that was the year the praties rotted in the field."

The merry blue eyes darkened with remembered pain. "And when we couldn't pay the rent, the land agent sent Daniel Sheehan and three men to turn us out and tumble the house. My mother was within a few days of her downlying. When my father would not move her, they knocked down the walls around her. The child came then, born dead, and my mother died with the birthing."

"And no one helped you?" I asked, shocked.

Sister Cecelia absently caressed her beads. "Those were bad times. The neighbors would have taken us in but they were afraid if they did the agent would have their cottages tumbled too. My father and brothers became roadlings, leaving me with the Sisters of Mercy. I never saw them again."

"That was all many years ago," I said uneasily. "Surely times have changed."

"Nothing will change," Sister Cecelia said. "Not till every last cursed Englishman is dead and gone from holy Irish soil."

I stared, startled, at my companion, at the old, wrinkled face that a moment before had seemed so kindly. The tiny compartment with the night sliding by the darkened windows, the tiny gas jet throwing an uneven light, had suddenly become filled with hate.

"But . . . but you wanted to return to Ireland."

"And why not?" she asked, surprised. "Where else should I die but in me own land when me time comes?" She settled herself more comfortably in her corner of the compartment. "And now I'm thinking it's a long night we have before us and we should be trying to get some sleep."

She fell asleep almost instantly, as a child drops off, but I couldn't shut my eyes. My thoughts, churning, would not let me rest. For the first time I began to wonder a little uneasily about Abbey Court and the people who lived there. Were the Fletcher family as indifferent as that landlord who had turned out Sister Cecelia and her family without a thought as to whether they lived or died? But that was more than fifty years ago, I reminded myself. This was 1882, almost the twentieth century. Surely such cruelties no longer existed.

Nevertheless, I was still wide awake when at three o'clock in the morning our train reached Holyhead. After the porters hustled our baggage and ourselves off the train at the pier, and the purser aboard the ship showed us to our comfortable cabins, I finally managed to sleep a little as we crossed the Irish Channel, but awoke again at first light.

Deciding that I might as well get dressed and go up on deck, I slipped quietly into my clothes so as not to awaken Sister Cecelia. Then, holding my cape against the chill wind whipping off the sea, I stood at the railing, peering through the gray opalescent light for my first glimpse of Ireland.

"It's an early riser you are, my child."

I turned, noticing for the first time the priest who stood not far from me, at the railing. When he moved closer to join me, I saw that he was old, but not as old as Sister Cecelia, and that his dark robe was shabby and worn.

"Good morning to you, Father," I said, sketching a hasty curtsy.

He smiled, pleased. "Och, it's from America you are. I thought so last night when I saw you and the good sister board the ship. I'm Father Jerome. And you're . . ."

"Meg O'Brien, Father, from Boston."

"A fine name," he beamed, "named for our blessed St. Margaret, whose birthday we'll be celebrating soon."

Since my Catholic education had been limited, I knew few of the saints' days and, in any case, my Christian name was not Margaret. Jamie had named me Maeve but the miners had never felt at ease with that name and I had been Maggie or Meg almost from the moment I could toddle. Before I could explain to the father though, he asked, "And is this your first trip to Ireland?"

"Yes, I'm visiting my brother, and Sister Cecelia is returning to her mother house outside of Dublin."

"Well, you'll find it's a grand land entirely," the priest nodded, and then, more slowly, "though it's a sad time to be visiting Dublin." At my blank stare, he asked, "Haven't you heard in America what's happened, the dreadful murders in Phoenix Park in the very heart of Dublin, not more than a month ago?"

Vaguely, I did remember the story being reported in the Boston newspapers but I had forgotten the details.

"A terrible tragedy," the priest said sadly. "The very day the new Chief Secretary to Ireland, Lord Frederick Cavendish, arrived in Dublin. He and his Under Secretary, a Mr. Burke, were taking a stroll in the park when they were set upon by a band of assassins and stabbed to death."

"Who would have done such a thing?" I asked, appalled.

"They say it's a new society called the Invincibles, a secret group of assassins. There are many such lawless bands roaming the countryside, I'm afraid, taking their vengeance wherever they can, killing cattle, burning houses, murdering land agents and process servers." He sighed. "It's as himself said when they imprisoned him in Kilmainham Jail, that Captain Moonlight would take his place."

"You mean Mr. Parnell? But I understood he was to be released from prison."

"Ay, but it may be too late to do any good. Violence has taken hold of the land and the English will not sit back and not take their own revenge."

My hands tightened on the rail. "Will it never end, Father, the hatred between English and Irish?"

"Ay, someday. Someday there must be an end to hating, God willing. But the roots go deep. You know your Irish history, lass?"

"Not a great deal," I admitted. "I know that the Normans invaded Ireland in the twelfth century and intermarried with the Irish, becoming more Irish than the Irish themselves. And then, under the reigns of Queen Mary, Henry VIII, and Elizabeth, colonies of British and Scottish settlers were brought into Ireland, taking the land away from the Irish landowners."

"Not only the land," Father Jerome corrected me. "Later, during Cromwell's invasion, over half the Irish people were killed or shipped off into slavery. More important, the Holy Catholic Church was taken away from the people. Monasteries were destroyed and all forms of Catholic worship forbidden. Then the terrible Penal Laws were enacted. Priests were treated like outlaws, and mass had to be conducted in hidden places, in hedge-rows, up in the hills, or secretly in private homes. . . . Priest hides, they were called, specially constructed with hidden bolt holes so that the priest could escape if his presence in the house was betrayed to the authorities. Even so, many priests were captured, tortured, and killed."

The priest stopped for lack of breath, his face flushed, as he apologized good-naturedly. "Ay, and I'm that sorry, it's lecturing you I am and we've hardly met. At least the terrible Penal Laws are no more, and I'd not have you thinking that all Englishmen are bad. Lord Ashford, who owns most of the country in which my parish lies, is a good man for all that he's English and Protestant. Not like some I could mention."

"Do you know the family of the Earl of Abbeymore?" I asked eagerly.

The priest nodded slowly. "Ay, I know of them. They live in the next county. Is it to Abbey Court you're going then?"

"My brother, Patrick O'Brien, is the husband of Regan Fletcher, cousin to the present Lord Fletcher. They're staying at Abbey Court."

"I'd heard that her young ladyship had married an American but I wasn't knowing his name. A great one for the horses is your sister-in-law. Always wins at the Dublin Horse Show, they say, and has a stud stable second to none in all Ireland."

"Have you met Lord Fletcher?"

"I've never had the honor," he said dryly. "I knew his father, the late Lord Michael Fletcher, a fine archaeologist, a scholarly man. He recovered many holy relics of ancient Ireland though it's my belief his father, old Lord Jason Fletcher, thought little of his son for his work, favoring more his older sons and his young brother, Cormac Fletcher."

"That would be Regan's father," I said. "You know him?"

"Ay, though I've not seen him lately," the priest said, then added dourly, "Even the Devil is slow to claim the soul of that one. During the terrible famine years, as land agent for old Lord Jason, more than thirty homes he tumbled, giving the poor souls a pittance and shipping them off to America—and some of the children enough like him to be his own, which many probably were, taking his pleasure where he chose." The priest's face shone with righteous vindication. "A pleasure he's not been taking lately, crippled as he's been these last years."

"But I thought—the Fletcher family are Catholics, aren't they?"

Father Jerome shrugged. "There are Catholics and Catholics, child. There are those that use the Church to suit their fancy as the Fletchers did. Half of old Daniel Fletcher's sons fought for James II, the Catholic King of England, at the Battle of the Boyne, gaining the oldest son an earldom in the bargain. The other sons fought against James II at that battle, so that when the cowardly James turned tail and ran, leaving the cream of Irish manhood to rot on the field, the Fletcher family still managed to hold onto the title and their estate." Then, grudgingly, "I'm not denying that in the last years there may not have been a good Catholic or two among them. The present earl's mother, Lady Margaret

Fletcher, by all accounts is a saintly woman."

"What of Regan's mother?" I asked curiously. "Did she live at Abbey Court too?"

"I never met her," the priest admitted. "Some say she was wild as a blue hare, brought from County Galway by Cormac. She died soon after Regan was born. Lady Margaret had the rearing of her own son, Kevin, along with Regan and her brother Sean, and a fine handful they both were, I'm thinking. Sean Fletcher is as much like his father as peas in a pod, a hard, godless man. Fortunate he'll be not to end up someday flat on his back, shot by an outraged husband."

I discovered I was clutching the ship railing again and I loosened my grip, wiping my damp palms with my handkerchief. "You're not making the Fletcher family sound too inviting a prospect, Father," I said, smiling weakly.

The priest did not return my smile; his face was somber, his voice grave. "I'd not rest easy knowing a sister of mine was going to live at Abbey Court. There's stories one hears . . ." He broke off abruptly, shaking his head. "But there, I should know better than to believe all the tales I hear. An Irishman is as full of words and tales as a pig has lice. And you tell me your brother is at Abbey Court. Well then, there'll be someone to see you come to no harm."

He leaned forward against the railing, his face brightening. "Ay, and here I'm blathering and you're missing the finest sight your eyes will ever see."

I followed his gaze to the shore, now dimly visible through the pearl-colored dawn. The sky was a hazy pink overhead, and through the silvery mist, rich green slopes rose verdantly, spilling lushly down to the sea.

The father's voice was hushed, almost reverent, as if it might have been the Holy Grail he was seeing. "There she is, child . . . there's Ireland."

5

I sniffed the air, delighted. "What is that sort of buttery smell?"

"That's peat and the sea and the sod of Ireland itself," the father explained. "No Irishman will ever be forgetting it."

"You've been away a long time?" I asked sympathetically.

"Ay, a long time," he agreed. "A fortnight."

Then Sister Cecelia came puffing up the stairs, looking for me. "The steward says we must hurry, Maggie, if we want morning tea."

There was only time for hurried introductions. Then the steward brought us a hasty breakfast of tea and scones before once again the porters rushed aboard and hustled off our luggage and ourselves onto a waiting train to Dublin. I had planned to escort Sister Cecelia to her mother house and spend the night in Dublin, proceeding in the morning to Abbeymore. Instead, Father Jerome very kindly offered to act as escort for Sister Cecelia. In addition, since there were several railroad stations in Dublin, he and Sister Cecelia insisted upon taking me to the proper station to catch my train for Abbeymore. There I sent a telegram to Patrick at Abbey Court announcing my earlier arrival, and said a fond good-by to Sister Cecelia, whose eyes shone suspiciously damp.

"You will be writing me now," she insisted. "I'll not sleep well till I know you're safe with your brother."

Father Jerome gave me his blessing and added, "If you should meet any trouble at your new home, my child, Father Vincent is the curate at Abbeymore. He's new and young but sound, I'm thinking."

"Trouble?" Sister Cecelia gave the priest a worried glance. "And what trouble would that be?"

Fortunately my train was getting ready to leave and there

was no time for explanations. Father Jerome found me and my luggage a first-class compartment where, since I was alone, I arranged my skirts discreetly around me and promptly fell asleep. I awoke several hours later with a start, feeling painfully stiff, not to mention ravenously hungry.

I soon discovered there was no dining coach on the train and no luncheon baskets were provided as had been done on the Irish Mail the night before. It made me irritable to miss a meal, not that it would hurt me to fast a little, I thought, looking gloomily down at my waist. No matter how tortuously tight I was laced, my waistline never managed to get down to the fashionable twenty inches.

Not only was hunger making angry murmurs in my stomach, but it was raining, a depressingly steady downpour hiding what scenery there was to be seen through the not too clean train windows. Occasionally I took my handkerchief and, clearing a hole in the mist, peered out the window whenever the rain showed signs of slackening. But the countryside seemed deserted. Now and then we passed a run-down-looking cottage with a thatched roof, or fields surrounded by stone walls. There were whitish blossoms in the field that I recognized as potato plants. Fiona had tried to plant a small garden behind whatever shack we lived in when I was young, and always, I remembered, she had planted potatoes.

More and more often, though, I saw the roofless remains of a cottage, or just a pile of rubble, a square of stones where a cottage had once stood, now filled with golden gorse and nettles. Once I saw the crumpled walls and half steeple of a church, and an even more elaborate ruin on a hillside that might have been a castle or a large home. There was something inexpressibly forlorn about the view, the deserted cottages, the crumbling ruins, like a landscape over which a terrible battle has been fought.

I glanced at the watch I wore pinned to my bodice and saw that we would be arriving at Abbeymore soon. I began to do what I could to make myself presentable. I was still wearing mourning black, of course, although I had allowed myself a touch of ivory satin trimming at the black velvet collar and cuffs of my alpaca traveling suit. There had been nothing livening I could do about my wrist-length, crepe-veiled bonnet, which I now took from my bandbox and secured to my head with two jet-tipped hatpins. At least, I thought, the hat hid much of my hair, which badly needed a good brushing.

Catching sight of myself in the train window, I couldn't help thinking, a little guiltily, that I would be glad when I could go into second mourning clothes. Fiona had looked dramatic in black with her creamy skin and golden-red hair but my face had a tendency to flush easily and, with my bright hair, black had a way of making me look and feel uncomfortably overheated.

At last the train was pulling to a stop at a tiny station platform. The rain had stopped. The porter helped me down the steps, then piled my luggage neatly on the platform. I looked around to see if I could find Patrick, my heart racing with excitement. The only person on the platform, though, was an elderly man in a great oversized frock coat who stared at me curiously.

After the train left, he approached me cautiously. "Is it a trap you'll be needing?"

"No, thank you. Someone is meeting me."

As I looked around the empty platform, disappointment had the taste of a sourball in my mouth. I had expected Patrick to meet me but if he, himself, hadn't been able to come to the station, surely he would send someone else from Abbey Court.

I sat on my small steamer trunk, as the sturdiest of my luggage, and waited five . . . ten . . . minutes. The sky above me had changed to a remarkable, almost translucent shade of blue. It was hard to imagine it had rained at all except for the grassy meadow beyond the station, which was coated with a crystal sheen of raindrops. The sun began to feel too warm, and my stomach rumbled unhappily. It had been a very light tea for breakfast and that many hours away now, I thought, stifling a feeling of righteous indignation. Still, there was probably a logical explanation—my telegram had gone astray, no doubt. It was foolish to continue sitting, uncomfortable in the sun and hungry.

I walked over to the old man, who got to his feet, watching me gravely. "I think I will hire that trap," I said.

He thought about my statement, then shook his head. "I have no trap. James O'Hara has but he's not for hire today. I have a handcart, if your ladyship's not going too great a distance."

"Abbey Court," I said. "Is it far from here?"

A look of consternation clouded the old man's face. "Abbey Court?" he repeated, blinking rapidly.

Was he deaf, I wondered, or only a little daft? "Abbey Court," I repeated. "I'm visiting my brother, Patrick O'Brien. Is the house far?"

He spoke slowly as if choosing each word with great care. "Not far, a mile and a bit."

"Well, then I think I'll walk," I said, suddenly making up my mind. I was stiff and achy from the train ride. I could use the exercise. "Would you bring my luggage to the house in your handcart?"

He looked uncomfortably to the right and left as if seeking assistance from someone but none was forthcoming. At the far end of the street I could see what looked like the beginnings of a small village but no people stirred.

"Which way?" I asked patiently. And at his blank look, I repeated, not so patiently, "Which way do I walk to get to Abbey Court?"

He gestured toward the meadow. "Follow the boreen through the field past Tom Welch's pasture and round Murphy's bog. You may have to climb a wall or two." He glanced down at my thin black leather shoes. "It could be a wee bit muddy."

"I'll manage," I assured him, wondering if it was safe to leave my luggage with the old man. There seemed no other solution, however, and I could always send someone back from Abbey Court once I reached there. I started off briskly enough down the small footpath that led first across the meadow, then through a narrow wooded area, and finally between stretches of pasture land all neatly lined with gray stone walls. In one pasture a cow grazed calmly, watching me with large velvet brown eyes. I passed two cottages but there were no signs of occupants although a bluish haze hung over the chimney of one cottage and I caught the smell of peat burning.

The afternoon sun had grown warmer. Soon I slipped my bonnet off my head, letting it hang down my back by its ties. Once or twice I came across walls I had to climb but they were low and I scrambled over them easily. I walked for about twenty minutes and when there was no sign of a house of the size of Abbey Court I began to wonder, worried, if I had taken a wrong turning.

Yet I hadn't seen any other path than the . . . what was it the old man had called it? . . . the boreen I was traveling. Another twenty minutes later the countryside began to change subtly, became more open. Instead of cultivated fields, the foliage took on a wild, unkempt look—there were sedges and reeds and heather and a thick, vivid green moss. The path beneath my feet had a soft, springy feel, like walking on a mattress, I thought, as I stopped a moment to admire a mass of yellow starry flowers growing a little way off the path, a carpet of gold flung across the green moss.

On an impulse I lifted my skirt above my ankles and stepped off the path to pick some of the flowers. I hadn't gone more than five feet when I felt the ground softening beneath me, and I heard a muddy, squishy sound. At first, I felt only annoyance that my shoes would be ruined. Then, as I took another step forward into the moss and felt the ground suddenly rise up around my ankles, I stopped short and decided I'd better get back to the path and forget about the flowers.

To my surprise, I found I couldn't seem to lift my foot up. The more I struggled, the deeper I sank into the mire. It was a disconcerting sensation, to feel solid ground give way slowly, inexorably, beneath me. I looked around, trying to find something to which I could cling. There was a shrub growing not far away that appeared well rooted. If I could reach that, I thought hopefully, perhaps I could pull myself free.

It was impossible to hold up my skirt and reach at the same time. There was nothing to do but let the hem of my skirt trail in the mud while I stretched my hands out toward the shrub.

Almost at the same moment I reached out, I heard the sound of a horse's hoofbeats on the path behind me and a man's voice calling out: "Keep still!"

I tried to turn to see the owner of the voice but the movement made me lose my precarious balance. I flailed my arms to keep from falling, and felt a clamminess against the calves of my legs as I sank deeper in the mud.

The voice was closer now, harsh with irritation. "Is it deaf you are as well as stupid? Did you not hear me tell you to hold still?"

I had turned enough so that I could see him now as he dismounted, a tall, evidently work-hardened, muscular man in simple homespun trousers and shirt. From what I could glimpse, his eyes seemed to be an unusual blue-green shade beneath heavy lids; his skin, swarthy; his black hair, short cut and curly. It was a face that somehow seemed more suited to a Mediterranean pirate than to an Irish tenant farmer. His face, I was also sure, had set many a maiden's heart a-fluttering but at the moment he was glaring at me, dark as a thundercloud, and I was too furious at my humiliating situation to feel anything but anger.

"Don't just stand there," I said with as much haughty dignity as I could muster under the circumstances. "Give me your hand."

"I'll not be ruining my boots too," he announced, studying carefully the ground next to the path. Then, warily avoiding the more vivid green moss, he stepped gingerly out onto a rock that brought him closer to me but not near enough to reach me with his hand. "Would you be wearing a shirt or suchlike under that jacket?" he asked hopefully.

I felt a flush sweep over my face and I sputtered, "My jacket . . . whatever for . . ."

He sighed. "Ay, I thought not." Then, before I had time to realize what he was about, he had stripped his shirt over his head and I caught a swift glimpse of brawny shoulders, a mass of black curly hair covering a broad chest, before I gasped and averted my shocked gaze.

"Slow now," he ordered. "Catch one end when I toss it to you."

Reluctantly I returned my glance and did as I was told. The first time I missed the catch, but the second time I caught a firm hold of a sleeve of his shirt.

"Hold tight now," he said. He pulled gradually at the impromptu rope, bracing himself on the rock. I felt myself being lifted slowly, heard the ripping of cloth, and then with one final effort he managed to reach my arms, hands fastening like irons on my wrists. Then I was jerked bodily with such force that I arrived at the rock barefooted, my shoes left behind in the bog.

The rock on which he and I stood was not overly large and was covered with a slippery moss. For a moment I clung to him to keep from falling backward before I gained a sound footing and hastily pulled myself free.

"Thank you," I said, annoyed at how my voice always sounded childishly breathless when I was flustered.

"Not at all," he replied curtly, and turning, he leaped agilely from the rock to the path. I followed more clumsily, the mud on my skirt hem weighing me down.

By the time I reached the path he had slipped his shirt back on and I saw the tear in the armhole. "Your shirt . . . oh, I am sorry. I'll pay for a new one, of course."

He didn't seem to hear me. He had given a low whistle and a roan mare came trotting up from where she had been calmly grazing. I don't pretend to be a judge of horseflesh but the mare was certainly no farmer's horse, and I wondered if the man worked at a nearby stable, perhaps even at Abbey Court.

I glanced back at the bog and felt a stirring of indignation. "The old man at the station should at least have warned me that this path was dangerous," I said, annoyed.

"Well now, I suppose the thought didn't strike him that anyone would be daft enough to pick posies in Murphy's bog."

I realized I was still clutching a few yellow flowers in my hand, and I let them fall to the path. A cold shiver like ice water trickled down my spine as I stared at my rescuer. "Is it possible I could have sunk . . ." My voice fell away; I did not want to put the terrifying picture into words.

" 'Tis like quicksand that gobbles up anything unwary enough to step into it," he assured me gravely. "I've heard tell of men cutting into the turf and finding the bodies of men trapped centuries before in the bog, body and clothes perfectly preserved. Once a man was even found still mounted on his horse."

I glanced up quickly, caught the spark of amusement in the blue-green eyes watching me, and realized he was laughing at me, or with me, for, unaccountably, I suddenly found myself laughing too. "I must look a fine sight," I said, glancing down at my mud-caked feet, my drooping skirt, and my hair undoubtedly flying in all directions.

He handed me a dry clump of grass. "Here, this will help with the cleaning until you can have a proper wash-up. And in the meantime maybe you'll be kind enough to tell me what you're doing out here in the middle of nowhere."

I concentrated on scrubbing some of the mud from my feet. "I was on my way to Abbey Court," I explained. "The old man at the station said it was just a mile and a bit, so I thought I'd walk. Do you know Abbey Court? Is it much farther?"

When he didn't answer immediately, I looked up and was surprised to discover that the dark, stormy look was all at once back on his face. As changeable as the Irish weather, I decided, one minute sunshine, the next clouds. Even his voice had changed. The soft, lilting Irish brogue was gone, a precise, cultivated intonation taking its place. "You have business at Abbey Court?"

"I'm visiting my brother, Mr. Patrick O'Brien," I said. "I had expected to be met at the station." My voice faltered beneath that dark gaze. "Is something wrong?"

41

"You've a dab of mud on your nose," he said, turning away. "Abbey Court is another mile from here. You'll learn in Ireland the bit is as long as the mile." He brought the roan to me, then, swinging easily up into the saddle, reached down a hand to me. "I'll take you there."

Before I could protest, he had swung me up and I was straddling the saddle behind him, my arms clasped tightly around his middle. "Hold on tight," he said. "I'm taking a short cut. We may have to jump a wall or two. Will you be all right?"

I nodded, rather enjoying the sensation, after I had gotten over the initial shock, of feeling the hardness of his back, the warmth of his body pressed so close to my own. He took a path through the woods on the far side of the bog and I hid my face against him to protect it from the whipping branches that snagged at my hair. He was an expert rider and the roan took a stone wall effortlessly before I even realized we were upon it. By the third wall, I had learned to relax and not brace myself against the shock of the landing.

At last the path turned off from the woods into a winding, hedge-lined road that finally passed between two great stone pillars, at which an iron gate swung open. There was a tiny cottage by the gate, a haze of peat moss hanging over it. I caught a glimpse of movement within the cottage and heard an odd wailing sound that sent shivers washing over me. Then the unnerving sound was behind us and we were galloping down a gravel drive and through a narrow, heavily wooded area that apparently acted as a screen. For suddenly, as we followed a long curve, the trees fell away and a house appeared at the end of the drive.

There was time for no more than a quick glimpse of a solid, square-cut stone façade and three tiers of windows overlooking a stone terrace that stretched across the whole front of the house and sloped down to the driveway. A curved screen of hemlocks and oaks pressed like thick pincers up to both sides of the house. My first impression was one of disappointment. Abbey Court was by no means the magnificent mansion I had imagined. It was simply a very large country house, larger than the homes I had known in Denver and Boston, but much more austere, without the elaborate jigsaw scrollwork, cupolas, and ornate cast-iron trim to which I was accustomed.

A servant came hurrying through the massive front door and down the gray stone steps. He took the reins of the roan, gazing at me curiously as I slid down from the saddle into the man's arms. My companion released me immediately, escorting me up the stairs and into a lofty front hall.

"Wait here," he ordered brusquely, and walked through a green baize door at the end of the large, square hall.

I glanced around me, curious. The entrance was more of an outsized room than a hallway. A dark slate-gray fireplace occupied one wall and old-fashioned rosewood chairs, covered in worn and faded gray and yellow striped fabric that Mother wouldn't have given house room to, stood in companionable clusters around the hall. There was no rug on the floor and my feet, clad only in thin stockings, were beginning to feel a trifle chilled when the man returned.

A woman was with him. She wore a black dress with a starched white apron tied around her thick waist. Her face was as pink and wrinkled and round as Sister Cecelia's but there the resemblance ended. For there was no merriment in the tiny eyes bedded in the plump cheeks, or any warmth in the narrow lips pulled taut in a look of perpetual ill humor. Her glance traveled from my tousled hair to my bedraggled face and lingered disdainfully on my muddy feet. I felt my face redden.

"Miss O'Toole, will you show Miss O'Brien to her room and make her comfortable," the man said.

Then, without giving me a chance to ask about Patrick, he turned away, opening one of the large doors that led off the hall and closing it quickly behind him. I had no choice but to follow the woman, who was apparently the housekeeper, up the uncarpeted oak staircase, past rows of unsmiling portraits, to a narrow art gallery branching off from the top of the stairs. We walked rapidly through the gallery into a passageway, then took a turn to the right. Near the middle of the corridor, Miss O'Toole stopped and opened a door, standing back so that I walked ahead of her into a spacious, high-ceilinged room.

Miss O'Toole did not enter the room. "I'll fetch you a jug of water. You'll want to wash up." She had a high-pitched voice that grated on the nerves but it was her eyes that most disconcerted me. They stared at me unblinkingly, a cold, pale gaze with no hint of friendliness, almost an open hostility.

Beneath that oddly intent gaze, I smiled nervously. "Thank you. I must look a fright. You see, I was walking here, when . . ."

"Mr. Sean told me," she interrupted, turning away abruptly. "I'll fetch the jug."

So my companion had been Sean Fletcher, I thought, staring at the closed door. I should have guessed he wasn't a servant or farmer. There had been too much arrogance about him, a ready air of authority as if he were used to giving, not taking, orders. And if Father Jerome was right, my reaction to the man's brooding dark handsomeness had been a typically female one with which Sean Fletcher was undoubtedly well acquainted.

Irritated at my foolish susceptibility, I determinedly pushed all thoughts of the man from my mind and studied my bedroom. Although the plaster work on the ceiling was an elaborate scroll of roses and cupids, the furnishings themselves were simple enough. There was a huge mahogany bed, a wing chair, a dressing table and washstand with a china bowl and basin, and at the two large windows hung green and white cretonne curtains, almost the same shade as the faded wallpaper.

A small fireplace provided the heat for the room. I had the definite impression from the chill in the air that heating with a furnace was unknown at Abbey Court. A door led into a largish dressing room, in which an old-fashioned wardrobe covered one wall. I opened the wardrobe, discovered it was empty, then closed it quickly against the unpleasant moldy smell.

Well, at least there was a pleasant vista from the windows, I thought, looking out over a broad expanse of green park and dense woodland. At a distance beyond the woodland there was a low, blue, almost lilac-colored range of mountains, where the sun was slowly setting. The sky had a milky hue, and the grass was such a vibrant green, crisscrossed with thin black shadows from the trees, that the whole landscape had an unreal, theatrical look. A flock of birds like bits of black paper soared and dipped above the trees, the only movement to meet my eye in the whole scene. Suddenly, for some reason I could not explain, the view no longer gave me pleasure, as if the warmth was being drained from my body the same way that light and color were being slowly drained from the day. When the knock came at the door, I turned eagerly. It was not Patrick, however, but Miss O'Toole returning with a steaming jug of hot water and a tray holding sandwiches and hot tea.

"I thought you might want a bite to eat." There was no warmth in her hospitality; it seemed automatic.

"Oh yes, thank you. I'm famished."

She put the jug and tray down but, instead of leaving, she stood staring at me, her plump hands clasped like tiny sausages in front of her apron. "You have nothing of your mother's looks about you," she said almost accusingly. "But the eyes. They have the same bold, shameless look about them."

At first I was too pleased to be indignant. "You knew Mother?"

"Is it that I'd be forgetting Fiona O'Neill, the black disgrace she brought to Abbey Court before she took her French leave?" Each word was a lovingly polished pellet flung at my face.

Before I could recover my wits she turned abruptly again to the door. "Heed me now. Mr. Sean said you was to stay in your room." The door clicked shut firmly behind her. If there had been a key, I had the feeling that she would have happily locked it.

I frowned at the closed door, anger rapidly replacing hunger. Ignoring my growling stomach, I flung myself into washing the dirt from my face, hands, and feet. There was little I could do about the hem of my dress except brush off as much mud as I could. My hair I pulled back ruthlessly, as if it were not my hair but something else I was attacking furiously. How dare I be ordered to stay in my room like a willful child? And where was Patrick? Well, Miss O'Toole and Sean Fletcher would discover I was not to be ordered about so easily.

I hesitated at the door, looking down at my bare feet, then shrugged. Patrick had seen me without shoes before. In the summer, as children in the mining camps, we neither could afford nor had use for shoes. I walked down the corridor, then made a wrong turning at the end and had to retrace my steps before I finally made my way again down the steep oak staircase.

The entrance hall was empty and I paused, uncertain, wondering which room to enter, when a young parlormaid came through the baize door and dropped me a startled curtsy. "What a fright you gave me, ma'am," she gasped. Her eyes widened at sight of my bare feet. "I didn't know there were visitors in the house."

"I'm looking for Mr. Patrick O'Brien," I said. "Can you tell me where I may find him?"

Her eyes still riveted to my feet, she gestured toward the room into which Sean Fletcher had disappeared. "Why, in there, ma'am, but does his lordship . . ."

I didn't wait to hear the rest of her question. Pushing open the door, I walked into what appeared to be a formal drawing room. It was difficult to tell because all the shades were drawn and the room lit by candlelight which did little to dispel the darkness.

I saw three people, two men and a woman, who turned startled faces in my direction as I walked toward them. One of the men was Sean Fletcher. He took a hesitant step forward, then stopped. For by then it was too late. I had already come far enough into the room to see the polished oak coffin with the silver candlesticks burning at the head and foot.

And in the coffin lay my brother Patrick.

6

I heard someone cry out. I didn't realize until later that that wild keen of pain had come from my own throat. Then all the candles in the room suddenly flickered and died and, with a great roaring in my ears, the darkness rushed over me.

I couldn't have been unconscious for more than a few seconds. The next thing I knew I was lying on a small couch and a man was kneeling beside me, rubbing my hands. At first his face was only a blur; then I was aware of pale, ascetic features, eyes the color of pewter, and light brown hair that fell across a high, slightly domed forehead.

When he saw that my eyes were open, he spoke in a stammering rush. "My dear Miss O'Brien . . . I . . . I can't tell you how sorry . . . that you should . . . find out about your . . . brother this way. It's inexcusable."

He cast an outraged look at Sean, who stood to one side, carefully removed from the scene, leaning nonchalantly against a table. The dark face was in shadow so I couldn't read the expression.

"You could at least have had the common decency to . . . to tell her . . . before this happened."

"I thought we agreed, Cousin, that it was your duty to tell her," Sean said, his voice flat. "And I did leave word that Miss O'Brien was to remain in her room."

"The good Lord have mercy, what difference does it make now whose fault it is?" It was the young woman speaking with a querulous impatience. "Fetch some brandy for my sister-in-law, Sean."

She stepped forward into the candlelight. My brother's widow was clothed entirely in black, but the mourning dress of a dull crepe was cut with such style that it might have been a fashionable gown. It suggested an unbelievably tiny waist and was flared at the hem, with a footing of black lace, delicate as a spider web, at the wrists and high neck.

I gazed up into that creamy, perfectly oval face and thought: Patrick had not exaggerated. His wife was extraordinarily beautiful. She must have been a few years younger than I, but somehow she appeared older, more sophisticated. Her shining black hair was gathered skillfully into curls that fell down her back. Her neck was slim and graceful, and her cheeks were a soft rose color that I suspected was artificially, if expertly, applied. Her heavy-lidded eyes very much resembled her brother's; they were the same striking aquamarine shade, with thick, lush lashes. At the moment, though, what I noticed most about my sister-in-law's eyes was that there was no touch of redness about them. If his widow had wept at Patrick's death, there was no trace of tears on her face. Hastily I pushed aside this uncharitable thought. Perhaps Regan was one of those women who kept her feelings deeply hidden, or who considered it a mark of ill breeding to show sorrow as lesser folk might do.

She leaned down and pressed her cheek against mine. Her skin felt cool and smelled of some heavy musk scent. "I'm Regan, of course," she murmured. "And I don't believe you've met my cousin, Lord Kevin Fletcher. . . ."

"Perhaps we should all introduce ourselves to Miss O'Brien."

I turned, startled, toward the sound of the voice. A second woman I hadn't even noticed was in the room stepped out of the shadows. It was no wonder I hadn't seen her. She was dressed all in black and her gown of some coarse woolen material was loose-fitting, more in the style of a nun's robe. A black, satin-edged, thick crepe veil reached down to her waist and almost completely hid her gray-flecked hair.

The man kneeling beside me got quickly to his feet and I saw that Kevin Fletcher was tall, taller than Sean Fletcher, but more slender, lightly boned and slightly round-shouldered. "Mother, this is Patrick's sister. Miss O'Brien, may I present the Lady Margaret Fletcher."

The woman lifted her veil and I looked for the first time into the face of the Dowager Countess of Abbeymore. She had pale, angular features, much like those of her son, but while there was about Lord Fletcher a touch of the young, romantic Lord Byron, his mother was simply a homely middle-aged woman. Her only exceptional feature was her eyes. They were a pale gray shade, and they shone with a glossy intensity that reminded me of the primitive paintings of saints, where the face is wooden but the eyes burn with an inner, all-consuming passion. They were not eyes that one could gaze comfortably into for very long. She leaned forward quickly and placed her cheek against mine as Regan had done. Her hand, thin and white and tapering, reached out from her long full sleeve and touched mine sympathetically, then swiftly withdrew.

"We have been looking forward to meeting you," she said softly. "Patrick spoke of you so often. . . ."

Before I could gather myself to rise to my feet and make a proper curtsy, Sean Fletcher came back into the room with a small glass of brandy. He frowned as he handed it to me.

"I'm not sure brandy is such a good idea. How long has it been since you've eaten, Miss O'Brien?"

I thought brandy was an excellent idea, however, and I swallowed the liquor quickly, choking a little as its warmth burned my throat. At least it gave me the strength to get to my feet.

"I believe you've already met my cousin, Sean Fletcher," Lord Fletcher began when Sean broke in brusquely.

"I think Miss O'Brien has had enough introductions for now, Kevin. She should be resting."

He spoke, I thought, as if he were the Earl of Abbeymore, accustomed to giving and having his orders obeyed here at Abbey Court. Lord Fletcher's face flushed boyishly beneath his pale skin but he said quietly, "Sean's right, Miss O'Brien. This must be a terrible shock for you. We can talk later."

"No." I shook my head, not sure how long the false,

warming strength from the brandy would last, knowing only that I couldn't leave this way, not yet. "I want to hear when . . . how Patrick died."

"His body was found yesterday, early yesterday afternoon around one o'clock," Lord Fletcher said reluctantly.

"Found?" I echoed. "I don't understand. He wasn't ill?"

Kevin Fletcher's face flushed a deeper pink; he cast a desperate glance at his cousin. Sean shrugged, his voice harsh. "There's no easy way of telling you, Miss O'Brien. Your brother died of a bullet wound. He was horseback riding alone and was shot from ambush."

For a second I was afraid I was going to faint again but I took a deep breath, my hands clenching into fists so that my fingernails gouged into the soft flesh of my palms. I would not let go, I told myself fiercely. Not until I heard the whole story.

"Why?" I blurted. "Who shot him?"

Lord Fletcher picked up the conversational reins again. "No one knows. There's an investigation being conducted, of course, and a search party has been looking for the assassin or assassins. I'm afraid, though, the feeling is"— the earl tugged uncomfortably at his ear lobe—"well, that it may have been Moonlighters or even one of the tenant farmers here at Abbey Court."

"I don't understand. Patrick wrote he was trying to help the tenants. Why should they want to kill him?"

There was an awkward silence that Sean finally broke, his face grim. "Terrorist groups like the Moonlighters don't always need logical reasons to kill, Miss O'Brien, and perhaps the tenants didn't have the wit to appreciate your brother's concern." His voice flattened. "Or there's always the possibility that the assassins mistook Patrick for me. He was riding my horse at the time."

I shivered, disbelieving, uncomprehending. How could a man be shot from ambush in broad daylight? What kind of people, what sort of country was this?

"We would have wired you immediately," Regan said quickly, "but Patrick had told us you were on your way here and we didn't know how to reach you. We thought you were arriving tomorrow or naturally there would have been someone at the station to meet you."

"I sent a wire, from Dublin," I said.

She frowned and bit her full lower lip. "So many telegrams of condolences have been arriving that I haven't had time to look through them all. Your wire must be among them."

"The funeral arrangements have all been made," Lady Fletcher said. "There'll be a three-day lying in state, today and tonight just for the immediate family. Father Vincent will be coming by this evening to lead the rosary. Tomorrow and the next day there will undoubtedly be a great many visitors, not just friends and dignitaries, but tenants and neighboring farm families and villagers from Abbeymore to pay their last respects. I'm sure you'll want to help receive them, as part of the family."

"Yes," I said weakly, not sure at all that at this point I wanted to meet hordes of strangers.

"The funeral mass will be at the parish church on Thursday. The bishop will, of course, preside at the solemn requiem mass and the solemn absolution. Burial will be in the cemetery by the family vault." The countess hesitated, then said tactfully, "You understand, because your brother was not a Fletcher, burial cannot be within the family vault itself."

"Yes, I understand," I murmured, but I didn't understand, not at all, I thought wildly. I didn't understand how she could speak of the burial of my beloved brother as if she were discussing a social occasion that must be ritualistically and formally scheduled every minute.

It was Lord Fletcher who sensed my bewilderment and interceded quietly, "I think, Mother, that the rest of the funeral arrangements can be discussed with Miss O'Brien tomorrow. I assume she'd like to be alone with her brother for a few minutes now."

I gave him a grateful glance.

Lady Fletcher offered graciously, "I'll stay with you, my child, if you wish."

I shook my head, mutely, and remained where I was until the door had closed behind them all. Then, slowly, I walked to where the coffin lay, and knelt to say a silent prayer.

Although I have never considered myself particularly devout, the prayer brought me a measure of peace, so that at last I could rise to my feet and bring myself to look down into Patrick's face, if not with acceptance of my loss, at least with an acceptance of sorts.

I lifted the net covering the casket and touched the soft golden-red hair for the last time, brushing back an errant lock that had fallen over his forehead. Absently I thought that now I would never know why Patrick's last letters had sounded so troubled. Well, whatever the trouble was, it would bother him no more. Some vile, cowardly creature skulking in the brush had taken care of that.

Now the tears I had been holding back blurred my eyes and poured down my cheeks. I brushed at them ineffectually with the back of my hand. These were not tears of sorrow, alone, but of anger, and a senseless fury shook me. I'd make him pay. Somehow, whoever it was, I'd run him down, see him hanged, if it was the last thing I did. . . .

Finally the storm passed and the wrenching sobs ended, leaving me exhausted, depleted of everything but an overwhelming weariness. Then, as I left the drawing room and entered again the vast entrance hall, I knew unhappily that wasn't all I felt. Sean Fletcher had been right. The brandy had not been a good idea, especially on an empty stomach.

I returned to my bedroom just in time to be sick in my washbowl. I was clinging weakly to the side of the table when I heard someone enter the room. A voice crooned softly to me as strong arms helped me to bed.

"Thank you," I whispered, and looked up into the face of the young maid I had met earlier in the entrance hall. Her brown hair was smoothed tightly back beneath a neat white cap with black streamers but several curls had managed to pull loose around a cheerful, red-cheeked face.

"My name's Rose," she said, "and I'm to look after you, they tell me, so we'll just take off your clothes and get you into bed where you should have been, I'm thinking, long ago." I saw that during my absence my luggage had arrived and unpacking had already begun. Rose slipped a nightgown over my head and tucked me between the covers with a hot water jug at my feet and a cool cloth on my forehead. Then she brought warm, golden toast and a sweet-tasting tea. " 'Tis camomile tea," she said. "And a little something in it that will give you a gentle sleep."

I don't know whether it was the tea or just plain exhaustion, but I fell asleep almost immediately and awoke the next morning, feeling as rested as if I'd slept for days.

There was a bad moment when memory of Patrick returned, like a knife twisting agonizingly just below my breastbone. For a moment I thought I might be sick again, then there was a soft knock at the door and Rose came bustling in, bearing a breakfast tray.

"Her ladyship thought you might be wanting breakfast in your room this morning." She put down an enormous tray with coffee, porridge and cream, eggs and slices of thick, pink ham. Now I know what they mean by a hearty Irish breakfast, I thought, appalled, certain that I would never be able to eat half of it. Thirty minutes later, however, when Rose returned with a hip bath, hot water, and fresh warm towels, I had finished every last morsel. "There's a room for bathing, down the corridor, that his lordship had put in last year," the maid said, "but it doesn't seem proper somehow and the water's never more than lukewarm."

So I bathed in the hip bath and then Rose patiently began brushing the tangles from my hair. My hair always did have a mind of its own and this morning it was more obstinate than usual about lying neatly in place. Finally Rose managed to confine it within a black net chignon, sighed triumphantly, and stepped back. "There now, it's cross-grained, that hair. No wonder it's bad luck to see a red-haired woman the first thing in the morning."

"Is it?" I asked curiously. "I didn't know that."

"To be sure," she said, and then added hastily, "although it's only the old ones who believe so."

I walked to the window after I had finished dressing, deliberately putting off the moment when I would have to go downstairs, meet the Fletchers again and—what was it the countess had said?—"receive visitors" by Patrick's coffin.

It was a beautiful morning, the sky a billowy blue with only a few puffs of clouds. Sunlight glistened across the lawn and in the trees so that each leaf and blade of grass had an enameled look. Toward the rear of Abbey Court, I could just glimpse a road curving like a white ribbon away from the house through a thicket of trees. Then, as I watched, at first disbelieving my eyes, I saw what appeared to be a stunted, black-clothed figure moving slowly down the winding road, slowly because I could have sworn whoever it was was not walking but crawling.

"Rose, who is that?" I asked, shocked.

She joined me at the window. "Och, that would be her ladyship, on her way to the old Abbey. What with your brother's death and all, it's forgetting I am this is the anniversary of the blessed martyrs' death." She crossed herself slowly.

I remembered now Mother's mentioning the ruins of an old abbey near Abbey Court, which I suppose was how the house had got its name. "What martyrs?" I asked, unable to remove my mesmerized gaze from that half figure inching painfully along the gravel road.

Rose's eyes widened, her voice disbelieving. "Sure and you've heard of them that died at the Abbey? When Captain Daniel Fletcher and his men burned Kilcallen Castle, the people from round about fled to the church at the old Abbey for safety. Most of the Abbey had been destroyed years before, but the church still stood and the people took refuge inside, old men and women and children. When the captain found them there, he ordered his soldiers to lock the door of the church and himself put a torch to the thatch roof. Then he and his men, like the blackhearted fiends from hell they were, stood and listened to the screams of the poor souls, burned alive inside the church, with no way of escaping."

I felt the muscles in my stomach jerk convulsively. "All of them . . . children too?"

Rose nodded somberly. "Ay, and a holy man among them, an old priest. They say that before the flames devoured him he swore that himself, nor any of the martyred souls that died with him, would ever rest until they were avenged. After her ladyship married the late Lord Fletcher, she made a vow that every year on the anniversary of the burning of the blessed martyrs she would make a pilgrimage to the Abbey on her knees, in penitence, and pray for the souls of those who died there that day. And each year, no matter the weather, she keeps that vow. A saint, her ladyship is. Sure and it's only her prayers that keeps them at peace."

"At peace?" I asked, startled, turning to face the maid.

Rose crossed herself fervently. "I've never heard them myself, thank the good Lord and Lady Fletcher's prayers. You'd not get me near the old Abbey after dark for all the gold in London. But there's others that have heard them, the terrible groans coming from the old Abbey, like souls in mortal torment. Just two nights ago, old Malachy, going home by the old abbey road, passing by the ruins of the Abbey, swore he heard cries that lifted the hairs on his head, before he took to his heels."

I sat down on the edge of the bed, more disturbed by Rose's story than I cared to admit. It wasn't that I believed in spirits who lived after death or in curses from beyond the grave. Old Malachy had doubtless been imbibing too freely at the local pub before his walk home that night past the old Abbey.

The look on Rose's face as she told me the tale of the burning of the church by Captain Fletcher was the same bitter look that had been on my mother's face when she spoke Cromwell's name. The hatred of the English was as fresh and alive in young Rose's mind as it had been in Mother's, a frightening legacy passed whole from one generation to the next, never allowed to be forgotten or forgiven.

Could it have been just such a blind hatred which had caused a man to lie in wait for my brother, to slowly squeeze the trigger and watch Patrick fall, mortally wounded, from his saddle, and then to run away and leave him to bleed to death there in the road?

"Are you feeling yourself, your ladyship?" Rose asked, her face worried. "It's sorry I am if I troubled you."

I shook my head and tried to smile. "No, I'm all right, Rose, and I'm not your ladyship. My name's Meg, or Miss O'Brien, if you'd rather."

"Very well, your la—" She giggled and put a hand up to her mouth. "Miss Meg. It's new I am to being a maid to a grand lady like yourself. My mother raised no higher than a lower parlormaid. She'll be that proud to hear of my new position."

I looked up into that open, round-cheeked face, all trace of old hatreds forgotten now, the eyes unclouded and innocent as the sky. Surely, I thought, if anyone, she would tell me the truth. I leaned forward and clasped her hand, my voice low. "Do you believe it was a tenant who killed my brother, Rose?"

The pink drained from her cheeks and she looked away from me, one hand twisting nervously at her neat white apron. "I'd not be knowing the true or lie of that. Sure and most of the tenants blessed the ground your brother walked on, the dear man. You think they were forgetting the shillings he'd slip them when their rent came due and their pockets were empty, or how he begged and fought with Mr. Sean to lower the rents?" She glanced away from me, then added reluctantly, "But there were those who remembered . . ."

A knock at the door interrupted whatever else she might have said. Miss O'Toole stood in the doorway, her mouth a thin, pinched line of disapproval as she scalded the young maid with a glance. "If you've finished here, Rose, there's work to be done downstairs."

"Yes, ma'am." She scuttled past me and out the door without a backward glance, as if relieved to get away.

I looked into the housekeeper's glassy, baleful eyes. Had

Patrick, too, felt the scorn of that glance? I wondered suddenly. Why? Why did she dislike me so? And I was all at once furious with myself for allowing the woman to intimidate me in this fashion. After all, if there was one thing I was supposed to have learned at finishing school, it was how to handle servants. I drew myself regally to my feet. "Was there something you wanted, Miss O'Toole?"

The woman seemed to coil back within herself, and I was reminded of a rattlesnake I had once come upon, and how for a few paralyzing seconds we had both frozen, each watching the other, waiting. But then, as today, it had not seemed the propitious moment to strike. The woman lowered her gaze, standing carefully to one side so that I would not touch her as I passed. "His lordship asked if you would join him in the library," she said.

7

I followed the housekeeper down the stairs into the entrance hall. She crossed the room and stopped before a door toward the rear of the hall. At her knock, I could hear a muffled answer. She stepped aside and allowed me to enter. It was a large, pleasant room, paneled in walnut and smelling of leather bindings, wood smoke, and lemon polish. Glassed-in bookcases lined the paneled walls, and the leather chairs over the years had burnished to a soft, golden butternut shade.

Lord Fletcher sat behind a black walnut desk, studying a book he held in his hands, absently pushing back a pair of spectacles which kept sliding down his long nose. When he saw me, he jerked off the spectacles and sprang to his feet.

"Miss O'Brien, it's good of you to see me. I hope you're feeling better this morning."

"Yes, thank you, much better."

He came around the desk and pulled out a chair. "Please sit down. My Uncle Cormac has asked to meet you but I thought perhaps we could talk a few minutes before I take you to him." He glanced at his pocket watch. "I don't believe visitors will be arriving for a while yet."

"Have you heard anything more about the investigation into Patrick's death?" I asked.

He shook his head as he returned to his chair behind the desk. "The magistrate of this county is a neighbor and good friend. I'm sure he's doing everything he can, but I'm afraid there's very little to go on. They think they know where the man or men must have hidden, in a gully near the road where your brother's body was found. However, the ground is heavily brushed there and covered with leaves so there wasn't even a footprint." He tapped his spectacles nervously on the desk top. "I am sorry. I wish I could offer you some hope but unfortunately the chances are good that the assassins will never be found. The Moonlighters have many friends among the countryside people, you see, who'll take them in and hide them."

"Do you believe your cousin was right, that it was he they meant to kill, not Patrick?"

Lord Fletcher frowned. "It's possible. My Uncle Cormac—actually, of course, he's my great-uncle, my grandfather's youngest brother—has been the estate agent for many years, even when my father and grandfather were alive. Despite his age and being tied to a wheel chair, he still acts in that capacity, although my Cousin Sean does most of the work of managing the estate now." He shrugged ruefully. "Land agents are seldom very popular with the tenants or with terrorists like the Moonlighters. They are blamed for every ill from the potato blight to too much or too little rain."

"But my brother was working for the tenants," I protested.

"I know. Patrick was a good, compassionate man. We were acquainted only a short time, but I'm proud to say we had become close friends. I was extremely fond of him. I still can't believe . . ." The earl's voice broke and he looked bleakly down at the desk top.

"He wrote me that you had been very kind," I said, filling the awkward silence.

A boyish smile of pleasure touched Lord Fletcher's face. "Did he now? How good of him. We had so much in common, you see, our love of art and literature. We talked for hours. I was particularly pleased to discover he shared my appreciation for the Pre-Raphaelite artists. I actually met Dante Gabriel Rossetti, you know, shortly before he died. The poor man was in a sad way then, his mind going, but a genius, yes, still a genius." He looked at me eagerly. "Did you share your brother's interest in art?"

I had to admit that my knowledge of art and artists was extremely limited. I didn't have Patrick's eye for technique and color, his passion for standing what seemed to me interminable lengths of time simply staring at a painting. "Patrick did write me that you had an outstanding collection."

"Not truly outstanding," Lord Fletcher said modestly. "At least, not yet. However, I do own a Botticelli and a Raphael of which I'm very proud, and several early paintings by Rossetti. I know there are those art critics who haven't a very high regard for the work of the Pre-Raphaelites but mostly it's simply rejection by society because Rossetti and his friends refused to conform to the strictures of narrow, bigoted minds."

He spoke heatedly and, I noticed, without a trace of a stammer, when he talked of his art collection. I wondered where his collection was hung. The paintings I had seen in the long gallery upstairs, as far as I could tell, had been family portraits.

"Perhaps one day you'd care to visit my collection," Lord Fletcher offered, almost shyly. "It's not far from here, in the tower."

"The tower?"

"When Kilcallen Castle was destroyed in the seventeenth century, only one tower was left standing. My father, Lord Michael, even before he became the earl, had begun restoring the tower, using it as an office and workshop for the discoveries he made in his archaeological digs at the old Abbey and elsewhere. I continued the work of restoration when I inherited the earldom. Fortunately the foundation of the tower is still sturdy and the walls are extremely thick. It's actually dryer than Abbey Court, making it a much safer location for my collection. As a matter of fact, I use a part of the tower as my living quarters when I'm staying at Abbey Court." His eyes once more were charged with sorrow. "Patrick often visited me there. Sometimes he would help me reach a decision about the purchase of a painting. He had a wonderful talent for separating the true and false in a work of art. I've often wondered, with the financial resources at his command, why he didn't become a collector himself."

I knew why. Patrick had hated possessions as much as Mother had loved them. My brother had looked with an amused eye and at times, I suspected, a quivering distaste at the ornate mansion in Denver and at the Boston brownstone, crowded to its flocked walls with overstuffed, clawed furniture, tasseled velvet draperies, and dried flowers under glass. As for collecting paintings, I remembered Patrick had once said that collecting works of art too often started out as a hobby and ended up as an obsession.

Before I could phrase a tactful reply to Lord Fletcher, though, he had pulled out his pocket watch and said, worried, "I suppose we should get along to Uncle Cormac. He hates to be kept waiting." He hesitated a moment, then smiled feebly. "I really should warn you, Miss O'Brien, that my uncle is . . . is quite a formidable person. You mustn't let anything he says upset you. It's just his way."

With these less than reassuring words, he escorted me into the corridor that led off from the main hall. As I followed him, I noticed what appeared to be a bricked-over door set into the end of the hall. Noting my gaze, Lord Fletcher explained, "Abbey Court was originally built in a square in the Italianate style, you know, with a central courtyard. However, the south wing was almost totally destroyed by a fire in 1849. What was left of the wing was torn down, and Abbey Court is U-shaped as you see it today."

He gave me a curious, questioning glance. "But then, of course, your mother must have told you all about the fire. She was quite the heroine of the day. If it hadn't been for her warning and Father's efforts, all of Abbey Court would have gone up in flames."

"No, I didn't know," I said slowly, and remembering the scar on Mother's arm, I wondered if it had had anything to do with the fire. "Mother never spoke to me of her life here at Abbey Court."

"Oh." I thought I saw a look of polite disbelief touch my companion's face; then we were retracing our steps back down the corridor. We stopped at a door across the great hall from the drawing room where Patrick lay. Lord Fletcher knocked and as we waited he said, "After my Uncle Cormac's accident, the family parlor was turned into a bedroom for him so he wouldn't have to bother with the stairs. However, he seldom leaves his room these days."

A manservant opened the door and Lord Fletcher turned as if he were about to leave me. Impulsively I reached out my hand, all at once frightened. "Aren't you staying?"

He hesitated, then, studying my face, said gently, "If you

wish, Miss O'Brien, but I rather had the impression that Uncle Cormac wanted to see you alone."

We were standing in a small anteroom and the servant led the way into a much larger bedroom. The furniture was of some dark wood and massive in size; the fourposter bed in the center of the room, with an odd rope and pulley contraption dangling above it, was enormous. As in all the rooms I had seen so far at Abbey Court, there were a great many large windows but, except at one window, all the curtains in this room were drawn. Before the one open window sat a man in a wheel chair, the sunlight falling upon him like the spotlight on a stage, so that he dominated all else in the room.

"Well, come closer," he commanded sharply. "Let me have a look at you."

I moved slowly forward and saw that Sean Fletcher stood to one side of his father, his hand resting lightly on the wheel chair. There was a gleam of amusement in his eyes as he watched me approach, as if he knew the effect his father had upon people and enjoyed watching the reaction of the helpless victims.

Then my eyes swung back to the man in the wheel chair. For all that his legs seemed shrunken and patently useless, he was a great hulk of a man, the shoulders and chest as broad and muscular as those of a miner who had spent his life swinging a pickax. He had the heavy-lidded eyes and high cheekbones that his son had inherited, but his color was florid, his hair a shock of gray. Despite the gray hair, though, when his eyes traveled over me I had the distinctly unpleasant feeling that I was being stripped down to my chemise.

Finally he growled, "You've none of Fiona's beauty."

I said, calmly enough, "So I've been told."

"Then it's your father you favor. Some bogtrotter who by a fool's luck stumbled and fell into a mountain of silver."

Now I did feel a quiver of anger. I thought of the years of frustration that my father had endured, the years of searching and failing and searching again; the claims that led nowhere, the veins that had petered out. Fool's luck, indeed! How many little, envious men had described prospectors who finally hit it rich that way.

I gazed at Cormac Fletcher coldly. "Jamie O'Brien may have been an uneducated man but when he was alive no man would have dared call him a fool and lived to tell about it afterward."

Behind me, I heard Lord Fletcher draw a deep, sharp breath but the old man cocked his head and chuckled. "At least you have your mother's spirit, my girl." He touched a thin, almost invisible scar that ran from his cheek to his chin. "I well remember the day she gave me this, fighting like a wildcat all the while, because I put my hands on her." He smiled, his mouth still red and sensuous, as if savoring the memory, his eyes bright with an ancient but still remembered lust. "Ah, *lian, lian,*" he murmured, and although I didn't understand the words, the meaning was only too clear.

My hands balled into fists at my side. When I was only seven or eight, a livery stable boy had teased me about my father's drinking and I had picked up a rock and would, I think, have brained the lad if Patrick hadn't pulled me away. I felt the same murderous rage now toward this obscene ruin of a man.

It was Sean who interrupted, who looked out the window and said, "Some of the mourners seem to be arriving early, Kevin. Lord Bailey's carriage is coming up the drive. Perhaps you should take Miss O'Brien into the drawing room."

"Yes . . . yes, of course." Lord Fletcher reached, relieved, for my arm when his uncle's booming voice stopped him in his tracks.

"One moment, my Lord Fletcher." Cormac Fletcher spoke the title with a contemptuous mock servility that brought a flush to his grandnephew's face. "Maybe before you go your lordship would do me the kindness to explain this." He thrust the wheel chair forward with one powerful, broad hand, while he waved a sheet of paper in the earl's face with the other.

Startled, Lord Fletcher took a step back and I saw that for a moment he looked like a frightened, guilty boy caught in a prank, before he smiled weakly and said, "It looks like a bill of sale."

"It is that . . . for another one of your fancy pictures . . . five hundred pounds!" Cormac Fletcher's voice exploded. "Have you taken complete leave of your senses? Haven't you been told often enough there's no money in the estate to be thrown away for such foolishness?"

Lord Fletcher cast me an embarrassed glance. "I don't think, Uncle, that Miss O'Brien is interested in family financial matters."

"And why not?" the old man snorted. "Isn't it her brother's

money paying for those wickedly expensive daubs of paint on canvas, for repairing that useless old ruin of a tower that should have been torn down long since." He stared at his grandnephew with an almost bewildered look of despair. "I'll never understand you. If it was a fine stallion you bought, or if you lost the money gambling or betting on the horses, or threw it away on some *dilsy* as any gentleman might . . . I had such high hopes for you." He shook his head sadly. "It's your mother I blame, pampering you, coddling you, whisking you off to the doctor every time you sneezed, ruining you entirely."

"The Lady Margaret is above reproach." Lord Fletcher's face stiffened angrily, and a spiteful note crept into his voice. "And don't forget she raised your son and daughter too."

Cormac Fletcher nodded shrewdly. "Ay, she's a saint to be sure but perhaps saints don't make the best mothers. Their minds are too much in the next world to make sense of this one." He wheeled suddenly upon his son, his voice like a whiplash cracking through the air. "And who gave you authority to pay this bill, Sean, and not a word to your old father first? I thought I'd beat more respect into you than that, or are you forgetting who's the estate manager here? Maybe it's getting too big for your boots you are."

I saw the muscles grow taut beneath Sean's olive skin, but his eyes were opaque, expressionless. "The painting had already been sent in good faith, Father," he said calmly. "It was too late to return it, and I saw no reason to . . ."

A soft knocking at the door interrupted him. A young parlormaid hurried in, giving the man in the wheel chair a quick, timorous curtsy before turning to Lord Fletcher. "It's the mourners, your lordship. They've started to arrive, and Miss Regan is waiting for you in the drawing room."

This time both Lord Fletcher and I did make it to the door before Cormac Fletcher's voice once more reached out and stopped us.

"It's sorry I am about your brother, Meg O'Brien." I turned, reluctantly, to face him. "There was much of Fiona in the lad, a softness, a gentleness that reminded me of his mother. It's sad he did not heed my warning not to interfere in matters he did not understand, or he might still be alive today."

I stared at the old man. What did he mean? It was almost as if he had known that Patrick was in danger. But then

Lord Fletcher had his hand on my arm and, murmuring that we must not keep the visitors waiting, he hurried me out the door.

8

Although I did not forget Cormac Fletcher's words, the next two days I was kept too busy during my brother's lying in state to give them more than a passing thought.

Hundreds of people filed past my brother's casket, including landed gentry from neighboring estates, Irish government officials, a few members of Parliament, and military officers in bright costumes from the nearby barracks. Only a few of them could have known Patrick personally. Their presence, I was sure, was a courtesy to the Earl of Abbeymore. Interspersed among the more illustrious visitors were a great many men, women, and children in worn garments, with work-hardened hands and faces. Many of the women cried loudly as they knelt a moment at the casket, somehow managing to juggle one child on a hip, while holding another by the hand, with two or three more trailing behind. The men's faces were sober with a ground-down defeated look; they walked with a shuffling gait. A few of the women stopped before me, clutching my hand and kissing it, murmuring their sorrow for "your ladyship." At first I tried to correct them but I soon realized the title was simply a term of respect, not an indication of my social station. Although it was impossible to gauge the sincerity of their sorrow over my brother's death, still it was hard to believe that any of them felt an enmity toward Patrick deep enough to drive them to murder.

Only once did I detect a reaction that seemed amiss. A rather unkempt red-haired, middle-aged woman, wailing more loudly than anyone else, stopped at the casket. Beside her stood a young man, obviously her son, with the same bright red hair worn longer than I was accustomed to seeing on a man. What particularly caught my attention, though, was the young man's striking good looks. His face reminded me of a Botticelli painting of an angel Patrick had once shown me, with the same fair skin and beautifully drawn, almost delicate features, oddly at contrast with a lithe, muscular body. When the young man knelt beside the coffin, however, the moment before he bent his head in prayer I could swear a pleased, crooked smile touched those perfectly formed lips.

When the family was given a break at lunchtime and the drawing room temporarily closed to visitors, I asked Regan about the red-haired man. She eyed me indifferently. "I'm sure I don't know who you mean. After all, there are more than fifty tenant families at Abbey Court."

"That many?" I asked, surprised.

"The demesne covers more than a thousand acres, including the tenant farms, the home farm, lake, grazing lands, and woodland," she replied. "I would have thought Patrick had written you all about the estate." The thick fringed eyelids lowered. "He certainly wrote you often enough."

Was it possible, I wondered uneasily, that Regan had been jealous of Patrick's affection for his family? In a strange way, the thought made me feel more friendly toward my sister-in-law. She wouldn't have been jealous unless she loved Patrick in the first place. And up to now I had seen no outward expression of grief mar that coolly beautiful face.

Then, that afternoon, something happened that once again raised doubts in my mind about the relationship between Patrick and his wife. During the first part of the afternoon only the household staff and outside workers at Abbey Court filed into the drawing room to pay their respects. Miss O'Toole, befitting her position as housekeeper, led the way with the youngest scullery lad bringing up the rear. Some of the staff I had begun to recognize. The only ones I was formally introduced to, though, were the butler, Jeremiah, and the head gardener, William—both tottering old men; the head groom, Tim Kennedy, a cocky bantam rooster of a man; and Brian Flaherty, the studmaster. There was a foxlike look about Mr. Flaherty's dark, mustached face that did not seem Irish at all and I couldn't help noticing that his well-cut suit fit too tightly, showing off his broad shoulders and narrow hips.

As he stopped to convey his condolences to each member of the family, it seemed to me he lingered a little longer than necessary before my brother's widow. And for the first time since I had met Regan, I saw a spark of animation in her face, although her eyelids, discreetly lowered, revealed nothing of what she might be thinking.

The briefly glimpsed incident might have concerned me more if I hadn't already been disturbed by the reaction of some of the older servants as they passed by my brother's coffin. Not that on the surface, at least, they weren't all properly respectful, but once or twice I caught a look of covert hostility before a glance was quickly lowered.

I tried to tell myself that I was imagining things; that I was too tired to see or think straight, which was certainly true. The terrible, final fact of my brother's death was hard enough to endure, without the ordeal of standing beside his coffin for two days, receiving the sympathy of countless numbers of strangers, some of whom I uncharitably suspected of coming only because of the excitement caused by the manner of my brother's death.

The second day of the lying in state, I was introduced to Father Vincent, who was much as Father Jerome had described him, young but already with an air of authority about him.

"A sad welcome for you to Ireland, my child," he said. "And a dreadful end for a young man with his life still stretching before him. Thirty-one years old, I believe . . ."

"Thirty-two, this March," I said.

He sighed. "I didn't know him well, I'm sorry to say, but there are many who spoke highly of his goodness, his Christian charity." His glance moved around the room, rested sternly on Sean Fletcher, who was talking to a most attractive young golden-haired woman. "There are those godless ones among us who have never learned the meaning of the words."

His gaze continued on to Lady Fletcher, who stood like some stark, black statue beside the coffin, a thick crepe veil hanging down her back. Her bloodless white hand reached out from the black folds of her sleeve to touch a shoulder, an outstretched hand, then returned quickly to be hidden once more in darkness. "Lady Fletcher was sorry you were unable to attend the rosary last evening," he said. "A remarkable woman. She has chosen to make the holy pilgrimage to Croagh Patrick again this year, although her doctor has warned her that the climb might prove too much for her."

At my mystified look, he said, surprised, "Surely, even

in America you've heard of the mountaintop where St. Patrick fasted for forty days and nights. On the last Sunday of July, before dawn, thousands of pilgrims climb the rocky slope in their bare feet to prove their devotion."

I looked again at the countess with a mixture of awe and respect, marveling at the depth of religious fervor that would force her to commit so many painful acts of penitence. Her stamina alone these last two days had amazed me. My own back ached from the constant standing as if an iron rod had been thrust down my spine, and the muscles in my face hurt with the strain of trying to keep the tears and grief from showing. Yet the face of Lady Fletcher had never once lost its look of serene composure and she had spent every waking moment beside Patrick's casket, in addition to one all-night vigil. I felt I could do no less than try to match her devotion, even though Patrick's widow had not been seen in the drawing room for the last several hours. It was announced that she was too grief-stricken to continue and would receive the more noted visitors in her private room. I suspected, however, it was weariness, not grief, that had overcome her.

Guiltily, I felt grateful myself the afternoon of the second day when the doors of the drawing room closed early and preparations were made to move the coffin to the parish church where services would be held in the morning.

I decided to by-pass afternoon tea with the Fletchers and return instead to my room where I could have some rest and privacy. It was not that each of the Fletchers, even Regan in her own way, hadn't tried to make me feel comfortable, but I was still very conscious of being the outsider in the family group. When I learned that Cormac Fletcher, in one of his rare appearances, planned to join the family, for tea, I did not regret my decision.

At the gallery on the second floor, I had paused a moment to study the family portraits when I sensed, rather than heard, footsteps behind me, and turned. Sean must have followed me from the drawing room, walking so softly I hadn't heard a sound.

"You won't be joining us for tea?" he asked. "Father will be disappointed."

"I didn't realize Mr. Fletcher's presence made it a command performance," I said tartly.

The heavy-lidded eyes studied me thoughtfully, then he smiled and gestured toward the portrait behind me. "No, but in his day it would have been. He made Cormac's wrath seem like a childish peccadillo."

I gazed, impressed in spite of myself, at the heavy-set glowering man in the portrait.

"Lord Jason Fletcher, the present earl's grandfather. He had strong feelings, shall we say, against lese majesty." A ripple of amusement ran through Sean Fletcher's voice. "I imagine he was also a sore trial to any pretty servant girl who caught his eye."

Deliberately I turned my gaze to the portrait hanging next to Lord Jason Fletcher's. "I'm surprised a woman with such strong character in her face would put up with such foolishness from a husband."

Sean Fletcher shook his head. "Oh, that's not Lady Caroline. That's Rosaleen, dark Rosaleen she was called, the real matriarch of the Fletcher family. Captain Daniel Fletcher, after he had razed Kilcallen Castle and killed off all the O'Neills he could find, took one look at the youngest daughter of the O'Neill family and carried her off, presumably kicking and screaming like the Sabine women of old." He smiled cynically. "At least that's the story that's been passed down for generations. For myself, I've always thought the young lady had a practical head on her shoulders and decided marriage was the only way to keep the O'Neill land. She was strong-minded enough to tame old Daniel, and she gave him six sons, three of whom she converted to Catholicism, one of whom brought the earldom to the family."

I looked more closely at the painting. Something about Rosaleen O'Neill Fletcher reminded me a little of my mother, not the features or coloring, but the stubborn set of the chin. Mother had inherited that, if nothing else, from her long-ago O'Neill ancestor. Remembering my mother and the relish that disgusting old man in the wheel chair had felt when he told me of trying to seduce her, I said bitingly, "It appears that assaulting helpless young women comes naturally to the men of your family. In the mining camps where I grew up, such men were regarded as lower than claim jumpers."

I saw I had struck home by the drooping of the eyelids, the darkening of Sean Fletcher's face, but before he could retaliate, I stepped around him, smiling sweetly. "Now if you'll excuse me, I am tired."

When I reached my bedroom, though, I realized it wasn't privacy I wanted so much as fresh air and sunshine and the earth beneath my feet. I had been closeted with death for too long. Snatching a shawl from my wardrobe, I flung it around my shoulders, then, pausing at the landing to make sure the entrance hall was deserted, I crept down the stairs and out the front door. With a childish sense of triumph, I looked around first to orient myself, then crossed the clipped lawn into the screen of trees that arched on either side of Abbey Court.

A narrow track ran through the woods, between the glossy-leafed laurel bushes, the smooth beech trees with their gray bark, and the dark green spruce. I had been hurrying as if afraid I might be pursued but now I slowed to a stroll, delighting in the sunlight that drifted down through the trees, dissolving into golden puddles at my feet. Pale pink primroses, trailing arbutus, and bluebells edged the path along with yarrow blossoms that bowed tipsily as if drunk with their own pungent odor. After a few minutes I came out of the narrow plantation of trees into an open meadow that sloped down to a horseshoe-shaped lake.

A cluster of gray-green willow trees brushed the water's edge with their trailing branches, and spiky reeds stood sentinel in a small stagnant inlet. When I reached the edge of the lake I stood very still, watching a school of minnows dart between the reeds. A heron completed a successful fishing expedition in the lake, then took off in a flopping, awkward flight over the treetops.

The sun felt delightfully warm on my face. I slipped the shawl from my shoulders and sat down on a mossy bank. The stillness was so complete that a lark's song overhead seemed to make circles in the silence like a pebble dropped into a pool. I could almost feel my nerves relaxing, and a drowsy languor crept over me as I stretched out on the ground, my shawl serving as a pillow beneath my head.

Narrowing my eyes against the sunlight, I looked up into a robin's-egg-blue sky, where clouds drifted like tufts of cotton. For a moment as I lay there I felt as though the earth were moving beneath me and the clouds standing still. The lark soared higher into the blue vault of the sky, the beauty of its song growing fainter and still fainter in the soft, lucent air.

My mind, emptied, felt wonderfully blank. I forgot everything, Patrick's cruel death, my own sense of unease since I had arrived at Abbey Court, that vile old man in the wheel chair, the glassy hatred in Miss O'Toole's eyes. There was only the deep, soothing silence. My eyes closed.

I awoke with a start and had risen to a seated position before I noticed two things: that a jacket had been placed across my shoulders and that Sean Fletcher was leaning against a tree, lazily looking down at me. "Aunt Margaret was worried. She sent me to look for you," he said, and then in the too thick, mocking brogue I was beginning to recognize, "Sure and you looked so peaceful, it seemed a pity to disturb you."

How long had I been asleep? I wondered. And then, embarrassed: What a queer one he must think me, first pulling me out of the bog, then finding me curled up like a waif, sound asleep on the grass.

"I'm sorry I caused concern. I should have left word with Rose."

I started to rise hastily, too hastily, and caught my heel in the hem of my skirt. Sean's hands reached down deftly and plucked me the rest of the way to my feet.

"Don't apologize, *alannah*," he said softly. "You look very nice asleep. Most women don't, you know."

I wasn't about to ask him how many women he had seen asleep. Too many, I had no doubt. He was still holding my hands casually but firmly, so that I could not pull free without struggling most ungracefully. Suddenly, unwillingly, I found myself remembering our first meeting, those moments riding pillion, my arms clutched tightly around his waist, my body pressed so close to that hard, flat back that my breasts ached.

There was a glitter of amusement in the heavy-lidded eyes; the voice was caressing, soft as silk. "Shall I tell you then what I was thinking, *alannah*, watching you sleeping like a babe?"

"No!" I said, flustered, disturbed in a way that I had never been before except perhaps in those uneasy, heavy moments before a storm breaks.

I glanced back toward Abbey Court but only the top floor could be seen above the screen of trees. No one would hear me if I called for help even if the whole idea weren't too humiliating to consider. Then, faintly, I heard a church bell tolling and, remembering Patrick, I jerked furiously at the viselike grip holding me. All else was forgotten but the need to see Patrick one more time, before they took the coffin to the church. Surely that was why Lady Fletcher had sent Sean to look for me.

The grip lessened but did not release my hands; the mocking brogue was gone from the voice. "It's too late, Meg

O'Brien," he said with a stiff gentleness, as if gentleness did not come easy to him. "They've already taken the coffin away. You should be glad it's over, for your brother's sake. We seldom saw eye to eye, Patrick and me, but I doubt if the grotesque charade of these last days would have been to his liking."

He was right, I thought numbly. Patrick had been too private a person not to have hated the open coffin, the strangers coming to stare at him. If they had been his friends it might have been different, but recalling the open curiosity and the veiled antagonism of some of the mourners, the lying in state seemed a pointless, even hypocritical ritual.

"Why?" I blurted, before I stopped to think. "Why did they dislike Patrick?"

I thought at first he wasn't going to answer me. His eyes searched my face, as if he were trying to make up his mind about something. Then he scowled and shrugged. "You're sure to hear the story from someone. It's been a long time, more than thirty years now, but you'll find the Irish have long memories. And there are still some in service at Abbey Court who were working at the house the day it happened. A small group of men, evicted tenant farmers mostly, planned an attack upon Abbey Court. They chose an evening when they thought the house was deserted. The youngest Fletcher son, Michael, had caught the fever and my uncle had taken his two oldest sons to London to keep them from the sickness. Lady Caroline insisted upon staying behind to nurse her son. Michael recovered but then his mother caught the fever and died within a matter of hours. The week before, my father had gone to London to fetch his brother back to Abbey Court, so Michael was alone at the house when the attack came.

"When the men crept up to the front of the house at dusk, Michael was waiting for them, watching from the ballroom windows, along with a few loyal servants. The attackers had only blackthorn sticks, stones, and torches. Michael fired off a volley over their heads and the men scattered. One man, though, before he ran off, broke a window in the rear of the house and threw a lighted torch inside. By the time the fire was discovered, the back wing of the house was already in flames.

"Michael and your mother, who was one of the servants who had stayed, did what they could but most of the servants soon fled. If my father hadn't returned just then and managed to rally the servants to help fight the fire, all of Abbey

69

Court probably would have burned to the ground."

"The men who attacked Abbey Court—what happened to them?"

"Troops from Kilcallen Barracks chased them down and they were captured, all six of them."

When I stared at him, still not understanding, he finished harshly, "Several of the men had relatives among the staff at Abbey Court. Miss O'Toole's young brother, Cullen, the ring-leader of the group, was the first man arrested."

"Oh." My throat felt dry, my mind dazed with horror. Yet the full horror was yet to come. "Patrick and I," I protested weakly, "we weren't even alive then."

Sean frowned impatiently, his face darkening. "No, but your mother was. Don't you understand? It was Fiona O'Neill who heard about the threat to Abbey Court and warned Michael Fletcher so that he was ready and waiting for the attack. There are many in Abbeymore who still believe that Fiona not only informed on the small group of attackers but gave their names to the soldiers so the six men could be hunted down and arrested. And finally hanged, one by one, in Abbeymore Square."

9

I was glad, then, that Sean Fletcher's hands held me with a grip that numbed my arms but at least kept my knees from collapsing under me.

Informer! What an ugly sound the word had. What an impossible name to give to Fiona, the most intensely loyal person I'd ever known. And yet a portion of the story must be true, I realized, remembering suddenly the scar on Mother's wrist. "Was my mother burned in the fire?" I asked.

"It's possible. A portion of the ceiling fell, trapping Michael, and your mother and another servant somehow managed to pull him free, badly burned but alive. However, your mother was apparently healthy enough to leave

Ireland shortly after the fire—rather abruptly," he added dryly.

"It was a fortunate chance, your father coming along when he did."

"It wasn't by chance at all," he corrected me. "When Cormac reached London he found the Fletcher family had suffered an additional, terrible tragedy. Lord Jason had taken his two eldest sons away from Abbey Court so they wouldn't catch the fever. Ironically, while out riding, their carriage ran away with them and overturned. They were both killed, the one brother, his back broken, lasting only a few days after his older brother. Uncle Jason, as you can imagine, was in a state of shock and died himself a year later. It was Cormac who had to return to Ireland and tell Michael that he was the new heir to the earldom."

I wasn't interested in the trials and tribulations of the Fletcher family. It was only my mother who concerned me, and the terrible lie that she could betray her own people.

"Why did Miss O'Toole stay on at Abbey Court?" I demanded. "And those others who had relatives hanged?"

Sean looked amused at my ignorance. "And what else could they do? Those were famine times, remember. Anyone who had a shilling to his name or a sack of oats put aside counted himself lucky. There were many with no food at all, who drank nettle tea and ate rats and weeds and grass and died with a green froth on their mouths. Whole families were found dead in their huts of the fever or starvation, and neighbors too weak, themselves, to bury them."

"But not the Earl of Abbeymore, nor your father, nor any of the Fletcher family," I said bitterly. "They didn't starve."

Sean Fletcher released my arms so abruptly that I swayed. His voice flattened. "No, I suppose my uncle and his sons lived very well in London. If it makes you feel any better, though, Lady Caroline never fled Abbey Court once, during the famine. She set up a soup kitchen in the back passageway of the house, feeding the roadlings, some so weak they crawled on their hands and knees to the door. And the fever she died of she didn't catch from her son; it was typhoid fever she contracted while nursing a tenant farmer's child. Your mother, so I've been told, stayed with Lady Caroline, nursing her till the end."

I felt hot with shame, knowing that I had struck out at Sean Fletcher only because of my own furious disbelief. I blinked back childish tears. "Fiona wouldn't . . . she couldn't have been an informer."

The coldness left his face like a glaze of ice melting. In two strides he was back at my side, his arms around me, cradling me gently. "Ah, *alannah*," he crooned softly, "none of us chooses our parents. And how old was your mother, seventeen years, eighteen? Terrible times make people do terrible things. Who knows what fears drove her?"

"No, I don't believe it!" Angrily, I thrust him away from me. It wasn't true. Fiona couldn't have informed on her own people, knowing surely what would happen to them, that she was betraying them to their deaths. "I'll never believe it," I cried.

Gathering up my skirt, I ran back toward the house. I thought I heard Sean call out after me but I didn't stop till I reached a back door. Pulling it open, I almost fell into a small common room, evidently used by the servants and filled with old boots and mackintoshes. Fortunately no one was about. I took a moment to catch my breath and regain my composure.

Nevertheless when I reached my bedroom Rose gave my face a quick, anxious glance, then hurriedly returned to inspecting a black Canton crepe gown. "Is this the dress you'll be wanting to wear tomorrow? It needs a bit of touching up and the sash seems to be missing."

I went to the window, staring at, without seeing the stretch of parkland, the shadows moving slowly across the waving treetops as a cluster of gray clouds chased each other across the sky. "The sash is probably still packed somewhere," I replied indifferently. "Have you opened all my cases?"

"No, ma'am." I heard the hesitation in Rose's voice and turned to look at her. Her face was pink with embarrassment and she spoke in a rush. "Miss O'Toole said I wasn't to bother unpacking all your trunks, that you wouldn't be staying long after the funeral." She shrugged apologetically. "She's a scalding class of tongue, that one, and a devil when she's crossed."

"It doesn't matter. I can wear the gown without the sash." It hadn't occurred to me before but what Miss O'Toole said was true enough. There would be no reason for my staying on at Abbey Court after the funeral. If Regan and I had struck up any sort of friendship the way I had hoped, things might be different. It was obvious, though, that my sister-in-law and I had little in common. I suspected that Regan had very few women friends.

Where would I go? I wondered, glad to turn my mind away from grief to more practical matters. I could return to Boston but, for all I knew, Mr. Adams might have already sold the house on Beacon Hill. In any case, Boston held few happy memories for me. I supposed I could travel, at least as long as my money lasted, but eventually I would have to find some sort of occupation. An aimless life would never appeal to me for long. I turned away wearily from the window. Well, there was no time to think about the future now. There was still the evening to get through, and my necessary appearance at the parish church, which, only dimly lit by candlelight, was made doubly depressing by the black velvet curtains hung at the windows and the black pall covering my brother's coffin.

I slept little that night. I dreamed of a faceless man crouching in ambush beside a road, waiting for a rider to come by, then raising the pistol and aiming it slowly, carefully, at the man on horseback. I tried to cry out a warning but, in the way of dreams, no sound came from my throat. The gun, firing, made no noise and the rider fell as if in slow motion to the road. When I rushed to his side, however, it wasn't Patrick lying there, dead in the road, but my mother, her tawny hair spilling like blood over the ground.

The dream stayed with me, even after I awoke the next morning, even as I sat in the small parish church, listening to the office of the dead being chanted. The long black hem-length crepe veil I and the other women mourners wore was like a shroud so I could barely see my brother's coffin.

My thoughts kept straying from the solemn requiem mass. Was it possible? I wondered. Could some brother or son or other relative of one of the men hanged in Abbeymore Square have lain in wait for Patrick, exacting his vengeance upon the son of the informer? Was that what Mother had been trying to tell me before she died, to warn Patrick that because of her betrayal he wouldn't be safe at Abbey Court?

The procession from the church to the graveyard was mercifully short. Although the turnout for Mother's funeral had been pitifully small, I could find no fault with the number of mourners who followed my brother's hearse by carriage and on foot to the small family graveyard just outside Abbey Court land. An impressive stone vault near the gateway had the Fletcher name on it, but the procession continued past the vault, past beautifully carved stone Celtic crosses, tilted every which way in the ground.

The procession finally halted at a freshly dug grave near a grove of spruce where the coffin was removed from the hearse. The black-plumed horses stood rigidly still.

I took only one look at the coffin, at the brass plaque on the lid reading: Patrick James O'Brien, Born March 15, 1850, Died June 2, 1882, then refused to look at it again. I concentrated on remembering Patrick as I had last seen him, laughing, vibrant, alive, the way I would always remember him.

The final absolution was said and the rosary recited, and people drifted to their carriages. Lord Fletcher rode with the widow, Sean with his aunt. Mr. Samuel Corcoran, my brother's solicitor, a small, desiccated-looking man to whom I had been introduced previously, assisted me into a third carriage.

He didn't speak on the short trip back to Abbey Court, for which I was grateful. The solicitor had, however, been invited to stay for lunch, which turned out to be a rather uncomfortable meal with only the solicitor, Lady Fletcher, her son, and myself present, and none of them making any more attempts at conversation than I did.

At the table, I brought up the matter of my leave-taking. I thought Mr. Corcoran gave me a sharp glance and both Lord Fletcher and his mother assured me that I shouldn't think of leaving, that I should stay as long as I wanted to. Although their manner was sincere enough, I couldn't help feeling that the invitation, like the funeral arrangements, was a formal, traditional ritual that must be strictly observed.

"Of course," Lady Fletcher murmured, "I'm afraid life here at Abbey Court will seem very quiet and dull to a young American woman like yourself."

After the tales of death and destruction I had heard about Abbey Court, and my brother's own violent death just a few days before, I would hardly have called life at Abbey Court quiet or dull, but I saw no reason to contradict the countess and simply kept quiet.

As soon as the meal ended I excused myself and had started to leave the dining room when I felt someone touch my arm. I turned to discover Mr. Corcoran had come hurrying after me. "You will be joining us, Miss O'Brien, in the study for the reading of your brother's will?"

He had a dry, reedy voice but it held a note of crisp authority and perforce I followed him back through the dining room into a small gem of a room I had not seen before. The walls were paneled in pine and intricately carved in a shafts-of-wheat and grapevine pattern. The fireplace mantel was of veined gray and white marble and the pattern of wheat and grapevines was repeated in the andirons. It was the only room I had seen at Abbey Court which looked as if it might have been recently redecorated. The colors in the flowered Persian rug were unfaded, the half-moon desk across from the fireplace seemed new, and the two paintings on the wall, instead of being age-dimmed portraits, were lovely French landscapes. The only drawback to the charm of the room was that, unlike the rest of the rooms in Abbey Court, it had no windows. A narrow, multicolored piece of stained glass was set into the outside wall, allowing ribbons of colored sunlight into the room, but the cut glass wall gas fixtures were an obvious necessity.

I saw that all of the family had already gathered in the room before me. Regan, in her widow's weeds but without the heavy veil, sat beside her father. Although Cormac Fletcher hadn't appeared at the funeral, he evidently found it possible to be at the will reading. Again I was conscious of the dominating quality of the man, despite his handicap, so that Kevin Fletcher and his mother, sitting next to each other, seemed pale, shadowy figures in comparison. Sean, as usual, was standing or rather leaning against the wall near his father and looked bored and a little impatient for the proceedings to begin.

I took a seat hastily, as far away from the family as possible in the small room, and Mr. Corcoran stood behind the half-moon desk. He cleared his throat and peered around the room. "It seems that everyone is present who should be. . . ."

"Get on with it, man," Cormac Fletcher interrupted shortly.

Surprisingly, the little man in the black frock coat was not intimidated. He gave Cormac Fletcher a long, cold look, then, clearing his throat one more time, picked up a document from the desk and began reading.

"I, Patrick James O'Brien, an American citizen, late of Boston, Massachusetts, presently residing at Abbey Court, Abbeymore, being of sound mind, memory, and understanding, hereby make this my last Will and Testament, revoking all previous Wills and Testaments at any time heretofore made by me. I appoint my Solicitor, Samuel Corcoran, as Executor and Trustee for this my Will. I direct said Executor to pay all my just debts, funeral and legal expenses and, after payment thereof, I direct as follows:

"I give, devise, and bequeath to my wife, Regan O'Brien, nee Fletcher, one half of all the funds of which I may die possessed and all my jewelry and personal possessions, with the exception of a silver pocket watch and a silver engraved Colt Revolver which I bequeath to my sister, Maeve Julia O'Brien of Boston, Massachusetts.

"In the event of my dying without issue, I give, devise and bequeath the remaining half of all the funds of which I may die possessed and all of my financial interest, held by a Deed of Trust, in the lands, stables, and properties of the estate of Abbey Court, Abbeymore, Ireland, along with interest, rents, and monies received therefrom, to my said sister, Maeve Julia O'Brien. I also hereby stipulate that to receive the above bequest of the Deed of Trust in the demesne of Abbey Court my sister must agree to assume the duties of assisting in the managing and overseeing of the lands, farms, stables, woodland, and other properties which fall under the Deed of Trust, as I have complete confidence in my sister's judgment, ability, and discretion to do so. . . ."

"That's a bloody, flaming piece of foolishness!" It was Sean's voice, cutting off the solicitor's expressionless reading of the will as if slashing at the man with a knife. He was no longer lounging against the wall but standing bolt upright, his face flushed, dark with anger.

Mr. Corcoran sighed. "I can assure you, Mr. Fletcher, the will is exactly as I am reading it and is quite legal. If you'll allow me to finish . . ."

In the same unemotional voice he continued reading.

"In the event my sister shall have predeceased me, or is unable or unwilling to fulfill the terms of the above bequest, then the bequest which would have gone to her shall be passed to the Sisters of Charity, St. Agnes Convent, Boston, Massachusetts.

"In witness whereof, I, the said Patrick James O'Brien,

have hereunto signed my name and affixed my seal the day and year first herein written."

The lawyer turned toward Sean. "If you'd care to examine the document, you'll see that it was signed properly in the presence of two witnesses, the local parish priest, Father Vincent, and the owner of, I believe, the local hostelry, Mr. James Kelly."

"But Patrick made his will on our honeymoon, when we were in Dublin on our way to London," Regan protested.

The solicitor inclined his head toward her respectfully. "That was an earlier will, Mrs. O'Brien. This will is signed May 22, 1882. At Mr. O'Brien's request, I came to Abbeymore on that date for the express purpose of drawing up a new will."

Cormac Fletcher's face was a bright crimson-purple, the cords in his powerful neck standing out like ropes. "It's a black Protestant trick," he stormed, "from a conniving Protestant lawyer. The boy would not sign away his estate from his rightful wife." Then, suspiciously, "And how much is there in the way of funds to be divided?"

"Very little, I'm afraid," Mr. Corcoran admitted. "The bulk of Mr. O'Brien's estate was the deed of trust covering the sizable sum of money loaned the Abbey Court estate upon his marriage to Miss Regan Fletcher."

For the first time I spoke. "When did you say the will was signed?"

"May 22, 1882."

That was less than two weeks before Patrick died, I thought, shocked. Why had he changed his will then? Surely he must have realized the terrible responsibility he was thrusting upon me. What did I know of managing an estate the size of Abbey Court? But then, of course, Patrick hadn't realized how soon I would be receiving the bequest. Probably he had assumed the terms of the will would not go into effect until some distant future time, until after I had arrived at Abbey Court and he had been able to discuss the terms of the will with me. Or—and the thought struck a chill through me—had Patrick somehow sensed that he was in danger? Had he tried to make sure that if anything did happen to him he could continue through me the protection of the rights of the tenant farmers at Abbey Court which he had begun?

Regan rose to her feet. She had never looked as beautiful as she did at that moment, her face white with anger, her eyes blazing, as she confronted the solicitor. "Does that will mean I no longer control the Abbey Court stud, that she"—she gestured contemptuously toward me—"owns my prize studs, Brian Boru and Heart's Delight?"

"Under the deed of trust, Miss O'Brien will not own them outright, Mrs. O'Brien," the solicitor explained carefully. "However, you might say she has a controlling interest in the stud as well as the pleasure stable. Only the house itself and the dower house, which are both entailed, do not fall under the deed of trust."

Regan whirled upon me and I shrank back before the fury of her wrath. "And what else should I have expected from your brother Patrick, with a mother who had no breeding, no better than an informer and a common thief!" She ran from the room, her black-edged handkerchief pressed to her face.

Sean had regained his composure. He bowed stiffly toward Mr. Corcoran, who had stood, impassive, under Regan's outburst. "I don't suppose you'll be needing our presence any longer so we'll be bidding you good day."

Cormac Fletcher opened his mouth but Sean, his voice colder than I had ever heard it, said quickly, "May I take you back to your room, Father?"

Without a glance in my direction, though the wheel chair came within a few inches of where I sat, he wheeled his father from the room.

I sat motionless, staring fixedly ahead at the paneled wall, my face still burning from the contempt in Regan's voice. It was too great a responsibility, I thought numbly. Patrick had no right to ask this of me.

It was Lady Fletcher who broke the strained silence. She rose to her feet and, crossing to my side, said in a regal manner that managed to be both disapproving and soothing, "I'm sorry, Miss O'Brien. Regan's behavior was inexcusable. I hope you'll accept my apology for her. Of course, she didn't mean what she said."

Lord Fletcher laughed sharply. "Oh, I'm sure Cousin Regan meant exactly what she said, Mother. For once in her life, dear little selfish, beautiful Regan has had her come-uppance. I wouldn't have missed it for the world. And did you see the look on Sean's face, and Uncle Cormac . . . priceless." He threw back his head and was laughing louder now, tears of delight streaming from his eyes.

"Kevin!"

It was a mere whisper but the laughter slowed to a chortle,

then died away completely. Kevin Fletcher wiped his eyes and nodded good-naturedly. "All right, Mother, I'll be good. I suppose the sad truth is, you and I are hoist on the same petard as Uncle Cormac and Sean." He got to his feet and gave me a sweeping, elaborate bow. "It seems, Miss O'Brien, that my Uncle Cormac and your brother's grieving widow greatly underrated Patrick's . . . what do you call it in America . . . Yankee shrewdness. Uncle Cormac thought he had Patrick in the palm of his hand, the way he has everyone else at Abbey Court, but it seems your brother had a trick up his own sleeve all the time."

I pulled myself to my feet and discovered I was trembling. "Please, Lord Fletcher, I asure you I knew nothing about my . . . my brother's plans. This is as great a shock to me as any of you."

He nodded gravely. "I believe you, Miss O'Brien. And now that Abbey Court is so deeply indebted to you, there's no longer any need to talk of your leaving. Miss O'Brien must stay here with us, don't you agree, Mother?"

The countess had replaced the heavy black crepe veil she had worn earlier at the funeral for a sheer black gauze veil which she wore tossed back now, so that it framed her graying hair and long, thin face. Her features looked as if they had been carved from a yellowish ivory. Even her pale deep-set eyes seemed drained of all color. She gave her son an uncertain glance. "Perhaps Miss O'Brien may decide not to accept the legacy, Kevin. It's a great burden for a young woman to bear, helping administer an estate the size of Abbey Court." She pressed my hand gently. "However, for as long as you decide to remain in Ireland, my child, you must consider Abbey Court your home. Now if you'll excuse me, I am a little tired."

"I'll be leaving too." I had forgotten Mr. Corcoran, who precisely folded the will and replaced it in a leather case he carried. "I'm staying on in Abbeymore for a few days, Miss O'Brien. I'll be talking with you tomorrow, if I may. Good day, Lady Fletcher, Lord Fletcher."

And then he was gone, too, and there was only Lord Fletcher and myself in the small study. He smiled sympathetically. "What I think we both need right now is a glass of sherry, Miss O'Brien. Would you care to join me?"

Before I could nod, he had rung for a servant who almost immediately reappeared with two cut crystal glasses of sherry on a silver tray.

I sipped the sherry gratefully, without speaking, and then

realized that Kevin Fletcher was studying me curiously over the rim of his glass. "Do you mind my asking you a question, Miss O'Brien?"

"Of course not."

"Do you plan to accept your brother's legacy?"

"I'm not sure," I said slowly. "You don't think I should?"

"It's not my place to advise you," he answered, flushing a little. He got to his feet and stood before the fireplace, his profile toward me, his hand tapping nervously at the mantelpiece. His fingers, I noticed, were long and tapered like his mother's. Then, speaking quickly, as if embarrassed by what he had to say, he continued, "Nevertheless, I do feel I'd be remiss if I didn't warn you that, by accepting, you'll be putting Uncle Cormac's and Cousin Sean's noses, shall we say, permanently out of joint. Uncle Cormac has run Abbey Court since my grandfather's time, and Sean, naturally, plans to follow in his father's footsteps. It's an unusual arrangement, I admit. Most estates hire a land agent to conduct their business, but Lord Jason, my grandfather, felt very strongly that the business of Abbey Court could be run more profitably and confidentially by keeping the financial affairs of the estate in the hands of the family. In any case, I'm sure neither Uncle Cormac nor Cousin Sean will appreciate a woman interfering in their domain, and I'm afraid . . ." He paused reluctantly, his mouth twisting in a rueful smile. "Well, as Patrick discovered, they cling strongly to their own methods of conducting estate business."

I remembered Cormac and Sean Fletcher's faces when the will had been read. Unless they were both extremely good actors, they had been as shocked as I was at the terms of my brother's will. Apparently they had confidently expected Patrick to leave the ownership of the deed of trust to his wife, which, in a manner of speaking, meant effectively canceling the debt and leaving the management of Abbey Court once more completely in their hands. I wondered suddenly what would have happened if they had known ahead of time that Patrick meant to change his will. Would that old man in the wheel chair have stopped, even at murder, to make sure his power continued unquestioned?

What I was thinking was repugnant to me, yet the seed of suspicion had been planted in my mind, and I knew it would not be destroyed but would continue to grow. Unless I could fulfill the vow I had made standing beside Patrick's coffin—somehow to bring to justice the man or men who brought about my brother's death—the doubt, the mistrust would always be there. And how could I hope to find Patrick's murderers if I didn't remain on at Abbey Court?

Replacing the empty glass on the silver salver, I rose to my feet. "Thank you for your advice, Lord Fletcher."

He studied my face, a sudden, sharp intelligence in his eyes that made me wonder about the nervous, hesitant manner. "You are refusing the legacy then?"

I spoke firmly, with more confidence than I was feeling. "No, as a matter of fact, I have decided, after all, to accept Patrick's bequest."

10

"Good." Lord Fletcher nodded, but whether he was actually pleased or not, it was impossible to tell. "Your brother, in a very short time, grew to love Abbey Court as if it were his own. I hope you do the same, Miss O'Brien. As you have probably guessed, I am very little involved in the day-to-day management of the estate." He shrugged with a wry helplessness. "If anything, I'm a worse businessman than my father was, but if there is any way I can help you, I hope you will call upon me."

"There is something, Lord Fletcher," I said slowly. "When my sister-in-law referred to my mother"—I hated even to remember that virulent accusation, yet forced myself to continue—"she called her a common thief."

Kevin Fletcher frowned uneasily. "Regan has a way of speaking without thinking when she's angry. It's best to forget what she said."

So he wasn't going to explain, I thought, and rising to my feet, turned purposefully to the door. "Well, perhaps one of the servants will know what she meant."

As I had expected, Lord Fletcher's dismayed voice stopped me at once. "Good Lord, Miss O'Brien, one doesn't discuss personal . . ." He broke off as I turned around and waited patiently. "Oh, very well." The fingers once more began their nervous tapping. "You recall the fire I mentioned that destroyed the south wing of Abbey Court some years ago?"

I nodded. "I understand the house was attacked before the fire and that it was my mother who warned Lord Fletcher's son that the attack was to take place."

"Yes, well, of course, my father couldn't know that the attackers would be driven away, that they might not succeed in breaking into Abbey Court. So he gave your mother some pieces of jewelry which she was to take to a safe place if the attackers did manage to get inside the house. For several weeks after the attack and the fire, my father was very ill from the burns he had suffered. When he thought again of the jewels, he checked the place where he had told Fiona to hide them. They weren't there. And, of course, by that time Fiona was gone, too, to America, so it was assumed . . ."

"That my mother stole the jewels and took them with her," I finished coldly.

Lord Fletcher flushed uncomfortably but said nothing.

"Where did your father tell Fiona to hide the jewels?"

"In the chapel." At my blank look, he gestured around him. "Here. This room was originally designed by Rosaleen Fletcher as a family chapel. You can see the wheat and grapevine, the Christian symbols, in the paneling. Naturally, during the times when Catholic worship was forbidden in Ireland, the room was used as a chapel only when it was safe. There's a small closet hidden in the wall where the priest could hide if the authorities should arrive unexpectedly. After 1829, when Catholics were again allowed to worship as they pleased, the priest hole was used as a hiding place for valuables. It still is, occasionally. It was in the closet that my father instructed Fiona to place the jewels."

"Fiona O'Brien," I said slowly and emphatically, "was never a thief."

Lord Fletcher spread his hands helplessly. "My dear Miss O'Brien, naturally I respect and honor your feelings of loyalty toward your mother. Your brother, when he first heard the story, reacted in exactly the same way. Still you must remember the terrible circumstances surrounding that particular day. Your mother was surely aware that it wasn't safe for her to remain in Ireland"—he paused tactfully—"after the part she had played in saving Abbey Court. The jewels, undoubtedly, must have seemed a heaven-sent passageway to a new life. Unfortunately, I doubt if the poor woman made much profit from the sale of the jewels. They weren't the family jewels, you understand. Fortunately those were in a bank vault in Dublin. The jewels in the case were relics Father had dug up, brooches and necklaces, beautiful pieces but of more historic than monetary value. Of course, I've never seen them myself but Father kept exact records of his findings and there are some very good drawings of the pieces in a book at the tower. I believe your mother was of some assistance to Lord Michael in the drawings he made, and in helping to clean the relics, that sort of thing."

"No one saw Fiona take the jewels, did they?" I persisted.

He sighed, looking as if he were anxious for this interview to be finished. "Yes, I'm afraid there was a witness of sorts. Uncle Cormac said Fiona had the jewel case in her possession when she left Abbey Court after the fire." At what must have been a stunned look on my face, he said gently, "I'm sorry, Miss O'Brien, to be the one to tell you this story. I would have thought your brother would have written . . ."

"No, Patrick never told me about the theft."

"Well, I'm sure he didn't want to distress you. I believe he, himself, only heard the story shortly after he received your wire about your mother's stroke. And you musn't concern yourself about the matter," he said firmly. "It's over and done with years ago. I never heard my father utter a word of reproach against your mother for the loss and you mustn't either. In fact, Abbey Court owes your mother a great debt of gratitude, more than the jewels could possibly have been worth." He put down his sherry glass and glanced at his watch. "Now if you'll excuse me, I think I'll drop by the dower house before tea. I thought my mother seemed overly tired. These last few days have been a great strain on her."

"Yes, of course." I stood aside to let him pass, then waited, taking one last look around the pleasant little study. Behind which piece of paneling, I wondered, was the priest hole where Mother was supposed to have placed the jewel case? It was no wonder, I realized now, that Patrick had been upset when he wrote me. Patrick had adored Fiona. Nothing in the world would convince him, any more than me, that Mother had been capable either of stealing or of betraying her friends and neighbors.

When I returned to my room, Rose was waiting for me. From the smug expression on her face, I gathered that she, and undoubtedly the rest of the staff, had already learned about my brother's will.

She bustled busily around the room, shaking out gowns and veils, opening hatboxes, unpacking gloves and shoes and shawls. "The old one has a bee in her ear now," she giggled. " 'Shall I unpack the rest of Miss O'Brien's things now,' I ask her, innocent as you please, and the look she gave me . . ." She shuddered in mock terror, "Sure it would curdle milk." At my silence, she bit her lip unhappily. "Och, my tongue's always running away with me. But it's proud you must be, knowing your brother held you so dear."

"Yes," I said, and to escape her lively glance, I turned away to the window. For I didn't feel proud at all. I felt apprehensive and uncertain, as I had when I was a child and realized that I had impulsively bitten off more than I could chew. And most disturbing of all, I felt vaguely frightened.

My fears were not allayed the next day when Mr. Corcoran sent a message, asking if he might call upon me at Abbey Court that afternoon at three. After I agreed to the meeting, I realized I wasn't sure in which room to receive the solicitor. I thought to speak to Lady Fletcher about it, but Rose told me the countess was not at Abbey Court.

"She lives in the dower house, down the road, very simple like, with just one maid," Rose explained, "ever since his lordship came of age. That way she can fast and pray without being disturbed." A look of awed respect lit the young maid's face. "A blessed saint, her ladyship is. Everyone in Abbeymore says so."

My sister-in-law was also unavailable, I was informed, confined to her room with a sick headache. I suspected that Regan had never had a headache in her life; that it was simply a polite way of asking me to stay away. That left only Lord Fletcher and Miss O'Toole to consult. Lord Fletcher, I was told, had gone to London for several weeks, and I would as soon have approached the housekeeper as a two-headed monster.

"You could use the small study, miss," Rose said helpfully. "Your brother always used it as his office like. He had permission from the earl to redecorate it the way he wanted."

"It's never used as a family chapel now?"

"Oh no, miss, not since her ladyship moved to the dower house. She has her own private chapel there, with the altarpiece and candles that used to be in the family chapel here."

So it was in the little study that Mr. Corcoran and I met, and over tea, he asked me much the same question as Lord Fletcher had, in much the same tone of voice. "You've decided then to accept the terms of your brother's will, Miss O'Brien?"

"Yes, although I'm not sure I completely understand about the deed of trust."

"It's simple enough," he said. "Your brother, at the time of his marriage, lent the Fletcher estate a stipulated sum of money to be insured by a lien upon the properties of the estate, excluding, of course, the house and the dower house. In return for the loan, your brother was to receive a certain percentage of the monies coming into the estate each year from rents, grazing fees, sale of timber and crops, and so forth. He also was to be allowed a limited amount of authority in the management of the estate. Under the will, you now stand in your brother's place."

"How limited was my brother's authority?"

"Well, Lord Fletcher, or his land agents through him, had the final word on the hiring or discharging of the land agents for the estate, the studmaster, head groomsman, the home farm manager, and other employees of the estate."

"Then Patrick could not have discharged Mr. Cormac Fletcher from his position as land agent?"

The solicitor answered promptly. "Not without Lord Fletcher's approval. I might add that, although Mr. Cormac Fletcher has a small financial interest of his own in the estate, he has no direct inheritance rights, unless, of course, the present earl should die without issue. However, Mr. Fletcher has always had considerable power given to him to run Abbey Court as he sees fit. The terms of your brother's will cannot completely change that."

"You don't approve of the terms of my brother's will?"

Mr. Corcoran gave me a level glance, his voice precise. "As to the original loan, my opinion wasn't asked nor would it have been listened to. A man very much in love as your brother was seldom listens to the voice of reason. As to his decision to revise his earlier will, yes, I did advise him against it, strongly. However, the day we met, Mr. O'Brien was, or appeared to be, extremely overwrought. And very insistent that I should follow his instructions exactly."

I felt the prickle of uneasiness returning. "You think he was wrong, leaving me the legacy he did?"

Mr. Corcoran shook his head gravely. "You seem a young woman of sound common sense, Miss O'Brien, but with all due respect, have you ever had anything to do with running an estate such as Abbey Court?"

"No," I admitted, "but Patrick knew that. I think all he wanted was to make sure—that the protection of the rights of the tenants, the policies he had begun, were continued if he should die."

"To be sure," Mr. Corcoran said dryly, perching on the edge of an overstuffed wing chair that threatened to enfold him. "It's unfortunate your brother wasn't as concerned for your well-being."

I looked across at the man, confused. "What do you mean?"

"Cormac Fletcher is not a man noted for his good nature. I don't suppose either he or his son will take kindly to your interfering in the affairs of the estate. Any more than he approved of your brother's interfering."

"My brother didn't interfere," I said indignantly. "He was interested in helping the tenant farmers, in protecting them from being misused."

"Very commendable," Mr. Corcoran said, smiling faintly. "But I rather doubt if Mr. Cormac Fletcher will take such a philanthropic view if you insist on following your brother's policies."

"Do you mean he'd physically harm me?" I demanded, setting my teacup down so abruptly that for a moment I was afraid I had cracked the delicate Dresden china.

Mr. Corcoran drew back sharply. "Not at all. There's no question of harm, Miss O'Brien. You misunderstand me. I'm merely pointing out that it won't be easy for you, working with either of the Fletchers." A trace of warmth, if that was possible, crept into his carefully emotionless voice. "I have four daughters, Miss O'Brien, one very close to your age. I'd give her the same advice I'm giving you. You should go home, back to your friends and family in Boston."

"I have no friends or family in Boston," I replied. Memory of the relief I had felt upon departing that city returned with such force that I added, without thinking, "And I have no intention of leaving Abbey Court until I discover why and by whom my brother was killed."

Now it was Mr. Corcoran who looked startled. "You can't be serious, Miss O'Brien. The authorities have searched thoroughly without success. How can you hope to do any better?"

"I have no idea," I admitted, regretting that I had brought up the matter. I had already guessed, correctly, what the solicitor's reaction would be. To change the subject, I said quickly, "And now perhaps you'll explain to me further the duties and responsibilities I'll be assuming at Abbey Court."

An hour later, my head surfeited with the facts and figures Mr. Corcoran had fed me, I escorted the solicitor to the door. As I bade him good-by on the terrace and he climbed into his waiting carriage, he turned toward me, the faint smile again on his face. "There's a saying we have here, Miss O'Brien. Little by little the castle is built. Nothing is done hastily in Ireland. And change doesn't come quickly either. You might remember that, when you're working with Mr. Fletcher."

The carriage rolled off down the driveway and I stood a moment, watching it go. Just for a moment I wished that I were in that carriage, leaving Abbey Court far behind me. Then I straightened and determinedly put the thought aside. Over the tops of the trees I could see the roofs of the stables, and I decided to visit them instead of returning to the house. As I approached the stable area, I saw that there was not one but three large stables, all of as fine a stonework as the house itself. Then, as I neared the closest stableyard, I noticed that my sister-in-law had evidently recovered from her headache. She was preparing to mount a black and white stallion that was being held by the studmaster, Brian Flaherty. His one hand clasped the reins, the other rested lightly on Regan's tiny waist.

I saw, before they did, Sean coming out of the stable office, his voice curt as he spoke to his sister. "Isn't it a little too soon for the grieving widow to go horseback riding, Regan?"

Brian Flaherty's hand fell away from my sister-in-law but Regan herself tossed her head, annoyed. "Oh, for heaven's sake, Sean, I'm not an old woman and I won't bury myself in my room. Isn't it bad enough that I have to wear ugly black clothes for a year and give up riding in the Dublin Horse Show when I'm sure Brian Boru would have been a prize winner?"

Then she saw me and had the grace to flush, although her voice lost none of its petulance, only taking on a slightly bitter tone. "Good day, sister-in-law. I see you couldn't wait to visit your new possessions. I suppose you know everything about horses and running a stud farm."

I bit back an angry retort, reminding myself that Regan from all accounts had done an excellent job in the past, handling the stud stable. Naturally she hated to give up managing her valuable and prized thoroughbreds to an outsider. "No," I said mildly. "I know very little about horses. Sometimes I rode with my father on prospecting trips in the mountains when I was young but that was usually astride a mule. And though I took lessons at Monsieur de Bussigny's riding school in Boston, I never did master riding sidesaddle. I didn't even bring a riding habit with me to Ireland."

"What a shame," Regan murmured, gazing from her own fashionable habit, with its hint of white at the neckline, to my waist, which was at least six inches larger than hers. "I'd loan you one of mine but, of course, it would have to be altered. . . ." Her voice trailed away pointedly.

"Perhaps you could forgo your ride, Regan, and show Miss O'Brien around the stables." Although Sean spoke quietly, it was more of a command than a request.

Regan gave her brother a defiant glance but something in his face made her change her mind and she said, cordially enough, "Very well, if she . . ."

I interrupted hastily, "Please don't bother. It's too nice a day to give up your ride. Some other time will do." Then, knowing if there was ever to be any friendship between Regan and myself, the first overture would have to come from me, I added in what I hoped was a humble enough voice, "I'd consider it a great service, Regan, if you'd continue managing the stable, certainly the stud stable, just as you always have."

For a moment the beautiful face behind the thin black gauze veil looked flustered. I almost thought I detected a spark of warmth but it was quickly gone. "Of course, as you wish," she said coldly. "And if you do decide to try riding, I'll have Tim Kennedy pick out a nice safe mount for you."

Then, without waiting for Mr. Flaherty's helping hand, she mounted with an easy grace and cantered off down the road away from Abbey Court. The studmaster cast an uncertain glance toward Sean, then, smiling a little tightly, leaped on his own mount and followed after her.

Sean gave a rueful shrug and turned to me. "Sometimes I think when Father was trying to beat some sense into Kevin and me he might have done the same with sister Regan. Or perhaps that's a prerogative a husband should have assumed."

He said the last with a smile but I bristled indignantly. "Patrick would never have struck a woman!"

To no one in particular, Regan's brother said softly, "Ay, more's the pity." Then he gave me his full attention. "And did you have a good visit with Mr. Corcoran?"

"Yes, thank you." I couldn't resist adding, "You don't share your father's distrust of my brother's solicitor?"

"Oh, Samuel Corcoran's all right, a practical man and a clever lawyer." A glint of amusement touched the eyes that in the sunlight looked more blue than green. "For all that he's a black Protestant."

He took my arm and we strolled back toward the terrace. "While I'm apologizing for Regan, I should add my own excuses for my behavior yesterday at the will reading. I can only say, in my own behalf, that it came as quite a shock to all of us, though, of course, your brother had a perfect right to dispose of his estate as he wished. Anyway, what's done is done, and there's no good trying to whistle back yesterday." He smiled down at me and I was once again conscious of the dark, easy charm of the man and the touch of his hand, warm through the sleeve of my gown. "Am I forgiven, Miss O'Brien?"

"There's nothing to forgive," I answered, knowing that I should remove my arm. I hardly needed his support to cross a perfectly level piece of land, but somehow found myself unable to refuse it.

"Then perhaps you'll allow me to show you the account books for the estate after dinner tonight in the office, around eight o'clock, if you won't be too tired."

"I'd like that, Mr. Fletcher, thank you," I said, surprised and pleased at the conciliatory gesture.

"And perhaps, since we'll be working closely together from now on, we might forget formality and use Christian names," he suggested.

I hesitated, although I was well aware that we had already gone past the first-name basis on the afternoon by the lake when he had called me . . . what was it now . . . *alannah*. I made a mental note to ask Rose what it meant, although I already half suspected its meaning.

He looked down at me, lifting an amused eyebrow. "Of course, if you're offended at my request, ma'am . . ."

The mock, too subservient manner made me smile in spite of myself. "No, Meg will be fine," I said briskly, as a servant held open the front door and stood aside to let us pass. "I'll see you at eight o'clock then, Sean, in the office."

11

That evening I ate alone with Lady Fletcher. Sean had his dinner with Cormac in his father's room as he evidently often did, and Lord Fletcher was still in London. Regan had not returned from her ride. She had sent back word that she was dining with friends and I wondered if Brian Flaherty had been included in the invitation. The studmaster had not returned from the ride either.

Lady Fletcher must have heard that I had been left to dine alone and at the last minute had shown up at the table, obviously to keep me company, although she ate none of the food and only sipped a little at a glass of wine.

The dining room at Abbey Court was a large, gloomy place. There was always a hint of chill in the air because the screen of trees pressed so close to the windows that little light penetrated into the room. The long table and chairs down the center of the room were of dark mahogany, but with the rapid change in Irish temperature and the dampness, the surfaces of the dining-room table and sideboard were constantly coated by a weathered, smoky look, as if the polish had misted over.

Despite Lady Fletcher's rather grim and forbidding appearance—she was, as usual, dressed completely in black— I was glad for her company. She apologized for Regan's non-appearance at the table, her voice sternly disapproving. "I hope you will excuse my niece's lack of discretion. It is, of course, far too early in her mourning for her to be dining out with friends. I'd ask Father Vincent to speak to her but I doubt if it would do much good. Even as a child, Regan was headstrong. Both she and Sean . . ." She shook her head sadly. "I tried to do my duty, to bring them up as if they were my own after their mother died, but it was like trying to hold the wind in your hand. And their father, unfortunately, was not the best influence. I warned him that

Regan was not ready for marriage, but he wouldn't listen."

I murmured something about Regan's being young.

"I was a year younger than Regan when I married my dear husband," the countess said. "And I hope I never failed in my duty to Lord Michael."

"You must have loved him very much, to marry so young."

If it were possible for that cool white face to look discomfited, I think Lady Fletcher might have been, for just a moment. "Why, no," she said candidly. "Actually I never planned to marry at all. I had hoped to enter a convent. My father, however, had made arrangements with the late Earl of Abbeymore, Lord Jason, that I should marry Simon, Michael's oldest brother. When he was regrettably killed in a carriage accident, I was betrothed to Michael instead."

"You had no choice in the matter?" I asked, shocked.

"Naturally not. One owes a duty to one's parents, and I was very young, of course, and not at all pretty. It was a most fortunate alliance for my family." Her voice softened wistfully. "Still, there have been times over the years when occasionally I wondered how it might have been if things had turned out differently. My husband, naturally, never expected to inherit the earldom—he was quite happy puttering around with his archaeological digs—and if I had been allowed to enter the convent and never come to Abbey Court . . ." The too thin mouth curved upward into a quick, fond smile. "But there was Kevin, of course, dear, sweet Kevin. He was always such a good, obedient boy and a child makes up for so much, don't you think?"

"Yes, I suppose so," I said slowly, and was grateful that the subject changed to other topics, to the pilgrimage that the countess was planning to make to Croagh Patrick. Later, though, as I prepared for my meeting with Sean in the office, I found myself trying to imagine how it would be to marry, as Lady Fletcher had, without love. Not that I was naïve enough to believe that such arranged marriages didn't happen, even among wealthy American families. After all, it was no secret that the Jerome family of New York had arranged their daughter Jennie's marriage to Lord Randolph Churchill.

Then Rose began to brush my hair and I forgot everything else but the meeting with Sean Fletcher that lay ahead of me. When she had finished, she stood back, frowning at little. " 'Tis a shame you cannot wear just a wee bit of color to perk up your face."

But I declined firmly and instead reached for a small

string of perfectly matched pearls Fiona had given me on my sixteenth birthday. Their gleaming luster matched the glow in my eyes as I took one final look at myself in the mirror. I didn't delude myself that I was beautiful. Yet there was an attractive color beneath my pale skin, a daring dab of corn-silk powder had made my freckles less obvious, and, thanks to Rose's brushing, my hair lay in smooth bright copper coils at the nape of my neck with a few curls allowed to escape to fringe my forehead. And a dark-colored gown does make you look more slender, I reminded myself hopefully.

"Is his lordship back from London then?" Rose asked, slipping a black shawl over my shoulders.

"Why, no, I'm having a . . . a business discussion with Mr. Sean Fletcher this evening."

A troubled look crossed Rose's open face before she said quickly, "Sure and he's a handsome man, for all he's black Irish, and not a one of them to be trusted. It's not all the poor man's fault, I'm thinking," she added hastily, "with the ladies buzzing around him like bees at a honeypot."

I pinched my cheeks to bring even more pinkness into them and asked teasingly, "What of Lord Fletcher? Doesn't he have young ladies buzzing around him too?"

"Oh yes, grand young ladies, but they're a different sort, not laughing and gay like Mr. Sean's ladies, more serious like and no end to their talking." Rose shook her head, baffled. "And me not being able to make head nor tail of what they're talking about."

I laughed, remembering that I had felt much the same way about the young women in whom Patrick had been interested. I wondered suddenly if that was what had attracted my brother to Regan: her beauty and temperament, such a blazing contrast to the more sober-minded women he had known.

It took me several minutes after I left my bedroom to find the estate office. It was lodged off a long narrow corridor in the back of the east wing, with an outside entrance for visitors and a back entrance for the family through the kitchen quarters. The room itself was small and simply furnished with a square, no-nonsense desk, two rather hard, uncomfortable chairs, shelves of leather-bound ledgers, a safe against the wall. There was one uncurtained window. It occurred to me that the cold austerity of the room might be deliberate, just as was the long narrow hallway the tenants had to walk before reaching the office.

Sean rose from behind the desk when I entered and if I had thought there might be any purpose other than business behind our meeting, his actions quickly dissuaded me. His manner was correctly, punctiliously polite, and if, in holding out a chair for me or handing me an account book, his hand brushed mine, it quickly fell away.

Rose needn't have worried, I thought, a little crossly, and then put all other thoughts out of my head but the subjects Sean was discussing with me. As it turned out, I needed all my wits about me. It was no simple matter, I soon discovered, the keeping of the accounts for Abbey Court. There were, in all, four to be kept. The first was the household account, which, Sean explained, "was originally kept by my aunt until she moved to the dower house. Regan should have assumed the responsibility but it fell instead on the shoulders of Miss O'Toole. She'll be happy for you to take it over," Sean assured me.

I wasn't too sure about that but made no comment as he continued, "Regan does keep the accounts for the stud stable although Brian Flaherty actually does the account work for her."

"He seems a very capable person," I said cautiously. "Is he a local man?"

"No, he's descended from a tinker family from Galway."

At my puzzled glance, he explained. "Tinkers are Ireland's gypsies with no particular home. Not Romany gypsies as in Europe but families that years ago were dispossessed from their land and took to the road. Most of them are excellent with horses. There are some tinkers who can break a horse by just whispering to the animal. At least, my sister believes so. But to get on to the other accounts, these are the two we handle here, the home farm account and, of course, the rents from the tenant farmers."

"What do you grow? I mean, on the home farm?"

"Oats mostly, and feed for the horses and dairy cattle. We have a sizable herd of dairy cattle and a small herd of sheep. There is a wool room below us where the wool is carded and spun. Some additional money comes in from land we've leased and from the woodland, although the trees haven't been thinned properly in the last years and new plantings are necessary. Whenever a tenant farmer leaves, we put the land to grazing or reforestation."

"Why do the families leave?"

Sean Fletcher leaned back in his chair, his voice relaxed, but I saw his hooded eyes watching me closely. "Oh, various reasons. Bad luck or bad management. Sometimes laziness or too much time spent at the local pub so that the farm work never gets done, or there are too many children so the rent money has to go for food. And then there's the potato blight. People always talk of the terrible blight and famine of '45, but there have been other years of potato blight, before and since, though not so widespread. And no one is any closer to solving the mystery of what causes the disease that turns the potatoes black and mushy so they're not only useless but poisonous."

"And if the tenants couldn't pay the rent, they were—turned out?"

The acerbity in my voice must have been self-evident, but Sean shrugged indifferently. "Father always gave them a grace period before the cottage was torn down, the land turned over to grazing or timber, and the family sent elsewhere." A grim smile quirked the corners of his mouth. "Of course, the Land Act passed last year has brought some small changes between landlord and tenant, not as many, naturally, as the tenants would have wished, but more, I think, than my father appreciates."

"It's your father's decision, then, when a family is turned out?"

Sean straightened in his chair, his face all at once harsh and cold. "We should make one thing clear before we begin, Meg. Cormac Fletcher is the estate agent at Abbey Court, not I. He makes the decisions. I not only work for him but pay him the respect due him as my father. I don't know how it is in America but in Ireland the father is the head of the household. His opinions and decisions are honored and obeyed, no matter how old or ill he might be. That's a fact your brother never seemed to grasp."

No, Patrick wouldn't, I thought. Not that Patrick hadn't respected Jamie but there had been more friendship in their relationship than blind obedience. Often I had heard Jamie and Patrick argue bitterly and Patrick would go his own way, but never had I seen any lessening of the love between them because of it.

"What of Lord Fletcher?" I asked. "Does he have no say in the running of Abbey Court? After all, the estate belongs to him."

I saw that this last shaft had struck home. Sean's face darkened, and for a moment I could see his father in his face, the same stubborn implacability, the hidden look of cunning in his eyes. When he spoke, though, his voice was flat. "Lord Fletcher has other interests. He wisely leaves the management of Abbey Court to Father, as his father did before him."

I decided to try a new tack. "If the potatoes are subject to this blight, perhaps the tenant farmers should raise some other crop," I ventured.

Sean flung back his head in a sudden, unexpected whoop of laughter. "An Irishman not raise potatoes? They'd as soon give up the Church. Oh, there are some who raise oats, have a pig, and try to keep a cow or two but the truth is the tenant farms are too small to raise cattle efficiently or much of anything else for that matter. And it's cattle that are the real future of Irish agriculture, not just dairy but beef cattle. With whatever spare cash I can lay my hands on, I've been increasing the beef and dairy herd at Abbey Court although Father wouldn't be happy if he knew . . ."

He broke off abruptly, and I lowered my head so he wouldn't see the smile on my face. So Sean Fletcher wasn't completely under his father's thumb!

Hastily he hauled the account books over to me at the desk. "You should become acquainted with these if you plan to continue working here," he said. For the next hour I dutifully studied row upon row of neatly drawn numbers, at first not able to make sense of them, but gradually I could see a pattern emerging. It was like discovering a hidden foundation that, although invisible, held up the whole massive structure of Abbey Court itself.

To my mind, the rents paid by the tenant farmers seemed too high although I said nothing, until I came to the wages paid the staff at Abbey Court. Then I couldn't resist saying, shocked, "Why, Rose only receives eight pounds a year!" I quickly, mentally translated pounds into American money. "That's less than forty dollars. Mother paid her maids at least twice that." As I read the amounts of wages paid the rest of the staff and farm workers, my indignation swelled. "No one in America would work for such low wages. No wonder there is such hatred and violence here."

"This isn't America," Sean pointed out calmly. "And don't forget the staff's wages include food and board and clothing. As a matter of fact, we pay better wages at Abbey Court than any of our neighbors in the county." He smiled grimly. "And it seems to me there was a long time in America when some people worked for no wages at all."

I frowned, puzzled, and then, understanding, "But those

were slaves. . . ."My voice trailed off.

"As for hatred and violence, I doubt if any one country has a monopoly on that. Wasn't your own President Garfield shot just last year in broad daylight in a railroad station? And it seems to me I've heard of a great deal of violence in your own country between white- and red-skinned Americans."

I started to reply angrily, then reminded myself of Mr. Corcoran's advice: "Little by little the castle is built." There was no point in antagonizing Sean Fletcher so early in the game, and I wasn't foolish enough to hope to make any changes in the running of the estate in one evening.

I hid a polite yawn behind my hand and glanced up at the clock on the wall. "I had no idea it was growing so late."

"We could continue tomorrow," Sean said, taking the hint. "I usually work with my father here in the office in the morning for an hour but he always leaves by eight. However, perhaps that's too early for you."

"Eight o'clock will be fine," I said, getting to my feet, deciding that one thing I definitely wanted to avoid, if possible, was any confrontation with Cormac Fletcher.

Sean took the gas lamp from the desk. "I'll light you to the main hall," he said.

I assured him that wasn't necessary but he brushed aside my objections and I was glad enough for his light in front of me as we made our way through the confusion of darkened passageways back to the main entrance hall. The front hall was only dimly lit with a few wall scones the servants had left burning and when Sean extinguished his lamp his face dissolved into a blurred shadow above mine. I could barely make out the shape of his mouth, the set of his shoulders. His tall dark figure somehow, before I realized it, had deliberately moved in front of me, blocking the way up the stairs.

His voice reached out, seeking me through the darkness. The lilting brogue that Sean Fletcher apparently turned off and on at will was soft as a caress. "I've a great curiosity about you, Meg O'Brien. Are they such clods, those men in Boston, that they let a lovely slip of a girl like yourself slide through their fingers? Or is there some handsome lad waiting impatiently for your return?"

I spoke briskly, trying to ignore the heavy, swollen feeling in my chest that made it hard to catch my breath. "Hardly a slip of a girl," I corrected him, "but no, there's no one waiting for me in Boston, patiently or impatiently."

I could sense, rather than see, Sean's glance travel over my sturdy, well-rounded body, finally resting at a point where my breasts betrayed their fullness above my corset cover, no matter how tightly I tried to bind them. His smile shone white in the darkness. "The more fools they are then," he laughed softly, "not appreciating what's before their very eyes. For myself, 'tis never been the size of a woman's waist that caught my eye."

I reached out and grasped the finial of the banister, gripping it so hard that the sharply carved surface cut into my palm. "It's been a long day, Sean . . . if you'll excuse me . . ."

"Ay, that it has." His glance fell away and, where his eyes had touched, my flesh felt suddenly, oddly cold. "I won't be keeping you from your bed, only I am sorry about one thing."

"And what is that?" I couldn't resist asking, curious.

"That I never saw you as a child, astride that mule. A grand sight that must have been!"

I hurried up the stairs, but the soft, teasing laughter was still in my ears when at last, smiling, I fell asleep.

The next weeks my days at Abbey Court fell into a set pattern. After Sean had his morning conference with his father, receiving his instructions for the day's work, we would spend the morning going over the account books together. I had thought I would find it boring, spending hours studying pages of figures. To my own surprise, I discovered it was fascinating. I had always had a good head for figures—in school arithmetic had been my favorite subject—and once Sean discovered I could add and subtract a row of figures in my head faster and more accurately than he could on paper, he turned more and more of the bookkeeping over to me. In the afternoon he would take me on inspection trips around the estate on a horse that, as Regan had promised, turned out to be a safe, placid old gray and white dappled mare.

Once we passed beyond the carefully tended park area around the house itself and through the woodland into the outer farm areas, the landscape became rougher. There were bogland and heaths, and rocks jutting out of the earth like the bones of some giant prehistoric creature. Small, mean-looking cottages with thatched roofs dotted the farmland. Once or twice Sean stopped at one of these cottages and introduced me to the family living there. The cottages, no more than hovels, had dirt floors and the cooking was done over turf-heated fireplaces. The smell of poverty was as strong as the scent of the turf that burned with hardly a flame in the hearths. If Sean expected me to be dismayed at what I saw, he was disappointed. Before Jamie hit it rich, the O'Brien family had lived in almost the same rude conditions in the mining camps, and I could still remember Mother baking endless loaves of bread to sell to the miners over much the same rude type of fireplace.

Sometimes a tenant farmer's wife with a gaunt face and a black shawl over her head and several children clinging to her skirt would come out of the cottage to stare at me. Then, with an innate sense of dignity and hospitality, she would ask "her ladyship" would she care for a jar of tea, although I was sure that what few leaves of tea they might have must be particularly treasured. More often than not the tenants spoke in the old Irish language, or a brogue so thick I had a hard time understanding what they said.

With Sean, their manner was never quite the same as it was toward me. When he spoke to them in Irish, they listened to him carefully, and although there was little warmth in their faces, there was a grudging respect, verging at times on fear.

As for my own relationship with Sean Fletcher, not since that first night in the hallway had he so much as touched my hand except to help me on or off Lady Jane, my long-suffering mount. Our discussions never again strayed into the personal but remained always on some aspect of estate management. Following Mr. Corcoran's advice, I had not tried to bring about any immediate changes in how the Fletchers, father and son, ran Abbey Court. I did, however, manage to coax Sean into allowing me to put curtains on the window of the office and install several comfortable chairs. And when James Leary came, hat in hand, one morning with a red face, admitting he'd spent the half-yearly rent money in the fine wake he'd held for his brother, I did slip out of the office and press the needed shillings into his hand to carry him over till the next rent period.

He thanked me profusely. " 'Tis the same good heart you have as your brother, God rest his soul. And may the villain who did that terrible deed burn in hell, as he deserves. And thank God it was none of us."

No, I thought, returning with a sober face to the office, now that I had met so many of the tenants at Abbey Court, I could never be convinced that any one of them had had a part in my brother's death. Yet why should outsiders, terrorists such as the Moonlighters, come upon Abbey Court land to wreak vengeance on a man they didn't even know? As for personal enemies, I couldn't imagine that anyone could hate Patrick enough to want him dead.

I was still thinking on it as Sean and I took our afternoon tour of the estate. I was feeling vaguely guilty because these last weeks, in working with Sean, I had let myself forget the reason I had stayed on at Abbey Court—to try to bring to justice my brother's murderer. Instead, reproachfully, I realized that often hours had gone by and I had never even thought of Patrick, had even felt stirrings of happiness instead of grief.

When Sean said, "Let's stay here a bit," I looked up, startled to see that we were stopped on a path by the edge of the lake. He helped me off Lady Jane but for the first time did not immediately release me. His hands lingered on my waist, and he growled, annoyed, "Damn those bloody corsets you women wear! It's like fondling an iron post."

I felt my face grow hot, my voice haughty. "A gentleman is not aware of a woman's inner garments."

He cocked an amused eyebrow at me. "Aren't you forgetting I have a sister, and don't you think I've heard her squealing in pain, hanging onto the bedpost while her maid laces her into those objects of torture?" He drew me slowly toward him, his voice softening. "I'll not have you mistreating your lovely flesh that way, *alannah*. You must promise me, once we're married, you'll never wear one of those things again."

"Married!" My voice was more a gasp of disbelief than of righteous indignation. "To you?"

Before I could protest further, I was being enfolded in an embrace that left hardly enough space for breath, much less words. My arms were pinned too tightly to my side for any struggle. But after the first shock of feeling his mouth on mine, there developed a most pleasant sensation through my body, which I discovered I didn't want to end.

When Sean finally released me and stepped back, an insufferable smug smile on his face, he asked, calmly enough, "And who else do you think you'd be marrying?"

With his arms and mouth no longer touching me, a measure of sanity returned. I could begin to think clearly again, at least clearly enough to sense the danger that his very presence thrust upon me. It was more than just the way my heart was racing, or a weakness in the knees. It was as if in one moment some vital part of myself had been stripped away, leaving me defenseless, completely vulnerable, a feeling I'd never known before. I stepped back. "I . . . I think we'd better . . . return to the house."

He scowled, his arms impatiently reaching out again. I shook my head, my voice steadier now. "Please, Sean, it's too soon."

He sighed and nodded regretfully. "I know you're in mourning, but I won't be apologizing for not waiting the proper length of time. I'm not a patient man, Meg O'Brien."

No, I thought, I know that. I wasn't even sure he was a particularly kind or compassionate man. And felt a stab of disquiet as I suddenly realized how little I did know about Sean Fletcher.

Yet when we reached the house and he turned to me, smiling, his hand warm on mine, and asked, "I'll see you then in the morning?" we both knew it was not a question but a promise.

I awoke early the next morning and, throwing back the covers, stretched blissfully. I had never felt so wonderfully, completely alive. It was as if the shock of Fiona's and Patrick's deaths so close together had frozen me into a sort of numbness, without my even realizing it. Now, as if recovering from frostbite, nerve endings and flesh had once again come stingingly to life.

The aching sense of loss was still there, would always be there, but there was an even stronger feeling of life reaching out to me, rushing by me, and if I didn't grasp it quickly it would be too late. Suddenly I couldn't wait to see Sean. All of yesterday's fears and uncertainties seemed foolish and inconsequential. I dressed myself without waiting for Rose to help me and, not bothering to eat breakfast, I fairly flew down the steps and through the back passageway to the office. I only stopped in mid-flight when I heard the booming voice of Cormac Fletcher coming through the half-open office door.

Having no desire to interfere in the morning conference between father and son, I had half turned away when all at once the words Cormac was saying swung me around, startled.

". . . so long to get the girl panting for the wedding banns. It only took your sister a few days to have Patrick jumping through hoops for her."

"The girl's not like her brother, you know." It was Sean's voice, with the cold, indifferent tone I had learned to recognize whenever he was annoyed.

"She's no prize beauty, that's true enough," Cormac Fletcher admitted. "Still, there's lovely flesh on her arms, not skinny as a scaldeen like some of the fine ladies you've fancied. A plain lass like that and a handsome gossoon like yourself, you'd think you'd have her wrapped around your finger in no time at all."

"There's no need to fret, Father." I could imagine the bored, slightly amused smile on Sean's face. "Abbey Court won't lose the O'Brien fortune a second time."

"Ay, it's not only the money," Cormac said darkly. "If we're not careful, she'll be poking and prying around, interfering in matters that are none of her concern."

Sean's voice hardened. "You can rest assured, Father, once we're married there'll be no more prying. I've made sure the girl's broken to the bit all right. I just don't like rushing my fences. . . ."

12

For a moment, standing in the dark hallway, I had the sensation that a clenched fist had thrust into my mid-section, knocking the wind out of me. I half bent over with the shock. Then I heard a whining sound from the office, the wheels of Cormac's wheel chair moving over the carpetless floor. The realization that any moment he and Sean would come through the doorway and discover me eavesdropping was enough to drive all else from my mind.

I fled past the slightly ajar office door and down the corridor which led to the outer door. Once outside, I glanced wildly around me. All I wanted was a place I could crawl into and hide. I saw an overgrown path, wide enough for a road, leading from the back east wing of Abbey Court, arching in a half circle around the screen of trees, and disappearing from view. It was the road I remembered Lady Fletcher using the morning I glimpsed her from my bedroom window making her penance pilgrimage. Picking up my skirt to keep my hem from the tall grass, still gray and heavy with dew, I ran down the road past the low stone wall encircling the kitchen and flower garden. A narrow wooden bridge at the garden's edge crossed over a deep gully on my right. Beyond the bridge, beechwood trees and oaks pressed almost to the edge of the gully itself.

Without thinking, I left the road and crossed the makeshift wooden bridge, several of the boards, rotted through, bouncing beneath my feet. At the edge of the woods I spied a narrow boreen leading off into the trees. Immediately I stepped onto this footpath, the woods seemed to close around me, much thicker and darker than the screen of trees between Abbey Court and the lake.

Velvety moss and fern edged across the path, making the ground treacherously slick underfoot. Brambles and dog rose, intertwined, sometimes almost blocked the way completely. Even if a steady stream of tears wasn't blinding my eyes, it would have been difficult to see my way along the path. Yet I couldn't stop myself from senselessly running, as if somehow I could flee the sound of Sean's voice; his words, trapped in my mind, repeated themselves endlessly, over and over again. No matter how I hurried, I was unable to escape them.

All at once the path widened and my foot tripped over a half-hidden root, the size of a small rope flung across the path. I felt myself falling unceremoniously to the ground. For several seconds I lay quite still, my knees aching from the impact, the palm of one hand scratched and bleeding. A part of me welcomed the pain. Physical pain was something real with which I could cope. It was the other pain I could not endure, the agony of rage and humiliation that left me shaken and helpless, blazing hot with anger one minute, icily cold with shame the next.

I don't know how long I lay there, my face pressed against the damp, musk-smelling earth. Finally the shuddering sobs diminished to occasional hiccups; the fever and chills had both gone, leaving only a blessed emptiness. Wearily I sat up and looked around me. For the first time I realized where I was. The old Abbey. Another few steps and the pathway abruptly ended at a tilted stone archway standing at the edge of the sunken ruins.

Curiosity overcame my misery and I pulled myself slowly to my feet. I was surprised to discover how much of the Abbey still stood. There were, of course, no roofs left, or floors or even doors, but there were high walls, crumbling in places, delineating where buildings had once stood, and fallen pillars and toppled archways outlined rooms and colonnades. On the stonework of arches and pillars, I could still see the carved monstrous heads of demons with twisted tails and mouths wide open, silently screaming at the sky.

Hitching my skirt up, I cautiously climbed to the top of a low wall, avoiding slippery patches of lichen, to get a better look inside the ruins. The Abbey had covered a large area, almost an acre of ground. The architectural layout, the arrangement of rooms, passageways, and gardens, could be discerned clearly, although great sunken depressions in the ground that once had been floors were now choked knee deep with broken rock, rubble, nettles, and weeds. Stone steps, hollowed in the center by the feet of generations of monks, led down into nothing. Deep recesses in the walls which had once housed tombs or statuary stood vacant; archways that once had enclosed heavy, studded doors stood empty.

And everywhere, running like green veins between the stones, or hanging in thick swag curtains partially concealing the violet-gray walls, were the ropes of ivy, the leaves burnished and glittering in the sunlight. Colonies of rooks apparently used the ivy as nesting areas and several of the large black birds dipped in the air above the ruins, making a raucous ca-ca-ca noise at my intrusion.

Deciding to take a closer look inside the ruins themselves, I started down a sloping layer of piled-up rock within the wall beneath me—and immediately set off a small rock slide, the chat tumbling and sliding noisily down onto the Abbey floor.

"Miss O'Brien!"

I caught my balance with difficulty and turned. Lord Fletcher approached the base of the wall. His face lifted to mine was filled with a concern that came very near to anger. "You shouldn't be climbing around on the walls of the Abbey. It's too dangerous. The stones have no mortar left between them. The smallest push can send a wall toppling." He held up his hands. "Here, let me help you down."

I accepted his proffered hands and clambered awkwardly down to the ground beside him. "I didn't know you had returned," I said, embarrassed at having been found in such an unladylike predicament.

"I arrived last evening and spent the night at the tower. I was taking a walk when I saw you on the wall and hurried to warn you." He hesitated, his gray eyes searching my face anxiously. "I don't mean to intrude, Miss O'Brien, but is anything wrong? Has someone said or done something to upset you?"

Unhappily, then, I remembered how I must look, my gown disheveled and grass-stained, my hair torn free from its chignon, my eyes no doubt red and puffy from crying. "No," I lied hastily, and then, knowing some explanation was necessary, added, "It's . . . it's Patrick . . . something reminded me . . ." I broke off, ducking my head guiltily, remembering how my face always gave me away when I lied.

Lord Fletcher, however, readily accepted the deception. He gave my hand a sympathetic squeeze before releasing it. "I envy you the close relationship that you and Patrick shared," he said wistfully. "Regan, Sean, and I grew up as children but we were never what you would call close. I'm afraid they considered me pretty much of a dull stick." His smile was brittle. "They got into all sorts of mischief and I usually ended up getting the blame. Uncle Cormac had a habit of thrashing first and asking questions later."

We were walking along the outer wall of the Abbey and had come to a section where the wall had completely vanished. "You can get a good view of the interior from here," Lord Fletcher said, stopping. "Your brother was very interested in antiquities. He used to spend hours climbing around these ruins and studying Father's notes. But then I suppose Patrick wrote you all about the Abbey."

"No, he never mentioned it," I said, a little surprised. I hadn't realized that Patrick, despite his knowledge of most phases of art, was interested in archaeology. Gazing down at the skeletal remains of what once had been a thriving and wealthy religious community, I confessed, "In fact, I don't even know which order built this Abbey."

"Cistercian," Lord Fletcher said promptly. "The monks came from France sometime in the twelfth century and built the Abbey on the ruins of an even older Celtic abbey the Vikings had destroyed centuries earlier. The Cistercian monks, as you may know, were excellent architects. They introduced the Gothic style of architecture to Ireland. Unfortunately, no examples of the rib vaulting they must have used in building this Abbey still remain."

I gazed at my companion, impressed. "You sound as if you know quite a bit about antiquities yourself."

"Not a great deal." He shook his head modestly. "Father was the authority in the family. He spent years excavating the Abbey when he was younger. After his marriage, though, his interests turned abroad. He made several trips to Egypt before he died. In addition to the drawings of the jewelry and other relics he discovered in the Abbey, he left behind a detailed plan of the layout of the buildings, or how it must have been when it was first built."

He gestured to the far right where an almost perfectly preserved wall hid a portion of the Abbey from view. "For example, he determined that the private chapel for the abbot lay next to the cloister arcade over there. The refectories and dormitories with gardens surrounding them lay below us. The Abbey church itself was built on that slight rise of land nearest that large fallen archway. The church must have been impressive in its time. You can still see where the altar stood."

I glanced where he pointed but all I could see were lines of irregular stonework and a great amount of rubble where one of the walls had fallen inward. "Was that the church Cromwell's men burned?" I asked, and then could have bitten my tongue for my thoughtlessness. After all, it was Lord Fletcher's ancestor, Captain Daniel Fletcher, who had led the raiding party and callously put the torch to the church with the congregation locked inside.

Lord Fletcher, however, did not seem embarrassed by my question. "No, the church that Captain Daniel Fletcher supposedly burned wasn't the original Cistercian church," he explained carefully. "That had been destroyed much earlier during the reign of Henry VIII. Only the walls had been left standing and it was never completely rebuilt, just a thatched roof placed over it and doors and windows installed." He smiled wryly. "I'm sure you've heard the tale of the deliberate burning of the church by Captain Fletcher. More than likely what actually happened was that the people did go to the church for protection when Cromwell's men arrived on the scene. A fire must have started somehow. With the candles used then and thatched roofs, fires were not at all uncommon. There were undoubtedly too many people crowded within the church and, in the crush to escape, probably the doors jammed shut. However, since the Irish dearly love to embroider their stories, that's not the account you'll hear today. Still, no matter how it happened, it was a great tragedy."

As we stood looking down into the Abbey sky, which had been a shimmering, translucent blue overhead, had darkened, one of those rapid changes of light I was becoming accustomed to, a constant part of the Irish weather and landscape. Clouds massed, black and sullen, over the ruins. Even the air felt all at once heavier. The violet color of the Abbey stones drained to a cold, depressing gray and the raucous cries of the rooks returning to their nests had a mournful, almost menacing sound.

One bird, annoyed at our standing too close to her nesting area, swooped so near where we stood that I could see the circle of bare white skin at the base of the bill. To my surprise, Lord Fletcher threw up his hands as if to protect his face and backed away abruptly. Only after the bird had circled away did he lower his hands and smile sheepishly at me. "I'm afraid I'm not a bird fancier, particularly not rooks. Such ugly, graceless birds. Do you know some of the old people hereabout actually believe that the souls of those poor people burned alive in the church are trapped in the rooks that nest here?"

I shivered beneath the black gown I wore, as if with a sudden chill. So much death, I thought, gazing down into the ruins, where once monks had moved through cloistered gardens in peace and tranquillity. Now there were only the rooks making their nests in the crumbling walls, filling the air with their discordant cries. Turning away quickly, I discovered that Lord Fletcher was standing quietly, watching me, a piercing intensity in his gray eyes that reminded me suddenly of his mother. Self-consciously and futilely, I tried to push my hair back within the confines of the chignon, murmuring hastily, "I really must be returning to Abbey Court."

"Oh." The earl looked disappointed. "I was hoping you might join me for a cup of tea at the tower." As my hand flew again, discomfited, to my hair, he added, "I hope you don't mind my saying that I think your hair looks charming, hanging loose that way. You remind me very much of a painting I'd like to show you while we're having tea." When I still hesitated, uncertain, his voice lost its warmth and took on a careful stiff aloofness. "Of course, if you'd rather not . . ."

Why, he's shy, I thought, surprised. Or maybe shy wasn't the right word. Wary, I thought slowly. I had the feeling that Kevin Fletcher seldom put himself into positions where he would have to face the humiliation of rejection. Then I realized that while I had been talking to him I had forgotten, at least temporarily, those cruel moments in the office corridor. Pain, revived by memory, clawed viciously at me again. How stupid I had been, how naïve to have let myself be deceived by Sean for a moment. Falling into his arms so easily like a silly, gawky schoolgirl . . . how he must have secretly laughed at me.

I spoke rapidly and with such eagerness that Lord Fletcher looked a little taken aback. "Yes, thank you, a cup of tea sounds delightful."

Quickly recovering, he took my arm to help me across the uneven stretch of meadow to a well-worn path that led through the woods directly away from the Abbey.

"Did you have a pleasant stay in London?" I asked with an almost feverish intensity. Anything to break the silence that had fallen between us.

"Yes, very pleasant. I attended a reception at Lady Wilde's. Unfortunately, her son Oscar wasn't able to be there. We were acquaintances in school, you know, Oscar and myself. He came to Magdalen College the year I was leaving. It was Wilde who first aroused my interest in the Pre-Raphaelite artists."

He spoke Mr. Wilde's name as if I should know him. I searched my mind frantically. The name did sound familiar. Then I remembered. Of course, Oscar Wilde, the celebrated Irish poet and playwright.

"Mr. Wilde recently returned from a lecture tour in America," Lord Fletcher said. "Perhaps you heard him speak in Boston."

"No." I shook my head, then smiled, remembering. "But Mr. Wilde did lecture at the Boston Music Hall last January. The Boston newspapers were filled with the story. It seems Mr. Wilde usually wears knee breeches and carries a sunflower or a lily when he lectures. That night he spoke in Boston, sixty Harvard students attended, all wearing knee breeches and carrying sunflowers as they marched down the aisle. Only it so happened that night Mr. Wilde wore ordinary evening clothes and you can imagine how ridiculous the students appeared!"

Lord Fletcher laughed, then shrugged, frowning a little. "Oscar was an eccentric, even in college. He used to be ragged unmercifully for the way he dressed, even the way he decorated his rooms. I remember once four students broke into his rooms to vandalize them, but they underestimated their victim. Oscar is not the weakling some think him and he threw the ruffians bodily down the steps, one by one. Of course, now he's the rage of London society. His attendance at a dinner or reception assures success for the hostess. I'm proud to say he's often been a guest at my town house in London."

The winding path through the woods had ended and I recognized where we were. It was the road that Sean and I had often taken on our way to visit the tenant farms. The dower house was not far down the road toward Abbey Court but I couldn't remember ever passing any tower as we came this way.

I looked toward my companion but he was already crossing the road. The wooded area continued on the other side of the road, and the footpath we followed now was very narrow, running for some distance parallel to the road.

I was trailing behind the earl when suddenly a gray stone, rounded wall loomed through the trees off toward my right. I stopped, surprised, realizing I must have ridden very close to the tower at least a dozen times and had never noticed it from the road behind its shield of trees.

The ground immediately around the tower had been cleared of underbrush and timber and was sunken a little, as if at one time a moat had been dug there and later filled in. There were narrow slits in the lower wall of the tower but near the crenelated top modern windows had been cut and glass installed.

"Well, here it is, Miss O'Brien, my tower," Lord Fletcher said with the same pride and enthusiasm in his voice, I thought, amused, as a small boy showing off his tree house.

"It's . . . it's most unusual," I murmured, trying to think of something polite to say without out and out lying. For the truth was the gray stone tower, rising so suddenly in the midst of the close-pressing trees, had an eerie Hansel and Gretel quality about it. At any moment I expected the wicked witch to come storming out of the portcullis.

Then I shook away such a childish fancy as Lord Fletcher reached for the heavy iron doorknob on the great studded door. Before he could touch the knob, however, the huge door swung quietly open. A young man with bright red hair, reaching almost to his shoulders, stood in the doorway. There was something familiar about his face—then I remembered the angelic-looking young man who, with an elderly lady, had paid his respects at my brother's lying in state.

"Good morning, my lord."

He stood aside to let us enter. Although he wore ordinary clothes instead of livery, the trousers and jacket were well cut and fit his slim body as if tailor-made. His eyes were as blue as my own but his lashes were darker and longer and had a way of veiling his glance so that one had the feeling he was watching surreptitiously from behind a curtain.

"Miss O'Brien and I will have tea in the gallery, Liam," Lord Fletcher said, his glance not meeting the young man's directly but roving restlessly around the room.

"Yes, my lord," the man answered, humbly enough, but just for a second the look on his face was not servile at all, and his voice seemed to hold a mocking, almost contemptuous note beneath the surface. I glanced quickly away, embarrassed.

"This was Father's workroom where he cleaned and catalogued his finds," Lord Fletcher said, gesturing around the circular room that made up the ground floor of the tower. "I've left it almost exactly as it was when he was alive."

There were only a few pieces of furniture in the room. The shelves were crowded with books and with brown bottles of chemicals all neatly labeled. There was a long worktable, much stained and scarred. Despite the modern gas lamps affixed to the stone walls, the room couldn't have been a very cheerful place in which to work, I thought. One could almost feel the clammy chill emanating from the ancient stone walls, and the small fireplace would have done little to help. Was it in this dank, cold place that Mother had worked, I wondered, helping Kevin's father remove the corrosion of years from the treasures he found in the Abbey?

But before I could question the present Lord Fletcher, he had directed me up the spiral stone staircase, which wound around the inner wall. "Be careful," he cautioned, following me. "I had the railing installed for safety but these are the original steps built into the tower. You can see they're badly worn."

Not only worn, I realized, but worn unevenly so that one had to watch one's feet carefully while making the ascent to the next level. Then I stepped through an opening onto the first floor of the tower and gave a cry of delight.

Unlike the ground floor, the walls here were painted a flat white above a black-paneled wainscoting. A handsome, soft-piled Axminster rug in a dozen shades of blue and green covered the floor, matching exactly a vase of blue and green peacock feather switches, as well as the robes of the medieval knight at prayer in a narrow stained-glass picture set into one wall. The furnishings in the room had a medieval air about them too—the high-backed, black-stained chairs with rush seats, the sideboard decorated with heraldic designs, even the elegant metal candlestick holders.

What caught and filled the eye with amazement, though, were the paintings hung all around the large circular room. Even I, untutored in art, recognized there was a small fortune in paintings here. I was sure I recognized the Raphael and the Botticelli that Lord Fletcher had mentioned, plus a Gainsborough landscape, along with the work of many other masters. I felt inundated, drowning in color that stirred the senses and boggled the mind with its richness.

"This was the painting I particularly wanted you to see."

Lord Fletcher took my hand and led me to the portrait of a young woman dressed in a flowing, graceful robe. The material was a brilliant blue against the almost death-white pallor of her flesh. Dazzling unbound red hair hung loose down her back, setting off a slender long neck and large dark eyes. One slim hand was languidly playing a lute and the other held a gold hand mirror.

"It's one of Dante Gabriel Rossetti's earlier paintings," Lord Fletcher said. "The model was his wife, Elizabeth Siddal. When she died at an early age, Rossetti was so overcome with grief that he placed all his love poems in her casket and buried them with her." Gently he picked up a strand of my hair and held it to the painting. "You can see the color is much the same. . . ."

The hair color might be the same as mine, I thought, mentally wincing, but not the boyishly slim hips, the delicate face, and reed-thin neck of the young woman in the painting. All at once I remembered Cormac's voice describing me, "she's no prize beauty," and I flushed and said, more caustically than I had intended, "The painting's lovely, Lord Fletcher, but the resemblance, unfortunately, ends with the hair."

"Don't!" The sharpness in his voice surprised me. Then he smiled faintly and shook his head, speaking more kindly but firmly. "Don't ever think less of yourself, Miss O'Brien, because others are blind around you. It's their loss, not yours."

I wasn't sure I understood what he meant but it was soothing to see the concern in the gray eyes that gazed down at me. Could Lord Fletcher have guessed what happened between Sean and me? I wondered suddenly. It was possible, I realized, with a twisting, painful sense of ignominy. I probably wasn't the first girl to fling herself into Sean

Fletcher's arms, believing every charming lie and smile. Perhaps I wasn't even the first girl Kevin Fletcher had consoled after she had bruised herself throwing herself at his cousin.

He continued, almost indifferently. "If it matters so much, there are tricks a woman can use to turn herself into the sort of artificial beauty society demands. A way of darkening eyebrows, reddening the lips, even making the waistline appear smaller." He smiled thoughtfully. "Although I think it would be a great shame to spoil the fresh natural charm you possess."

His hand had moved from my hair and lay against the bare skin above the ruched neckline of my gown. We were standing so close that I caught the light flowery scent of the shaving soap he used, and noticed for the first time the sharp indentation in his full lower lip, the pinpoints, like golden fire, deep in his eyes. Always before when we had met, although unfailingly gracious toward me, he had seemed reserved, carefully keeping his distance. Now all at once he was no longer the rather too formal tenth Earl of Abbeymore but only a man like any other, perhaps in some ways as lonely as I was. Where his hand rested lightly on my neck, I could feel a pulse pounding.

I suppose I was still in a state of emotional shock, or perhaps it was only my battered pride desperately needing reassurance—all I know was that if Kevin Fletcher had taken one step toward me at that moment I would have gone, unresistant, into his arms.

Somewhere, behind us, the servant, Liam, spoke: "Would you care for your tea to be served now, my lord?"

13

I had completely forgotten that the servant was in the room. Hastily I stepped a more decorous distance from

Lord Fletcher and pretended to be very busy examining the Rossetti painting.

If Lord Fletcher was abashed at the presence of the man he gave no sign. Only a trace of annoyance crept into his carefully modulated voice as he said, "Put the tea things on the table, Liam. Miss O'Brien and I will serve ourselves."

The man disappeared behind a lacquered screen where evidently the tea had been prepared. He returned promptly with a blue and white china tea service in a Delft design, and a plate of tiny biscuits. After he had placed them on a low table before the paneled wood sofa he stood waiting.

The irritation became plainer in the earl's voice, the slight stammer returning. "I . . . I said we'd serve ourselves . . . Liam. You . . . can go. I won't be . . . needing you any more today."

"Yes, my lord." The man ducked his head meekly but not before his eyes raked my face with such open hostility that I was sure Lord Fletcher must notice. Could Liam, I wondered uneasily, be another one of the Abbey Court people who had had a relative involved in the attack on the house and who still blamed my mother for their betrayal and capture?

I glanced at my host questioningly after the servant left. Lord Fletcher shrugged. "You'll have to excuse Liam. He's not my regular manservant. Carmody and his mother are tenant farmers, but since I don't like servants here at the tower, I've hired him to come in occasionally to tidy up the place. He's a bright boy but I'm afraid, at times, he fancies himself too much." He escorted me to the sofa. "Will you pour, Miss O'Brien?" Then he smiled and shook his head. "Surely by now it should be Kevin and Meg, don't you agree?"

"I was christened Maeve."

"Maeve . . ." He nodded approvingly. "I like it. It suits you better than Meg. There was a famous Irish queen with that name, you know, Queen Maeve of Connaught. And after all, you are a descendant of royalty, aren't you—the O'Neills who once owned Kilcallen Castle and all of the Abbey Court land."

His voice was gently teasing. I suspected he was trying to put me at ease, as if he, too, had sensed the unusual closeness we had shared for a moment and was trying to build a bridge between us from that uncertain emotional peak. As I poured the tea into the fragile blue and white cups I found myself wondering about Kevin Fletcher. He was a strangely contradictory man, one minute with all the poise and arrogance of inherited wealth and position; the next, shyly sensitive, even a little unsure of himself. How did he occupy his time here at Abbey Court, I wondered, when he wasn't working at the tower with his paintings? He didn't involve himself in the business of running the estate, and he obviously wasn't a religious fanatic like his mother. His artistic tastes were not shared by his uncle or cousin, nor could I imagine him enjoying the hunting and fishing which I was sure were the main pursuits of the other country gentry in the neighborhood.

"Do you go to London often?" I asked.

"As often as I can," he admitted cheerfully. "I keep a flat in Dublin, as well as a town house in Bloomsbury, not the most fashionable section of London, but even so, Uncle Cormac grouses continually about the expense. He doesn't understand how I have to get away from Abbey Court at times. The atmosphere, the people, even the climate, they stifle me. You can't imagine how cold and damp Ireland can be in the winter. Still I make it a point to return to Abbey Court at regular intervals, if only to"—he hesitated, then finished lamely—"keep an eye on things."

By "things," I wondered if he meant his Uncle Cormac and Cousin Sean. I handed him a cup of tea and then, although I knew it was an impertinent question, asked, "Have you ever thought of taking a more active interest in running the demesne?"

Kevin shook his head, amused. "Can't you see me scurrying around collecting rents, keeping accounts, deciding when the oats should be harvested and cattle butchered? No, I freely confess I have absolutely no talent for business or farming. I leave all that to Uncle Cormac and Cousin Sean." He smiled, thin-lipped. "In any case, I doubt if Uncle Cormac would welcome interference from me, any more than he did from your brother."

And you're afraid of your uncle, I thought, averting my glance, embarrassed that Kevin might guess what I was thinking. Yet I knew it was true. I had seen the fear in Kevin's face the morning he faced his uncle over the disputed bill of sale. Not that I blamed him. It would take a strong person to stand up to Cormac Fletcher. Despite the wheel chair, he was a man who knew how to threaten people, to grind any opposition into dust. When Kevin was younger, Cormac Fletcher had used a whip; now he used words, but the effect was the same.

I remembered my own sense of helpless anger when he had spoken about my mother with that lascivious smirk on his face. The anger I felt then returned full force so that I spoke without thinking. "You should get rid of him!"

Kevin lifted a surprised eyebrow. "I can't do that," he said, mildly reproving. "Whatever else Cormac is, he's a Fletcher. One doesn't go around dispossessing a member of one's own family. Particularly when there's the remote possibility that Uncle Cormac could be the eleventh Earl of Abbeymore—that is, if I should be unfortunate enough to die without leaving a male heir. Of course, Uncle Cormac is old now and the doctors say he can't live much longer. But there's always Sean."

He sipped his tea thoughtfully. "I suppose it must be frustrating to be always just one step removed from the earldom. How much more convenient if I were out of the way completely before I ever learned the joys of fatherhood."

At my shocked look, he laughed abruptly, his gray eyes suddenly as chill as if a hoarfrost had settled over his face. "Don't worry, my dear. I can assure you I have every intention of marrying and presenting my uncle with a bouncing grandnephew, if only to enjoy the look of outrage on his face—and Cousin Sean's."

I cradled my teacup in my hand, welcoming its warmth. It was as if I had suddenly glimpsed in Kevin Fletcher a ruthlessness that in its own way matched Cormac Fletcher's. And all at once the beautiful tower room with its sun-drenched colors seemed icy, the men and women in the paintings, for all their sensuous beauty, oddly cold and sexless.

Kevin put down his cup, his voice softening apologetically. "I'm sorry. I have no right boring you with dull family matters." His face brightened. "Since you like Mr. Rossetti's painting, perhaps you'd care to hear some of his poetry. Patrick was very fond of the Pre-Raphaelite poets, Rossetti, Swinburne, Meredith, but then I suppose you know that."

Not giving me a chance to confess that I didn't know my brother's taste in poetry, he hurried to a bookshelf and returned with a slim volume bound in blue morocco.

"I remember, after he heard of his mother's death, Patrick would sit in that same sofa where you are now, for hours, talking about her. I never saw a man so grief-stricken. No doubt he felt guilty that he had been so far away when she died. Sometimes I'd read aloud to him. It seemed to help. There was one poem by Christina Rossetti, Dante's sister, he particularly liked." He found the poem in the book and began to read.

"When I am dead, my dearest,
   Sing no sad songs for me. . . ."

I listened, my throat tightening with remembered grief, and I understood why Patrick had felt the poem a fitting epitaph for Fiona. She had been such a joyously alive person. She would have hated her children moping around, lamenting her death.

When Kevin finished the poem he read another, this time by a man named Swinburne. Although I was swept along by the sensuous rhythm and the lush images in the poetry, the longer I listened the more I began to feel an uneasy depression, as if the poetry, like the painting of the pale-skinned, red-haired beauty, was without joy or warmth or passion, a celebration not of life but of death.

How strange to think of Patrick, who had always reached for life with both hands, sitting here in this room listening to these poems of despair and death. And why, I wondered suddenly, hadn't he turned to his wife in his grief? Or had his marriage, with the honeymoon hardly over, already begun to deteriorate? It was distasteful thinking of Patrick this way, as if my brother were a stranger, someone I thought I had known well but didn't really know at all.

I was relieved when Kevin at last closed the book, saying regretfully, "I'd forgotten. When I stopped by Abbey Court last night, Sean told me that Regan has asked some friends over for luncheon today and Mother thinks Sean and I should be there, for propriety's sake, I gather. It's much too early for a widow to be entertaining, even quietly, but when Regan makes up her mind . . ." He shook his head helplessly. "You'll be there, I hope."

Oh no, I thought, suddenly panic-stricken at the thought of seeing Sean. I couldn't face him. Not yet. I would make some excuse, stay away, but then I realized in despair that I couldn't hide forever. Sooner or later I would have to face Sean again and it would be easier in a group of people than alone.

"Yes, I'll be there," I said, hoping my voice didn't betray my lack of enthusiasm as I followed my host down the stairs. At the door, he insisted I take the book of poetry with me and then, as we stood a moment in the thick grass just outside the door, he said quietly, "If you'll allow me, I'll make sure I'm your luncheon partner and Sean is seated at the other end of the table."

I felt myself flushing. How transparent I must be, I thought. My face must have shown an instant unease when Sean's name was mentioned. I would have to learn to be more careful, to mask my feelings better if I were to sit at the same luncheon table with Sean. If Kevin had guessed, others might too.

"Thank you," I said gratefully. "I'd like that. And thank you for the tea. I . . . oh!"

I looked down at the ground where a young, floppy-eared dog was tugging at the hem of my skirt.

Kevin laughed and swooped up the dog, no longer a puppy but not yet full grown, into his arms. "This is Rory, part Irish setter and part hound, I believe, no one knows for sure. The mother, a purebred setter, belongs to the gamekeeper. He got rid of the rest of the litter and was getting ready to drown this one when I happened along and talked him into letting me have the pup. Not that it took much persuasion."

"He's adorable," I said, scratching the silky red hair behind one ear, while golden-brown eyes gravely studied my face.

"Would you like to have him? I don't have the time to take care of him properly and he'd be company for you at Abbey Court." Kevin put the young dog down and he promptly returned to pulling at the hem of my skirt. Kevin smiled. "He seems attached to you already. He's housebroken and has reasonably good manners."

"I don't think I should," I protested feebly, but my heart wasn't in the protest. When I finally walked away from the tower, Rory trotted along behind me, without stopping once to look back. After I had gone a short distance down the road I turned and glanced back toward the tower. Already the trees had hidden it from view, as if it had never existed at all or, like the bewitched tower it seemed, it could appear and disappear at will.

When I reached the house I picked Rory up in my arms—all rangy legs and tail—and, covering him as best as I could with my shawl, hurried him through the green baize door and up the back stairway to my room.

Rose was waiting for me and, after giving an exclamation of surprise at our new guest, cuddled Rory in her arms.

He settled there quite comfortably as if it were his due. "Och, the little darling," she crooned. "And where will we be after hiding him, miss? Herself will have a fit if she finds a dog in the house."

I hadn't thought of the housekeeper's displeasure over my keeping a pet and decided that discretion for the moment was the better part of valor. "We'll keep him closed in the dressing room when we're not around," I said. "Do you think you could find him something to eat while I change for lunch?"

"I'll just slip down to the kitchen and come right back. I've already laid out your dress." Tactfully the girl did not mention the disreputable state of my hair or the traces of grass and earth on the skirt of the dress I was wearing.

By the time I had washed and slipped into fresh undergarments she was back with bread and bacon for Rory, who gulped down the food and then promptly curled up in a ball and went to sleep.

The uncut black velvet gown Rose had chosen seemed a little formal for luncheon but there wasn't time to choose another. Also I had forgotten it was a gown I could wear only if I were very tightly laced. Even so, the fitted bodice emphasized the rounded fullness of my breasts more than I thought proper. Rose's face was flushed red with exertion when she finished tugging at the laces of my corset, while I hung onto the bedpost and bit my lip to keep from crying aloud as the breath squeezed out of me.

" 'Tis a great shame," Rose said, after she had slipped the gown over my head and hooked up the back. "There's a lovely sherry trifle for lunch and, as tight as you're laced, you won't be able to swallow a mouthful."

"I'll manage," I said, but as I hurried down the steps I only hoped I would be able to breathe, much less eat. The family and guests were already gathered in the drawing room when I entered. I saw Sean at once, his back half turned toward me so that I caught only the darkly handsome profile. His head was bent toward a young, golden-haired woman who was talking in an animated fashion, her hand resting possessively on his arm. Then Sean lifted his head, saw me, and smiled.

I felt a sharp stitch of pain in my side that had nothing to do with my tight lacing, and remembered suddenly a line from a love poem that Kevin had read to me that morning in the tower:

And circled pain about with pleasure,
And girdled pleasure about with pain.

That was how I felt when my eyes met Sean's: pain and pleasure so intermingled it was impossible to tell where one began and the other ended. A weakness filled me, pinning me helplessly to the spot where I stood, as I saw Sean start toward me. Then there was a hand on my arm and Kevin asked quietly, "May I take you into the dining room, Maeve? I believe they're ready to serve."

"Yes." My voice sounded breathless. I clutched Kevin's arm. "Yes, thank you." As I turned away, I saw Sean stop short, a bewildered look on his face.

The rest of the guests followed Lord Fletcher and me into the dining room. Kevin had arranged the table as he had promised. I sat to the right of him at the head of the table. Since Lady Fletcher wasn't present, Regan sat in the hostess seat at the far end. The animated young woman sat next to Sean, still talking happily.

Once or twice I saw Sean glance toward me, a quizzical, half-annoyed look on his face, but always, if our eyes met, I glanced quickly away. Lord Fletcher was involved in a conversation with a woman guest on his left so I had perforce to turn my attention to the portly gentleman on my right. He had the ramrod look of a retired military man with eyes as flat and dull as lead pellets. At the moment he seemed deeply engrossed in his own thoughts.

When he recalled I was sitting beside him he mumbled an apology. "Afraid I was woolgathering, remembering the last time I had lunch here at Abbey Court, the day they found that young American's body. Bad day, that. We had only started eating, one o'clock—I remember looking at my watch—when the studmaster came in and fetched Lord Fletcher and his cousin from the table. I guessed at once something was wrong. Wondered why Regan's husband hadn't appeared at the table, guest of honor so to speak. Atrocious manners, even for an American. Still, horrible to think about, our sitting here enjoying ourselves at the table, at the same time some bloody blackguard was out there in the brush, waiting to shoot down an unarmed man . . ."

Kevin must have overheard the last part of the conversation, for he turned toward me abruptly, his voice clipped as he stared coldly at my luncheon partner. "Major Gill, I don't believe you've had the honor of meeting Regan's sister-in-law. Miss O'Brien, may I present Major Ralph Gill, a neighbor of ours."

A bright red stained the major's face in splotches; his plump mouth opened and shut quickly. "My deepest apologies, ma'am," he choked. "If I had known, I would never have brought up such an unhappy subject."

"No, please, Major," I said quickly. "I never heard the... the full story of my brother's death. I'm interested in knowing how Patrick's body happened to be found."

The major cast Lord Fletcher an uncertain glance, then cleared his throat nervously. "No secret about that, Miss O'Brien. It was shortly after we sat down to lunch that Sean's horse, minus his rider, came back to the stable. The groomsman noticed blood on the saddle and got in touch with the earl immediately. We started out on search parties at once . . . Lord Fletcher, Sean, myself, but Mr. O'Toole, the gamekeeper, had already found your brother in the road. He was still barely alive and Mr. O'Toole took him to the cottage of a nearby tenant who has had some experience in tending the sick. Unfortunately there was nothing she could do for your brother. It was remarkable, with the location of the wound, that he lasted as long as he did."

He glared angrily at me, the ends of his walrus mustache quivering. "Dastardly cowardly act, shooting a man from ambush. But then what can you expect? Lazy, undisciplined lot, the most of these people, homes filthy as pigsties and the owners not much cleaner."

I thought of the tenants I had met at Abbey Court, living in one-room sod cottages with mud floors and leaking roofs, cottages that sheltered a whole family, with the nearest water a creek or a well several cottages away. How did the major expect them to bathe every day?

Swallowing the angry retort that sprang to my lips, I forced myself to ask instead, "You did say it was Sean's horse that came back to the stable, Major? Why should you all assume then it was my brother who was in trouble?"

The major spoke slowly with the patronizing air I suspected he used with all females and other incompetents. "Well, it couldn't have been Sean, now could it, Miss O'Brien? He was sitting right here at the table at the time with my daughter Mindy." He gestured proudly toward the young blonde woman seated next to Sean, so close her arm kept brushing his, I noticed. He chuckled fondly. "Looks like they're on much better terms today, though. Mad as a wet hen, Mindy was, with Sean Fletcher that last lunch we had here. She'd expected that he'd go riding with Regan and myself that morning but Sean begged off at the last minute; work to do at the office. Then Regan's horse threw a shoe and she had to return to the stable, and there was poor Mindy, stuck riding with her father. Not her cup of tea, not at all. . . ." He laughed in little snorts.

"Patrick didn't ride with Regan that morning then?"

"No." The major's eyes shifted uncomfortably away from me. "No business of mine, of course, but I rather think he and Regan had had a lovers' spat. Regan looked as if she were out for blood when she joined us at the stable that morning. But when we came back to Abbey Court after our ride, she insisted we stay for lunch and meet her husband. Shouldn't have stayed, of course. House and servants in an uproar, getting ready for a party that evening. Then when your brother didn't show up for lunch, deucedly awkward for Regan."

Kevin, who had been listening with a pained expression on his face, said coldly, "You might say it was rather more awkward for Patrick, Major."

The major pulled, discomfited, at his mustache, his voice half strangled in his throat. "Yes, yes, very true . . ." and he turned with evident relief to begin a conversation with the partner on his right.

Kevin was watching me and I saw the look of disdain, almost contempt, that darkened the gray eyes as he asked, "If you were so eager to know more details about Patrick's death, why didn't you ask me?"

I felt my face burn. Did Kevin think it was only some morbid female curiosity that had made me question the major? "I'm sorry, Kevin," I replied, my voice steady even as I gripped my hands together under the table to keep them from trembling. "I didn't mean to embarrass you, but as long as the authorities seem unable to find Patrick's murderer, I'll naturally continue to be interested in the circumstances surrounding his death."

"I see." Kevin's voice was thoughtful, as if I had revealed a side of my character he hadn't been aware of before. Then he smiled, a stiff smile, but a smile nevertheless. "Of course you must do what you think best but I'd appreciate it if, in the future, you'd confine your questioning to the family. I'm sure we can tell you anything you feel you must know."

Then he lightly but quickly changed the subject. The rest of the meal we chatted amiably enough but I was glad when lunch was finished and I was able to excuse myself from a ride that Regan was arranging for the guests, pleading a headache. I had made my escape to the front hall when a hand grasped my shoulder and spun me roughly around. I looked up into Sean's face. He stared at me, baffled. "Where were you this morning?" he asked irritably. "I looked all over for you."

"I was at the tower, having tea with Lord Fletcher."

He seemed taken aback at my answer but then, recovering, grinned sardonically. "Well, that must have been a fine dull morning. No doubt it was poetry he read aloud to you while you sipped your tea."

"I don't see that where or how Kevin and I occupied ourselves is any concern of yours," I snapped, pleased at the anger that strengthened me to face him down.

"Oh, so it's Kevin now, is it?" Sean said softly. But for all the softness in his voice, I could sense the anger in him, to match my own. I stepped back until I came up hard against the wall and could move no farther. Then, as I watched, I could almost see him regain control of himself. The anger faded, replaced by a tenderness and the rich, sensual timbre in his voice brought back memories of another time, another place. His hands dropped coaxingly to my waist. "I missed you this morning, *alannah*," he murmured. "I thought this afternoon we could take a ride together, just the two of us. There's a pretty little stream I know of, a fine, private place we can be alone . . ."

At his touch, I felt a swift melting inside of me, a delicious faintness, so that pulling myself free of his hands was as difficult as it had been that first morning, freeing myself from the bog. I had to force myself to remember that other voice, hard, calculating: ". . . the girl's broken to the bit all right. . . ."

I wrenched myself away from his grasp. "No!"

At my exclamation, he drew back and his expression for the first time was uncertain.

I gathered my skirt and turned toward the stairs. "You'll excuse me," I said coldly. "I have other plans for the afternoon."

Then as I turned I saw Regan come into the hall. Her lustrous blue-green eyes took in the situation at a glance. She laughed silkily, her voice lightly, maliciously amused as she said, "Why, Brother Sean, I do believe you're losing that devastating charm of yours."

14

The pained look on Sean's face as I turned and fled up the stairs should have assuaged my wounded pride. Instead, as I burst into my room, startling Rose, who was playing on the floor with Rory, I felt treacherously near tears.

The maid scrambled hastily to her feet while Rory gave a yelp of delight at seeing me and began pulling happily at the black velvet sash on my dress. "I took him out for a run, miss, while you were at lunch," Rose said. "Tim, at the stable, gave me a leash. Rory's that fast, he almost got away from me."

I sat down in the small wing chair by the window and, holding the dog in my lap, began absently to stroke the long, silky ears. "There'll be hair all over your dress, miss," Rose warned.

"It doesn't matter." There was something very comforting about the small warm body pressed close to mine, the uncomplicated love that gazed up at me from the soft brown eyes.

Rose gave me a worried glance. "It's sick you've made yourself, laced so tight."

I shook my head and, wanting to think of something else, anything but the way Sean had looked, I asked the maid, "You were here at Abbey Court, weren't you, Rose, the day my brother was killed?"

"That I was, miss. It's a day I'd not be forgetting. Not just your poor brother being found dead that way, may he rest in peace"—she crossed herself hastily—"but Miss Regan was giving a party that evening and the old one was in a rare snit. The whole staff was turned out, cleaning the house from top to bottom, and nothing done to suit her. Then she found a bottle of ink spilled in the small study, and . . ."

"Did you see Mr. O'Brien that morning?" I interrupted, not interested in Miss O'Toole's domestic crises.

She thought a moment, then nodded. "He came through the dining room while I was polishing the silver, on his way back to the little study where he had his desk, you know. To be sure, the only way you can get to the room is through the drawing room and dining room. He could not have passed without my seeing him. Very pleasant he was to me, as always, wishing me a good morning . . ."

"Do you remember what time he left, to go for the ride?"

Rose shook her head. "I'd not be knowing that. After I finished the silver I was sent to help turn out the guest rooms upstairs. Maybe one of the others saw him leave. The servants were in and out of the drawing and dining rooms all morning, except when we all took our morning tea in the kitchen."

"Where exactly was his body found? Was it far from Abbey Court?"

Rose began to look uneasy and I felt a twinge of guilt, remembering Kevin's request. Still, I rationalized, a servant could almost be considered a member of the family.

"Not far at all, miss. On the old road that runs just this side of the Abbey."

"I didn't know there was another road through the wooded area."

"Oh yes, miss. It's not used much any more. When the late earl rebuilt the tower, he built a fine new road through the woodland so he could get to the tower and the dower house more easily. But some of the tenants still use the old road to come to the office."

"And this house they took Patrick to after . . . after he was found." My voice faltered a moment. "It's near where he was shot?"

"Not what you'd call near." Rose frowned, considering. "Mary Shaugnassy's cottage is on the far side of the woods where the tenant farms begin. Not that Mary Shaugnassy does much farming any more. She makes a few shillings healing with her herbs and potions, those that can't afford to go to the doctor in town. And if you need tending and haven't two pennies to rub together, she'll ease you for nothing out of the goodness of her heart. But then, sure, you've heard your mother speak of Mary Shaugnassy."

"No," I replied, puzzled. "Why should she?"

"Why, it's just they were such good friends, Fiona O'Neill and Mary Shaugnassy. After the fire, when every door was closed to your mother, it was to Mary's cottage she went and Mary took her in, though there were those who spoke out against her for it. But Mary Shaugnassy is not one to pay any heed to gossip or threats."

"Threats?" I sat up so quickly that Rory almost tumbled off my lap.

Rose's rounded cheeks grew pink. "It was a bad time, and there were those who might have done your mother harm if they could have found her, and Mary Shaugnassy, too, for harboring her."

Carefully I deposited Rory on the floor and got to my feet. "I think, Rose, I should pay a visit to Miss Shaugnassy. How do I find her cottage?"

"Why, it's just the other side of the woods. First you pass the Carmody cottage, a terrible disgrace it is, too, run down so because young Liam is too high and mighty to turn his hand to common work, and his mother more happy with her poteen than cleaning. Then there's the Widow Hagerty's farm, although they say she's close to snaring her fourth husband, and how she does it I'll never understand, snaggle-toothed as she is . . ."

I waited impatiently for Rose to complete the personal family history of all the tenant cottages I would pass. Although it was unreasonable to expect that Mary Shaugnassy could tell me anything she hadn't already told the authorities, I was consumed with a sudden feverish desire to meet the woman who had been my mother's friend.

At last I broke into Rose's monologue. "Miss Shaugnassy's cottage, Rose? How will I recognize it?"

"Sure and you can't miss it. Neat as a pin it is and with the prettiest garden around it." She gazed at me, worried. "But you're not thinking of going there now, miss? The guests will be coming back for tea after their ride. You'll be expected to join them."

And furthermore, I remembered belatedly, I had begged off from joining Regan's friends because of a headache. I could hardly show up now at the stable and go off for a ride by myself. I rubbed absently at my forehead. Perhaps the lie had been father to the fact, or otherwise everything that had happened to me that day was suddenly catching up with me, causing a nerve in my temple to pound.

"Perhaps it can wait until morning," I agreed reluctantly.

"A lie-down is what you need," Rose said firmly. "Your face is all peaked-looking."

Her nimble fingers unhooked the back of my dress and unlaced my corset. I took a deep, grateful breath, rubbing ineffectually at the ugly red marks pressed into my skin by the whalebone stays. Then, as I climbed into bed, I noticed that the sky had once again turned gray and threatening. Regan and her guests, which I supposed included the major and his daughter Mindy, might end up being soaked if they went for their ride, I thought, and wondered what Mindy Gill would look like with all those blonde curls hanging limp and straight around her face. On that uncharitable thought, I fell fast asleep.

Rose woke me in time for tea. She informed me as I dressed that the rain had not only interrupted the ride, but several of the guests who lived a distance away would be staying the night at Abbey Court because the rain had made the side roads impassable. Unexpected overnight guests, however, did not seem to be unusual at Abbey Court. As I walked down the hall toward the gallery I saw that several of the unused bedrooms in my wing were already being prepared by servants.

This time when I entered the drawing room I saw with a sinking feeling that Kevin was not in the room. Apparently he felt he had done his duty by appearing at lunch. To my surprise, Regan appeared at my side and shortly thereafter the studmaster joined us, making a not very cozy threesome. Although they carefully included me in their conversation, which centered mostly on who would be taking the various honors at the upcoming Dublin Horse Show, I had the distinct sensation of being forced unwillingly into behaving as a rather reluctant chaperone. The fact that Mr. Flaherty had been included in the tea at all was raising the eyebrows of some of the guests. He must be a singularly difficult position to maintain at Abbey Court, I decided, for the studmaster was neither a servant nor of high enough social position to be considered a member of the gentry.

For my own part, I was trying very hard not to notice that Sean and Miss Mindy Gill, who, along with her father, would be two of the guests staying the night, spent a good deal of time very close together, whispering and laughing.

All in all, it made for a most awkward hour and finally, after what seemed an interminable time, the guests who were able to return to their homes began to leave so they wouldn't be caught on the road after dark. Those who were spending the night drifted off to their rooms, with talk of arranging for cards later in the library, after a late supper. Since the only card game I knew was poker, which I doubted they would be playing, I excused myself early and went to my room.

I planned to curl up in bed with the book of poetry Kevin had lent me, but Rory indicated by whimpering at the door that he preferred a short run before retiring. Slipping a cape over my gown, and using the back stairs, I stepped gingerly out into the darkness. Rory tugged frantically at the end of his leash, almost pulling me off my feet. It was still raining, a faint drizzle now, and the ground was muddy underfoot no matter how carefully I tried to urge Rory to stay near the path.

By the time we returned to the house both my shoes and Rory's paws and the ends of his ears as well were coated with mud. Our path up the stairs and down the hall into my bedroom left distinct muddy tracks. I supposed I would hear about that tomorrow from Miss O'Toole but at the moment I was too tired to care.

Undressing quickly, I closed Rory into the dressing room—he was supposed to be housebroken but I decided not to take the chance his first night in a strange house—and climbed into bed, reaching for the book of Mr. Rossetti's poems. Despite the rain, it was a warm evening, reminding me of summer nights in Boston, except here at Abbey Court there was no sound of carriages trundling noisily by on the cobblestone street below my window. There was, I realized, listening, no sound at all except the soft murmuring rain. I had forgotten how quiet summer nights in the country could be, or how exposed and lonely such nights made you feel.

I wondered suddenly where Sean was and if Mindy Gill was with him. I remembered the husky timbre in Sean's voice when he whispered, "*alannah*," and was he whispering the same words to Mindy now, his hands spanning her tiny waist—she was so short she would have to stand on tiptoe to kiss him.

I drew in a ragged breath, shocked myself at the pain the thought of Sean and Mindy together brought me, despising him and yet despising myself more for having been such a gullible little fool. Then, knowing that if I let myself think about Sean any longer I would never sleep, I tried to concentrate on Mr. Rossetti's poetry. Unfortunately his poems seemed to be concerned mostly with melancholy death or unrequited love and only managed to make me feel more miserable. At last I put the book aside, turned out the lamp and, for the first time in years, allowed myself the luxury of crying myself to sleep.

How long I slept or what awakened me I would never know. Perhaps it was the sound of Rory whimpering behind the dressing-room door. All I knew was that I awoke and realized instantly that I was not alone in the room. I lay very still, my eyes wide open, vaguely aware of the curtain moving restlessly in a light breeze. The rain had stopped but the sky must still have been overcast, for no hint of moonlight entered the open window. The room lay in darkness around me.

I told myself I was imagining things but my senses knew differently. My whole body stretched taut, waiting, watching, listening. The darkness around my bed seemed to have weight and thickness, pressing against me. I could barely make out the wing chair by the window and the oval dressing table. I caught the faint scent of lavender in the bed linen, heard the whispering rustle of the breeze through the curtain—and another even fainter sound I could not place at first—a slight, creaking noise.

My eyes flew to the hall door. Although the hallway was as dark as the bedroom, I could have sworn that the door stood open. And that something or someone stood there in the half-open door, watching me, a blurred, indefinable shape but somehow blacker than the darkness around it.

For a moment I lay frozen, afraid to draw a breath in case even that small sound might betray me. Then the darkness at the door stirred, became a narrow, tall shape, and seemed to dip toward me. I screamed and in one motion flung back the covers and leaped from the bed. Fleeing into the dressing room, I slammed the door shut behind me. I had collapsed in a heap on the floor when something rough and moist touched my hand, startling me into a second cry of terror. Then I realized it was Rory, a tiny bundle of trembling fur and soft, whining, frightened noises, trying to crawl into my lap. I pulled him close and we both crouched, motionless, listening for whatever it was on the other side of that door.

"Miss O'Brien? Miss O'Brien, are you all right?"

Someone was knocking at my bedroom door. Cautiously I opened the dressing-room door and peered out. I could see light sliding beneath the hall door, securely closed now. The pounding on the door became more demanding, and a man's voice raised irritably.

"Miss O'Brien, are you there?"

I pulled open the door and Major Gill stood in the hall,

holding a lamp. He was wearing a borrowed nightshirt that was too short for him, exposing a great amount of hairy leg. I looked beyond him, down the hall toward the stairs. "Did you see him?" I asked eagerly.

"See who?" The major looked around bewildered. "I heard you scream, loud enough to wake the dead. Couldn't find my lamp at first, then I wasn't sure in which room they had put you. But there was no one in the hall, not that I could see. A prowler, was it? Did you get a good look at him?"

"No," I said slowly. It all seemed incredible, like a bad dream. "I woke up and he was standing there." Or had it been a man? Could it have been a woman just as well? The fear was already fading, like a dream slipping away when you awake.

Mindy came down the hall, yawning sleepily. She had stopped to slip on a robe and put her hair in some semblance of order, which was more, I suddenly realized, than I could say for myself. "What's the commotion, Papa?" She glanced at me curiously. "I thought I heard a scream."

"Miss O'Brien almost caught a prowler in her room," her father said. "She says he left by the hall but I can't say I saw him."

"Oh?" Mindy gave me an arch look. "Anyone we know?"

I flushed uncomfortably. "I couldn't see his face. It was too dark. It was just a . . . a shadow by the door."

The major straightened with brisk authority. "Well, mustn't dawdle here while the fellow gets away. Wake up Sean and the servants, get up a search party."

"No, please, don't bother," I pleaded, suddenly envisioning how ridiculous I would sound trying to explain my nebulous visitor to a skeptical Sean, to the curious servants.

"Nonsense, no bother." The glow of the hunt was in the major's face. "Can't allow these impudent ruffians . . ."

"Oh, Papa, for heaven's sake." It was Mindy who understood, who gave me an amused glance. "There wasn't any prowler, don't you see? Miss O'Brien was probably having a bad dream and woke up and imagined she saw someone in the room. Isn't that right, Miss O'Brien?"

"Yes, I suppose so." I took a deep breath. Of course, Mindy had to be right. I had awakened, still half asleep, and some trick of the shadows had made me believe I saw a dark figure standing at the door. After all, if it were a prowler, why should he come to my room when there was all that valuable silver flatware down in the dining room?

The major was still looking outraged at having been deprived of his search party when I closed the door. It had begun to rain again, a soft, insistent patting sound at the window, but the air in the room no longer had a balmy softness. There was a definite chill. I lit my bed lamp, then turned to look at the hall door. How real it had all seemed for a moment, I couldn't help thinking. The dark shadow standing there, the terror that had gripped me, as if something evil, hate-filled, were reaching out to engulf me.

I shivered and pushed the morbid thought quickly aside. Nevertheless this time before I climbed into bed I brought a delighted Rory into the bedroom with me and kept my bed lamp turned low. Rory's contented half snores and the soft buzz of the lamp were the last sounds I remembered before I again fell asleep.

15

I slept late the next morning and awoke with a start. I remembered the nightmare immediately. My glance flew to the hall door. Of course there was nothing there. There had never been anything there, I told myself sternly. Yet, when I closed my eyes, for a moment I saw clearly, imprisoned against my eyelids, the dark shadowy figure swooping down upon me. . . .

A soft knocking came at the door. Rose, I was sure, wanted to discover if I was awake and more than likely was anxious to hear all about my "prowler." I could wish otherwise but I had no doubt that the servants, as well as everyone else at Abbey Court, had heard from the major and his daughter about the disturbance I had caused last night. When the door opened a crack I kept my eyes tightly shut, feigning sleep. As fond as I was of Rose, I had no desire to discuss last night, even with her. Rory, however, was delighted to see the visitor. I could hear his paws sliding over the hardwood floor toward the door. Then the door closed and once again there was silence.

I waited a few minutes, then got out of bed, fetching from the wardrobe the riding habit that Regan had lent me. I hadn't forgotten my plan to visit Mary Shaugnassy. If nothing else, it gave me a good excuse to avoid working in the office this morning and facing Sean again.

I finished brushing my hair into some sort of order, then turned away from my mirror, noticing guiltily the mud tracks my boots and Rory's paws had made on the floor the night before. Several untidy clumps of earth and grass had dried between the door and the foot of the bed. At least, I decided, I could get rid of them before Rose returned. I knelt down, then stopped and took a closer look. In the center of one dried clod of dirt I saw what looked like the sole print from a shoe, too large for my boot. The footprint of my mysterious visitor from last night, I thought, but then I'd never heard of dream prowlers leaving footprints behind.

Deciding that my imagination was working overtime, I quickly brushed the dried mud into the wastebasket and continued on my way downstairs. I was happy to find the dining room deserted. Food still stood on the sideboard, however, and I served myself, eating the lukewarm porridge and cold toast hastily, then hurried out to the stable.

The stableboy, who brought me my horse told me that the overnight guests had left early that morning, Miss Regan riding along with them, and that yes, he thought the back road by the Abbey was passable, even after yesterday's downpour. After he helped me mount, I waited a minute, reins in hand. Lady Jane was never eager to rush off and stood quietly while I asked the boy, "Have you worked at Abbey Court long?"

"Yes, my lady, more than a year now," he said proudly.

"Then you were here, working at the stable, the morning Mr. O'Brien was killed?"

The boy was too flustered at my question to do more than gape at me stupidly. Behind him I saw Brian Flaherty step out of the shadows inside the stable office door. I wondered how long he had been standing there. There was something about the man, and about the way he looked at me, his gaze lingering on the tightness of my riding habit—Regan's borrowed habit could only be let out so much—that made me feel ill at ease. His voice, as always, was properly respectful, almost too much so when he spoke. "I was at the stable that morning, Miss O'Brien." He gestured the stableboy away. "Maybe I can answer your questions."

He came over to Lady Jane, stroking her mane gently, caressingly. He had large, spatula-shaped hands, a worker's hands, but the nails were clean and carefully polished. I gazed at the hands as if unpleasantly hypnotized by them, sensing their touch would be incredibly light and skillful on a skittish horse—or a woman. Then I felt my face redden at what I was thinking and forced myself to meet Brian Flaherty's eyes. There was a sheer animal virility about the studmaster that I supposed some women found attractive but that faintly repelled me, or perhaps it was only that the dark eyes seemed to be secretly laughing at me. Had the story of my fright last night reached the stables already? I wondered. If so, I could imagine how the story had been exaggerated and embellished with each new telling.

"What was it you wanted to know about that morning, Miss O'Brien?"

My hand tightened on the reins but I refused to drop my gaze, as if a challenge had passed between us. "Only why my brother happened to be riding Mr. Sean Fletcher's horse. Didn't he have a mount of his own?"

"That he did. Miss Regan herself picked the gray stallion for him, a fine beast, only he was laid up that morning with a lame hock."

"Then someone saw my brother at the stable that morning when he came to get Mr. Sean's horse?"

"As far as we know, your brother never came by the stable that morning. None of the groomsmen or stableboys remember seeing him."

"How did he get Mr. Fletcher's horse then?" I asked, but I knew the answer before I had finished the question. Working with Sean, I had discovered that each morning around eleven o'clock his horse was saddled and brought over to be tied outside the office, in case Sean should need him.

I frowned, still puzzled. "I don't understand. You mean my brother took Mr. Fletcher's horse and no one saw him do it?"

Brian nodded. "That area of the yard outside the office is screened from the rest of the house. Mr. Sean likes his privacy."

"It was Mr. Fletcher, though, who gave my brother permission to ride his horse?" I insisted.

The studmaster shrugged. "You'll have to ask Mr. Sean about that. It's my understanding he told the magistrate he didn't even know his horse was missing until I came into the dining room to tell Lord Fletcher that Sean's roan had come back to the stable without a rider and with blood on the saddle and mane."

"I don't believe it," I protested indignantly. "Patrick wouldn't borrow a man's horse without asking him first."

Without realizing it, my hand had tightened, jerking at the rein, startling Lady Jane, who tossed her head nervously.

The studmaster reached out to quiet her. "Easy does it, Miss O'Brien," he cautioned me, his voice amused. "Lady Jane is like most fillies. She frightens easily. You'll have her taking off down the road like a ghost was at her heels." He gazed up at me innocently. "And were there any more questions I can answer for you?"

"No, thank you," I said coldly. "Good day, Mr. Flaherty."

I tapped Lady Jane's neck lightly with my crop and she trotted down the road, circling around the screen of trees and onto the back Abbey road. It wasn't until we had ridden past the Abbey and into the wooded area on the other side of the ruins that my anger finally simmered down and I slowed Lady Jane to a walk. It was foolish to let Brian Flaherty upset me, as if I had been the butt of a joke he had hugely enjoyed.

In any case, one thing seemed sure. The studmaster had seemed as puzzled by Patrick's action in taking Sean's horse that last morning as I was. I would never have thought that Patrick would borrow a man's property without his permission. And suddenly I was reminded again of the uncomfortable sensation I had felt in the tower yesterday—that my brother had become a stranger to me. Was it possible Patrick could have changed so much in a few short months? I was still puzzling unhappily over the matter when I reached the edge of the woods and noticed a haze of smoke hanging in the air ahead of me. Not the blue turf smoke that hung inevitably over the rude cottages. This was thicker, blacker.

I spurred Lady Jane forward but by the time I reached the scene the cottage was already almost completely destroyed by the fire. A few men in work clothes were pushing down the remains of a wall, still standing. To one side of the burned cottage, I was conscious of a woman's sorrowful cries, thin and high-pitched: "My home, all the home I've ever had since my dear man brought me here on me wedding night."

I recognized the woman but before I could put a name to her my eyes were caught elsewhere. Sean stood to one side of the small clearing and it was obvious he was directing the men in their job of deliberately tearing down the last cottage wall. His face was impassive. If he heard the woman he gave no indication. His voice, sharp and impatient, rose above the wailing. "Hurry it up now, we haven't all day."

I slid off Lady Jane so quickly I caught the heel of my boot in my riding skirt and ripped it free without even looking at the tear I had made. "Sean! What's going on here?"

He turned toward me. The impassive look did not alter, only his body seemed to tense warily. "This is no concern of yours, Meg," he said shortly. "I suggest you go on about your business."

"This is my business," I said hotly. "Why wasn't I told you planned to tumble this cottage? Are you evicting the Carmodys?"

"I am," he said calmly. "And if you'd cared to show up at the office this morning, I would have told you then. The rent on this farm hasn't been paid for over a year. They haven't even tried to put a potato in the ground and they've been warned three times what would happen."

"But you . . . you can't do this . . . this is their home." I was stuttering with anger. "You can't just turn them out!"

I glanced over at the woman and saw that she wasn't alone. The red-haired young man, Liam Carmody, stood with his mother. His gaze met mine, his face set blankly. He didn't touch his mother and when she reached for his hand he drew quickly away, as if he had mentally, if not physically, removed himself from what was happening around him.

I reached into the pocket of my riding skirt and took out all the coins I found there. I felt sick, with pity and embarrassment for the boy, at the humiliation he must be feeling, forced to stand by helplessly and watch his home destroyed before his eyes. "I'll speak to Lord Fletcher," I told him. "I'm sure he'll do something about this but in the meantime . . ." I handed him the coins.

If I had been dismayed at the hatred in Liam's eyes watching me in the tower yesterday morning, it was nothing to what I felt now. A blind fury tore away the mask of indifference from his face. His hands tightened on the coins, then he contemptuously flung them at my feet.

"I want none of your charity."

His mother gave her son a shocked glance, then, still wailing, fell to her knees and began to gather up the coins.

"Thank you, my lady, may the saints bless you for the goodness of your heart."

When Liam flung the coins at me, I saw Sean start forward, his face darkening, but then he stopped and instead crossed to my side. Taking my arm in a viselike grip, he propelled me toward my horse.

Since there was no way I could break away without making a scene—the three workers had already stopped their task and were watching curiously—I allowed Sean to help me mount. Then, gathering up the reins, I looked down at him, coldly furious. How could I have ever imagined I had glimpsed any warmth or tenderness in that face? He was as ruthless as, if not worse than, his father. At least Cormac had the frustration of being tied to a wheel chair to account for his callous cruelty. For Sean, there was no excuse.

"This isn't the end of this matter," I said softly, so the others couldn't overhear. "I intend to tell Lord Fletcher everything that happened here today."

"That's your privilege," Sean said and then, catching the rein so Lady Jane couldn't move, asked, "And where might you be going by yourself on a fine morning like this?"

"Not that it's any of your business," I replied curtly, "but I plan to visit Mary Shaugnassy's cottage."

For a moment I thought I saw a discomfited look cross Sean's face, but it was quickly gone, and he said irritably, "I saw you talking to Major Gill at lunch yesterday. What stories was the old windbag telling you? He's got a tongue that wags at both ends and never quits."

"He was telling me how my brother died, while you were all enjoying a fine lunch," I said viciously, wanting to hurt him the way he had hurt me. "How no one stopped to ask why Patrick was late, or worry when he didn't appear at lunch. Perhaps if you'd looked for him sooner . . ." My voice broke and I bit my lip savagely, refusing to cry in front of him.

Sean stepped back, letting my reins fall. His voice was suddenly weary, his face emptied of all expression. "Leave it be, Meg. Why torment yourself this way? It won't bring Patrick back."

"No, but it may find his murderer for me," I replied, and this time I put the spurs to poor Lady Jane, and we galloped away before I could say something more I might regret later.

16

Within a matter of five minutes I had found Mary Shaugnassy's cottage. It was exactly as Rose had described it. Although outwardly little different from the other farm houses, its roof was newly thatched and purple fuschias and pink and red roses scrambled in profusion over the low stone wall surrounding the house. Almost the moment I knocked, the door opened as if my hostess had watched me ride up to the door.

She did not curtsy as the other tenant women did when they met me, nor did she seem surprised to see me. Her eyes, a milky blue in a much-wrinkled face, studied me gravely.

"Miss Shaugnassy? I'm Meg O'Brien, Fiona's daughter . . ."

"Aren't there eyes in me head?" she asked, her toothless mouth quirking in a childish smile of pleasure. "Do you think I'd not recognize Fiona's child? Only the hair is different. Fiona's was never so red."

She reached out a gnarled hand and touched my face gently. "It seems only yesterday Fiona and me were together." She stepped back. "Och, here I let you stand in the door while I natter on. I was just wetting the tea . . . come in . . . come in . . ."

The room at first seemed dark after the bright sunshine outdoors, but it was not an unpleasant darkness. A small fire burning in the hearth, a St. Bridget's cross of reeds hanging over the door, and a clock ticking busily on the wall gave the room the cozy warmth of a thrush's nest.

Miss Shaugnassy busied herself preparing the tea with water from a kettle suspended over the hearth, then sliced thick pieces of soda bread. There was only one wooden chair and a bench in front of the fireplace and she insisted I take the chair, as she placed a steaming cup of tea before me.

"They tell me Fiona's dead now," she said, crossing herself slowly as she sat down on the bench across from me. "God rest her soul, a peaceful death, I hope, in a soft bed in the grand house they say she owned in America. That was always her dream, you know, to be a great lady and live in a fine house, from the first day she came to work at Abbey Court for Lady Caroline, and treated more like a daughter she was than a servant. I worked in the kitchen myself, then, but I remember Fiona was always favored by her ladyship, taught to read and write and talk almost like gentry. I blame Lady Caroline for putting ideas in Fiona's head that had no place there. The poor lonely lady she was, left to sit at home while her husband, Lord Jason, was off chasing any lass he could lay his hands on. The only son who spent any time with his mother, was the youngest, Lord Michael, when he wasn't out digging in the dirt like a mole. It's no wonder she treated Fiona like the daughter she never had. And Fiona, och, she lapped it up like a kitten with cream. I warned her no good would come of it, a pretty young girl in the same house with those godless Fletcher men, and she needn't count on Lady Caroline, poor timid thing, to keep her safe. But Fiona, she would just laugh at me and pretend not to hear or say she could take care of herself."

The old woman stopped a moment to sip her tea, while I had not even touched mine, so engrossed was I in the story she was telling. "I remember one day she came to my cottage, no longer a child and pretty as a sunset, but her shift was all torn and her shoulder bruised. When I asked her who had done that cruel thing to her, she said it was Cormas Fletcher but I shouldn't worry, he wouldn't touch her again. That his nephew, Michael, had stood between them. . . ."

"Yes," I said, my voice strained. "Cormac Fletcher boasted to me how he had attacked my mother."

Mary Shaugnassy shook her head, marveling. "A grand fight that must have been. Fiona would never have given in easily. She must have put her mark on him for all that Cormac was a great brawn of a man then. They tell me he sits tied to that chair of his now, half a man." A hint of a smile touched the clouded blue eyes. "Not, mind you, that there wasn't a time when plenty of lasses came running if Cormac so much as beckoned. A handsome man he was, with a way about him. Only your mother would have none of him. Too much alike they were, I think, proud and stubborn, both with dreams like itches that would not let them rest—Fiona to be a grand lady and Cormac to be the Earl of Abbeymore and own all of Abbey Court."

I stirred restlessly, a little annoyed at the assumption that my mother had anything in common with that hulking, tyrannical man at Abbey Court. Yet in a way what Mary Shaugnassy said had the ring of truth. All through Fiona's life must have run the desire that was planted in her as a child when, starving and homeless, she had first seen the grandeur of Abbey Court. It was then she must have made up her mind that someday she, too, would be a grand lady and own such a house. It was a dream that had never left her, or my father, in peace.

"I was told Lady Caroline died of the fever," I said, to change the subject from Cormac.

"Ay." A sadness drifted like a cloud over my companion's face. Her eyes seemed to be looking inward to horrors that were beyond description. "It was like God's curse was on us all, poor and rich alike. Lord Fletcher and his two oldest sons fled to London to escape the fever, leaving Lady Caroline behind to nurse young Michael. Then she took the fever too. Fiona sent for me but there was precious little I could do for her except fetch the priest."

She moaned softly in memory, rocking back and forth on her bench. "The terrible sights I saw then, I still dream about them. The roadlings coming to my door, almost naked, the children with their stomachs all swollen, the bones sticking through the skin, and not a bit of food I had to give them. Those families still strong enough, Cormac sent out the men to tear down their cottages, gave them enough money to pay their passage to America, and off they'd go with their bed ticks and a bit of the old sod in a handkerchief. And many died in the holds of the filthy ships and were dumped overboard, no decent sod over their head but the sharks to eat them."

"What of the families who wouldn't go to America?"

Mary Shaugnassy shrugged bitterly, pulling her shawl more tightly over her shoulders. "Och, and it made no difference. The cottages were tumbled just the same and the people turned out on the road to beg, except there was none to beg from. His lordship was safe and snug and fat in London with his fine house and carriages, and the Abbey Court land and rents were his, what he could get of it. He wouldn't even pay the passage money to America. It was his younger brother Cormac who paid it out of his own pocket. No wonder the people turned upon Abbey Court. The night I saw the flames leaping from the windows of the house, I thought it was God's judgment, at last, upon the Fletcher's. It was that old devil. Daniel Fletcher, you know, who first brought the curse of Cromwell upon us."

I was afraid she would start on the old grievances that arose whenever Cromwell's name was mentioned and I said hastily, "I've been told that Mother was at Abbey Court during the attack on the house."

Mary nodded. "That she was. Her ladyship had died of the fever but Lord Michael—of course, he didn't know then he would be inheriting the title—had recovered, but he was still weak."

"They say"—I found it difficult to form the words—"that it was Mother who informed on the men who set fire to the house."

My hostess straightened, her eyes awash wtih anger. "Not to me they don't, not to Mary Shaugnassy's face! Sure and I can believe she warned Lord Michael that the men were coming with torches. She had a soft spot in her heart for him. He always treated her kindly, for all that he spent most of his time digging in the ground or with his nose in a book. But she would never have gone to the soldiers and named names. There was no treachery in the heart of Fiona O'Neill. And those who say so are black liars."

"And the jewel case," I said, delighted to find at last an ally, who believed in Mother's innocence. "She didn't have it with her when she came to your cottage after the fire?"

"She had naught with her," Mary Shaugnassy said, poking at the fire so that it sent up a shower of golden sparks. "Only a shawl over her shoulders and the dress on her back."

"Cormac Fletcher swears that Fiona had the jewel case with her when he last saw her, leaving Abbey Court. Did she say nothing to you about the jewels?"

"We had little enough time for talking, half out of my mind I was with worry about her, and those that would gladly see her dead if they found her. If she had any jewels she must have got rid of them somewhere for safekeeping before she came to my door. I did what I could for her, put poultices on her poor burned arm, and never told a living soul she was at my cottage, but they found out just the same. It was a miracle I came back early from mass and saw the man bent over the straw tick where your mother was lying, my best feather pillow pushed down over her face. I screamed and when he saw me he threw me aside and ran from the house."

I leaned forward, fascinated. This was a bit of information I hadn't known about; that not only had threats been made against Fiona but an actual attempt on her life. "You didn't recognize the man?"

Mary turned away from me to stare into the fire. "It was too dark. I couldn't see his face. I told Cormac Fletcher so, when he came."

"Cormac came here . . . to the cottage?" I asked, startled.

"Ay, early one morning, and sent me out of the house so he could talk to your mother alone. I heard her cry out once, such a cry of sorrow I never want to hear again. Then Cormac came and told me to help Fiona get ready, that he was taking her to Cobh and putting her on the first ship to America. His face was black as night and he would say nothing more. I went into the cottage. Fiona had already tied in a shawl the few pieces of clothes Cormac had brought her, her face pale as death, but not a tear in her eye. 'I'm on my way to America, Mary,' she said. 'There's nothing more to hold me here in this accursed land.' And it was me who cried and clung to her. She was like my own flesh and blood, the only friend I had left, to see her go fair pulled the heart out of my body. I remember she said I shouldn't carry on so, that America had streets paved with gold and one day she'd be rich, richer than the Fletchers, with a grander house than Abbey Court, and she'd be a fine lady and everyone bowing to her in the street. Then off she went in Cormac's carriage and not one look back."

"You never heard from her at all?"

"No, and no one else in the village did. I thought she was dead. Until her son showed up in Abbeymore one day, looking as rich as any earl, making a glory in the street with his grand clothes and fine manners."

She leaned forward and touched my cup. "Och, and your tea's cold. There's no comfort there." She refilled my cup, then said suddenly, "He came to see me, you know, when he first heard the black lies about his mother."

"What did he want?" I asked.

Over the teacup, the blue eyes met mine. I had thought Mary Shaugnassy a kind if rather garrulous, not too bright old woman. Now, looking into those knowing eyes, I wondered if I had under-estimated the woman. "The same as yourself, I'm thinking," she said shrewdly, "asking the same questions, hoping to clear Fiona's name. Fiona was on her deathbed then and he could not question her, so he came to me, her best friend. And I'll tell you the same now as I told him then, I cannot help you."

She sighed and looked deep into the pale golden flame. "*Mo leir*," she murmured softly, "what harm can foolish people with loose tongues do to your blessed mother now? Only your brother would not heed my words. And what did it bring him, all his searching, but death, and nothing I could do to stop it."

I shivered and edged closer to the fire, all at once remembering Sean's words. "Leave it be. . . ." Had it been a warning, too, the same as Mary had tried to give Patrick?

"They told me it was Moonlighters who killed Patrick. Are you saying it was someone else who shot him?"

"I've said no such thing." She looked sharply at me, cocking her head. "You'll be putting words in me mouth."

"They brought Patrick here, didn't they, after they found him? Did he say anything, anything at all, before he died?"

"He was unconscious, *alannah*," she said sadly. "I saw at once there was nothing I could do when I cut away his shirt. The bullet had gone straight through him, but he'd lost so much blood, you see. I cleansed the wound as best I could, made him comfortable, but it was a miracle he lived as long as he did. Perhaps if his wound had been tended sooner . . ." Her voice died away as she got to her feet and went to a cupboard next to the fireplace. "This is something that rightly I should have given to your brother's widow long since. I haven't touched it since that day."

She took a piece of what looked like white cloth from the cupboard and placed it in my hand. Then I recognized what it was. A fine cambric shirt, torn and stained with a sooty blackness and stiff with blood, dried a dark brown color.

She glanced uneasily into my face. "Perhaps it was wrong to show it to you but it's been lying heavy on my conscience, that I should keep what isn't mine." She reached out her hand. "Let me burn it, child."

"No." My hand tightened possessively on the cloth. There was something about the shirt that teased at a memory, hidden away in a corner of my mind. "Have you shown this shirt to anyone?"

Mary Shaugnassy shrugged her shoulders with a peasant's unwillingness to become involved with those in authority. "No one ever asked, not the magistrate or his men who stomped mud all over my clean floor, after they took your brother's body away." She touched my hand lightly. "It's no use grieving, child. It's God's will." She crossed herself slowly. "May your brother rest in peace."

"It is not God's will," I cried, furious, jerking to my feet. "Not that Patrick should be shot from ambush and lie in the dirt, bleeding to death, with no one to help him and his murderer getting off scot free. I won't believe it!"

I was outside the door before I realized my rudeness and turned apologetically to my hostess, who had followed me, dragging one leg, out into her front garden. "I'm sorry," I said, shaking my head. "I had no right shouting at you. You've been very kind. There is one thing more. No one has told me exactly where it was my brother was shot."

"Just past the ruins of the Abbey on the old road, where the gully crosses near a great oak tree," she answered.

I mounted my horse. I could still see in the distance the spiraling trail of black smoke from the tumbled cottage. My companion followed my gaze, her voice troubled. "I'll be going to the Widow Carmody to give what comfort I can. She has the curse of drink on her, poor soul."

"Mr. Fletcher had no right to evict the Carmody family," I said. "I intend to speak to Lord Fletcher about it."

"Ay, he's a hard man, Sean Fletcher," Mary agreed. "There's much of old Carmac in the son. Still, he's a just man, in his way. He'll tide you over if you have a bit of bad luck, and if you make your farm better, he'll not raise the rent on you like some do." She gave me a sly, questioning glance. "And they say he has the devil's own way of whistling the heart from a girl, just like his father."

I felt my face grow hot, wondering how much gossip had already spread among the tenants about the times I had spent riding with Sean. Hastily I picked up Lady Jane's reins. "Thank you for the tea, Miss Shaugnassy. And if you remember anything else about . . . about the day my brother died, you'll let me know?"

A shadow slipped across her face, no larger than a cloud moving over a still, clear pool. "There is nothing more I can tell you, Meg O'Brien," she answered with a quiet dignity. "Only may God lift the darkness in your soul. Good day to you."

"Good day, Miss Shaugnassy."

I had gone only a short distance when I wished I had thought to ask the woman if she had any idea what Cormac had said to my mother the morning he had come to fetch her from the cottage. Except, I thought, frowning, even if Mary knew, I doubted she would have told me. I wondered what else she might not be telling me. Mary Shaugnassy had been my mother's friend but she was as dependent as any of the other tenants upon the Fletchers for her home and food and land. She could be evicted as easily as the Widow Carmody if she incurred their displeasure by spreading scandal about a member of the family. No, if I wanted to know what had happened between Fiona and Cormac that morning, I would have to ask Cormac myself.

I passed the Carmody cottage and saw that everyone had gone except one workman, who poked disinterested at the still smoldering ashes, to make sure the fire didn't spread into the grass. I continued down the road, letting Lady Jane keep her own slow, plodding pace. As we passed into the wooded area again, the dark trees arched overhead like a cathedral vault and the air became chill and heavy with the scent of damp earth and moss and rotting trunks of trees.

My thoughts, however, weren't on my surroundings. I had Patrick's shirt tucked beneath my saddle and my eyes fastened on it. I tried to force myself to remember what there was about it that plagued me. But the more I tried, the more the memory eluded me.

I was still concentrating on the shirt when I passed the old Abbey ruins, briefly glimpsed through the trees, and came in sight of a huge old oak tree at the edge of a gully. As I slipped off my horse I could see where over a period of years the earth in the gully wall had eroded away, exposing tangled, weblike roots of trees. It was a good place for an ambush. There was enough brush between the gully and the road to provide sufficient cover for whoever might hide there, waiting. In fact, the murderer needn't have waited in the gully at all. Both sides of the road were thick with trees and brush and undergrowth.

I stepped a little way off the road upon a tiny path that led deeper into the woods. I wasn't sure what I was looking for or what I expected to find. Surely the magistrate and his men must have searched the area thoroughly and any tracks left by the assassin would have long since been washed away. I didn't suppose there would have been too much in the way of tracks anyway. The ground was thickly layered with leaves. Even Gray Shadow, the old Indian who had hunted occasionally with Father and me, would have had a hard time tracking through cover like this.

I had gone only a few feet off the road when I heard a branch snap behind me, a rustling sound that I thought at first was some small animal. At the same moment a small branch over my head seemed to explode and dissolve, showering me with bark and twigs. I heard the report of the gun a split second later.

Instinctively I froze, even before a man's voice called out, "Don't move!"

I heard footsteps crashing through the brush and a man's voice, closer now. "What the hell are you doing here?"

I turned to face a thin little man with a balding head and a deeply creased forehead. He had the look of a mischievous gnome, or was it leprechauns they called them in Ireland? I could almost believe he was one of the little people—he seemed to have appeared from nowhere—until I saw he carried a gun over his arm. Two dogs advanced toward me, growling deep in their throats. My knees were still shaking but anger was replacing fear and I demanded, "What do you think you're doing, shooting without knowing what you're shooting at? You might have killed me."

The man smiled good-naturedly but the smile did not touch the pale green eyes. "No danger of that, Miss O'Brien. I always hit my target. You might say I was in a bit of a rush to catch your attention."

"Well, you certainly did that," I said grimly. "Now do you mind telling me why?"

He stepped around me warily, motioning the dogs back with one wave of his hand. Then, taking a long stick, he brushed aside the matted leaves directly on the ground before me, exposing a shallow, wide hole.

It was not the pit, though, that brought a sharp cry of revulsion to my lips. It was the gleaming saw-tooth metal jaws of a trap that waited, like a gaping, obscene mouth, at the bottom of the pit.

17

I tore my glance away from the hidden trap. If I had taken only a few more steps forward, I thought, swallowing hard . . . I imagine those viciously sharp blades snapping shut.

"What . . . what sort of animal do you trap?" I asked.

The man chuckled. "Sure and it's not for animals, Miss O'Brien. It's a mantrap, for poachers. That's why it's not safe to go wandering through the woods, the way you were doing. I've other traps hidden around, as well as spring guns set so cleverly in brushwood you'd never see them till it was too late. It's best you stay on the road."

Twice now the man had used my name and yet I couldn't remember our meeting, for all there was something familiar about the set of the mouth and the high, thin voice. At my questioning glance, he doffed his hat and introduced himself. "I'm Seamus O'Toole, Miss O'Brien, the gamekeeper at Abbey Court. We met at your brother's wake but then no doubt you have better things to do than remember the likes of me." Although his voice was jovial, there was a nastiness beneath it, and suddenly I realized why his face had seemed familiar.

"Are you related to Miss O'Toole?" I asked.

"That I am," he nodded, still smiling. "The old harridan's my sister." He paused. "And Cullen O'Toole was my brother."

Almost imperceptibly, the good-natured expression altered. Just for a moment something ugly peeked out from behind the jovial, smiling mask. "You've heard the name before, I'm thinking, or perhaps it slipped your mind too."

I spoke slowly, carefully. "He was one of the men who attacked Abbey Court, wasn't he, and was caught and hanged afterward."

"Not hanged," the man corrected me. "Flogged to death." He shrugged as if amused. "Poor Cullen. He never did have the luck. For the others, a nice, quick hanging but for Cullen, him that they caught first, it took him three hours, they say to die under the lash."

My stomach was churning as if I were going to be sick. It was an effort to speak. "How could you stay on with the Fletchers, afterward?" I asked, concentrating my gaze on the man's thin lips. I was unable to look into the pale green eyes, and the hatred I knew I would see there.

"Well, now, it wasn't the Fletchers who did the flogging," he said, as if surprised at my question. "It was the soldiers from the barracks. And the one who betrayed the names of the men in the first place to the soldiers so they were caught at all. There wasn't any harm in young Cullen, you understand, seventeen years old he was, and too much hunger and poteen in him or he'd never have done such a wild, foolish thing."

I forced myself to look the man full in the face, wondering why there should be something even more frightening about his loose smile than there was in the open hostility in his sister's face when she stared at me. "I'm sorry about your brother, Mr. O'Toole," I said. "But surely you can't hold my brother or me responsible for what happened to Cullen."

"Now why should you be thinking that?" he asked with a mock amazement. "Seamus O'Toole was never a man to hold a grudge. Ask anyone in Abbeymore. Now my sister, Molly, I can't be answering for. A woman nurses her grievances; they never forget, now do they?"

I turned and walked briskly back to the road, wanting to get away from the gamekeeper, but he followed me at once, the dogs close at his heels. "Was there anything I could do for you, Miss O'Brien?" he asked. "Was there something, perhaps, you lost in the brush?"

"No, thank you." I started to mount Lady Jane, then suddenly remembering, swung around to face the man again. "You were the one who found Patrick, weren't you?"

He leaned easily against his gun, a long, old-fashioned double-barreled fowling piece. "That I did, a terrible sight he was, too, just there, almost where you're standing."

I refused to look down at the road, sensing that that was what the man wanted me to do. "Was he able to talk at all when you found him?"

"Well, now, you might say he wasn't in the mood for conversation at the time," he replied with rough good humor.

I flinched, thinking that, of the two O'Tooles, I was beginning to find Miss O'Toole the more likable. There was nothing I would have enjoyed more than to turn my back on the man and ride away, but I steeled myself to continue.

"Did you know my brother?"

"You wouldn't be calling us close friends," the gamekeeper said, pursing his mouth thoughtfully. "We had a little argument about my work. He didn't approve of my traps, called them cruel and inhuman."

"They are!" I blurted indignantly. "They wouldn't be permitted in America."

"Well, I wouldn't be knowing about that, now would I?" he asked reasonably. "But if it wasn't for my little traps, the poachers would steal Abbey Court blind, that I do know.

There wouldn't be a pheasant, partridge, or grouse, not to mention rabbit, left in the woods and old Cormac wouldn't like that, no, he wouldn't like that at all." He smiled so that his thin lips pulled tight over a row of badgerlike, protruding teeth. "Not that I'm saying anything against America, mind you. I've always had in the back of my mind the thought I'd like to go there myself someday. New York City. Now that's a grand place, I've heard."

"Did they find the cartridge?"

He stared at me blankly.

"The cartridge from the murderer's gun," I said impatiently. "Surely the magistrate or his men must have looked for it."

The smile, I noticed, became a little fixed around the edges. "Oh yes, they looked for it," he said. "With the way the ground is, though, with the leaves and underbrush and soft mud, they weren't likely to find it, if there was a cartridge at all to find. Your brother was killed by one shot. There was no need at all for the Moonlighter to remove the cartridge and put in another shot."

"If it was a Moonlighter," I said.

Now the smile did disappear. The gamekeeper's bony hands, unusually large for such a small man, tightened on the barrel of his gun. "You're not thinking that me or my sister would risk the hangman's noose for the likes of your brother?" The voice became rasping as a dull knife. "If you're looking for those that would gladly have seen your brother dead, there's others at Abbey Court with more reason than the O'Tooles."

"What others?" I demanded.

Seamus O'Toole shook his head, the smile slipping easily back, only a feral look still lurked behind the pale green eyes. "Now do I look a great fool, Miss O'Brien? Do you think I've so little wits about that me that I'd be caught slandering the gentry? Me with a fine job and a cozy cottage all my own." He glanced up at the darkening sky. "It'll be wet soon. You'd best get back to the house. And mind you, stay on the roads next time." He winked roguishly. "My traps haven't the sense to tell the difference between a poor old sod of a poacher and a grand lady."

I glanced at him sharply. Was there a threat behind those words? But it was impossible to tell from the man's cheerful smile. I mounted quickly before Seamus O'Toole's large, hamhock hands could reach out and help me, and spurred Lady Jane forward.

The gamekeeper had been right about one thing. I hadn't gone more than a few feet when the rain began in torrents. By the time I reached Abbey Court I was soaked to the skin. Fortunately, the cambric shirt, carefully tucked beneath my saddle, remained dry. As a servant came hurrying out the front door to take the reins of Lady Jane, I grabbed the shirt and dashed up the steps into the front hall, almost colliding with Kevin, who was crossing the hall from the drawing room.

"I was looking for you," he said, worried, catching my arms to keep us from running into each other. "Your maid told me you'd gone riding. You shouldn't ride alone, Maeve."

"Why not?" I asked. "It's safe, isn't it?"

"Safe?" He looked startled. "Yes, of course, but I understood from Regan you weren't an experienced rider. I was concerned you might have been thrown. I was about to send the groomsmen out to look for you." His glance fell to the floor and I saw I had dropped Patrick's shirt when he grasped my arms. "What's this?" he asked, picking up the shirt gingerly and handing it to me.

"It's the shirt Patrick was wearing when he was shot," I explained. "Mary Shaugnassy gave it to me. She said she had meant to return it to the widow, but—"

"I can assure you Regan won't be interested in seeing it," Kevin interrupted. "Frankly, I can't imagine why you should want it either. Isn't it a bit, well, morbid?" He glanced at the shirt, winced slightly, and looked quickly away. "I know you and Patrick were close, but don't you think this is going a bit too far?"

I could feel the angry protest flaring up in me, and he flung up his hands in abject surrender. "All right, let's not quarrel." He smiled. "That's why I was looking for you in the first place, to apologize for my abominable behavior at lunch yesterday. I suppose Major Gill set me off. I can't abide the man. He's such a stiff-necked bore. If it weren't for Sean's being taken with the Gill daughter, they wouldn't be asked to Abbey Court."

Instantly, I remembered the intimate, possessive way she had touched his arm, and pain cramped me like a most unpleasant stomach-ache. Who would have thought jealousy could hurt so? I thought, surprised.

Mistaking the stricken expression on my face for a chill, Kevin said quickly, "How stupid of me to keep you standing like this. You should get out of those wet clothes. Will you be coming down to lunch?"

"No, I think I'll ask Rose to bring a tray to my room. It's been a tiring morning."

"That's probably a sensible idea, though I'll miss you," Kevin said, and then hesitantly, "I had hoped that we could go riding together tomorrow afternoon, that is, if I'm forgiven for snapping at you yesterday."

"Of course you are, and thank you for the invitation," I said, feeling faintly guilty because the truth was I wasn't too tired to join the family at lunch. I simply wanted time to be alone and think.

Once in my room, I stripped off my wet clothes and, after drying myself, slipped into a flannel robe and went to sit at my favorite spot by the window. Rory immediately came over to join me, looking up at me politely, his tail wagging expectantly, until I lifted him into my lap. We shared the lunch that Rose brought me and then she put on Rory's leash, to take him out for a run.

"Has Miss O'Toole discovered Rory yet?" I asked as the girl started for the door, Rory yanking happily at the leash.

"That she has." Rose grinned impishly. "This morning she caught me with him on the back stairs. 'And what is that creature doing here?' she asked, with fire in her eyes. And without blinking, I answered, 'Why, he's a gift from his lordship to Miss O'Brien. I don't suppose you'll be having any objections to that,' and I swept by her like I was Queen Victoria and Rory the crown jewels."

"I met Miss O'Toole's brother this morning," I said.

"Seamus O'Toole?" Rose frowned. "Sure and he's an awkward man. Always smiling like honey in his mouth but shivers go up me back when he looks at me."

"Those traps of his are horrible. They could kill someone."

"Och, well, all the gentry keep traps in their woods to catch poachers," Rose said, unperturbed. "During the famine years, even the wild game sickened and died. It's just the last years they started coming back, if poachers don't get them first. Still, with Seamus and his traps, it's different somehow, almost like he takes pleasure in catching a man in one of his devilish contraptions. There's several men in the village maimed for life because of Seamus O'Toole."

"I don't understand why the Fletchers keep a man like that around," I protested.

Rose shrugged. "Didn't you know that it was O'Toole who helped your mother pull his lordship from the terrible fire, when all the other servants had run off? When the late earl sickened and died, on his deathbed he made her ladyship promise that she'd keep Seamus O'Toole on at Abbey Court for as long as he lived, in gratitude for what he did that day. And her ladyship isn't one to forget a solemn deathbed promise."

Then Rory, restless at having to wait so long, ended the conversation by giving a frustrated yipe and headed for the door, pulling Rose along behind him.

After they had left, I resumed my staring out the window. The rain had stopped and the sullen gray skies were once again a sparkling blue. A fine golden glow covered the landscape; the mountains in the distance were the color of heliotrope, the deep woods a dozen shades of green that changed before my eyes in patterns of dark and light. Next to Colorado, I thought, I had never seen a land of such entrancing beauty as Ireland. But while Colorado's snow-capped mountains were dramatic, Ireland's beauty was quieter, a brooding loveliness that stirred the senses first to happiness, then to despair. No wonder Patrick had fallen in love with the country, and how Fiona must have hated to leave. Yet she had left just the same, driven away by Cormac Fletcher.

I picked up Patrick's shirt and spread it on my lap, still trying to recall what there was about it that bothered me. It was an expensive hand-sewn shirt but that was to be expected. Patrick had been as much a dandy about his clothes as Jamie. I smiled in memory. Not even the best tailor in the world, though, could disguise Jamie's burly shoulders and thick or make him look anything but what he was—a hard-rock miner who had struck it rich.

My hand stroked the soft material, and a lump of unshed tears as big as a stone stuck in my throat. Both were gone now, Jamie and Patrick, both ironically meeting violent deaths, shot down in cold blood.

My hand clutched the shirt fabric. I stared down at the ugly stains, the dried blood, and the black powder burns from the bullet entering Patrick's body through the shirt. Then, as if it were happening all over again, I could see them carrying Jamie home, his fine white shirt stained with the same black sooty powder. But Jamie had been shot while seated at a card table, I remembered, licking at my lips that had suddenly gone dry. Only a man shot at close range would have such extensive powder burns on his clothes.

And, according to all accounts, Patrick had been shot from a distance, from ambush, while he had been riding horseback. How then could Patrick's shirt have powder burns on it?

I got to my feet and began to pace back and forth, excitement like a fever burning inside me, my thoughts leap-frogging dizzily. Now that I thought about it, why had Patrick gone off riding alone at all? Surely he had known he was expected for lunch and there would be guests present. Why go off instead for a ride down a seldom-used back road?

A knocking at the door cut short my speculations and I shoved the shirt under a pillow on the bed before opening the door. The housekeeper stood in the doorway, her plump sausage fingers folded across her ample stomach. Her mouth, so much like her brother's, was pinched in tightly at the corners, her plump face, as always, coldly hostile. "Mr. Cormac would like to see you in his room," she said shortly.

It was not a question but a command. I felt a spurt of resentment. Then, remembering that I had some questions of my own to ask Cormac, I nodded distantly and said, "Very well, after I've changed my clothes."

A half hour later I once again stood before Cormac Fletcher in the dark-paneled room, only this time the man was not in his chair but in his bed, and we were alone. He had imperiously gestured his manservant and Miss O'Toole to leave. Either Sean had declined or hadn't been asked to attend this meeting.

Almost the second the door closed behind the servants he turned to face me and I saw that he had lost weight. The flesh hung loosely from his neck, and his skin was an odd yellowish shade. There were dark shadows beneath his eyes. His voice, however, held no sign of weakness as he boomed out accusingly, "They tell me you've been visiting Mary Shaugnassy."

Who had told him? I wondered. One of the O'Tooles, Sean? Certainly not Mary herself. I felt a flicker of indignation, wondering how long I had been spied upon, how long my actions had been reported back to Cormac Fletcher. He had not asked me to sit and I stood beside the bed like a schoolgirl called to task before the headmaster.

I determined not to let the man put me at a disadvantage and asked calmly, "May I sit down?"

The eyelids lowered. He looked discomfited and frowned impatiently. "Sit down . . . sit down."

I chose a chair, slowly pulled it next to the bed, and carefully adjusted my skirt around me, taking my time with every movement, until Cormac began making rumbling noises deep in his throat and I decided I had pushed him far enough. "Was there any reason why I shouldn't visit Miss Shaugnassy?" I asked, widening my eyes innocently. "After all, she was my mother's friend and the last person to see my brother alive."

"What foolishness did the old woman tell you?"

I debated whether or not to mention Patrick's shirt with the powder stains, then decided against it. Although my face would never let me become a good poker player, I at least knew enough to keep an ace in the hole. "She told me my brother was unconscious until he died," I said slowly. "There was nothing she could do for him."

I thought the grizzled head relaxed a little against the pillows. "And what else did you expect?" he demanded. "Don't you think the magistrate and his men asked questions till they were blue in the face about your brother's death? In the future, I'll have no more of your running around the demesne, bothering the tenants, interfering in what is none of your concern."

I stiffened angrily. "The tenants of Abbey Court are my concern. My brother's legacy to me made them my concern."

"Your brother was a fool! He thought he could step into my shoes and change overnight the way matters have been run at Abbey Court for centuries. He tried to turn a lot of backward, ignorant farmers into American freeholders, as good a chance as changing milk horses into thoroughbreds." He studied me beneath lowered lids. His voice changed and softened, becoming a cruel parody of the coaxing, sensual voice the young Cormac Fletcher must have employed on his courting expeditions. "You have more sense than your brother. I knew it the moment I laid eyes on you. You're not a foolish addlepated schoolgirl or a dry-as-dust spinster. It's a man you're needing to bring you pleasure and give you children. I'll not be knowing what went wrong between Sean and yourself. I admit the boy's too high-spirited at times but you have the hands to tame him, I'm sure."

"I have no intention of marrying your son," I said icily. "Ever. Nor would I marry a man who'd sink so low that he'd burn down a house and stand by while a widow and her son were evicted from the only house they've ever known."

Cormac Fletcher blinked, then his eyebrows lifted. "And whose cottage might that be?" he asked cautiously.

"Why, the Widow Carmody, of course," I said indignantly. "Don't pretend you didn't give the order to your son to tumble the Carmody cottage. I warn you, I won't allow such a thing to happen again." Then suddenly I realized the old man wasn't pretending. He didn't know about the eviction of the Carmody family. So it had been all Sean's idea, I thought, sickened. My earlier suspicions had been right. Cormac might bluster and shout and give orders but it was all a sham. It was Sean Fletcher who ran Abbey Court now, not his father.

Perhaps it was the trick of light cast by the shadows from the gas lamp over the bed, but suddenly Cormac Fletcher looked old and shrunken, the lion's head too heavy for the aged, scrawny neck. The hands clutching a bit of blanket were convulsed not in anger but in the rheumatic, painful squeezing of a sick old man. And all at once, despite myself, I felt sorry for the crumpled wreck of a man who lay trapped in his bed, still pretending to be the master of the demesne but surely knowing all the time it was pretense.

He must have sensed my pity, for his face grew livid. Grabbing the ropes on the pulley above his head, he yanked himself erect, his voice growling with anger. "You'll warn *me*, Cormac Fletcher, a bit of a girl like yourself! It's me that's warning you. Stop meddling in matters that are none of your concern, or I'll send you packing, the same way I sent your mother."

"Did you threaten Fiona, too, when you came to Miss Shaugnassy's cottage?" I asked, forgetting discretion in anger. "Is that why she left for America the morning after someone tried to smother her in her bed?"

"There was no need to threaten her," Cormac said, a deliberate, taunting smile on his face. "I simply told her Michael was dead."

I rose from my chair and stared, disbelieving, down at the man. "How could you? How could you tell such a cruel lie?"

For a moment the old man had the grace to look ashamed, then he scowled indifferently. "Michael could easily have died, burned badly as he was. It was for her own good I sent her away, a woman made for loving like Fiona, and Michael with ice water in his veins. Even if he knew what to do with a woman, and had the courage to take her, no happiness would have come of it. His father had already made plans for Michael to marry his dead brother's fiancée, Lady Margaret. Fiona was too proud a woman to sit around and watch that happen."

I glared at the man, my voice shaking. "That's not the reason you lied to her, is it? The truth is, if you couldn't have Fiona, you had to make sure that Michael didn't have her either."

Cormac Fletcher studied me for a long moment without speaking. His heavy-lidded eyes, with all emotion hidden, reminded me all at once of Sean. Then he chuckled softly and shook his head as he asked, "Do you think a few scratches or screams or Michael with arms like twigs would stop me? What makes you think I didn't have Fiona?"

18

The sound of Cormac Fletcher's laughter followed me as I ran from the room, afraid of what I might say or do if I stayed a moment longer. When I reached my own bedroom I was still trembling with fury. Even Rory sensed something was wrong, and after a few playful nips at my ankle brought no response he sighed and crawled beneath the bed and went to sleep.

When Rose came to my door a few minutes later she took one look at my flushed face and asked, "Would you like me to brush your hair, Miss Meg? Miss Regan's maid says that her lady finds that very soothing like when she's upset."

It would take more than hair brushing to calm me, I thought grimly. I remembered the fine stream of oaths I had often overheard in the mining camps when I was young—before Mother could cover my ears and whisk me away—and I could understand now why men indulged in such vulgar, if descriptive, language. There were a few choice expletives I would have liked to call Cormac Fletcher if I hadn't been a lady.

Rose hesitated, then said quickly, "You mustn't mind old Cormac, miss. Most of the time, it's the pain talking.

They say every waking moment he's in terrible agony and not a drop of medicine he'll take for it. Father Vincent says it's God's punishment for the wicked life the old man's led." Her voice dropped to a delighted whisper. "There's five or six I could name around Abbey Court that have the look of Cormac Fletcher about them."

And Sean, I wondered bitterly, was the son following in his father's footsteps? I had seen the way the young women's eyes followed him when we visited the tenant farms. Yet, much as I detested Cormac Fletcher, there was something distasteful about gossiping about him this way with a servant and I asked, "What was it you wanted, Rose?"

"Och, and I almost forgot. A messenger from your solicitor's office brought these for you to sign, if you please."

Enclosed with the legal document was a short letter from Mr. Corcoran, expressing his apologies for being unable to come to Abbey Court himself. He hoped I was encountering no difficulties in working with the estate agents and he would be happy to assist me in any way he could, if I should have any questions about my brother's estate.

I signed and returned the documents to the waiting messenger, thinking wryly that the difficulties I had encountered with Sean were not the sort I cared to confide to my solicitor. In any case, as far as the estate accounts went, Sean had been most co-operative in showing me everything I wanted to see.

As I lay in bed that night, unable to fall asleep, I wondered if I should write to Mr. Corcoran about Patrick's shirt and the powder marks on it. I doubted, however, if it would do any good. Lawyers, I had already learned from my association with Mr. Adams in Boston, were a notoriously conservative breed, hesitant to muddy up still waters. I would need more evidence than powder stains to convince Mr. Corcoran that a new investigation should be made into Patrick's death.

And what other evidence did I have? I had the feeling, constantly with me, that something was awry, out of place, but I was not able to put my finger on what was wrong. I remembered the sly look on the gamekeeper's foxlike face, the rasping malevolence in his voice: "If you're looking for those that would gladly have seen your brother dead, there's others at Abbey Court with more reason than the O'Tooles."

When sleep finally did come, it was light and fitful. Once

I awakened, aroused by a soft, thumping sound. My eyes flew at once to the hall door, my heart pounding. There was nothing there, only a shadow caused by a curtain blowing in the rising wind. And the thumping noise was Rory beneath the bed, scratching vigorously at a flea.

Disgusted at my own timidity, I went to lower the window. As I drew the curtains, I noticed a pinpoint of light moving slowly in the woods in the direction of the old Abbey. When I looked a second time, however, the light was gone. Old Malachy, I thought, returning home late from the pub, probably filled with poteen. I smiled to myself, remembering the nights when I had helped put Jamie, in the same condition, quietly to bed, so Fiona would not hear.

I slept late the next morning and dawdled over breakfast, putting off as long as possible the moment when I knew I must walk back to the office and sit at the desk, only a handsbreadth away from Sean. Still, that moment, awkward as I was sure it would be, could not be put off indefinitely, so finally, reluctantly, I sipped the last of my coffee and got slowly to my feet.

As I made my way back through the servants' area and kitchen, I instructed myself carefully on how I would behave when I saw Sean. I would be gracious but cool, I decided, so there would be no question in Sean's mind that from now on our meetings would be conducted in a strictly businesslike atmosphere. And I would also make it very clear that there would be no more eviction of tenants. It occurred to me then that I had forgotten to tell Kevin about the tumbling of the Carmody cottage. I was positive he wouldn't approve. Well, I would talk to him about it this afternoon when we went riding.

Then, as I reached the door of the office, I realized there was no need to tell Kevin. He already knew. I could hear voices raised in anger and when I entered the room I saw Sean and Kevin facing each other across the desk, both too intent on their own heated discussion to notice my presence.

Kevin's face was scarlet; he spoke with the slight stammer he always had when he was upset. "I . . . I won't have it, I warn you. Liam Carmody and his mother . . . must have their home . . . back."

If Kevin was literally beside himself with rage, however, only the flatness of Sean's voice and the impassive, almost indifferent look on his face, as if all emotion had been stamped away, betrayed his tightly controlled anger. "Mrs.

Carmody has been sent to stay with her sister in Limerick where she'll be much better off than relying on her worthless son for her daily food. As for Liam Carmody, I've told him he's not to set foot on Abbey Court land again."

"I . . . I should have been told. There was no need. I would have . . . paid the rent."

"No doubt, but the Carmodys are off Abbey Court land now and they stay off. Let's have no misunderstanding about that."

I listened, startled. It almost sounded as if Sean were threatening his cousin.

Kevin must have thought so too, for his voice grew shriller and a murderous fury distorted his face. His hand, trembling, tightened on the paperweight. "How . . . how dare you! You have no right!"

Sean shrugged contemptuously. "Take your complaint to Cormac." He smiled coldly. "Or would you rather I spoke to him?"

I must have made some sound, for they both saw me at the same time. Kevin tried to smile but it was a painful grimace. Then he murmured a greeting, brushed by me, and hurried from the room.

If Sean was disturbed by the scene I had just witnessed he gave no sign. He rose quickly to his feet and held my chair out for me with a smile. "Well, this is a pleasant surprise. I was afraid you had decided to give up the tedious job of working with the accounts."

"Not at all," I said coldly. "May I see the accounts for the tenant farms, please?"

He handed me the ledger with a flourish as if he were mocking my businesslike manner. When his hand accidentally touched mine, I drew it away so quickly he lifted an amused eyebrow but said nothing.

Looking through the entries for the Carmody farm, I saw that, at least, Sean had been right about one thing. No rent payment had been made on the farm for over a year. Then, glancing through other entries for the day before, I saw that the sum of twenty-five shillings had been advanced to James Leary. "It was a loan to Mrs. Leary," Sean explained. He leaned back in his chair, a glint of amusement in his eyes. "I assume you have no objections."

"But I already gave Mr. Leary fifty—" I broke off, embarrassed, because, of course, I hadn't entered my loan to James Leary in the ledger.

"Fifty shillings," Sean finished for me. "Wasn't that the

amount you gave James Leary for the rent, which I understand from his wife she promptly spent at the nearest pub, getting into a grand fight with his friends in the bargain." He added dryly, "If there's anything an Irishman enjoys more than fighting the English, it's fighting among themselves."

"Now I suppose you'll be evicting the Learys too?"

At the contempt in my voice, Sean's eyes narrowed but he shrugged indifferently. "Why should I? Mrs. Leary and her two sons are hard workers. It's not their fault if James would rather talk revolution than turn his hand to farming. It's a common enough failing among Irishmen."

"You're Irish yourself!"

"Anglo-Irish," he corrected me. "The Fletchers have only lived in this country for three hundred years, so naturally we're still not considered truly Irish."

"Can you blame James Leary?" I asked. "When you think of how the English have treated the Irish people for generations, why wouldn't he plot revolution?" Then I had a sudden flash of intuition. "Wouldn't you, if you were in his place?"

Sean nodded thoughtfully. "I might," he agreed. "Only my job happens to be to manage Abbey Court, preferably at a profit, for the Earl of Abbeymore. Or at the least to keep it from going under." He gestured toward the ledgers. "You've seen the accounts. You know the precarious financial condition of the estate. What you haven't seen are the great mansions, many just like Abbey Court, settling into ruin all over Ireland. Farmlands are being wasted, nettles and weeds are growing where snug cottages once stood and families made a living—if not a luxurious one, then enough, at least, to keep their children from starving or begging in the street. What famine and absentee and indifferent management didn't destroy, the Encumbered Estates Court took." His voice tightened harshly. "Well, I intend to see that doesn't happen here. Abbey Court will, God willing, still be around for the eleventh Earl of Abbeymore to inherit."

Why? I almost demanded. It's not your land, not your title. Then I bit back the words, remembering what Mary Shaugnassy had told me of the dream Cormac Fletcher had to one day inherit the earldom. Did Sean have the same dream? In many ways the Fletchers, father and son, already owned Abbey Court. Certainly their word was law in running the estate. Even Kevin's protest against the tumbling of the Carmody cottage had been futile.

But Patrick had not been like Kevin, I realized suddenly. My brother would never have knuckled under to Cormac or Sean Fletcher. After all, it was O'Brien money loaned to Abbey Court that had saved the estate from financial ruin. And if Patrick had somehow learned, as I had, of Cormac's treatment of Fiona, I was sure my brother would have been more than ever determined to wrest the management from Cormac. How far, I wondered, would the old man have gone to make sure the estate stayed in his hands? As far as murder?

Although a man in a wheel chair couldn't possibly have hidden in the gully, gun in hand, waiting for his victim, the old man could have bribed someone to kill in his place. He could have turned to someone he trusted and didn't need to bribe, I thought uncomfortably, gazing at Sean—someone close to the old man who was accustomed to doing his bidding without question.

My thoughts were leading me down a dark road. I felt my face grow warm and Sean, watching me, said slowly, "It seems strange, your championing the cause of the revolutionaries, after the way your brother died, at the hands of terrorists."

"You don't know that." At Sean's searching glance, I said bitterly, "After all, no one bothered to look very hard, did they, for Patrick's murderer?"

"You're mistaken," Sean said sharply. "There was an autopsy and a hearing. The verdict was death by person or persons unknown. The magistrate, Lord Jeremy Fleming, I admit is a good friend of the late earl and naturally was interested in causing the family as little notoriety as possible but, whatever you may think, I assure you his investigation was thorough and complete."

Not quite complete, I thought, remembering the powder-stained shirt Mary Shaugnassy had given me. For a moment I almost thought of telling Sean about the incriminating evidence that proved Patrick had been shot at close range, but I held my tongue in time.

"Of course, if you have some new information to present," Sean said and waited.

His glance was too probing, the stare seemed to pin me to my chair so that it was an effort to force my eyes away, back to the ledger books on the desk. The lines of figures blurred before my eyes.

"No, of course not. How could I? Shall we get back to

the accounts for yesterday?" I spoke in a rush, and the rest of the morning we concentrated on the work at hand, but once or twice I looked up to see Sean studying me, his glance thoughtful, speculative.

Around noon I glanced at my watch and rose quickly to my feet. "I think that is all the accounts I will have time for today. If you'll excuse me . . ."

Sean reached the door before I did, his arm casually stretched across the opening, effectively blocking my exit. His face was no longer watchful but smiling, his voice warm and coaxing. "There's an inn on the other side of Abbey-more that serves freshly made Stilton cheese and hot scones thick with raisins and dripping butter, so rich they melt in your mouth. I could have the carriage brought around and we could be there in half an hour."

"Thank you," I said hastily, "but I have another engagement."

"I see." It was plain, however, from the brief, bewildered look that crossed his face that he didn't see at all; that being rejected by a woman was a new, unsettling experience for Sean Fletcher. I watched pride struggle with uncertainty, then he bowed mockingly and stepped aside. "Another tête-à-tête in the tower with Kevin, listening to poetry by Rosetti, I suppose. Isn't that Kevin's current favorite? Some-how I hadn't pictured you as such a moonstruck romantic, Meg."

"Lord Fletcher and I are going riding," I said. "And your opinion of Mr. Rosetti's poetry is of no particular interest to me. I would hardly expect you to understand the feelings of a man who loved a woman so completely that when she died he buried his poetry with her."

"And had the grave exhumed nine years later so he could retrieve the poems and publish them," Sean commented dryly. "Or didn't Kevin mention that? Or the fact that the lady in question was so happily in love that she committed suicide with an overdose of laudanum."

I flushed, annoyed. "I had no idea you were such an authority on literature."

"Oh, I never made it to Oxford, like Kevin, but Cormac saw I had a few terms at Trinity in Dublin." His voice changed into the lilting, teasing brogue, his eyes laughing at me. "For myself, though, I've always thought spouting poetry to a woman was a grand waste of time, when there are so many more interesting things to do."

Although he made no move toward me, I stepped quickly

back, my voice tart. "Yes, I've heard of the great interest your father and you have taken in the young women at Abbey Court."

His arm dropped, but he continued lounging against the doorframe, watching me, smiling, his voice lazily indifferent. "I won't be making apologies for my father. Cormac Fletcher needs no man to defend him. As for myself, I've never taken what wasn't freely given." His smile faded. "Perhaps you should do less running around the countryside, listening to old gossips like Mary Shaugnassy. What other fine tales did she tell you?" The last question was spoken in an offhand fashion but I sensed he was waiting, with more than casual interest, for my answer.

I had no desire to cause trouble for Mary Shaugnassy and I replied, "She told me nothing that's not common knowledge. Mother came to her cottage for shelter; someone tried to kill her there, and the next day your father came and sent Fiona away."

"And your brother Patrick. What did she tell you about him?"

"Only that Patrick died without regaining consciousness," I answered. Then, feigning innocence, "What else is there to tell?"

"Nothing, of course, only talking's the one thing in great supply here in Ireland." Sean smiled grimly. "The priests love to say that drink is the curse of the Irish. Myself, I've always thought it was the love of talking. You'd be wise, Meg, not to listen to a lot of idle tongues wagging."

"I'm not in the habit of listening to gossip," I said haughtily. "Now if you don't mind, I am in a hurry. . . ."

Although I rushed through lunch, Kevin was already mounted and waiting for me when I arrived, breathless, at the stable.

He was dressed in formal riding regalia, which made my second-hand outfit seem dowdy in comparison, and the sleek black mare he rode made Lady Jane seem even more suited to pulling milk pails. As we followed the road leading past the dower house and through the wooded area, Kevin turned and caught me admiring his finely etched profile above the white stock he wore. "I should apologize for this morning," he said hesitantly. "I cut a rather foolish figure in the office with Cousin Sean. I'm sorry you had to see."

"You were right to say what you did. Will you talk to your uncle?"

He nodded. "But I doubt if it will do any good. Sean's

already had the men out planting trees at the Carmody farm this morning. However, I have told Liam he can continue working for me at the tower. It seems the least I could do and he can pick up some wages that way." He gave me a sidelong, boyish grin. "I'd appreciate it if you wouldn't mention Liam's job to Sean. No need to cause poor Liam more trouble."

We were passing into the more deeply wooded area now, the tower far behind us, when a rabbit suddenly shot out from the brush and darted across the road. The small animal reminded me of my run-in with the gamekeeper yesterday. "There's something else I wish you would speak to your uncle about," I said. I told him of my meeting with Mr. O'Toole and the dangerous trap into which I had almost walked.

Kevin scowled, stiffening in his saddle. "Seamus has been warned not to use mantraps. I'll have Sean talk to him, although sometimes I think he secretly encourages the man in their use. But it's my fault too. I should have warned you of the danger of straying off the paths. If you like to walk, there is a safe path that follows this road. It runs from the gamekeeper's cottage past the tower, and then you can take the path through the woods to the road that leads to the office. I often walk it myself in the mornings."

I wondered if Kevin would actually talk to Sean about the gamekeeper. Although there were flashes of stubborn strength in Kevin that made me sometimes suspect the weakness and the uncertainty were a sham, most of the time he seemed quite content to sit passively to one side, without interfering in the running of Abbey Court.

It was too pleasant a day, though, to debate my companion's character, or lack of it, and I concentrated instead on the sunlight filtering downward through the trees and a bird call falling like a riffle of music through the hushed quiet. Kevin talked entertainingly about his days at Oxford, his fellow students and tutors, and I could sense his pleasure in those days. After a half hour's ride he suggested we stop and walk a little. "There's a small stream that circles not far from here, and a lovely shaded glade. Perhaps you'd care to see it."

Was this the same hidden glade Sean had wanted to take me to? I wondered. I felt a pinch of pain as if I had touched an exposed nerve. I smiled at my companion with determined brightness. "I'd like that," I said.

Kevin helped me dismount, his hands lingering a moment

longer than necessary on my waist. Then, smiling intently, he reached up and removed my top hat and the bit of veil across my face. He touched the mass of my hair caught into a coil at the nape of my neck.

"May I?" he asked.

I hesitated a moment, then nodded, feeling oddly disjointed, as if I were standing to one side, watching myself. Very slowly, one by one, Kevin gently removed my tortoise hairpins. When I felt my hair fall loosely, like a shawl around my shoulders, a conviction possessed me more strongly than if Kevin had taken me into his arms in an embrace that I had committed myself.

Neither of us spoke a word as we walked quietly down a path through the trees, the boreen so layered with crushed, disintegrating leaves that our feet made no sound. Which is why, when we came to a break in the path, the two occupants already in the glade, my brother's widow and Brian Flaherty, neither saw nor heard our approach.

19

My first startled impression was that Regan was fighting off the studmaster. Her riding jacket and shirt were opened down the front, half pulled off, exposing a softly rounded, white shoulder. She seemed to be struggling against the man's embrace, her face absorbed in some intense, inner concentration, her eyes narrowed, glittering.

Brian Flaherty caught one of Regan's outflung hands, her fingers curled as if to scratch his face, and twisted it cruelly behind her back. His dark head descended, and he buried his face in her breast. Regan's lovely straight back arched suddenly forward, a soft moan of pain, or was it pleasure, sounding deep in her throat. Then her free arm tightened around the studmaster, pulling him down onto the thick grass, his body covering hers from view—before I turned my embarrassed gaze away. I hurried after Kevin back down the path, as quickly as we had come.

When we reached the horses, who were standing, nibbling at the grass, I caught a glimpse of Kevin's face. It was white with mingled shock and revulsion. "My God," he muttered thickly, "like animals rutting in the woods. Poor Patrick, to think he was married to that slut. How ghastly for him."

I finally found my voice and felt the heat of embarrassment drain from my face, leaving my skin icy cold. "You think Patrick knew . . . about them?"

"Of course he knew," he said bitterly. "He must have guessed what Regan was like, even on the honeymoon. After they returned, I sensed something was wrong between them, but naturally we never spoke of it. No gentleman would. What a hell she must have put him through."

"Yet he loved her," I said slowly. "He wouldn't have married her otherwise."

"Oh, your brother fell neatly into Regan's trap all right. Cormac and Sean saw to that. No sooner did Cormac hear that there was a wealthy American visiting in Abbeymore than he set Regan on him. Of course he didn't know, at first, that Patrick was Fiona's son, but it didn't really matter. All that mattered was Patrick's money. I was away in London at the time they met or perhaps I could have warned Patrick. Regan has always been wild. There was a groomsman she ran away with when she was only fifteen, but Cormac found them, thrashed the boy half to death, and brought Regan back. By the time I returned to Abbey Court for the wedding, though, it was too late. Patrick was walking around in a daze, as if he were bewitched. No one could have saved him."

Kevin lifted his hands toward me, then let them fall helplessly to his side. "I can't ask you to forgive me for this, Meg. I wouldn't blame you for despising me, for bringing you here today. . . ."

"You couldn't have known they'd be here," I said dully. And I suppose I had already guessed the truth, partly. I shivered suddenly as if a chill wind had passed over me. "Please, Kevin, let's get away from here."

He helped me remount, then rode silently beside me, back to Abbey Court. After we left the horses at the stable, he took my hand as we walked toward the house, as if he wanted me to know he was there beside me, even though we didn't speak.

At the front door he asked, "Why don't you come to

the tower with me? We could have a sherry and talk, if you like. I hate to see you look so . . . stricken."

"I'm all right," I said. "I think I'll be better alone."

He nodded, then reached up to rest the palm of his hand gently against my cheek, his voice tender. "It doesn't have to be that way between a man and a woman, what you saw. . . ."

But I didn't want to hear any more. I walked away from him into the house, leaning against the great, oversized door for a moment after I had closed it behind me. Almost without thinking, I went through the drawing and dining rooms, back into the little chapel that Patrick had turned into his study. Somehow, ever since I had come to Abbey Court, I had felt closest to Patrick in this room.

Today, however, I found no comfort in the study and I paced, anguished, back and forth. How long had it been going on between Regan and Brian? I wondered. Before she met Patrick and afterward too? Had Patrick accidentally wandered into the same sort of scene Kevin and I had witnessed? Was that why he had decided suddenly to change his will, leaving the bulk of his estate to me with only a token inheritance to his wife? And Cormac, who must have confidently expected to control his son-in-law's wealth through Regan, had lost his last hold on Patrick.

Even as I was trying to think rationally, to sort out what must have happened between Patrick and Regan, the scene in the glade kept returning, no matter how I tried to shut it from my mind. I remembered the look of rapture on Regan's face in the shimmering, dappled sunlight, the two dark bodies intertwining in the grass, and what was even more disturbing, the bitter envy I had felt for one split second as I stood there watching them. Only it was Sean's arms I had imagined tight around me. I could even feel the springy, sweet-smelling grass beneath me, and Sean's mouth hard on mine. . . .

I felt my body grow hot with shame at the memory and I began to walk faster. What was happening to me? I wondered, frightened. I must think of something else, anything else. My eyes wandered around the small study, so beautifully, carefully decorated, each piece of furniture obviously, lovingly hand-picked by Patrick. Even the crewelwork on the chairs was the green vine leaves and golden wheat of the carving on the paneled walls. Only the rug, I thought absently, although beautiful, did not fit the rest of the room. The colors were wrong and it was too small.

I stopped my pacing to study a stretch of paneling at one side of the fireplace and ran my fingers idly over an ear of wheat, still as fresh-looking as if it had been carved yesterday instead of more than a century before. The priest hole must be hidden behind this section of the wall, I decided. It was the only wall that didn't front on another room or on the exterior of the house. I wondered where the entrance to the room was concealed. Probably it involved some special piece of paneling that had to be pushed or lifted, although each carved piece looked exactly like its neighbor.

Tentatively I ran my fingers over the grape leaves and the stalks of wheat, pushing and probing with no result. I tapped on the wall with my hand. It did have a faintly hollow sound. Once again I began the painstaking search with my fingers, going over each square of wall, inch by inch.

I was examining a section just below eye level when my fingers passed over an ear of wheat, hesitated, and backtracked to touch the ear again. For one moment a small section of the wheat ear had felt different, cold to the touch and not curved, but flat. I could have sworn my fingertips had touched metal. Excited, I fetched a lamp from the desk.

There *was* something different about that particular piece of paneling. I could see clearly now the small, flattened piece of gray, leadlike metal imbedded in the center of the wheat ear, almost invisible to the eyes unless one were studying the wall as carefully as I was. I pushed at the piece of metal hopefully, but nothing happened. No door swung silently open. The panel didn't move at all. Frustrated, I studied the indentation caused by the metal more closely. Obviously the metal didn't belong in the paneling. I couldn't imagine the original woodcarver placing it there. Thoughtfully I touched the pellet of gray metal again, and all at once, as if my fingertips had memories of their own, I suddenly recognized what it was.

Turning quickly to the desk, I found a long silver letter opener. Slowly, painstakingly, so as not to damage the wood around it, I dug into the paneling. Finally I was able to pull the piece of metal free and hold it in my hand. And knew I had guessed right. Even crushed as it was by its impact into the wall, the round-nosed piece of lead I held in my hand was, nevertheless, a bullet.

"And what might you be looking for?"

I jumped and, turning, saw Miss O'Toole standing in the

doorway, watching me suspiciously. My hand tightened around the bullet, and I restrained a nervous impulse to hide it behind my back. "I . . . I was admiring the paneling."

Disdainfully she rejected the lie. "If it's the priest hole you're looking for, there's no need. The family no longer keeps anything of value there."

Light-fingered, like her mother, were the unspoken words between us and I felt my face flame with indignation and embarrassment. Curiosity, however, overcame pride and I said, "You know how to open the door then?"

"It's no great secret." She crossed the room to where I stood and pressed a corner piece of paneling that edged the fireplace flue. The small paneling swung open enough for me to see a knotted rope hanging inside. She pulled at the rope and a section of the wall slid open behind me, exposing a small empty room, not much larger than a closet but big enough for a man to stand inside, if he didn't mind being cramped. Quickly Miss O'Toole pulled the rope again and the door, creaking noisily, slid shut.

"If you're satisfied," she said, her eyes raking my face, enjoying my discomfort, "I'll be about my business."

She had almost reached the door when I recovered my composure enough to ask: "Miss O'Toole, has this room ever been used as a gun room?"

She turned, surprised, momentarily thrown off guard. "Never. Until the day Lady Fletcher moved to the dower house, it was always the family chapel. Then it was a sitting room until your brother decided he was too grand to share the estate office with Mr. Sean and had to have an office of his own."

"My brother chose all the furnishings?"

"That he did, had to pick out everything himself, nothing else would suit him."

"The rug too?"

Miss O'Toole's thin lips almost disappeared into an aggrieved frown. "No, not the rug," she admitted grudgingly. "One of the maids spilled ink all over the rug he picked out. I had another one brought down from the attic to take its place."

I dimly remember Rose's mentioning the ruined rug. "That was the day my brother was killed, wasn't it, the day the ink was spilled on the rug?" I asked slowly.

"That it was, and I sacked Bridget Murphy the same day for her clumsiness. A perfect ruin the rug was and nothing could be done with it. I tried everything I could . . ."

"I'm sure you did, Miss O'Toole," I said, my voice placating. "Running a house the size of Abbey Court must be a very difficult job."

"That it is, and each year the girleens going into service are lazier and more dim-witted than the last." Mollified, she relented enough to add, "If it's guns you're after, the case is kept in the library under lock and key. Her ladyship would never allow them in the house otherwise." The housekeeper scowled darkly in sudden memory. "Only your brother, when he took over this room, always kept a gun in the desk, though why a decent, God-fearing man should . . ."

I had half turned toward the desk when she said sharply, "You'll not be finding it there now. After he died, I cleaned out everything in the room that belonged to your brother and gave it all to Miss Regan." Suspicion began to congeal on the housekeeper's face as she eyed me. "And if you have any more questions, you'll be after asking her, not me," she finished flatly.

I doubted if my sister-in-law would be any more co-operative than Miss O'Toole was in answering my questions —if anything, Regan seemed to go out of her way to avoid my presence. Nevertheless that evening I made a point of joining the family in the dining room for dinner. Usually the evening meal at Abbey Court was not well attended, but this evening I was lucky. Everyone was at table with the exception of Cormac Fletcher and Lord Fletcher. Lady Fletcher murmured an apology for Kevin's absence. "A slight indisposition, he's subject to chills, you know, like his father."

I thought it more likely that Kevin's indisposition was an aversion to facing Regan across the dining table, after the scene we had witnessed in the glade that afternoon. My sister-in-law never looked more beautiful than she did that evening. Her eyes shone softly, her skin glowed, and she spoke to me in a friendlier fashion than usual. "How did you enjoy your ride today, Meg?" she asked gaily. "I saw the stableboys rubbing down Lady Jane and Kevin's mare, so I assumed you two had been off somewhere together."

There was a teasing note in her voice, as if intimating that my ride with Kevin had had a slightly illicit air about it.

"It was very pleasant, thank you," I replied, and couldn't resist adding a barb. "It's lovely in the woods this time of the year."

The color in her face heightened as she glanced at me sharply, then she gave a careless shrug. "How anyone could enjoy riding Lady Jane, I'll never know. It must be like riding a rocking chair. We must see to your getting a better mount. I'll ask Mr. Flaherty to find something more suitable. He might even give you a few riding lessons."

Sean, who had been the last to join us at the table, interrupted curtly. "Brian Flaherty has more important things to do than give riding lessons, Regan. As a matter of fact, has it never occurred to you that your riding with him every day interferes with his regular duties, not to mention causing talk in the neighborhood?"

Regan frowned indifferently. "Oh, the old gossips will always talk about something. And my riding alone wouldn't be proper either." She gave her brother a spiteful glance. "The trouble with you, Sean, is that your nose is out of joint because you've lost your riding companion to Kevin."

Sean's face reddened and their aunt spoke quickly. "Children . . . children. There will be no quarreling at the table. But Sean is right, Regan. I have been meaning to speak to you about your daily rides with Mr. Flaherty. After all, it isn't as if he were a member of the family." Then, before the petulance in Regan's face blew up into a full-scale storm Lady Fletcher changed the subject hastily. "Did you stop by Major Gill's this afternoon, Regan? Was there any news?"

Regan subsided sulkily. "There was just talk about those Moonlighters who stopped Lord Kendrick's process server on the Abbeymore Road."

"The poor man, he wasn't killed?" Lady Fletcher asked anxiously.

Regan suddenly giggled. "No, they stripped him of his clothes and burned them, along with the eviction papers he carried, and sent him on his way, stark naked. Of course, the next day armed constables arrived and turned the families out anyway, though they had to fight their way through a crowd to do it. You can be sure Parnell will be complaining loud and long in Parliament about the immorality of Irish landlords when he hears of it." She sniffed disdainfully. "As if that gentleman has any right to talk about morality."

"What do you mean?" I asked, giving Regan a surprised glance. "We've always heard in America that Mr. Parnell's character was above reproach."

"Well then, you Americans are a naïve lot," Regan

laughed. "It's common knowledge in Dublin that Mr. Parnell is keeping a woman named Kitty O'Shea and that she had his baby while he was in prison, for all that she's married to another man. Fortunately, the child died at birth."

"I don't believe it!" I said, shocked.

"Oh, it's true enough," Sean said grimly, "although what a man's private life has to do with his ability and competence as a leader, I wouldn't be knowing. One thing is certain. Once the gossip about Parnell's paramour becomes public property, all the fine people and priests who called Parnell Ireland's savior will turn upon him and tear him to pieces."

"Naturally the Church cannot condone adultery, Sean." Lady Fletcher's face was outraged. Then, glancing at the butler and maid, she added a warning: "A dinner table is, in any case, not the proper place to discuss such a subject."

So, although I would have liked to hear more on the subject, the rest of the meal was spent on topics of conversation sufficiently innocuous to please even the countess. As we left the table, however, I hurried after Regan, catching up with her on the upper gallery landing by the portrait of Rosaleen O'Neill Fletcher.

"May I speak to you for a minute, Regan? It's about the gun Patrick left me in his will."

"You really do insist upon having your last pound of flesh, don't you?" she asked, her cheeks flushing. "Isn't it enough that Patrick gave you everything that should by rights have been mine?"

I decided this wasn't the polite moment to mention that, in spite of her less than circumspect behavior, Patrick hadn't left her penniless. Instead I said mildly, "It's just that the gun has a sentimental attachment for me. The silver used in the engraving came from the first load of silver Jamie took from the Silver Lady Mine."

She tossed her head impatiently. "Oh, very well. I haven't any use for it anyhow."

I followed her down a side hall which was in the opposite wing from my room. I had already learned that Sean's room was at the extreme end of this wing but the rest of the bedrooms, except for Regan's, were empty. When I walked into my sister-in-law's rooms, I couldn't resist staring around curiously. Regan had left me standing in a small sitting room but I could glimpse through a half-open door a lushly decorated bedroom. She had chosen a red velvet bedspread, there were gold tassels at the scarlet damask window curtains, and a black lacquer Chinese Chippendale dressing table was covered untidily with a multitude of bottles and discarded jewelry. A dressing robe lay in a crumpled heap on the floor and several pairs of shoes were scattered by the bed. I tried to imagine Patrick, who had been unusually neat for a man, living in such a constant state of confusion and knew why he had made the small study into his own private hideaway.

I could hear Regan rummaging through dresser drawers, and a wardrobe door banging shut. At last she returned with Patrick's gun in her hand. I recognized it instantly. Jamie had had the "Peacemaker," as it was called, especially made for Patrick, down to the extra-length barrel and the silver engraved grip.

I even knew the size and shape of the bullets that were hand-molded for the gun. And unless there was another Colt .45 at Abbey Court, I would swear the bullet I had found in the study wall came from the revolver Regan now held in her hand.

20

I hadn't realized I had been staring at the gun without speaking until Regan impatiently thrust it into my hands. "This is the gun Patrick wanted you to have, isn't it? I'm afraid you'll have to do without the watch mentioned in the will. Patrick was wearing it the day he died. The watch wasn't found afterward. I suppose the men who murdered him stole it."

"Yes, this is the gun." It was the first time I had heard that Patrick's body had been robbed. Somehow this did not seem to fit, yet what was more logical than that a murderer should also be a thief?

I shifted the revolver awkwardly into my left hand and let it hang by my side. Regan did not ask me to sit down and I was clearly not expected to stay. But it was the first time my sister-in-law and I had been alone together since I had arrived at Abbey Court. I felt as if there were things that should be said between us, only after the scene I had glimpsed by the stream that afternoon, I wasn't sure how to begin.

"I understand Patrick kept this gun in the study," I said hesitantly.

"How did you . . . ?" Regan stopped and smiled thinly. "Of course, the servants. I had no idea Americans had such a love of backstairs gossip. I suppose if the servants told you that, it must be true. I haven't any idea where Patrick kept the gun. I haven't laid eyes on it since, let me see . . . since our honeymoon."

"Patrick took a gun with him on his honeymoon?" I asked, surprised.

"Patrick gave me a diamond necklace and matching teardrop earrings for a wedding present," Regan explained. "I was worried about traveling with such valuable pieces. Patrick told me not to be concerned and showed me the gun. Then in Paris he bought me an emerald necklace that matched a gown I had made at Worth's. I wore it the night Patrick took me to Maxim's." She laughed in memory, her eyes sparkling. "Naturally, Patrick didn't want to take me there. He said it wasn't proper, but I insisted. The man at the next table thought I was a *cocotte* and flirted with me so outrageously that Patrick was furious with me. Of course, we made up later. Patrick's tempers never did last long. And after that we went to Venice and Rome . . ."

There was a tenderness in Regan's voice, a softness in the curve of her mouth, as she spoke of her honeymoon. Had she loved Patrick then? I wondered. Or had it all been a pose from the beginning?

"And then you came back to Abbey Court?" I prodded gently.

The glow faded, the petulant look returning, pulling down the corners of her mouth. With age, I thought, staring at my sister-in-law, those lines would finally deepen into a perpetual ugly frown of discontent. "Yes, we came back. Patrick grew tired of traveling. He was anxious to return to Abbey Court. So we returned . . . and everything changed."

"Changed? How?"

Regan paused, as if she was sorry she had spoken, then she smoothed her skirt carefully. "Patrick found other interests," she said at last.

Another woman . . . Patrick? "I don't believe it," I blurted.

She read my face and shook her head scornfully. "No, not another woman. I could have managed that. It was Abbey Court. Patrick was obsessed with the house, the estate, and he made everyone furious with him for stirring up the tenants. And if he wasn't quarreling with Sean and Father about the tenants, he was digging around in the Abbey. He no longer had any time for me. He even started sleeping in the next room." She shrugged disdainfully, her eyelashes making dark half-moons on her cheeks. "But by then it no longer mattered. I had found other interests too."

"Brian Flaherty?"

The contempt in my voice made the color rush to Regan's face. "How undemocratic you are, my dear sister-in-law," she jeered lightly. "What's so much more degrading about the son of a tinker than the son of a bogtrotter and kitchen-maid turned thief and traitor?"

What happened next, I think, shocked me even more than it did Regan. With the open palm of my right hand I slapped my sister-in-law soundly across the flushed cheek. The sound of the blow echoed and re-echoed in the tiny sitting room.

I knew I should apologize at once. I had behaved childishly, no matter the provocation. Regan had every right to be furious with me. Oddly enough, though, my brother's widow didn't seem to be angry.

Absently she rubbed her cheek where I had struck her and gazed at me through lowered eyes. For a moment I saw her resemblance to her brother Sean, the tightly curbed anger somehow making it more formidable.

Then she smiled sweetly, her voice low and amused. "I think, Meg O'Brien, you're going to be even sorrier than your brother that you ever came to Abbey Court."

With a graceful flourish, she walked around me to open the door. She held it open and waited. There seemed nothing I could say that would make any difference. I walked out and the door closed very quietly behind me.

Once in the hall, I took a deep breath, trying to quiet an uneasy panic that made my heart race. It was foolish to be frightened of a young girl like my sister-in-law. What could she possibly do to hurt me? She might be snappish and disagreeable and try to make my life uncomfortable here at Abbey Court, but then she'd always done that.

Still clutching Patrick's revolver—half hidden against the fold of my skirt in case anyone should come along the passageway and see me—I made my way back to my room. Rory was overjoyed at my arrival, but I had no time to play with him, despite his blandishments of bringing me his favorite bone. Going to the wardrobe, I reached to the top shelf and retrieved the cambric shirt and the smashed bullet, placed them and the silver-plated gun side by side on the bed.

Heaven knows, it was little enough to go on to track down a murderer. I couldn't even be sure if the three items could be tied together at all. Yet somehow I was sure there was a connection. The conviction was growing stronger within me that it was no Moonlighter, no chance stranger, who had taken Patrick's life.

I picked up the revolver and the bullet and held them under the gas lamp so I could examine them more closely. There was no doubt in my mind that the bullet I had dug from the wall panel in the study had come from a Colt .45. I would check the Fletcher gun case in the morning but, though the Colt was a popular gun in America, I doubted if one had found its way to Abbey Court and the possession of the Fletcher family.

Of course, it was possible that Patrick himself had accidentally fired the gun within the study. Possible, but not probable. Patrick was too experienced in handling guns, particularly the Colt, to have it go off accidentally. I examined the gun more closely and saw with a rising excitement that the cylinder still held a spent cartridge, and the interior of the gun barrel a gummy residue. Whoever had fired the revolver last had been in too much of a hurry to reject the spent cartridge or to clean the gun after firing. Patrick had been well taught by Jamie to clean a gun carefully after each use, particularly a gun he prized as highly as this one.

But if Patrick had not fired the revolved, then who had?

I was still pondering the question as I undressed for bed. I didn't ring for Rose to come and assist me, although as I gave Rory a good night pat and climbed between the sheets I decided that I could have used a soothing cup of Rose's camomile tea. I suspected that sleep would not come easily that night.

To my surprise, though, I slept with such soundness that I overslept the next morning and awoke to the sound of rain tapping at the windows, followed promptly by Rose's quiet knocking at the door.

The girl didn't seem depressed by the gray day, and her voice was cheerful as she helped me dress. "A fine soft day it is, miss."

I thought it an unpleasant wet day but had already discovered that the Irish viewed their weather in a more philosophical light than I did. I hurried through breakfast but when I reached the office Sean was already hard at work. As I passed through the hall and entered the office I wrinkled my nose at the faint, offensive odor in the air.

Sean looked up from the account books and caught my expression. "It's the kitchen drains," he said. "They always smell their worst on days like this. They should have been cleaned out months ago but unless you can find some money in the household accounts . . ."

A week before, I had secured, over Miss O'Toole's protests, the household account books. "I'm sure you'll find them in order," she said defensively. "There's no one that dares say Molly O'Toole touches a penny that's not her own."

I assured her that her honesty was not in question. I simply wanted to become acquainted with the costs of running the house. What I had discovered left me stunned. I had thought it expensive to maintain the house on Beacon Hill, but the costs of running a huge old mansion like Abbey Court—with its dozens of servants, its never ending need for repairs, not to mention the expense of the pleasure stable and Kevin's flat in Dublin and town house in London —made the expenses of the Beacon Hill house pale in comparison.

I pulled the household account book toward me unhappily. "Perhaps if we let a few of the servants go," I murmured, yet I dreaded the thought, knowing how important even a small-paying job was to the very survival of the men and women in service at Abbey Court.

I glanced up to discover that Sean was leaning back in his chair, watching me. He smiled ruefully and said, "I hate to admit it, Meg O'Brien, but I was wrong about you. I thought that after a few days you'd be bored with all the account work that comes with managing the estate. Your brother certainly was. I never could get him to spend more than ten minutes looking over the ledgers or trying to make sense of them. In fact, I can't recall his spending more than a half hour in this office in all the time he was at Abbey Court."

As always when Patrick was criticized, I felt myself bristling protectively, even though I suspected that Sean was telling the truth. Patrick would find working with figures dull, and I couldn't see all his nervous energy, his seeking, restless mind, being chained for hours at a time to account books.

"I've been told my brother preferred using the small study as his office," I said.

Sean nodded grimly. "At least, there, he didn't smell the drains, or the tenants coming straight from the fields with the manure on their boots and their clothes not washed in weeks."

"Patrick wasn't a snob," I protested at once.

"No, he wasn't," Sean unexpectedly agreed. "If anything, he leaned too far in the other direction. All the tenants knew they could go to him with a hard-luck story and your brother would have his hand in his pocket before they were finished."

"What's wrong with that?" I demanded stiffly. "Charity isn't a crime."

"No, to be sure, charity fills the stomach," Sean acknowledged. "Unfortunately, it does little to stiffen a man's spine. Patrick and I had a little discussion on that point once. I don't think I convinced him." He smiled wryly. "Your brother was a very stubborn man, about many things."

"Did you see Patrick, the day he was killed?" I hadn't expected to ask that question, and found myself waiting, almost fearfully, for Sean's reply.

"I talked with him for a few minutes in his study." I saw the amusement in his glance. "I'm surprised you haven't learned that already from the servants."

I flushed, the jab hitting too close to home for comfort. "Is that when he asked if he could borrow your horse?" I tried to make my voice casual, but I saw Sean stiffen warily.

"I don't recall the subject coming up at all. Why do you ask?"

"Doesn't it seem strange to you that Patrick would borrow your horse without asking your permission?"

He shrugged indifferently. "I never thought about it, one way or the other. He'd often admired my roan. I told him he could borrow the mare whenever he wanted. Your brother was an excellent horseman."

"Then you saw him take your horse that morning?"

Now I didn't mistake the sharpness edging Sean's voice. "How could I, sitting here at this desk with my back to the window? I didn't realize the horse was gone until word was brought at lunch that she's come back to the stable without a rider." A brittleness descended over Sean's face, as if he were finding my questions as distasteful as I had found the odor from the drains. "Now if you haven't any more questions, perhaps you won't mind if I get back to work."

Oh, I had more questions, I thought, staring rebelliously at the bent head, the crisp black hair, remembering only too vividly the feel of those wiry curls beneath my fingers. I wanted to know what Sean and Patrick had talked about that last morning, and who else had visited Patrick in the study the day he died, but I knew it was no use questioning Sean. I would have to find out some other way.

After lunch it was still raining so a horseback ride was out of the question. Feeling frustrated and housebound, I wandered into the library to check the gun case. As I had expected, all the guns in the case were British made, mostly large-bore fowling pieces. They would all have used a much larger size ammunition than the bullet I had dug out of the study wall. I was studying the collection when the butler came into the library with a note for me from Kevin, obviously written in haste.

Dearest Maeve,

I have decided to go up to London for a few days. I hate leaving you on such short notice but perhaps it is for the best—to give us both time to think. I am sure you've already sensed that my feelings toward you have grown beyond those of an affectionate friend. I hesitate to say more for fear that you may not share my sentiment or return the deep regard with which I hold you. I would like to believe that I am in your thoughts while I am away, as you will constantly be in mine.

I half smiled at the stilted language, even as I felt a faint stirring of guilt. I suppose I had realized that Kevin's feelings toward me these last day had changed and deepened. Hadn't I perhaps even encouraged him? It had been reassuring, if selfish on my part, to know that he was there to turn to if I needed him; flattering to feel that when I was with him it didn't matter that I wasn't slim and elegant and beautiful. But it had never occurred to me to think any further. After all, Kevin wasn't just any young man to come courting. His son would be the eleventh Earl of Abbeymore and his wife would be the Countess of Abbeymore. A thought slipped wickedly through my mind. Wouldn't the first families of Boston be set back on their heels if Fiona O'Brien's snubbed and rejected daughter came home a countess?

"Was there an answer?" Jeremiah stood waiting, patiently.

"No, no answer." I folded the note and slipped it into my skirt pocket. Returning to the front hall, I hesitated, uncertain what to do next to occupy my time. Then I remembered that I had not yet visited the ballroom on the top floor of Abbey Court, and I decided this was as good a day as any to explore.

The staircase to the top floor of the house was not as grand as the richly ornamented stairs from the entrance hall to the gallery. Perhaps the original builders of Abbey Court had begun to run out of money and started cutting costs. Whatever the reason, the plain straight chairs didn't prepare me for the long empty room that met my eye when I reached the ballroom landing.

Even empty of furniture, the elaborate Italianate plastered ceiling, the French crystal chandeliers, and the parquet floor spoke clearly of money having been poured into creating this ballroom. A marble fireplace stood at either end of the room but their hearths had a swept-clean, untouched look about them. In fact, the whole room appeared neglected, as if it had not been used in years. The windows needed washing, the parquet floor was dull, a piece of plaster from the ceiling littered the floor—and yet . . . I frowned, puzzled. The room to my mind had a familiar feel about it. It was as if I knew exactly how it would look: the floor and windows would be polished and gleaming, the candles lit . . .

Had Mother ever described the room to me? I couldn't remember. I did recall her saying that you could see the Irish Sea on a clear day from the Abbey Court ballroom. Had she spent much time here, I wondered, the pretty young maid who had once been more than a servant but much less than a family member? Had she watched from some secluded corner the balls held in this room, the women in their shimmering gowns, their jewels dazzling, and vowed that some day she would wear such gowns and jewels?

I drew in my breath sharply. All at once I understood

why the room had seemed familiar. On a smaller scale, Mother had built an identical ballroom on the third floor of our Beacon Hill mansion. How could I ever forget the night of my coming-out party when I had stood at the doorway, squeezed into a white satin and ninon gown two sizes too small, wearing too many jewels, and my stomach tied into knots. I could still feel the smile frozen on my face as I had clumsily tried to make conversation with the fringes of Boston society, with the young men Mother and Patrick had coaxed and bribed into attending. I had almost hated Mother before that evening finally, mercifully ended.

Pushing the memory back into a corner of my mind, I walked quickly down the long room, my footsteps echoing hollowly in the emptiness. As I passed the row of uncurtained, arched windows, the gray slanting rain seemed to reach into the room itself, as if I were walking through the murky depths of the sea.

I stopped at the last window. From here I could glimpse, just barely through the wall of rain, the screen of lime and ash and beech trees curving in a graceful semicircle toward the front of the house. It must have been from those trees, I thought, that the attackers had crept up to Abbey Court, and perhaps at this very window that Michael Fletcher, Fiona, and the few remaining servants had silently watched their approached through the gathering dusk. What had Fiona felt then, I wondered—fear, grief, self-reproach? Yet even if she had given the warning to Michael, there would have been no need for her to name names. And in the shadowy darkness at this distance, the faces of the men couldn't have been visible to the watchers. But someone had placed names to those faces, so that the authorities had been able to round them up one by one and hang them one by one.

I stepped back from the window, feeling suddenly chilled. Goose flesh prickled my arms. All at once Abbey Court, with all its windows, seemed too open. There were no sheltered nooks to keep out bad dreams and terrible memories, there was no safe place to hide.

Leaving the ballroom quickly, I returned to the ground floor and to the one room in which I always felt comforted. At least in the little study there were no curtainless windows with a depressing view of gray skies and soughing rain. The damp cold, though, had even crept in here, and I knelt before the fireplace, poking a small peat fire into burning more briskly.

Rose found me huddling there by the fireplace, trying to warm myself. She took one look at my face and said, "It's a nice hot cup of tea you're wanting. The day's turned awkward."

She returned with a tea tray and thin slices of fruitcake. I sipped the tea gratefully, and then, remembering, asked slowly, "You were in the dining room, weren't you, Rose, that last morning? Do you remember if anyone visited my brother here in the study?"

Under the small mobcap of white muslin she always wore, her forehead furrowed thoughtfully. "I can't be saying for sure. There was Mr. Sean. I remember because he looked like he was in a rare temper and never a word to me as he passed."

"No one else?"

She thought again and shook her head. "Mind you, I wasn't here the whole time. Some of the others cleaning the drawing room might have noticed the comings and goings. Myself, I had my hands full, what with Miss O'Toole in an uproar and then, later, storming at poor Bridget over the spilled inkstand and the poor lass beside herself, swearing she never so much as touched the ink."

"Did you believe her?"

Rose nodded firmly. "Bridget Murphy would not lie if the good Lord himself asked her to."

"Then it must have been one of the other ser—"

My voice broke off. The teacup I was holding dropped from my hand, hit the edge of the table, and shattered into a dozen pieces, like bits of eggshell, at my feet.

As if it were happening this very moment before my eyes, I saw Patrick die. Not ambushed on a back road but in this room, shot at close range with his own revolver, the bullet passing through his body and burying itself in the paneled wall, his body flung backward at the impact, then crumpling, slowly, to the floor. And the final horror of all—the body dragged from this room and the inkwell hastily spilled to cover the telltale blood that must have stained the rug where Patrick lay.

21

"Are you all right, miss?" Rose knelt beside me, picking up the pieces of broken china from the carpet. "You look as if you've caught a chill."

I took a shaky breath. I felt as if I had been wrenched back from a different time, a different scene. It was difficult to focus my eyes and thoughts on Rose. "I'm sorry about the cup," I said mechanically.

"Don't be troubling yourself," Rose said cheerfully. " 'Tis only second best china."

I got slowly to my feet. "I think you may be right, Rose. I do feel—chilled."

Not chilled, I thought, rubbing my arms with my hands. My blood felt frozen in my veins, as if all the heat had drained from my body and I would never feel warm again.

Rose bustled ahead of me up the stairs, lighting a fire in my bedroom fireplace. When I refused to get into bed she insisted upon wrapping me in an afghan and placed a hot stoneware bottle at my feet. She was equally insistent that I have dinner on a tray in my room, saying, "Not one of the family will be at table anyway. Her ladyship won't come out on a day like this and Mr. Sean has gone to pick up Miss Regan from the Gills', so she won't be alone on the road after dark."

She hovered over me as I picked at the cold roast beef she had brought me, and an apple tart covered in thick, clotted cream. Fortunately she didn't notice as I surreptitiously fed most of the beef to Rory, who was half hidden under the afghan at my feet.

Finally she left, taking Rory with her for his nightly run. I had been waiting impatiently for her to leave but, once she was gone, I wished she was back. For the moment the door closed behind her silence settled around me and pictures crowded into my head. One picture in particular.

As a child—I couldn't have been more than eight or nine years old—I had seen a miner shot down by his partner in a sudden drunken rage. I will never forget the look in the man's eyes, not anger, or pain, but a childish look of surprise, the muscles of the face slackening into a grotesque emptiness. Had that same look of stunned disbelief filled Patrick's face for that split second before he fell, mortally wounded, to the floor? And Patrick's murderer—what had he felt? How had he looked, staring down at my brother? What expression had filled his face?

Shivering, I drew the afghan more closely around me. Perhaps I was wrong, I thought hopefully. Perhaps what I imagined had died as they said, ambushed on a back-country road. For if my brother had been killed in the small study, then his murderer could not be a stranger but someone with easy access to Abbey Court, whose presence in the house would not be questioned. Someone who had visited Patrick in the study that last morning . . .

Sean! Quickly I rejected the thought. After all, even if Sean had been seen going into Patrick's study, he wasn't the only one in the house that morning. Or the only person who resented Patrick's presence at Abbey Court. There was Cormac, who had wanted Patrick away from Abbey Court perhaps even more than his son did. And even a man in a wheel chair can aim and fire a gun.

Then there were the O'Tooles, brother and sister, who had never forgiven Fiona for their brother's death. The gamekeeper could come and go freely at Abbey Court, and there was no doubt the housekeeper had been very much in evidence in the house that morning. It was Miss O'Toole, also, who had discovered the ink stains on the study rug and blamed the housemaid, Bridget. She could just as easily have spilled the ink herself to cover the bloodstains on the rug

Nor could I forget Regan and the studmaster. Patrick alive, must have been an inconvenience and a worry to the two of them, but as a wealthy widow Regan could have both her freedom and her lover. Brian Flaherty had already told me he had spent the morning at the stable, which meant he could have slipped into the house without anyone noticing. And Regan, I remembered, according to Major Gill, had not stayed with his daughter Mindy and the major when they rode that morning. Regan's horse had supposedly thrown a shoe and she had had to return to Abbey Court.

It occurred to me that even Kevin, in a way, would

have benefited from Patrick's death. It was actually Lord Fletcher who was in debt to Patrick for the large sum of money my brother had lent the estate. If Patrick were dead and Regan inherited his estate, as everyone had assumed she would, the debt to all intents and purposes would have been wiped out. And Kevin, too, had been at Abbey Court that morning. At least, he had appeared at the luncheon table.

Shamefaced, I rose to my feet and, tugging the afghan around me to keep from stumbling over it, began to pace up and down before the fireplace. What was I doing? Wasn't it despicable enough that I was deliberately labeling one of the Fletchers, or their servants, a murderer, without including Kevin? Of all the Fletchers, he was the only one who had been genuinely, deeply grieved at Patrick's death. I should as well suspect Lady Fletcher. . . .

When Rose returned with Rory a half hour later I was standing staring, without seeing, out the bedroom window. She touched my forehead gently but her voice was scolding. "Why, you're feverish, Miss Meg. You should have been in bed long ago."

Meekly, I let her help me out of my dress into my nightclothes and sipped obediently at the camomile tea she brought, which had an oddly bitter taste.

" 'Tis only a bit of quinine to cool a fever," the maid said firmly.

At the door she hesitated. "You're sure now you won't be wanting me? I was going over to Mike McCarthy's wake, but there'll be a grand crowd there and they won't be missing me."

"No, run along. All I need is a good night's rest and I'll be fine," I assured her.

I turned down the lamp beside the bed but the room was still not completely dark. The long Irish twilight had taken on a misty blue tone, half day, half night. I heard a heron cry down by the lake but sounding so near that the mournful cry seemed to be in the room with me, quivering in the air, like the keening I had heard at the gatehouse the day I arrived at Abbey Court.

I closed my eyes, determinedly, trying to put the scene in the study out of my mind. I could be mistaken. There could be some simple, logical explanation for the bullet in the wall panel, the fired gun, the spilled inkwell, even the powder-marked shirt. But my mind was too tired to grope any further for answers that lay somewhere, tantalizing, just beyond my reach. And finally I slept.

This time when I awoke, suddenly, in the middle of the night, there was no moment of drowsy confusion. I knew at once what had awakened me. The dark shadowy figure stood beside my bed, hovering like some loathsome black bird of prey. His face was shrouded but it was not his face that caught and held my horrified gaze. It was his hands, holding something pale and plump . . . a pillow. For one split second I remembered Fiona's near death at Mary Shaugnassy's cottage. Perhaps I was meant to remember. Perhaps I was meant to feel that one moment of pure, unadulterated terror, paralyzing me, so that I could not lift my head, much less scream, before the pillow, soft and yielding, smelling faintly, sweetly of lavender, pressed swiftly downward, covering my face.

Even as I was remembering Fiona, though . . . reliving the same heart-stopping fear she must have felt . . . instinct took over and I flailed wildly upward with my hands, trying to force the obstruction away from my face, pushing at arms that, like immovable stone pillars, thrust the pillow down harder over my mouth and nose. I tried to suck in air when there was no air. My throat burned, my lungs ached with the effort. There was a drumming in my ears that was my heart swelling, pounding against my rib cage. But no matter how I fought, the clinging, murderous softness only pressed harder, a dead weight crushing me, suffocating me, forcing me down into a swirling darkness.

Then dimly, blessedly, I realized the weight covering my face had lifted a little. I felt a miraculous trickle of air like a drop of life-giving water run down my seared throat. At the same moment I heard, as if from a great distance, Rory's half bark, half playful snarl as he awakened and dived out from under the bed, attacking a fascinating target. For a moment, as if thrown off guard, the arms pressing the pillow over my face relaxed their pressure. But a second was all I needed.

I flung myself out of the bed. The door to the hall stood open, only a few feet from the bed, but it wasn't a distance that could be measured in feet. It was an endless stretch, an infinity of space to be covered. Every second I was sure the soft, smothering darkness would envelop me again, pulling me back to that lavendar-scented death.

I could hear scuffling noises behind me, an angry, muffled curse, mingled with Rory's excited, happy growling. Then I was through the door and running down the dark hallway.

I tried to scream but my throat was too raw. All that came out was a frightened whimper. At one end of the long gallery, I could see the staircase, palely moonlit from the Venetian glass window at the mid-landing. I plummeted down the steps, tripping in my haste over the hem of my nightgown, staggering, almost falling, and catching myself in time. Then I was in the entrance hall, the cold polished floor burning like ice against my bare feet. The gas lamps on the wall had been extinguished. The only light was the moonglow from the landing, the clumps of furniture making blacker shapes in the darkness. I half turned toward the rear of the hall, to the green baize door leading to the kitchen and servants' quarters, when I heard footsteps on the stairs behind me. I whirled and shrank back against the wall.

The drawing-room door was the nearest one to me, standing open. I darted into the room without thinking, only looking for a place to crawl into and hide. The drawing room was darker than the hall, and I realized my white nightgown would stand out like a flame. Desperately my eyes searched for shelter and found an ornate, overstuffed sofa. I dropped behind it, crouching to the floor to make myself as small as possible. I heard the footsteps come to the threshold of the room, then hesitate. Suddenly I heard another sound, a quick, softly bumping noise down the stairs, the scampering of paws over a hardwood floor. The darkness was no barrier to Rory. Within a matter of seconds he had sought me out, found me, as if he were playing a game of hide-and-seek. He gave small, ecstatic yipes of triumph as he bounded behind the sofa, thrusting his soft nose into my hand to be petted for his cleverness. Helplessly, I tried to silence him, but it was too late.

As if Rory were a magnet, the footsteps began again, moving suowly, inexorably directly toward the sofa. Despairingly I closed my eyes, waiting, unable even to scream. The footsteps came to the sofa and stopped. Nothing happened. I could feel the clammy chill of death like an ice-cold hand caress my face, then pass by. The sound of the footsteps continued again, more quickly now, down the long drawing room. Then I heard, far away, another sound, a grating noise that I couldn't at once identify and, after that, silence.

Cautiously I opened my eyes but remained where I was. My body felt stiff, as if my bones would crack and break if I moved. Then the silence was broken again, and I knew then why my assailant had not stayed. I heard it now, too —carriage wheels throwing up gravel, stopping with a jingle of harness before the stone staircase at the edge of the terrace.

I heard a door open and I rose to my knees to see a yawning servant with a lamp in his hand come hurrying through the front hall. He unbolted and swung open the front door. Slowly, my legs trembling, I pulled myself to my feet, clinging for support to the edge of the sofa.

Through the half-opened drawing-room door I could see Regan, with Sean behind her, walk into the hall, their shadows caught in the lamplight falling before them.

Regan's voice was irritable. "I don't know why we had to come home just because you were bored with Mindy. I'm sure I would have won that last hand if—"

Her voice fell away as she stared, speechless, at what must have seemed an apparition suddenly appearing before her in the drawing-room doorway. Over Regan's shoulder I saw Sean's face, at first as startled as his sister's in the lamplight. Then he moved away quickly from the circle of light, his face hidden in the darkness as if the features had suddenly gone blank. I felt him beside me, his arm slipping around my waist, supporting me as he helped me to a chair. "What is it, Meg?" His voice sounded harsh, angry. "What's happened?"

It was painful to speak but I knew I must. There might still be time to catch the man. "In my room . . . someone . . . tried to kill me . . . followed me down here . . ." My throat was bruised and I spoke in spurts.

Sean turned to the gaping servant. "Bring another lamp and come with me," he ordered.

I saw them move slowly through the room, testing the windows, holding the lamps high to light the corners where a man might be hidden. They disappeared finally into the dining room where I could no longer see them and returned within a few minutes. "You're positive he came in here, Meg?" Sean's face was puzzled now, uncertain.

"I'm positive. He must have gone out one of the windows."

"The windows are all locked on the inside, miss," the servant said, giving me a curious glance.

"There was one open in the dining room," Sean said thoughtfully, "but anyone going out that window would need wings. It's a good fifteen-foot drop to the ground on that side of the house." He turned to the manservant. "You'd better rouse Miss O'Brien's maid."

I grabbed at Sean's hand. "You're going to keep looking, aren't you? He can't have gone far."

Regan had come into the drawing room, putting her hand to her mouth to hide a yawn. "Don't tell me the invisible prowler has struck again." When Sean turned to her, scowling, she tossed her head, annoyed. "Oh, don't look so grim, Sean. Don't you remember? Mindy told us about Meg's imagining there was a man in her room, the night they stayed here. She's had another bad dream, that's all." She smiled archly. "Or perhaps it's just wishful thinking. . . ."

"I didn't imagine it and it wasn't a dream. He put a pillow over my face. He tried to kill me!" I heard my voice rising hysterically.

"How fortunate you managed to escape without a scratch," Regan murmured, her glittering eyes roving skeptically over my unmarked face, my nightgown without a rent or tear.

Sean frowned hesitantly. "Sometimes a dream can seem very real, Meg, even after we awake."

"It wasn't a dream! Why won't you believe me?" I wanted to fling myself at them, to pummel with my fists their cool, disbelieving faces. "If you won't wake the servants and start a search, I will!"

I started for the bellpull by the door but Sean reached out and caught my arm, his voice embarrassed. "For God's sake, Meg, get hold of yourself. If there was someone, he must be gone by now. There's no need to alarm the whole household."

I glared angrily from Sean to Regan. "You want him to get away, don't you? Maybe you even arranged the whole thing!"

I heard Regan take a quick, outraged breath, saw Sean's face stiffen. "That's enough, Meg," he said sharply. "You're upset. You don't know what you're saying."

"And is it an early grave you're wanting, standing around in your bare feet and no robe at all?" Rose hurried into the room, giving Sean a furious glance as if blaming him for my condition.

Sean spoke carefully. "You had better take Miss O'Brien back to her room, Rose. She doesn't seem quite herself."

"And should she be?" she demanded, her voice scolding. "Didn't I put her to bed myself with one of Mary Shaugnassy's potions? You can take one look at Miss Meg's face and see that she's feverish. Warm in her own bed is where she should be."

Sean nodded, as if relieved. "I think Rose is right, Meg. Your face is flushed and your hands are like ice." Before I could open my mouth to protest further he had pulled off his jacket and placed it around my shoulders. "And it's off to bed you're going," he said firmly. Then his arms were around me and I was being lifted, carried through the hall and up the broad staircase. I struggled to free myself but it was as useless as my efforts had been to free myself from the implacable arms that had held the pillow over my face. Only this time, instead of lavender, I was aware of the mixed scent of whisky and tobacco and the scratchy, tweed stuff of Sean's coat.

The minute we crossed the threshold of my room, I saw the pillow lying on the floor by my bed where my attacker must have dropped it. Instantly all those moments of horror returned to terrorize me. I felt again the feathery softness clogging my mouth and nostrils, the painful, burning gasps for breath tearing at my throat. A lightheadedness swept over me, a dread certainty possessing me that the man had not left after all but was still here, waiting in my room, invisible to all but myself.

I am not clear about what happened after that, except I know I behaved very badly. I screamed and fought like a wild woman, striking out at Rose and Sean, who were trying to hold me down on the bed. Then someone was forcing some bitter black concoction down my throat and a feeling of listlessness took hold of me, a weakness that brought tears streaming soundlessly down my face. I no longer struggled or made any outcry and finally, exhausted, I slept.

22

For the next two days I suffered a minor recurrence of the congestion of the lungs that had sent me to my bed immediately after my mother's funeral. I had the same high fever and sudden chills, then the headache and deep cough that remained with me for several days after the fever finally broke. I was vaguely aware that a doctor, a gruff-voiced man smelling of peppermints, had been sent for but it was Rose who apparently stayed by my bedside the whole time. And it was Rose's face I first saw when I opened my eyes the third morning and found her slumped, half asleep, in a chair by my bed.

When I stirred, she came awake instantly. As she leaned over the bed to tuck the covers more tightly around me, I saw the faint black and blue mark on her cheek. "Did I do that?" I asked, mortified.

She clucked indifferently. "I've had worse. It was the fever making you act so wildlike, the doctor says."

She was talking too rapidly, carefully avoiding looking directly at me. I understood. So it was the fever being blamed for my erratic behavior, for my showing up downstairs in my nightclothes in the middle of the night, making outlandish accusations.

I only wished I believed it had been the fever, I thought unhappily. What a blessed relief it would have been to discover that the man who had tried to smother me had been only a figment of my delirium, not an actual person. The memory, though, was still too clear in my mind. Nothing would convince me that those few terrifying minutes had never happened, that if it hadn't been for Rory . . .

All at once I realized the dog wasn't in the room and I asked, suddenly fearful, "Where's Rory? Is he all right?"

"Sure and he's fine," Rose assured me. "I've been keeping him down in my room. I'll bring him up as soon as you've taken a little broth. And her ladyship is anxious to see you when you're feeling stronger. She's been that worried about you."

It was another day before I felt well enough for visitors, except for Rory, who, sensing that something was wrong, lay quietly beside my bed, thumping his tail occasionally against the floor to let me know he was there. And, as it turned out, my first visitor was not Lady Fletcher but Sean.

Upon his entrance, Rose curtsied quickly and left. I noticed, however, that she carefully left the door ajar several inches and, with her low opinion of the black Irish, I didn't doubt but what she was hovering not far from the door, in case I should need her.

"How are you feeling today?" Sean asked, standing with his feet braced, his voice a little too hearty.

"Much better," I said, and stifled the stab of vanity that made me pleased that for a change Sean wasn't seeing me in drab black. I wore a white ruffled bed jacket and Rose had brushed my hair that morning and tied it back loosely with a blue ribbon. Then, remembering my last metting with Sean, I felt a flood of color rush into my cheeks. "I believe I owe you an apology."

"Don't mention it," Sean said. He rubbed his jaw reflectively and grinned. "Not that you don't have a strong right uppercut that would put James Leary himself to shame." He studied my face approvingly. "I'm pleased to see you looking so fine."

"I should be up and about in a day or two."

"Well now, there's no great hurry about that." He pulled a chair to the side of the bed and sat down. Rory immediately came to him, rolling over on his back, so that Sean could rub absently at his stomach with the toe of his boot. "I've been thinking it might do you a world of good to get away from Abbey Court for a while. I understand this is your first trip abroad. It seems a shame to spend all your time here in Ireland before you return home."

I straightened, eying him suspiciously. "I wasn't aware that I was going home."

"Not immediately, of course, but then I don't suppose you were planning on staying here in Ireland indefinitely, were you? After all, your roots are still in America. Or were you thinking of giving up your American citizenship?"

"Of course not!" I frankly hadn't thought that far ahead, although I suppose I had always realized that, despite my finacial interest in Abbey Court, I was still a guest here, not a permanent lodger. "It's just that under the terms of my brother's will . . ."

Sean interrupted quickly. "I'm sure your solicitor, Mr. Corcoran, would agree that you're entitled to a holiday away from your duties, the same as anyone else. You've been under a great strain these last weeks. It's no wonder that you—" He broke off, looking embarrassed.

"I did not imagine that someone tried to kill me," I said, setting my chin stubbornly. "And if you had sent a search party out right away, the way I wanted, the man might have been caught. You said yourself, the dining-room window was open."

"I looked very carefully under that window the next morning, Meg," Sean said. "If the man didn't break a leg making a jump like that, he'd have certainly left his footprints behind. There were none at all."

"He *was* there. I saw him walk by me. I didn't imagine it."

"And out through the wall, no doubt," Sean finished, leaning back in his chair so that it was balanced precariously on two legs. "Anyway it's all over with now. We can forget about it."

"The same way everyone's forgotten about finding Patrick's murderer," I said bitterly.

A muscle in Sean's cheek jerked. "Your brother was killed by assassins on a deserted road. It was a terrible tragedy to be sure, but that's all it was. In God's name, why can't you accept his death for what it was, instead of trying to make a great mystery out of it?"

Stung by his anger, I felt my own hackles rising and spoke in a heated rush. "Because I don't believe Patrick was killed on a back road! I believe he was shot at close range in the study with his own gun. I found the bullet that killed him in the paneling and saw the powder marks on Patrick's shirt."

Immediately I regretted my outburst. I had had no intention of letting anyone at Abbey Court, particularly Sean, know what I had learned about Patrick's death. At least, not until the appropriate moment arose, and this was hardly that moment.

Sean rose so abruptly that the chair tipped over, falling with a crash to the floor and sending Rory scurrying under the bed. "You can't be serious! It makes no sense at all. If Patrick was shot in the study, then how did his body end up on the Abbey road?" The soft brogue became softer, taunting me. "Or are you thinking that, with all the servants running in and out of the drawing and dining rooms that morning, the murderer simply slung Patrick over his shoulder like a sack of oats and walked out the front door like a grand fool for anyone to see?"

"I don't know how his body got out of the study," I admitted.

"Of course you don't," Sean replied, furious. "Because it never happened that way. Why do you insist on pursuing this futile crusade of yours to find Patrick's murderer? What will it bring you but more grief?"

"Sean! Have you taken leave of your senses?" Lady Fletcher came rustling into the room, her long black gown sweeping the floor. "Miss O'Brien is barely recovered from a serious illness and you're yelling at her so I could hear you down the hall."

Sean shrugged, his voice subsiding to a growl. "I'm sorry, Aunt Margaret, but there are times when Miss O'Brien would try the patience of a saint!" Then he turned and stalked out of the room.

The countess sighed and picked up the chair. "You must forgive Sean, my dear. His temper has always been a terrible burden to him. I prayed that as he grew older . . ." She spread her hands in a delicate gesture of despair. "I hope he didn't upset you."

She sat down, her straight spine carefully not touching the back of the chair, her thin, emaciated hands with their almost transparent skin clasped loosely in her lap.

"We've all been greatly concerned about you," she continued gravely. "As Dr. McBride pointed out, our Irish climate can be particularly dangerous to anyone with weak lungs."

"Please don't worry about me, Lady Fletcher. I'm actually very healthy. It was only a sudden chill coming on top of the"—I paused, wondering how much Kevin's mother knew—"the shock," I finished lamely.

The pale face remained smooth, expressionless, as she spoke. "Sean told me of your experience, that you believe someone tried to kill you by smothering you with a pillow the same way your mother was attacked." A faint crack appeared in the composure, a fissure of curiosity opening. "Can you describe what he looked like?"

Since the countess was the first person to take seriously the fact that I really had been attacked, I was only too happy to oblige. "It was too dark to see him clearly. He was more like a shadow. I never could see his face but I'm sure he wore black—"

Lady Fletcher interrupted sharply. "Like a priest?"

"A priest?" I looked at her bewildered.

She continued eagerly. "You've heard of the holy man who died in the Abbey fire with the other martyrs and the oath of vengeance he took?"

A sudden, preposterous idea took hold of me. "You can't seriously believe that what I saw was some sort of a . . . a spirit?" I stammered.

The blue-white skin had an unpleasant sheen; Lady Fletcher's eyes burned into mine, her voice low. "I know the Holy Church doesn't encourage the belief in spirits of the next world returning to visit this world." She leaned forward and I caught the scent of wax and incense, as if her gown and skin were impregnated with the odor. "But surely if there is divine grace there is also divine retribution. Who are we to say how that retribution shall be exacted? Why not through the unhappy spirits of those who were martyred and most sinned against while they were on earth? What better instrument to take divine vengeance upon the wicked than a man of the cloth?"

"Lady Fletcher!" I had to stop that voice with its undercurrent of a terrible desperate fear of a God who was without mercy or compassion. "I can assure you it wasn't a spirit who tried to kill me. He was very much alive."

She ignored my words, sighing deeply and gazing at me, perplexed. "What I don't understand is, why you? Surely there are others in this house who have sinned more greatly, who deserve God's wrath."

"I don't know why," I said, suddenly, helplessly remembering again the cruel, deliberate strength of those arms pressing the pillow over my face. Why should anyone want me dead? Vengeance for the six men hanged in the square at Abbeymore? The same ancient, long-festering hatred that had cut Patrick down? Or was it something else, some reason I didn't even suspect? Perhaps that was the most frightening thought of all. That someone hated me enough to kill me and I didn't even know why.

The countess must have seen the reflection of her own fear mirrored in my eyes. With an almost physical effort, I saw her pull together the ragged edges of her self-control, her pale marble face once more composing itself into serene lines. "Forgive me, my dear," she said softly. "I've tired you with all my foolish talk. Dr. McBride is right, of course. He sad it was the fever playing tricks on your mind. He suggested that as soon as you were strong enough you should take a holiday, somewhere warm and sunny. The south of France is lovely at this time of year."

She got to her feet and stood beside my bed looking down at me. Seeing her there in her plain black woolen gown, it occurred to me that in the darkness Lady Fletcher could easily resemble my assailant. The thought brought a guilty flush of shame to my face and I said hastily, "You mustn't be concerned about me. I'll be fine in a day or two."

"I do worry," she said, smiling and touching my face lightly. "I feel responsible for you. And I think the best thing for you now is to rest quietly for a few days and then get away from Abbey Court for a while."

After she left I remembered that had been Sean's advice too. Advice or warning? I wondered uneasily.

For several gray, rainy days I remained in my bed, following Lady Fletcher's suggestion, not because of any physical weakness—I felt stronger every day—but a simpler, more cowardly reason. I was afraid. There was no bolt on my bedroom door and I was delighted when Rose, over my feeble protests, insisted upon sleeping on a trundle bed in my dressing room at night. Nevertheless, the numbing fear stayed with me. I awoke with it in the morning and fell asleep with the fear, beside me, at night. Twice I lurched awake in the middle of the night, drenched with perspiration, my throat aching, fighting for breath, as if something black and heavy sat on my chest.

And then one morning I awoke to find the bedroom awash in sunlight so that my eyes squinted against the brightness as against the shimmering glare of the sea. The sunlight not only filled the room but warmed the dark, terror-filled corners of my mind. I got out of bed and, taking a hard look at myself in my dressing-table mirror, didn't like at all what I saw. I could imagine Jamie's annoyance if he could have seen me cowering in my room. "Haven't I taught you better than that, Maeve O'Brien?" he would have roared. "Rabbits hide in burrows. An O'Brien stands up to his enemies."

The trouble was, I thought ruefully, as I insisted, over Rose's objections, that I wanted to dress and have breakfast downstairs, that I didn't know who my enemy was. It was one thing to fight back against the known; it was another to stand up to a faceless stranger who could, unfortunately, be anyone at Abbey Court.

When Miss O'Toole herself served me a late breakfast, muttering darkly all the while about "the cook being destroyed with the labor of preparing meals at all hours," I found myself wondering if there were enough strength in the housekeeper's arms, plump as a partridge's legs, to snuff the life out of me.

After breakfast, when I strolled out toward the stable, I glimpsed Regan and the studmaster standing close together, deep in conversation. They pulled apart immediately they saw me, Regan's mouth dipping in a guilty pout, Brian's dark, satyric face gazing at me with a brooding intensity, much as I had imagined the expression on my attacker's face as he watched me struggle, in vain, against the smothering pillow.

I didn't stop to talk. I nodded a greeting and, returning

to the terrace, rested a moment on the low stone wall. Rory came bounding around a corner of the house, skidding to a stop beside me, and then leaned his head companionably against my knee, as I patted him absently. I had sat there only a few minutes when I had the crawling sensation at the nape of my neck that someone was staring at me. I turned quickly. A curtain in Cormac's bedroom window twitched shut, but not before I glimpsed the dark bulk of Cormac Fletcher seated in his wheel chair at the window.

The sun on my face all at once no longer felt warm, as if a cloud had drifted across the lucent blue sky. I drew Rory closer to me. No matter the wicked life Cormac Fletcher undoubtedly had led, what a terrible fate for a virile, active man, to spend his last days in constant pain, confined to a wheel chair. I could almost sympathize with his frustration; first, scheming so carefully to snare Regan a wealthy, presumably easily managed husband, and then to have his son-in-law attempt to take over the running of Abbey Court, to threaten Cormac himself. It must have been doubly galling, after Patrick was providentially disposed of, to have me appear on the scene and take my brother's place.

I frowned. Now that I thought of it, wasn't it too much of a co-incidence that someone should try to kill me after I had made it clear to Cormac that I would not be seduced into a prearranged marriage with his son? Was it then, I wondered, that Cormac had decided he must devise another way of ridding Abbey Court of my unwelcome presence?

Quickly, I rose to my feet and whistled to Rory, who had wandered away on the scent of a rabbit. He came flying back and we left the front of the house, making our way to the rear area where the fourth wing of the house had stood, before the fire. I passed by the office window and saw Sean at his desk, his back to me. He would be writing figures into an account book and I could picture his forehead knotted in concentration, and his shoulders hunched forward in a small-boy way. It occurred to me that an active man like Sean must dislike the bookkeeping part of his job as much as Patrick had, and I felt all at once guilty that I wasn't there in the office, helping him.

Then I remembered our last meeting and the angry words that had passed between us. I hurried down the back farm road away from Abbey Court. How could I even be sure that Sean wasn't in the conspiracy with his father? Of course, Sean couldn't have visited my room himself, but that didn't mean he couldn't have hired someone else to act in his place. Someone who might already have a grudge to pay against Fiona's daughter.

Rory raced ahead of me down the road and crossed the bridge over the gully that led toward the ruins of the Abbey. At the bridge I hesitated, looking apprehensively back toward the house. Although I had whipped up my courage to leave my bedroom, it was one thing to walk out on an open road in broad daylight and another thing to venture out of sight of the house.

Rory stopped on the far side of the bridge, barking at me impatiently, then darted off into the woods.

"Rory!" Panic stabbed through me as I remembered the traps that Seamus had set for poachers in the woods. If they could mutilate a man, what could they do to one small dog?

I hurried across the bridge and saw to my relief that Rory had not plunged off into the woods but was following the boreen toward the Abbey ruins. By the time I reached the crumbling walls to retrieve him, he had scrambled down among the fallen stones intent on some small prey.

"Rory, come back here," I scolded, but he didn't even look in my direction, digging furiously into a corner of the wall by an empty, arched doorway. I started to climb down into the ruins to retrieve him bodily, then I recalled Kevin's warning about the unsafe condition of the walls and decided it would be more sensible to wait for Rory to grow tired of the hunt.

The walk had tired me more than I realized. I settled myself gratefully on a rock ledge, lulled into a stupor by the warmth of the sun, feeling drowsily content for the first time in days. Still, when I heard a slight rustling sound in the trees before me, I jumped almost instinctively to my feet. My eyes searched the thick underbrush, my heart pounding. It was only some small animal scuttling away through the trees, I told myself, but even as I thought this, I was calling, "Rory!"

A different note in my voice finally caught the dog's attention. He lifted his head, then began climbing up the rocks toward me, setting off a minor rock slide as he did. As soon as he reached the crack in the wall I grabbed him in my arms and ran down the path, not stopping till, flushed and out of breath, I reached the bridge.

Only then, feeling more than a little ridiculous, did I

put Rory down and cast one backward glance toward the Abbey through the dark screen of trees. So much, I thought wryly, for my vaunted O'Brien courage!

23

I walked slowly back to the house, Rory gamboling at my heels, nipping at the hem of my skirt. As soon as I reached the front hall of Abbey Court, however, he disappeared through the baize door leading to the kitchen. Rose had already told me that Rory had managed to become great friends with the cook.

I started up the stairs, then stopped when the library door opened and Lord Fletcher stepped into the hall.

"Kevin, how good to see you!" I was surprised myself at the rush of pleasure I felt, an irrational sense of relief surging through me. Now that Kevin was here, everything would be all right. I hurried down the steps to him. "When did you get back?"

"Not more than a half hour ago." He took my hand, pressing it gently. His pale scholarly face flushed with pleasure at the warmth of my greeting but his eyes searched my own, anxiously. "I'm delighted to see you looking so well. I was away from London, visiting friends, so I didn't get Mother's letter, telling me you were ill, until yesterday. Naturally, I started for Abbey Court at once. Then, when I arrived, your maid told me she didn't know where you were."

I was touched by the concern in his voice at the lines of weariness in his face. For the first time since I had met him, Kevin was not dressed impeccably. His suit was crumpled from travel, as if he hadn't taken time to change before coming to look for me. "I was visiting the Abbey," I explained.

"The Abbey?" He seemed startled. "But why? I mean, should you be walking that far?"

"I'll be perfectly fine," I laughed, "once everyone stops trying to make an invalid out of me."

"Well, you make a ravishing invalid." There was such open admiration in his silvery gray eyes that I felt momentarily flustered, although, due to my illness and the fact that I hadn't had a solid meal in days. I had no doubt I was beginning to resemble the wan pale ladies in Mr. Rosetti's paintings.

He gestured toward the library. "Could we talk for a minute?"

"Of course." I followed him into the room and saw with surprise a bottle of brandy and a half-emptied glass on a silver tray. Following my gaze, Kevin shrugged sheepishly. "I admit it's a little early in the day but a man can be forgiven for needing a touch of liquid courage at a time like this." He closed the door and turned to face me, his voice suddenly worried. "You did get the message I sent you when I left?"

I began to feel ill at ease. "Yes, but I'm afraid I . . ."

He took my hand. "No, don't say anything, not yet. What I have to tell you won't take long. You see, I found out while I was in London that I didn't need any more time to think about us. When Mother sent me word of your illness, I knew then. I had lost Patrick, the best friend I'd ever had. I'm not going to take the chance of losing you too."

When I again tried to speak, he said quickly, "Naturally, I don't expect you to feel the same toward me, not right away. I haven't any illusions about myself. I know I'm not the type to set a young girl's heart fluttering. And I must confess I've found most women bore me with their silly chatter and vapors. Somehow, though, I've felt completely at ease with you from the beginning, and I've sensed you felt the same. I think we could be happy." He smiled wryly. "Once you become accustomed to the idea of being the Countess of Abbeymore, which I admit, at times, will be a blasted nuisance." Watching my face, his expression sobered. A glow of perspiration coated his forehead and a slight stammer jerked at his voice. "Or per . . . perhaps you find the whole idea of . . . marriage to me unattractive."

"Oh no," I protested, embarrassed. I could guess the effort it was costing Kevin to make the proposal, to drop his reserve and leave himself open and vulnerable to rejection. "It's . . . well, everything that's happened these last days. I haven't had time to think about anything else."

He frowned, puzzled. "I saw Sean for a few minutes

when I arrived. He told me what happened the night you became ill. And some wild story about your finding powder marks on Patrick's shirt and a bullet in the wall of the study."

"I did find a bullet!"

"Oh, I believe you," he assured me, picking up his half-finished glass of brandy. "Very likely one of the servants cleaning the study found the gun in the desk and couldn't resist handling it. Then when it went off accidentally, naturally he never told anyone what happened for fear of being sacked. As for the powder marks on the shirt . . ." He shook his head thoughtfully. "I suppose it's possible Patrick wasn't shot from ambush as we thought. He could have been stopped by the men, he could have dismounted and tried to reason with them. It probably never entered his mind that they'd actually shoot him. Then when they left him for dead there on the road, he must have tried to remount his horse but didn't have the strength, which would explain the bloodstains on the saddle."

His eyes filled with pain as he looked at me, his voice was unhappy. "I'm sorry, my dear, but sooner or later you're going to have to face the truth. We'll probably never know exactly how Patrick died."

At his calmly logical explanation for the bullet and the powder marks, I felt a sense of letdown so intense it was like a vast emptiness. I grabbed desperately at my last straw. "And the man who tried to kill me? I suppose you can explain him away too, or do you believe, like your mother, he was some sort of apparition?"

Kevin shrugged uncertainty. "Sean says it was the fever."

"It wasn't the fever. I swear to you he was real."

Kevin spoke softly, thoughtfully. "I imagine he could have been quite real."

I stared at him. "What do you mean?"

He looked away, his face uncomfortable. "I haven't any right saying this, of course, without any proof, but I know Regan. Creeping into your room at night, trying to frighten you, is the sort of childish, malicious prank that she would pull. Not," he added hastily, "that I believe she would have actually meant to harm you. It would just be her way of getting even, for your receiving the lion's share of Patrick's estate."

And for my slapping her? I wondered, remembering the icy look on Regan's face that day in her sitting room. "But Regan couldn't have been the man," I protested. "She was coming up the drive in the carriage when I last saw him in the drawing room."

"Oh, not Regan herself," Kevin said, his voice suddenly explosive. "Brian Flaherty! The man would do anything for Regan, if she so much as crooked her finger at him. If I could prove he was involved in such a cruel hoax . . ." He began to stride, agitated, back and forth. "I should have had Sean get rid of him long ago. He's already made Regan the laughingstock of the county, the way they've been carrying on."

The murderous anger in Kevin's face reminded me of the day he had confronted Sean in the office over the tumbling of the Carmody cottage. It shocked me now as it did then.

"Please, Kevin," I murmured. "It doesn't matter now."

"Of course it matters! When I think of the hell you've been put through . . ." He had stopped before me, and all at once his arms were around me, my head seeming to fit naturally into the curve of his shoulder. Then even more naturally, it seemed, our lips met, at first tentatively, lightly. Then Kevin's arms tightened, his mouth demanding, insistent upon mine.

When he released me he whispered, "Oh, my dear, let me take care of you. I won't let you be frightened or hurt again, I promise you."

Although his voice was gentle, I sensed the sharpness of steel beneath, and knew he meant what he said. As if seeking the safe ground, something within me reached out to him. The fear I had been carrying like a tightly coiled spring inside me loosened, and I thought: If we were married, I wouldn't wake in the middle of the night, terrified at the thought of some dark shadowy figure hovering over my bed. Whoever had tried to kill me might have the nerve to frighten Meg O'Brien, but not the Countess of Abbeymore. If I were Kevin's wife, even Regan would think twice before trying anything nasty. After all, she and Sean and Cormac, too, for all their possessive airs about Abbey Court, still lived here at the sufferance of Lord Fletcher.

At my hesitation, Kevin lifted my chin so I had to look him full in the face. "You're not still thinking about Patrick?" he asked. "You have to promise me that you'll try to forget the way he died and remember only the happy times. Don't you think that's what Patrick would have wanted?"

"Yes," I said slowly.

He leaned down and kissed me lightly but his voice was jubilant. "Anyway, once we're married, I won't give you time to brood. We won't even have to live at Abbey Court if you don't want to. We can take a house in London, larger, naturally, than the one I have now so we can entertain properly. And we'll travel. There are so many wonderful places I can show you, darling. And you can show me America. I've always wanted to visit there. We could spend some time in Boston. You must have friends there."

I smiled inwardly. I had no doubt that if I returned to Boston as the Countess of Abbeymore I would have many friends. I could reopen the house on Beacon Hill, I thought suddenly, and give the parties and balls for which Mother had designed the house. Only this time Fiona O'Brian's daughter would be accepted by a society that had refused to acknowledge her presence before.

"You will think about it, my love?" There was an urgency in Kevin's voice that was flattering, and with his eyes intent on my face, I think he already guessed what my answer would be. I didn't pretend to myself that what I had felt in Kevin's arms was the same as when Sean held me. Or that marriage to Kevin would ever be more than one gentle affection and quiet, mutual concern. Still, in the long run, wasn't that better, more lasting, than what I would have known with Sean? If I didn't experience the wild ecstasy, then neither would I have to endure those ugly moments of doubt and suspicion when I would inevitably wonder if some other woman had caught Sean's wandering eye. And if Kevin would never demand more of me than I was willing to give, wasn't that easier than marriage to a man like Sean Fletcher, who would never be satisfied with second best?

"Yes, Kevin, I'll think about it," I promised.

That night my sleep was again troubled but not because of any nightmares. Finally, restlessly, I got out of bed and went to stand at the window, glancing almost automatically toward where the Abbey slumbered, caught up in its everlasting sleep. The silver sliver of a moon rode so low in the sky above the Abbey that it was tangled in the treetops.

I should be happy, I told myself fiercely. Kevin was a fine man, much better than I deserved. And I knew myself well enough to know that I wouldn't be happy living the rest of my life alone. I wanted a home of my own, a family, children around me, a man in my bed to turn to at night.

Why then did I feel this nagging sense of loss, of betrayal, when it was all within my grasp? I had only to reach out.

As for Patrick's death, I was forced to admit that what Kevin had said made sense. It was pointless to continue the search for my brother's killer, as futile as trying to clear Fiona's name. Strange how the two incidents seemed to join together in my mind, like the links in a chain. If Fiona hadn't come to Abbey Court there would have been no accusations of theft and betrayal, forcing her to flee to America. And if she hadn't gone to America she would never have met Jamie, and there would have been no Silver Lady Mine, no money to turn Patrick into a gentleman of means who could return to Ireland and finally, ironically, meet the very fate here at Abbey Court that Fiona had fled.

Perhaps that was all there was to it, I though, an ironic twist of fate, without reason or logic. I should know by now that life didn't always have neat, happy endings.

Rory came crawling out from under the bed to join me at the window, yawning sleepily but politely. He was growing bigger every day. Already I could see the full-grown dog he would soon become, the silky fur less red, more golden in color, the chest filling out, the legs less rangy. I reached down to give him a quick hug and as I did so I saw through the trees in the direction of the Abbey a flicker of light. I stiffened, watching the light bob off through the trees. Rory, sensing my unease, growled deep in his throat.

I tugged gently at his ear. "It's all right, boy. If it's not old Malachy, it's probably someone trying a bit of night poaching. We'd better go back to bed. There's no sense in both of us losing sleep."

The next day was Sunday. The Fletcher family always went en masse to Sunday services in two carriages, followed by the servants on foot. Ordinarily, I would have accompanied them but this morning I had other plans. My illness gave me the excuse to sleep late, and when I awoke I could tell from the stillness in the halls that the servants had already left for mass. I dressed quickly, then went down the stairs, closing an aggrieved Rory in my bedroom.

Despite Kevin's logical explanations, there was still one point about the appearance and disappearance of my assailant that puzzled me. If, as Sean claimed, there had been no footprints on the ground outside the dining-room windows and the drawing-room windows had been locked, then how had he left the house? The answer, I was convinced, lay in the small study, and more particularly in the priest's hole. I remembered Father Jerome telling me aboard ship that such hidden rooms often had escape shafts or bolt holes so that, if the searchers came too close, the priest could use the hidden passageway to escape further into the house, or out of the house completely. Perhaps my prowler had done the same.

Walking quickly through the dining room, I opened the study door. The room was deep in shadows with a greenish glow where light filtered in through the stained glass wall. I took a lamp and lit it, then found the panel the housekeeper had pushed. The strip of wood gave easily under pressure, and I reached in and pulled at the knotted rope. I had had only a quick look inside the priest's hole before but now I took my time and examined the small room carefully. The floor was of brick like the fireplace hearth, and the walls were of unpainted oak, solid oak, I discovered after I had pounded on them in vain for several minutes. The ceiling proved equally solid and inpenetrable.

Frustrated, I stepped back out of the room, gave the rope a yank, and the door slid shut. So much, I thought irritably, for romantic ideas of secret passages. If there had ever been any, they had oviously long ago been walled shut. And just as obviously I had let my imagination run away with me again.

Kevin was right. I would have to stop looking for answers when there were none to be had, because I knew, guiltily, that it wasn't only the answer to my assailant's disappearance I had been seeking. For if I could prove that a man could leave the study without being seen, then why not Patrick's body?

Someone cleared his throat behind me. I turned to see Jeremiah, the butler, standing in the doorway.

"I thought everyone had gone to mass," I said, startled.

"I'm a Protestant, miss," he said, unruffled. "I didn't mean to intrude but I thought I heard a knocking in here."

My face grew warm beneath his respectful, if questioning gaze, but I couldn't think of any ready answer without appearing more foolish than I felt.

He glanced around the room, his gaze finally centering on the stained glass panel. "I thought perhaps you were having difficulty opening the window."

"Window?" I set my lamp down abruptly. "What window is that?"

He gestured to the stained glass behind me. "Why, that window, of course, miss."

"I thought . . . isn't that set into the wall?"

"Oh no, miss. It's a bit tricky to open, though. If you'll allow me . . ." He ran his fingers expertly up beneath the rim of the stained glass, pressed what must have been a latch set into the border, and pushed. The window made a rusty, complaining noise as it slowly swung outward. The butler turned, wiping flakes of rust from his hands. "Needs a bit of greasing. I don't suppose it's been opened in years. Was there anything else, miss?"

"No, thank you." He was wrong, I thought. It hadn't been years since the window had been opened. I recognized that grating sound the window had made when it swung open, the same noise I had heard when I had hidden, terrified, in the drawing room and death had passed within a hairsbreadth of me.

After the butler had gone, closing the door behind him, I crossed quickly to the open window and looked out. The sill of the window was at the most three feet above the ground. A man could easily climb out the window, swing it shut after him, then disappear into the screen of trees that pressed within a few feet of the wall of the house.

I leaned farther out the window and could see the sun glinting against the windows of the kitchen area. I glimpsed the winding gully that cut through the woods before it curved alongside the road leading to the Abbey. The depression was deeper and wider here, edged by tiny saplings. I wondered what the gully had been used for originally— perhaps it had been part of an old drainage system. Even now there was a few inches of water, black and dank-smelling, in the bottom of the ditch.

A sudden breeze wafted the unpleasant odor toward me and I started to close the window, then stopped. The breeze had also set the long, tangled grass beneath the window to waving. For a moment something deep in the grass caught and reflected a ray of sunlight, shining like a crystal drop of dew, only larger, brighter.

My curiosity got the better of me. Without stopping to think how I'd get back inside the window, I hoisted my skirt and swung my leg over the window sill, balanced a moment at the window's edge, then dropped without a sound to the soft, marshy ground. The breeze had died as quickly as it had arisen. It took several minutes of searching on my hands and knees through the grass, still heavy with dew, before I found what I was seeking.

Then I felt it, hard and cold beneath my hand. I lifted it up and the sun's rays caught it again, glittering against the untarnished silver surface. I didn't have to open the watch lid to read the inscription. I knew it by heart. "To Patrick with love from his father, March 15, 1871."

It was the silver watch Jamie had given Patrick on my brother's twenty-first birthday.

24

It had been easy enough to climb out of the study window. I discovered it was much more difficult to climb back inside. The ground sloped gradually away from the wall toward the gully. Although I could reach the sill with my hands, I wasn't strong enough to lift myself up and over the sill. Finally, giving up, I swung the window shut from the outside and made my way through the edge of the trees to the front of the house.

By the time I reached the low stone wall on the terrace the hem of my gown was damp and my thin slippers were soaked through. I knew I should change into dry clothes but somehow I couldn't force myself to go back inside Abbey Court. The white Connemara stone walls seemed to loom menacingly behind me, the numerous windows like blank, empty eyes. The whole aspect of the house was cold and forbidding.

I sank down upon the stone wall, clutching the watch in my hand, and stared out across the park. It was Patrick I was seeing, though, lying crumpled in the waving grass beneath the stained glass window, his body dumped so unceremoniously that the watch he always carried in his pocket must have fallen out, to lie hidden in the grass.

As if I were unable to stop myself, my mind conjured up pictures—my brother, still barely alive, lying there helpless, his blood soaking the soft, damp earth, turning the grass red—then horror engulfed me and my mind went mercifully blank. I felt all at once numb, past all feeling, as if there were, finally, thoughts too painful for the mind to endure.

The low voices behind me were no more than unimportant sounds that I ignored, that couldn't penetrate the invisible wall I had flung up around me, until Cormac's angry voice boomed like a fist from the partially opened window of his bedroom. "Take your damn blood money then and go to hell, but don't be showing your face around me again."

I had forgotten that only Cormac of all the Fletcher family never attended mass. But who was with him? Surely he wasn't yelling at dignified, harmless Jeremiah in that fashion.

A few seconds later the front door opened and Seamus O'Toole stepped out onto the terrace. When he saw me he smiled jauntily, whipping off his hat and giving me an elaborate bow. "And a fine morning to ye, Miss O'Brien. Have you ever seen such a glorious day?"

I was in no mood to enter into a conversation with the game-keeper, of all people. "Good day, Mr. O'Toole," I said, getting quickly to my feet. I started to walk by him into the house. As I passed him, his hand reached out and grasped my wrist, his voice dropping softly. "Perhaps we could talk for a few minutes, if you'd be willing."

He glanced toward the window of Cormac's room and laughed uneasily. "Let's move a wee bit away. No need for the old man to hear us and a rare foul mood he's in this morning."

I allowed him to lead me toward the edge of the terrace near the drawing-room windows, then pulled my hand free. "What is it you wanted?"

His small green eyes shone with roguish good humor. "Well now, what I want is a fine little pub in America. I have a cousin, you see, who owns one in New York and he's willing to sell it to me, at a good price. There's a grand future for a man in America, not like here in Ireland, and I'm thinking a man should take advantage of his opportunities."

"What has that to do with me?"

"Only that I've heard talk that you're interested in how your poor brother died, may the saints rest his soul . . . asking questions of Mary Shaugnassy and suchlike." He gave me a conspiratorial wink. "But there's others who might tell you more, like my sister Molly, who happened to be outside the study when Mr. Sean came visiting your brother that morning."

"I know Mr. Fletcher was with my brother that morning. He told me so himself."

"Ay, but did he tell you they had a grand fight? My sister swears she never heard the like, Mr. Patrick giving Mr. Sean his walking papers, you might say, and Mr. Sean saying he'd see him in hell first, begging your pardon for the language, miss, but those were his exact words. Molly will swear to that." He nodded, pleased. "Well now, I thought that might be of interest to you, and there's more I could tell you. A man who works in the woods all day learns to walk quietly, before a poacher can take off, you know, and he sees more than others might see, like the morning your brother died."

"If you know anything about Mr. O'Brien's death, you should have told the magistrate," I said indignantly.

"Sure and where's the profit in that?" he asked, grinning broadly, but his eyes in the sunlight were the green color of slime growing at the edge of ponds. All at once I was revolted by the man, half convinced he was bluffing anyway, the way his gaze kept sidling away from me. Even the story of Patrick threatening to sack Sean could be a lie. After all, Mr. Corcoran had told me that my brother didn't have the power to disgrace Sean without Kevin's consent.

"And how much profit do you expect to make from me, Mr. O'Toole?" I didn't bother to hide the contempt in my voice. "Enough to buy yourself a pub in New York?"

The laughter died from his face, and suddenly I sensed that beneath the man's easy smile and laughter he was frightened to death. "I need that money, before God I do," he whispered hoarsely. "I have to leave this place and soon. I'll not end up like your brother."

Then, abruptly, the voice changed again, the face once more jovial as he tipped his hand to his forehead and said, "And a good day to you, Miss O'Brien."

I turned, startled, to see the carriages coming up the driveway, returning from church. By the time I had turned back again the gamekeeper was gone, disappearing as quietly as one of the animals in the woods he patrolled so rigorously.

To my dismay I saw there were other carriages arriving too, guests apparently invited for lunch. I remembered my bedraggled skirt, and how I must look. I tried to retreat to the house, but it was too late. Kevin came quickly to me, slipping an arm possessively around my waist while he made introductions. I saw that Sean, standing to one side, had noticed the gesture and his face darkened before he turned and strode away. It was Lady Fletcher who, when Regan led the company to the stable to show off a new mare she had bought, drew me to one side, murmuring, "I'm sure you'll want to change for lunch, my dear. Kevin will be expecting you to help entertain his guests."

I looked up at her quickly and knew that Kevin had told her about his proposal of marriage. Was she pleased, I wondered uneasily, or disappointed? Well, hardly pleased, I thought, considering that her son was planning to marry a woman whose mother had once been a servant at Abbey Court. I certainly couldn't have been the aristocratic daughter-in-law Lady Fletcher had envisioned for her son, the mother of her grandchildren. Yet I was equally sure that, no matter how she felt, never by word or gesture would the countess show her disapproval.

Awkwardly I searched for the right words to reassure Kevin's mother. "Lady Fletcher, I can understand how you must feel . . ."

She didn't allow me to finish but stepped forward quickly and kissed me lightly on the cheek. When she drew back, I saw that there were years of happiness in her eyes and that she was smiling. "You must call me Lady Margaret, my dear. I can't tell you how delighted I am at the news. It has always been my fondest wish to see Kevin married. I'm sure you'll make him very happy. What more could a mother want?" She gave me a gentle shove toward the stairs. "Now run along, child, and change. The engagement can't be announced, of course, until your mourning period is finished, but you might as well become accustomed to acting as the hostess here at Abbey Court."

When I quickly changed my clothes, however, and came downstairs—just in time, as the guests had started to move into the dining room—I saw there was no question of my acting as hostess, at least not that day. Kevin took his place at the head of the table and Regan immediately sat in the hostess seat at the end of the table.

I saw Kevin frown as if he were about to speak, but I caught his eye and shook my head. Regan had taken on the duties of hostess at Abbey Court probably ever since Lady Margaret had withdrawn more and more to the dower house. I suspected that she wouldn't look kindly upon my usurping her position, and I had no desire to have another run-in with my sister-in-law, particularly not in front of guests. I sat to the right of Kevin and tried to make bright conversation but social chatter never came easily for me and the meal seemed to drag endlessly. Sean, I noticed, wasn't enjoying the lunch either. He drank a good many glasses of port, and the more he drank the quieter and more brooding he became. I was aware of his eyes watching me so intensely that I felt my face flush. I was embarrassed, and hoped that the other guests didn't notice.

After lunch the guests drifted into the library and the talk turned political, at least among the men. The women sat together discussing the latest fashions and how difficult it was to train a decent servant. I found the conversation boring and discovered I was eavesdropping upon the men's conversation, which wasn't difficult with Major Gill shouting angrily at the top of his voice, "Biggest mistake Parliament ever made, passing the Land Act and releasing that scoundrel, Parnell, from prison. You watch my words. He'll only stir up more trouble among the tenants, him and his hired assassins in the Land League."

Father Vincent said mildly, "It was my understanding that under the Kilmainham Treaty Parnell signed when he left prison, he agreed to use his influence against the outrages, the murders and intimidation of the landlords by members of the League."

"Bah!" the major scoffed. "With all the money pouring into the League from misguided fools in America, you think the members will listen to Parnell?" He saw that he had my attention and he turned to me, his voice accusing. "Isn't it true, Miss O'Brien? You've only recently left America. Doesn't every ne'er-do-well Irishman there support the Irish Land League?"

I could feel my temper rising and I kept my voice steady with difficulty. "Most Irish-Americans have enough trouble supporting themselves, but, yes, I'm sure most of them support what the League stands for—'the land of Ireland for the people of Ireland.'"

At my quote from one of Parnell's speeches, I saw Kevin's face freeze and heard outraged gasps from several of the ladies, while the gentlemen frowned. Unhappily I realized I had been tactless, if not openly rude. The Irish National Land League, which had been set up to help the Irish tenant farmers, was obviously anathema to the Anglo-Irish landlords present. Sean, lounging back in a chair half asleep, opened his eyes and smiled mockingly at me across the room, as if enjoying my discomfiture. Kevin hastily changed the subject and not much later the party broke up. The guests murmured their good-boys graciously to me at the door but I couldn't help noticing the coldness in their eyes.

Later, after everyone had left, Kevin drew me to one side. He studied my face, concerned. "Are you feeling all right, my dear?"

"Yes, I'm fine," I said, wondering if I should apologize for my behavior. After all, the guests had been Kevin's friends and when we were married they would be my friends too. I would have to learn to curb my tongue.

Kevin looked as if he were about to make some comment, then said instead, "I noticed you were talking to Seamus O'Toole when we drove up. I hope he didn't say anything to upset you."

"No . . ." And then, remembering Patrick's silver watch I had found in the grass, I reached eagerly for his hand. "There is something I want to speak to you about, Kevin, something I found this morning."

"Of course, darling," he said, gazing at me a little absently. "But can it possibly wait until tomorrow? Mother is expecting me at the dower house. She breaks her fast on Sundays to have tea with me in the afternoon." He smiled shyly. "I told her about us. I hope you don't mind."

"No, I don't mind but what I have to tell you—"

"I have a splendid idea," he interrupted. "Why don't you have luncheon with me at the tower tomorrow? Liam is quite a good cook and we can have the whole afternoon to talk and make plans."

I bit my lower lip, staring down at the floor. The truth was that I always felt uncomfortable around Liam Carmody, particularly since the episode of the cottage tumbling. "I'm not sure I can," I said slowly. "I had planned to start work in the office again in the morning."

Kevin lifted a surprised eyebrow. "Surely you won't be working at the books any longer, now that we're to be married! It wouldn't look right, would it, the Countess of Abbeymore doing the work of a grubby little clerk?"

"It isn't a clerk's work," I pointed out. "And according to Patrick's will, I am supposed to assist in the management of the estate."

"Oh, that." Kevin shrugged indifferent. "I'm sure something can be worked out without your spending hours closeted in an office alone with . . ."

He left the rest of the sentence unspoken but I knew what he implied. Alone in an office with a man who wasn't my husband. And I began to realize that, beneath all of Kevin's liberal philosophies about life and art, he was in many ways as staunchly conservative as any of the men at the luncheon. Even my remark about the Land League had shaken him, I suspected. But of course he was right about my working in the office alone with Sean. It would simply be asking for trouble to continue the practice after I was married. Even if it was only Sean's pride that was hurt, I doubted if he was a man to take rejection easily. And a little thing like a wedding band wouldn't stand in his way. No, it was better if I stayed as far away as possible from Sean from now on. I tried to ignore the sudden catch of pain at the thought.

I realized that Kevin was waiting a little impatiently for my answer and I said submissively, "No, I suppose it wouldn't be proper."

"I'll see you tomorrow, then, at the tower?"

"Tomorrow," I agreed, lifting my face for his kiss, but when his lips touched mine and immediately started to pull away I found myself clinging to him, refusing to let him go. "Please stay," I whispered.

I felt vaguely shocked at my own unladylike behavior but it didn't seem to matter. All that mattered was that for a few minutes I desperately needed Kevin's closeness to blot Sean's face from my mind, to still the sudden, nagging uncertainty.

Gently but firmly Kevin freed himself, his voice, embarrassed. "My dear, you know I'd rather stay." Then, reluctantly, "I suppose I could make some excuse to Mother."

I felt my cheeks flaming as I straightened the bodice of my gown, which had been pulled away. "No, of course you mustn't do that," I said, not looking at hm. "I was being childish."

He still hesitated, frowning. "If it's important, what you have to tell me, I could stay a few minutes longer."

"No." As much as I had wanted him to remain with me, now I couldn't wait for him to leave. It wasn't only the humiliating memory of how I had thrown myself at him. Suddenly, belatedly, it occurred to me how difficult it was going to be, telling Kevin about my finding Patrick's watch. Kevin had explained away the bullet in the study wall and the powder marks on the shirt, but how could he explain away where I had found Patrick's watch—at least a mile from where my brother was supposed to have been killed? Even more damaging, how did I tactfully tell my future husband that I suspected a member of his own family was a murderer? No matter that Kevin was not overly fond of his uncle and cousins, nevertheless, he had a strong sense of family honor. He would not relish the Fletcher name being dragged through the scandal of a court inquiry.

I forced myself to smile. "No, it can wait. We can talk tomorrow."

After Kevin had gone I turned and walked slowly up the broad staircase, the decision I must make like a yoke on my shoulders. Tomorrow would be better, I told myself hopefully. Surely by tomorrow I should be able to think of some painless way of telling Kevin the truth.

25

By the next morning, however, I was no closer to thinking of an easy way to tell Kevin of my latest discovery. I even found myself wondering whether I should say anything to him at all. Wasn't it possible that Patrick could have dropped his watch where I had discovered it, perhaps days before his death? Then I remembered that Regan had said that Patrick had had the watch with him that last morning.

No, even the long arm of coincidence could stretch only so far—Patrick's gun being accidentally shot off in the study; his shirt powder-burned because supposedly he had been foolhardy enough to get off his horse and try to reason with armed men, instead of obeying the natural instinct to spur his horse forward and escape; even the ink being providentially spilled by a careless servant the same morning that Patrick died. And there was always the chance that the gamekeeper hadn't been bluffing, that he had actually seen something in the woods the morning my brother was killed. Even Kevin must see that the magistrate should question Mr. O'Toole. . . .

But would Kevin forgive me? I wondered unhappily.

Would he ever look at me again without remembering the dowry of suspicion and mistrust I was bringing to the marriage? If I cared for him, how could I hurt him this way? And not just Kevin, I thought, flinching, there was Lady Margaret. Could those frail shoulders bear an additional burden of guilt, more penances she must punish herself with for the wicked deeds of a member of the Fletcher family?

I was so deep in my own misery that I wasn't listening to Rose's chatter as she laid out my morning gown and brushed my hair. She had had Sunday afternoon off to visit her parents and had taken Rory with her to show him off. "My father said he was a fine, smart dog and Jim said he hoped we could have one just like Rory when we marry."

Rose beamed happily, "Ay, though naught's settled yet, Jim having his mother and two sisters to look after, but Father and Jim talked of it."

I had met Jim O'Connor, a serious-faced farmer, twice Rose's age. "I'm so pleased for you, Rose. Will the wedding be soon?"

"We hope to announce our pledge on St. Stephen's Day," she said proudly. " 'Tis a custom for young people to go from cottage to cottage on that day, singing songs and carrying holly and ivy and ribbon. The couples who pledge themselves that day continue their courting until Shrovetide."

St. Stephen's Day—there was something I had heard recently about that saint's day—then I remembered. It was the day, Sister Cecelia had told me, Patrick was born. "It's a long time to wait to announce your engagement, all the way till March," I teased.

Rose clucked disapprovingly. "St. Stephen's Day is the twenty-sixth of December, miss. Everyone knows that."

Not everyone, I thought absently. Not someone like myself who hadn't been brought up with a Catholic education. And then the shock hit me, so that for a moment I simply stared at Rose, while the full effect of her words rocked me.

In the O'Brien household Patrick's birthday had always been celebrated on March 15, but if my brother was actually born on December 26, St. Stephen's Day, then—I figured backward rapidly—Fiona would have already been pregnant when she boarded the ship at Cobh, and at least three months pregnant when she married Jamie in June aboard the same ship.

It had to be a mistake, I thought. Sister Cecelia was an old woman. She had remembered the date wrong. Except I knew very well that, despite her age, the nun's mind was as sharp and clear as anyone's. In any case, it would be easy enough to check. The convent in Boston probably kept some sort of records, though for my brother and myself there had never been any reason to doubt Fiona's word that Patrick had been born on the date she told us. For Fiona, it would have been a white lie to save Patrick from the shame of illegitimacy. Undoubtedly Jamie, loving Fiona as he did, had been happy to go along with the deception and accept Patrick as his own son.

I stared, white-faced, at my reflection in the mirror. What was I doing? I thought, shocked. How could I accept so readily the fact that Patrick was not my brother but my half brother? There had to be a faster way of learning the truth than writing to Boston. I couldn't wait for weeks, I decided. There was one person closer at hand who could tell me the truth about Patrick's parentage. . . .

I got quickly to my feet. "Rose, I want you to go to the stable and have them bring the trap around for me."

"But you're not dressed yet, miss. And you've not had your breakfast."

"Never mind. I can finish dressing by myself and I'll eat later."

She stopped at the door. "You'll wear a shawl then? It's turned chill out."

"Yes," I said impatiently. "Now hurry."

My fingers were all thumbs as I hooked my dress up the front of the bodice, pulling so hard at the tiny black satin ribbon that bound the collar that one of the ribbons broke. Irritably I reached into my jewel box for a pin to hold the collar closed and picked up the copy of the ancient Celtic brooch that had been Mother's favorite. I jabbed myself twice with the point of the brooch before I finally managed to secure it in place, wondering, frustrated, how I had ever managed to dress myself in the old days without the help of a maid.

Finally I started out the door and, remembering at the last moment my promise to Rose, grabbed my shawl from the bed and hurried down the steps. As I crossed the hall Regan came out of the drawing room. She was dressed for riding. Behind the sheer black veil her eyes were shadowed, her skin waxy white.

When she saw me she hesitated and then held out her

hand. "I understand best wishes are in order," she murmured.

At first I thought she was angry and then realized that the news of my engagement to Lord Fletcher seemed secretly to amuse her. I could see the glitter of laughter behind the thick, dark lashes. She shook her head with mock sadness. "Poor Sean. I don't think he's ever been jilted before. Naturally he's crushed."

"If he is," I replied tartly, "I'm sure he'll recover rapidly." Then, not wanting to waste any time exchanging barbed remarks with my sister-in-law, I nodded good morning and started to walk past her.

"Meg!"

I stopped, surprised, at the note or urgency in Regan's voice. She stared straight at me, looking like a troubled small girl who had carried a prank too far without realizing it, and now was afraid to face the consequences.

"What is it?"

She shrugged her shoulders, her mouth drooping sulkily. "Nothing. Nothing at all."

I continued out onto the terrace. The trap was in the driveway, the stableboy waiting to help me into the small carriage. Before I picked up the reins I drew my shawl more closely around my shoulders. Rose was right. It was a chill, foggy day, the clouds gray and sullen overhead. I was glad I had decided not to ride Lady Jane. I didn't welcome being caught in the rain again.

As I drove away from Abbey Court down the back Abbey road, the grayness seemed to press down upon the earth, smothering all sound. Even the birds were silent. Once I reached the wooded area, the trees on either side of the road were almost hidden by the mist drifting quietly as ghosts between the branches.

Then from somewhere deep in the woods I heard a thin, high-pitched scream like a soul in mortal agony. The air around me trembled with the sound, which stopped as abruptly as it had started. Some animal caught in one of the gamekeeper's traps, I thought, shivering, and drew my shawl more tightly around me. I urged the horse to a faster trot, resolutely keeping my eyes on the road. One thing I was sure of, I thought angrily, once I was married to Kevin, there would be no more traps of any kind in the Abbey Court woods.

When I reached Mary Shaugnassy's cottage I saw that she was working in her garden. She straightened with difficulty when I drove up, and wiped her hands on her skirt as she came to greet me, "Should you be out on such a raw day, child? They tell me you've been ill."

"I'm fine," I assured her. "Could we talk for a few minutes?"

"Come in . . . come in. I'll just put the tea on. You look as if you could do with a bit of warming."

Once inside the cottage, she insisted on serving me not only a cup of hot tea but thick slices of bread, and would have fed me more but I declined, knowing that eggs and ham were not that easily come by for a tenant at Abbey Court.

At last, after I insisted, she sat down across from me, her hands folded in her lap, looking somehow awkward as if they were not used to being still.

"What is it you're wanting?" she asked, curious. "If it's about your poor mother, I've told ye all I could."

"Not everything," I said, watching her face closely. "You didn't tell me Fiona was carrying a child when she left Abbey Court."

The toothless mouth collapsed inward, the eyes charged with dismay. If I had doubted that Mother was already pregnant with Patrick when she left Ireland, then I doubted no longer.

"You knew, didn't you?" I asked accusingly. "Fiona told you."

"Never she did," she said, shaking her head. "Not a word. But I've birthed too many not to know the signs."

"Then you don't know the father—" I stopped, because there was no need to ask that question. Mary Shaugnassy and I both knew who the father was.

"It was Cormas Fletcher, wasn't it? Is that why he came to your cottage, when he sent Fiona off to America?"

"I'll wager he never knew. Fiona O'Brien had too much pride in her. She would never have told him she was carrying his child." Her glance turned upon me was gently reproachful. "You should know your own mother better than that."

No, I thought, Cormac couldn't have known that Patrick was his son. Unscrupulous as the old man was, he still would never encouraged Patrick's marriage to Regan if he had known the truth.

"You should have stopped Patrick's marriage!"

"How could I do such a thing?" she asked helplessly. "It was already done when I heard of it." Her shoulders slumped as if her body were settling into itself. "It was a terrible weight on my mind, but what could I do? I had only my suspicions. When I decided, at last, I had to tell Father Vincent, that very day they brought your poor brother to me. There seemed no need then to . . ."

She lifted her head, hearing before I did the voices calling outside the cottage. We had both risen to our feet when the door burst open and two men staggered in, bent over with the weight of the burden they carried between them.

"It's Seamus O'Toole, Mary," the older man panted, his face crimson from exertion, as he carefully lowered the gamekeeper onto the floor before the fire. "The poor devil was caught in one of his own traps. Mike and me found him, screaming like a stuck pig, on the path."

I took one look at the gamekeeper, the bloodied stump of a leg, the small green eyes glazing with pain and fury, the mouth gaping wide in a round, red O. The sounds that came from that mouth, the high ululating, mindless screams, pounded into my skull, following me as I dashed from the room and for a few minutes was violently sick in Mary Shaugnassy's garden.

When I was able, I returned inside the cottage. The terrible cries had mercifully stopped. The gamekeeper had been moved onto a pallet in a corner of the room; the two men stood hunched together talking quietly before the fire. "The old fox would never have fallen into one of his own traps. Some poacher moved it, to be sure, where he'd not be expecting it. . . ."

Mary turned from the pallet to the men. "Don't stand there gossiping like old biddies. Fetch the doctor and Father Vincent, and be quick about it."

I forced myself to join her, willed myself to look down at the bleached, lifeless face, the straw pallet already soaked red with blood from the mangled leg. "Is there anything I can do?"

"There's a brown bottle in the wee cabinet by the door and some clean cloths," she ordered. "And a blanket from my bed in the loft."

I brought them to her and watched as she worked quickly, trying to stanch the flow of blood, finally covering the man with the blanket and spooning some of the brown liquid into his mouth, the lips closed now and sagging in the corners.

"Will he die?" I asked softly. It seemed incredible to me that the man was still alive.

Mary pulled herself wearily to her feet. "I've seen worse than him live to dance a jig with a wooden leg. If the shock doesn't kill him or the poisoning in the blood."

"How do you suppose it happened?"

"That's a thing I'd not be knowing. But there's many a poacher crippled in one of those traps of O'Toole's who'd be pleased to get a bit of his own back." She studied my face, her voice kind. "You've done all you can, child. You'd best get back to the big house and tell them what's happened."

"Yes," I said, wondering, wearily, as I climbed into the trap and picked up the reins, how I would find the words to tell the Fletchers of this newest tragedy to strike Abbey Court.

When I reached the house, however, and went almost automatically to the office to find Sean, I saw that I wouldn't have to tell him. He already knew. He was pulling on his jacket when I came into the room. "Mike Kelly stopped by and told me," he said. "I've sent Flaherty to town to fetch the doctor and the priest." Then he saw my face and said quickly, "I'm sorry. I forgot you were at Mary's cottage when they brought Seamus there. Are you all right?"

"Yes, I'm all right," I said, but my voice sounded thin and I felt, suddenly, the room dipping curiously beneath my feet.

Sean came around the desk and pushed me gently down into a chair. "It couldn't have been a pleasant sight. Would you like some brandy?"

"No." I took a deep breath and felt the fluttering like butterfly wings in my stomach grow quiet. "I'd like to see the latest account for the estate, please."

He looked startled. "Now! Why?" And then, shrugging, he handed me the tall ledger. "You'll notice the entries are all up to date," he said dryly.

I glanced at the last written page of the book, then up at Sean. "I don't see any entry for the sum of money your father gave Mr. O'Toole yesterday morning. It couldn't have been his wages. The gamekeeper was paid last month."

But by now Sean was on guard, his face carefully expressionless. "If it's not entered in the account book," he said, "then the money must have been a personal matter between Father and O'Toole."

Despite my determination to remain as calm and composed as Sean, I could hear the anger creeping into my voice. "A personal matter? Or blackmail? Money to keep

217

the gamekeeper quiet so he wouldn't tell what he knew about Patrick's death? Maybe he even helped move Patrick's body from the grass outside the study window to the Abbey road, or saw the man who did the moving. And was Miss O'Toole paid, too, not to tell about the quarrel you and Patrick had that morning in the study?"

I saw I had finally struck a nerve. Sean's face darkened so that only the two muscles around his mouth stood out, white and taut. "I'll not deny we quarreled," he said slowly. "Patrick had some wild notion that he could dismiss me and manage Abbey Court himself. There was no way that could be allowed to happen. He would have run the estate into the ground in a matter of months."

"So you killed him . . . you or your father ·. . . or Seamus, and afterward the body was removed from the study through the stained glass window, put on your horse, taken through the gully to the Abbey road and left there, so it would look as though he'd been killed by Moonlighters."

"Be careful, Meg." Sean's voice was all at once deadly cold. His opaque eyes held no warmth, no warmth at all. "Be careful what you're saying."

There was no way short of throttling me that he could have stopped me now. "And when I came to Abbey Court and your father's plan to get you to marry me didn't work, he decided to send Seamus to my room, hoping to frighten me away from Abbey Court before I learned too much, poking and prying. Isn't that what he called it? Or was my visitor your idea?"

Sean didn't speak for several seconds. I shall never forget the way he looked, as if there was nothing between us now but hatred so intense that I could feel it quivering in the air between us. He sat on the edge of the desk, swinging his leg thoughtfully. "So you overheard the conversation between Father and me that morning. I wondered, later, when you started throwing yourself at Kevin."

"I didn't throw myself at Kevin!" I retorted, furious. "And at least he's not marrying me for the O'Brien fortune, the way you were perfectly willing to do."

Even now, paradoxically, I found myself hoping that Sean would somehow miraculously explain away the conversation I had overheard; that he hadn't cold-bloodedly on his father's orders set out to seduce me into marriage.

Instead of denying my accusation, though, he frowned and said, "It's true then, what Regan told me. You're going to be a grand fool and marry Kevin." He studied my face almost pityingly. "Does a title mean so much to you then? Do you think being called the Countess of Abbeymore will change you into one of those fashionable, bloodless women that Kevin fancies, any more than a fortune of silver could change your mother into a great lady?"

The scorn in his voice stung me, even more so because what he said was partly true. I rose to my feet. "I have no intention of discussing my marriage with you," I said haughtily. "How could you possibly understand what I feel for Kevin?"

I started for the door but, without a sound, Sean was there before me, his hand on my arm, swinging me around to face him. "Because I know you, Meg O'Brien," he said tautly. "We're the same, you and I. We love or we hate. There's no comfortable in-between for us. And we're cursed with the same stubbornness—the way you wouldn't give up finding out the truth about Patrick; the way I'll never give up what belongs to me here at Abbey Court."

For one split second, I could have pulled free from his grasp but, treacherously, my body betrayed me. And then it was too late. His mouth was hard on mine, his hands dropping, resting above my waist, his fingers stroking lightly, caressingly where my breasts began to swell above my corset. My hands lifted as if to push him away but instead faltered around him, pulling him closer. For one endless moment nothing else mattered in the world but our being together. The feeling possessed me that if I were to let go I would fall off the edge of an abyss into nothingness.

Until, finally, I opened my eyes and saw Kevin standing in the doorway of the office. His face was still and cold and white as death.

26

Looking into Kevin's eyes, I saw the same revulsion I had glimpsed that afternoon when we discovered Regan and

Brian together in the glade. My face burned and I stepped away from Sean.

Kevin broke the awkward silence, stammering slightly, his voice excruciatingly polite. "For . . . forgive me for intruding. I . . . I heard about Seamus and came to . . . to ask if there were anything I . . . could do." He took a step forward. "I believe you . . . dropped your shawl, Miss O'Brien." He picked it off the floor and handed it to me, carefully not touching me, only his eyes fastened on me, narrowing suddenly, as in pain.

Then he turned and walked out the door, his back ramrod straight. I couldn't let him go, not this way, and called out, "Kevin!" but Sean caught my wrist and held me when I would have gone after him.

"No," he said harshly. "It's better this way."

I looked up at him, bewildered by the coldness in his eyes, the mouth set cruelly when a moment before there had been only tenderness and warmth. And felt all at once sickened, not at Sean but at myself. How could I have so shamelessly betrayed Kevin and all his kindnesses to me? More important, how could I have forgotten so easily how Patrick had died? What sort of besotted, mindless fool had I become? I knew the contempt Kevin must feel for me was not half the contempt I felt for myself.

Sean was still holding my wrist. "Let me go," I said.

He scowled down at me, his face angry. "Not until we've talked. You wanted to know the truth about Patrick, though God knows I tried to stop you from finding out. Now you're going to hear it, whether you like it or not."

I wrenched my wrist free, rubbing at the skin where he had held me, as if to rid myself of his touch. "I know the truth. I won't listen to any more of your lies."

Sean sat down again on the edge of the desk, his smile coldly, lazily amused. "You mean those wild accusations you made about Cormac and me? You don't actually believe the magistrate will pay any attention to the ravings of a rather hysterical young woman, obviously overly distraught at her brother's death?"

He was right, I thought dully. There was no point in going to the magistrate, who was in any case a close friend of the Fletcher family. "No, not the magistrate," I said, pulling my shawl around my shoulder, feeling suddenly cold to the bone. "I think, however, my solicitor will listen to me, once I tell him the whole story. Even he might wonder about the argument you and my brother had in the study that last morning, and how Patrick's watch that he was wearing when he died came to be outside the study window."

A flickering, like heat lightning, flashed for a moment in Sean's eyes. He hadn't known about my finding the watch, I realized triumphantly, and I continued, gaining confidence. "And if Mr. Corcoran won't listen, Patrick was still an American citizen with some influential friends in diplomatic circles. Our consulate in Dublin should be interested in what I have to tell them."

"You'd go that far?" Sean asked, then, studying my face, nodded grimly. "Yes, I suppose you would." He got to his feet, his eyes never leaving my face. "Well, then it appears we have nothing more to say to each other, do we? If you'll excuse me, I'll go see how Seamus is faring. Lady Margaret will want to know."

After he left the room I discovered I was shaking so that it was necessary for me to hold tightly to the balustrade as I climbed the staircase to my room. Rose and Rory were waiting for me when I entered. Rose's eyes were shining, her face pink with excitement. "Have you heard the news, miss, about O'Toole? Caught in one of his own traps, they say, a terrible sight, one of his legs cut off."

Then she saw my face and fell silent.

"I'd like a bath, Rose," I said. "Hot water, as hot as possible."

"Yes, miss," she said. Her glance fell to my skirt and her eyes widened, shocked. "Whatever happened to your gown? It's all stained. . . ."

"Never mind about my dress," I said sharply. "Just fetch the bath water."

After a subdued and quiet Rose filled the hip bath with steaming hot water, I scrubbed myself till my skin felt raw, and toweled myself fiercely dry. Then I rang for Rose and handed her the gown I had worn that morning.

"I don't want to see this again, Rose. You can do what you want with it."

"Och, the stains can be removed," she assured me. "I'll just dip it in cold water."

"I said I don't want to see it again!" My voice trembled and I turned away. I would not cry, I thought angrily. It was too late for tears. And there wasn't time.

"I want you to fetch my trunks and my carpetbag, Rose, and then find out when the next train for Dublin leaves from Abbeymore."

"Why, that would be tomorrow at noon. It's the one his lordship always takes when he goes to Dublin." She hesitated, her face unhappy. "Will you be gone long?"

"I don't know, at least a week or two, perhaps longer." Perhaps forever, I thought. Why not face the truth? There would no longer be a welcome for me at Abbey Court, not after what I planned to do. I could hardly expect the Fletchers to extend their hospitality to the person who was bringing scandal and disgrace upon them. As for my continuing to fulfill the terms of Patrick's will, I'd have to talk to Mr. Corcoran about that. It would, of course, be impossible for me to work any longer in the same house with Sean and Cormac, much less the same office. Except, I thought suddenly, pain jabbing me in the chest, if the new investigation into Patrick's death discovered what I suspected it would, then Sean and Cormac wouldn't be at Abbey Court either.

I thrust the thought aside, just as I refused to think any further beyond my trip to Dublin, where I would go afterward, how I would live. All I knew for certain was that it was time I chose my own way, learned to live my own life, not Fiona's dreams for me, or even the surrogate life Patrick had forced me into through his will.

I felt something moist and cold touch my hand and, looking down, saw Rory, sitting back on his haunches, his soft brown eyes gazing up at me, worried, as if he sensed I was leaving. Rory, too, I thought in helpless misery. I had lost so much. How could I lose him too? Yet how could I take him with me, not knowing where I would be going after Dublin? Except undoubtedly there would be hotel rooms, hardly happy surroundings for a young, active dog.

I knelt down and stroked the dog's silky coat, scratching him at the spot he liked, just behind the right, floppy ear. "You'll look after him for me, won't you, Rose?" I looked up at the girl pleadingly. "Perhaps later, when I'm settled, I can send for him."

"That I will, miss," she promised, her own eyes suspiciously bright. "He'll miss you, though. And so will I, ever so much."

In another minute we'd both be in tears, I thought. I got hastily to my feet, forcing my voice to brisk neutrality. "Thank you, Rose. I know I'll miss you too. Will you bring the bags now? I have a message to write that I want you to take to Lord Fletcher, and then I'll help you with the packing."

I spent an hour trying to decide what to say in my note to Kevin, and then, in the end, it was done in a few short sentences. What was the use of asking him to forgive the unforgivable? I simply told him that I was leaving for Dublin the next day on the noon train and that I would send for my trunks and the rest of my belongings later, and that if he needed to reach me he could write me in care of Mr. Corcoran at his law offices in Dublin.

I gave the letter to Rose to be delivered. I didn't expect any answer and I received none.

The rest of the day I spent deciding which clothes to take with me to Dublin and which to place in my trunks to be shipped later. I was glad for the diversion, the small decisions that had to be made, which took my mind off the larger decisions I didn't want to think about. Just how much should I tell my solicitor? Was it necessary to inform him that in all probability Patrick was the son of Fiona and Cormac, conceived in rape; that, without knowing it, Sean might have very well plotted the death of his own half brother? There had been sufficient disgrace attached to Fiona's name. Why should I betray now the secret that she had so carefully hidden all her life? No, I decided it was better not to say anything about Patrick's parentage. What I would have to tell Mr. Corcoran was damaging enough.

I had dinner served in my room that evening. Rose took a long time to bring up the tray and when she finally returned her eyes were dancing with excitement. "The kitchen's all in an uproar. The magistrate's men have called the staff together, asking all sorts of questions about old Seamus."

"Surely they don't suspect a member of the staff of being the poacher?" I asked, surprised.

Rose shook her head. "The cook told me there's talk now that it wasn't a poacher who moved the trap. O'Toole received a message from Mr. Sean last night, asking him to come to the estate office at nine o'clock this morning. You see, if Seamus hadn't received the message, he would never have walked from his cottage to the office this morning? And then he wouldn't have fallen into the trap that was hidden and waiting for him there on the path. The magistrate thinks the message could only have been sent by someone here at the house who had a grudge against poor Seamus." Rose placed the tray on the table before the fireplace, adding almost cheerfully, "Sure and you'd not have to look far to find someone with a grudge againset the old devil." Then she hastily crossed herself. "May the blessed saints forgive me."

"Mr. O'Toole is dead then?" I asked, my hands clenched in my lap.

"Not yet, but they say he'll not last the night. The blood poisoning has set in." Rose poured the dark brown tea with a flourish. "A fine wake that will be. Molly O'Toole will have to pay dear for her brother's keening."

I had lost my appetite and had to force myself to sip at the tea. So Seamus O'Toole would never have his pub in New York after all, I thought, remembering our conversation on the terrace. And I remembered something else suddenly, uneasily, about that old conversation. I recalled the look of fear that had pinched the gamekeeper's ferret face, and the hoarse voice saying, "I have to leave this place and soon. I'll not end up like your brother."

"Is the ham too salty then?" Rose asked anxiously, watching me toy with my food.

"I'm not hungry," I said slowly. Rose had brought up a bowl of bread and milk for Rory and I placed it on the floor for him. He finished the milk in three swipes of his pink tongue, then looked up at me inquiringly, as if wondering if that was all.

"How do they know, Rose, that Mr. O'Toole received any message?" I asked. "Did he tell someone? Is he able to talk?"

"Oh no, miss, not so to make any sense. They say he's half out of his mind with the pain. It was the magistrate's men who found the piece of paper on a table in his cottage. Signed with Mr. Sean's name, it was, and near enough to his writing to fool old Seamus."

"How can they be sure Mr. Sean didn't send the message?"

Rose looked startled. "Why, because he said he didn't send it, miss. And why should he lie? Sure and Mr. Sean would have no reason to want O'Toole dead?"

Oh, he might have a reason, I thought grimly. If Seamus O'Toole had been blackmailing Sean and his father, it was possible that the father or son had decided to permanently silence the gamekeeper. And blame the man's death on poachers, the same way Patrick's death had been conveniently blamed on Moonlighters.

For a few moments I debated whether or not to go to the magistrate with my suspicions but then realized it would be an exercise in futility. It would be my word against Sean's and Cormac's, and why should anyone believe me, a woman and a stranger in the country, against respected members of the gentry? No, it would be best to follow my original plan, to go to Dublin and tell Mr. Corcoran everything I knew or suspected, and let him decide the best way to handle the matter. The Fletchers had no hold over Mr. Corcoran, and the magistrate would not be able to brush aside Dublin's request for a more thorough investigation into Patrick's and the gamekeeper's deaths.

In any case, going to the local authorities with my story would mean delaying my departure from Abbey Court, perhaps even running the risk of seeing Sean again. And that was a risk I didn't dare to take. The sooner I left Abbey Court the better. Without wanting to delve too deeply into what lay behind my pressing sense of urgency to leave Abbey Court, I rose quickly to my feet. "It's getting late, Rose," I yawned. "We'd better finish the packing. There won't be time in the morning."

When we had finally closed the last trunk and snapped shut my carpetbag satchel, I could hardly keep my eyes open. Rory had already given up on us and was curled in a ball, fast asleep, beside the bed.

"You'll want me to sleep in the dressing room, won't you?" Rose asked.

I hesitated. I knew the bed in the small room wasn't very comfortable. I supposed I was being foolish to believe that I might be in any danger. After all, three mysterious deaths in a row at Abbey Court would be too much for even the friendliest of magistrates to swallow. And yet—I gazed uneasily at the bedroom door without a lock. "Would you mind, Rose?"

She assured me she didn't mind and in fact, by the time I had read in bed for a while, finally turning off my own gas lamp, my eyelids drooping, I could already hear the sound of her light snoring through the open dressing-room door. I had thought I would have trouble falling asleep. Instead, as soon as I put my head down on the pillow and closed my eyes, sleep swept over me like a wave.

I slept so heavily that when I awoke the next morning I felt dull-eyed and thick-headed. Rory must have felt the same, for when I reached down to pet him he blinked his eyes drowsily, then promptly closed them again.

The bed in the dressing room was empty so I knew that Rose, at least, was stirring. In a few minutes she knocked softly at the door, then came in to help me dress.

Her face was sober as she helped me slip into my black

traveling gown, and I guessed what she would say before she told me. "It's Mr. O'Toole. He died early this morning."

"Did he . . . was he conscious at the end?"

"I wouldn't be knowing that. Father Vincent and Mr. Sean sat with him all night at Mary Shaugnassy's cottage. They daren't move him, you see."

"How is Miss O'Toole taking it?"

Rose shrugged. "Carrying on as if she's lost her nearest and dearest. And everyone knows brother and sister never had a kind word to say about each other when old Seamus was alive. Still, death has a way of making people forget old ills, hasn't it now? Even Mr. Cormac, when he heard the news about O'Toole, shut himself in his room, refusing to see anybody."

I was guiltily glad of that piece of news. I had been dreading the thought of saying my good-bys to Cormac Fletcher. Undoubtedly Sean had told his father of my plan to take my accusations to Dublin. Cormac would hardly be pleased that I was attempting to bring about a new investigation into Patrick's death.

When I reached the drawing room on my way to breakfact, I discovered that I wouldn't have to face Regan either. Through the tall windows I could see my sister-in-law on horseback, heading toward the tower road. She seldom came back from her morning rides till mid-morning. By then I would be at the train station in Abbeymore.

After breakfast the butler brought me a message. "Her ladyship asks if you might visit her at the dower house before your leave-taking, if it's convenient."

Unpleasant or not, I knew this was one good-by I couldn't forgo. Lady Margaret had been too kind to me to rudely leave Abbey Court without even thanking her or saying good-by.

I went up to my room to fetch my hat and cape from Rose. As she adjusted the gauze mourning veil over my face, her eyes were red as if she had been crying. "It's a sad day," she mourned. "I'll miss you sore and there are others who will too. We'll not be forgetting."

"I won't forget you, either, Rose," I promised, and then we were hugging each other, and both of us crying, not mistress and servant, but two friends, parting. Finally Rory, sympathetically, began to howl and we fell to laughing.

"There now," Rose fussed when we calmed down. "I've mussed your veil. What will Lady Fletcher think to see you with your hat all crooked? And you won't be forgetting your cape?"

She followed me down the stairs with Rory close behind, taking two steps at a leap to our one. I glanced at the watch pinned on my bodice. "I'll be going straight to the station from the dower house, Rose. Would you have my bags placed in the carriage and ask the coachman to wait for me in the drive?"

"Are you walking to the dower house then?"

"I might as well. It will only take a few minutes and I can use the exercise. My head feels as if it were stuffed with cotton wool." I became aware of Rory, watching me eagerly, as if it he knew there was a walk in the offing and didn't want to be overlooked. "Oh, very well," I said, unable to resist that beseeching look. "You can come along. You probably could use the exercise too."

When I reached the dower house, though, I realized that Rory presented a problem. I didn't want to take him inside the house and I didn't want to leave him untied outside. The woods were too invitingly close.

The maid who answered my knock at the dower house solved my problem by fetching a length of rope and tying Rory to the boot scraper. She was an older servant, one I hadn't seen before, with a rather blank look to her face and thin as a railbird, as if she endured the same fasts as her mistress.

She ushered me into a small front hall, asked me to wait, and disappeared up the narrow, uncarpeted staircase. It was my first visit to the dower house and I looked around curiously. Abbey Court, despite its furniture from every conceivable period, still had an opulent, if slightly worn, charm. The furnishings of the dower house, however, were sparse, the chairs uncomfortably hard-looking, the color of the wallpaper an ugly faded brown and puce. Also, unlike those at Abbey Court, the windows in the dower house were narrow and heavily draped, effectively blocking out the sunlight and leaving the rooms shadowed in a perpetual chill gloom.

I noticed a small chapel to one side of the hall. The white marble altar with a pair of golden candlesticks, gleaming through the dimness, drew me closer. The beautifully embroidered altar cloth had stitches so tiny it was difficult to imagine the sewing having been done by human hands. Above the altar a wooden figure of Christ was nailed on the cross. There was such a lifelike, writhing look of agony on his face that I could bear to look at the cross for only a few seconds before I dropped my gaze.

I started to genuflect quickly, then stopped and drew back, appalled. The top altar rail, padded with red velvet, had been lifted, and I saw another rail beneath. The second rail was studded with row upon row of nails, needle-sharp and stained a rusted brown, as if with blood.

27

"It was kind of you to come, my dear."

Lady Margaret stood in the archway of the small chapel. She was dressed in her usual loose-fitting black gown and, with her hair pulled back severely, her white face seemed to float, disembodied, in the dimly lit room.

She gestured behind her. "Perhaps you would be more comfortable in my sitting room."

I followed her into another small room off the hallway, but this room, at least, had a fieplace at which a peat fire had been laid. Since I had noticed no sign of heat in the rest of the house, I assumed the fire was in my honor. Gratefully I sat as close to the small flame as possible, trying to put out of my mind the memory of the altar rail in the chapel.

"I thought you might like a fire," Lady Margaret murmured. "I visited New York once, you know, several years ago. I found the houses unbearably warm, very unhealthy, I would imagine. Still, I suppose it's all in what one grows accustomed to."

I had the impression she was making conversation, trying to put me at ease. I stole a look at her profile and wondered how much Kevin's mother had been told. Did she know the reason I was going to Dublin and seeing my solicitor? Had Kevin told her about Sean and me? It was impossible to tell from her serenely composed manner.

Then, unexpectedly, she said, "Seamus O'Toole died this morning."

"Yes, I know."

"It was not an easy death." She turned to face me and her eyes reminded me of the candles in the chapel, flickering in the darkness. Where her glance touched my face, my skin seemed to burn. "God's wrath is terrible when it falls upon the wicked," she said softly.

I shifted, all at once uncomfortable at the direction the conversation was taking. "I understood Mr. O'Toole and your husband were friends."

Lady Margaret stiffened. For the moment the aura of saintly reserve fell away and there was only the Dowager Countess of Abbeymore, giving me a haughty glance down her long, patrician nose. "Lord Michael was never friendly with Mr. O'Toole," she said coldly. "Mr. O'Toole was a servant."

I chose my next words carefully. "I've been told the magistrate is looking into Mr. O'Toole's death, asking questions of the staff."

Lady Margaret's gaze never wavered but the frail white hands resting in her lap closed together. "Mr. O'Toole's death was an unfortunate accident. The magistrate is exceeding his authority. I shall ask Kevin to speak to him. He has no right bothering the staff."

"But someone moved the trap," I insisted doggedly. "And someone had to write the note, sending for Mr. O'Toole."

Lady Margaret flinched. "Not one of the servants," she said softly, her voice so low I could barely hear her. "Only a half dozen of them can so much as write their own names."

I stared at the woman, struck silent by what she was not saying, what I suspected she would never allow herself to say aloud to anyone. I leaned forward and reached for her hand. "Lady Margaret," I said urgently, "if you have any information at all about Mr. O'Toole's death, you should tell the authorities."

The muscles in her face contracted so that the lines deepening across her forehead stood out, a blue vein in her temple throbbed. Then a deep sigh, or rather a shudder, passed through her body, and she stiffened, withdrawing her hand from my touch. "My dear child, what could I possibly know of such matters?" she murmured.

Defeated, I sank back in my chair. After all, what had I expected? Even if Lady Margaret suspected that a member of her own family had killed the gamekeeper, loyalty to family name and honor had been bred into her. And if her conscience bothered her, she could always inflict a punishing, tortuous penance upon herself, relying on God's wrath to take care of evildoers. Fortunately divine retribution operated without the scandal of a jury trial or newspaper headlines.

Lady Margaret was watching me anxiously. "Forgive me, my child, all this unpleasantness is, of course, none of your concern. I'm forgetting why I asked you here this morning. Kevin tells me you are going to visit Dublin for a few days. He asked me to tell you that he has arranged rooms for you at the Shelbourne Hotel. And I've some letters of introduction for you to friends of ours in Dublin." She frowned a little unhappily. "The Shelbourne is a fine hotel and I'm sure you'll be comfortable there, but I'd be happier if you were staying in a private home, or, at least, have a maid with you."

"I'm sure I'll be all right, Lady Margaret," I assured her, feeling a rush of gratitude toward Kevin. I had stupidly forgotten about making a hotel reservation and was relieved that I would not have to worry about finding a place to stay. I was even more relieved to realize that evidently Kevin hadn't told his mother that my leaving Abbey Court wasn't temporary but permanent. It was better this way, I decided. After a week or so, when I didn't return, Kevin could break the news to Lady Margaret that I wasn't coming back. By that time, if I had been able to force a new, full-scale investigation into Patrick's death, I was sure Lady Margaret would have no desire to have me back at Abbey Court, in any case.

Lady Margaret reached for the little silver bell beside her chair. "Would you care for tea, my dear? I believe Jessica made some of those little scones this morning that I notice you particularly enjoy."

"No, thank you." I rose quickly to my feet, feeling all at once shamefully hypocritical. "I must be going. My train leaves in an hour."

"Yes, of course." She walked with me to the door. "Do have a pleasant trip. Kevin was desolate at not being able to accompany you to the station but, what with Mr. O'Toole's death, naturally he felt it his duty to remain here at Abbey Court until the matter is settled."

Impulsively I embraced her, wishing I didn't have to leave this way, with so much deception between us. "Thank you, Lady Margaret, for everything. I'll always be grateful."

The body beneath the black woolen gown in my arms felt weightless, almost boneless. She drew back from my grasp graciously, but effortlessly as smoke. Was it human passion of any kind she could not endure, I wondered, or was it my touch? The drawn white face once more wore its serene, reserved mask, the gray eyes for all their intensity were as devoid of warmth now as chips of marble.

"Good-by, my dear," she said, and closed the door behind me.

After the darkness of the dower house, the sunlight blinded me. I blinked and looked around, dismayed. Where was Rory? The rope with which I had tied him was still attached to the boot scraper but there was no eager, leggy young dog pulling at the other end, trying to jump up on me.

I thought irritably that he must have pulled free and gone chasing off into the woods. I followed the road down to where the path cut through the woodland from the tower to the Abbey, walking a few feet down the path and calling Rory's name. If he was within earshot, I knew that in another few seconds he would come bounding out of the woods, looking the picture of perfect innocence, his tongue lolling happily.

"Rory . . . here, boy . . . Rory!"

No matter how loudly I called, my voice was almost instantly swallowed up by the lush thickness of the oak and beech trees around me, and the inches-thick matting of leaves beneath my feet. Frowning, I glanced at my watch. I still had more than enough time to get to the station but I could imagine what my dress and hair would look like if I went plowing through the woods in search of one errant dog.

I supposed the sensible thing to do was walk back to the house and tell Rose what had happened. She could send some of the servants out to look for the dog. I had half turned toward the road when I heard a sound that froze me to the spot where I stood. It was the high-pitched, yipping cry of an animal in pain.

"Rory!"

The silence wrapped around me again but this time my ears strained to catch the slightest noise, the merest whimper. The cry came again, louder, an agonized howling, weakening, dying away even as I bolted down the path toward the point from which the sound seemed to be coming.

Pictures crowded my mind. All that loving exuberance, that frantic enjoyment of life, crushed within the jaws of a trap, the silky, golden-red fur stained with blood, the dog struggling to free himself while the teeth clamped cruelly through muscle and bone, the soft brown eyes glazing with bewildered pain.

I forced myself to stop again, to listen and peer into the darkened woods where the sun's rays fell charily as golden coins, slipping through a web of branches, disappearing into the thick brush beneath. The musk of moldering branches and decaying leaves choked my nostrils.

When a scratching, rustling sound in the underbrush to the right of the path broke the silence, I plunged off the path through the low-hanging branches of scrub oak. A patch of wild roses tore at my skirt before I paused, breathless, in a small clearing, calling again. "Rory!"

More wild roses dotted one edge of the clearing, making a fine sheltered nest for some wild thing. As I stood, very still, staring into the clustered branches, I saw the shine of a small animal's eyes staring back. A ferret or fox, I realized, and disappointment squeezed my throat dry.

The silence and the darkness seemed to press against me, the lichen-coated trees a thick curtain beyond which it was impossible to see more than in few inches. For one panicky moment I wasn't sure in which direction the path lay. Then I got hold of myself, annoyed. The Abbey Court woods were thick, but not that wide between the tower road and the old Abbey.

Locating the sun through the treetops, I got my direction firmly in mind and turned confidently back toward where the path should be. Then without warning, I felt myself falling through a thick layer of leaves. My feet couldn't have sunk more than a few inches into the hole dug out by a decayed root. It was only a second or two, but long enough for terror to lift the hairs on my head, as if I were feeling the razor claws of a trap clamping around my ankle. I pulled myself free and practically flew the rest of the way back to the safety of the path.

Once on the path again, I took a deep ragged breath. It wasn't any good. It would be foolish for me to attempt to search the woods in the slim hope of finding one small dog, not only foolish but dangerous. Even with Seamus O'Toole gone, the traps he had placed so cunningly still lurked in the woods—the spring gun set into a tree, the claw trap hidden underfoot, waiting to maim and mutilate the unwary poacher.

Then, as I stood hesitating, I heard again the frantic howl of pain. Suddenly now I was sure of the direction—it was straight down the path directly ahead of me. The Abbey,

I thought, relieved. Of course. Why hadn't I thought of it sooner? I should have remembered how fond Rory was of digging around in the rocky crevices. He must have fallen or been trapped somehow within the ruins.

In a matter of minutes I had reached the crumbling walls and found the jagged opening which provided the best view of the interior of the cloister.

"Rory!"

A joyful barking greeted my call this time, as if the dog knew that rescue was near. I studied the fallen rock inside of the wall where I stood. Great tilted slabs of stone and rocks, almost like steps, led downward. It shouldn't be too difficult a descent, I decided. I had climbed down much more hazardous mountain paths as a child.

Taking off my cape and bonnet, I placed them neatly, along with my reticule, on top of the wall out of harm's way. Then, inching up my skirt, I began the slow, careful passage downward over the uneven stones, avoiding the slippery patches of moss and ducking several rooks that flashed upward into the air in front of me, screaming raucously at being disturbed.

At the foot of the rocky stairs I stood in what must have once been the cloister gardens. I could barely make out the now almost obliterated geometrically placed paths. Weeds and nettles stood where once carefully tended flowers and vegetables had grown. Rory's sharp, eager barking was closer now, just the other side of the half-fallen wall ahead of me, shielding the remains of the refectory from my view.

I hurried forward, circling a depression in the ground— the lower floor of some room that was now filled with rubble and weeds and broken stone columns. A crooked archway stood at one corner of the wall, a curtain of ivy falling across it.

Cautiously I pushed the ivy aside. It was darker on this side of the wall. The trees grew closer to the edge at this end of the Abbey, casting deep black shadows inside the ruins. Even the air felt colder and had a faint unpleasant odor as if some animal had died near the ruins. I waited until my eyes grew accustomed to the gloom and saw that there was another smaller, sunken area on this side of the wall, perhaps twenty feet square. The part of the wall still standing seemed in reasonably good condition, with elaborate carvings and deep niches. The bases of the columns that held up the archway were richly ornamented with monster faces, gargoyles and demons, half animal and half human. A stone staircase went down into the sunken area from a paved walk. This had been a colonnade, perhaps, under which monks had once strolled, meditating, but now the roof of the colonnade was gone. Only a tall crumbling wall remained.

Something about the place—perhaps it was the clammy chill in the air—reminded me suddenly of the cold, damp chapel in the dower house. All at once I couldn't wait to find Rory and leave.

I skirted the edge of the depression, moving very gingerly over the broken pavement, trying not to touch the leaning columns on one side of me or the loose broken rock slide from the half-fallen wall on the other side.

Finally I had to stop, the sunken staircase a barrier across my path. The narrow steps were hollowed as they descended into a stair well but still in good condition; the walls of the well were cracked and veined with moss. A partial rock slide had cut off the ambulatory on the wall side of the stairway so there was no way I could edge around it unless I climbed over the crumpled mass of rocks.

I studied the pile of stones uneasily, trying to decide if they would bear my weight without slipping. There was no mortar left that I could see, just thick swags of ivy extending back to what must have been the end of the colonnade. One large stone pillar still miraculously remained whole and upright at the corner though so covered with lichen it appeared to be carved from emerald. It was darker by the column, which was shrouded in the shadow cast by a gnarled beech tree overhead. Then I saw a movement in the darkness and heard a scratching, rustling sound, a muffled yipe.

"Rory!"

At that moment something hurtled toward me along the colonnade, leaping easily the open space over the stair well. The next minute Rory was almost knocking me over with the ecstasy of his greeting, trying to lick any portion of me that he could reach with his tongue, making delighted, growling sounds deep in his throat.

I knelt down, hugging the wiggling, excited body to me, running my hands over the red-gold fur, trying to feel where he might be hurt. "Rory, you bad boy," I scolded, half-angry, half relieved. "What a lot of trouble you've caused me. Where have you . . ."

My heart lurched inside me and my voice died away. Slowly, still holding Rory, I got to my feet. For something else stood in the corner by the green column—the dark, elongated shadow of a man, watching me.

28

In that split second terror gripped me as it had the day I had looked down into one of Seamus O'Toole's traps. I couldn't breathe, mush less move. Then the man stepped out of the darkness cast by the wall above him and, picking his way a little clumsily over the fallen rock, came close enough to me so that I could see his face.

I gave a gasp of relief. "Oh, it's you, Kevin. I thought for a moment it was—" And stopped, discomfited.

"Sean?" In the shadowy light filtering through the beech tree, Kevin's pale face had a greenish cast. His voice was thin, mocking. "Is that why you looked so frightened? And so soon after that touching scene I witnessed in the office."

"It's . . . it's just that I didn't know anyone else was here." I stammered. "I was looking for Rory." At mention of his name, the dog began to try to pull free from my arms. I knelt and set him down, glad for the chance to hide my face and gather my wits. Kevin must have heard Rory barking, too, and come to investigate. That was why he was here, wasn't it? Only why hadn't he called out to me? Probably he was as embarrassed as I was at our meeting unexpectedly this way.

I straightened slowly, wondering what I possibly could say to ease the awkwardness of the situation. If only, I thought, I'd gone straight from the dower house to the carriage! "I've asked Rose to look after Rory but I'll send for him, of course, as soon as I'm settled. She's as fond of him as I am. . . ." I knew I was babbling, gazing at a point just above Kevin's shoulder so I wouldn't have to look into his face. Unconsciously I gathered my skirt about me for a quick flight as soon as I could gracefully withdraw.

Kevin's abrupt harsh laugh disconcerted me. My eyes swung to his face, startled. "It won't do any more, my dear," he said, shaking his head. "The ingenuous air, the naïve, innocent smile. Oh, I admit you do it all very well. At first I really did believe Patrick had told you nothing in his letters. Or perhaps I just wanted to believe you. It was easier that way. Liam said I was a fool to trust you. And he was right. He usually is, about women."

"I . . . I don't understand. What letters?"

Kevin frowned impatiently. "Come now, you don't really think I believe you found the jewel case without any help, after Liam and I spent weeks searching for it here in the Abbey. Or did your mother tell you before she died? Even if Patrick hadn't spent so much time here in the Abbey, I would have guessed Fiona must have hidden the case here. She had to pass the Abbey on her way to Mary Shaugnassy's cottage that day after the fire at Abbey Court. Where could she find a better, safer place? I suppose she planned to return and collect the jewels later, but Uncle Cormac whisked her away from the Shaugnassy cottage before she had the chance. And before Seamus could finish the job Father sent him to do," he added bitterly.

Although most of his words made no sense, I grasped at the last sentence eagerly. "Then it was Seamus at Mary Shaugnassy's cottage, the man who tried to kill her." A mingled disbelief and horror shook my voice. "Why? Why should your father want to have Fiona murdered?"

"Not murder," Kevin said, his face twisting with a delicate distaste at the word. "My father was too tenderhearted for that. I assume he told O'Toole to get rid of Fiona, to get her out of the country. After all, what else could he do? Can you imagine the impossible position he was in, married to a servant girl, and then to suddenly receive word that his brothers were dead, that he was next in line to inherit the earldom? He had no choice. No doubt Fiona had tricked him into marriage in the first place. Women have ways of doing that. I suppose working so much alone with Father in the tower, helping him with the artifacts he had discovered, Fiona found many ways to make herself . . . agreeable."

Kevin's smile was an unpleasant leer and I felt a flush of anger rise in my cheeks. As if Mother would trick anyone into marriage, I thought furiously. For a moment I was too angry at Kevin's nasty insinuation to grasp what else he was saying. Not Cormac, I thought, bewildered. It had never been Cormac, always Michael. And I remembered the special softness in Mother's voice when she told me about the Abbeymore brooch, as if she had been speaking of a man, not a piece of metal. It had been Michael's name on her lips when she died, the husband she thought had been killed in the Abbey Court fire. All those months they had worked together in the tower, the scholarly recluse who must have married Fiona secretly in a sudden fit of rash courage, and then never found the same courage to stand up to his father and admit the truth. Did he know, I wondered, that when he meant to send Fiona away she was carrying his child, or would it have made any difference? There was Lady Margaret waiting in the wings, his dead brother's fiancée, with wealth and social position, a much more suitable wife for the next Earl of Abbeymore than an Irish servant girl.

"I'm sure it was O'Toole's idea, not Father's, to get rid of Fiona permanently. After what happened to his brother Cullen, Seamus had no love for your mother, as you can imagine." Regret tinged Kevin's voice. "It's a shame, really, that he botched the job. It would have been much simpler all the way round if he had rid Abbey Court of Fiona O'Neill once and for all. The thought of her, alive somewhere, must have hung over Father like a cloud all the rest of his life, never knowing if someday she might suddenly show up again, marriage lines in hand. I don't suppose he even knew that Fiona hadn't taken them with her; that her marriage lines were buried in the jewel case, along with the Abbey jewels."

"He told you—his son—all this?" I asked, shocked.

"Naturally not! I was only a boy when he died." Something cracked in Kevin's face, the icy reserve shattering violently as if under a pressure too great to be borne. "Part of it I learned from O'Toole when he tried a bit of blackmail on me. The rest your brother Patrick told me."

"Patrick couldn't have known," I protested. "How could he? Mother would never have told him."

"Oh, he knew all right. He couldn't let it rest, you see, that his precious mother was a thief. He was determined to find the jewels and clear her name. He spent half his time scrambling around here in the Abbey ruins, the *auld kil* . . ."

"*Auld kil*." I repeated the words softly. Fiona's words, when she was dying. And I remembered I had written Patrick everything Mother had said at the end. Patrick had understood what the words meant, even though I didn't.

Kevin gestured around him. "The *auld kil*—the old chapel—that's where we're standing. It's the oldest part of the Abbey, the private chapel where the abbot himself worshiped. But you knew that, didn't you? Patrick must have written you. Why keep pretending? This is where Patrick found the case, isn't it, with the jewels and marriage lines inside? And it's where he buried it again, before he told me what he had found. He didn't have the document on him. We searched him thoroughly—afterward."

"No!" I cried the word aloud, a cry of anguished rejection. "You couldn't—not Patrick—you were his friend."

For a moment Kevin seemed at a loss, the color draining from his face. Then he spoke in a rush. "You must understand. I never meant for him to die. It was an accident. I was very fond of Patrick. I had hoped he felt the same. Those hours we spent together at the tower were some of the happiest in my life. He was like a young chevalier, slim and golden and handsome, and that wonderfully clear, lucid mind. All that beauty wasted on Regan."

"He loved Regan!"

A spitefulness sharpened Kevin's voice. "Perhaps, in the beginning, until I told him a few hard truths about his young, pure bride. Then he saw her clearly, as I had long ago. She disgusted him, the sight of her, the touch of her. He turned more and more to me. At first I was afraid to say or do anything. I wasn't completely sure, you see, how he felt. For all his sophistication, Patrick was in many ways completely innocent. Such exquisite pain for me to be near him, not knowing."

"No, please, no, I don't want to hear any more." I thought I was screaming the words but no sound came from my lips. This was a horror I sensed without understanding, without being able to put it into words. A vague memory stirred in my mind of a young scion of a proud Boston family suddenly whisked away to Europe, the whispered gossip that had reached my bewildered young ears, and Mother, looking embarrassed, speaking sotto voce of perversion and sin, and Patrick, not so much embarrassed as saddened, murmuring, "Poor fellow."

Not Patrick, I thought. My God, not Patrick!

Kevin continued compulsively, as if he could not stop himself even if he had wanted to. "The morning your brother asked me to come see him privately in the study, his note sounded urgent. I thought—I hoped he wanted to speak of us, but instead he asked me again if I would agree to let Sean go as agent for the estate. He even had some ridiculous idea of allowing the tenants to use their rent money to buy their own farms over a period of years."

Kevin flung out his arms, exasperated. "Naturally I couldn't permit that. The idea was preposterous. What did he think would happen to me if I let a lot of dirty, ignorant peasants own Abbey Court land? He would destroy Abbey Court. I tried to reason with him. I swear I tried. Then— I only wanted to make him understand how deeply I cared for him—I said things. I suppose I shouldn't have. And suddenly he was livid with rage. I'd never seen him so angry. He came out from behind the desk and struck at me with his fist. No one, not even Uncle Cormac, had ever hit me in the face. I was terrified and retreated back behind the desk, afraid he'd hit me again. Then he told me. He had found the jewel case and the marriage lines almost a week before. The document that proved my mother's marriage was invalid; that Father had already had a wife when he married her. My own claim to Abbey Court and the earldom might not be legal if it could be proven I was illegitimate. Patrick told me he had planned to keep silent, for my sake and Lady Margaret's. But now he'd changed his mind. I wasn't fit to be the Earl of Abbeymore. He said— terrible things. I was frantic. There was my inheritance to think about, my position, and Mother.

"Then I saw the desk drawer was half open and Patrick's gun was there. I didn't mean to use it, only to frighten him, force him to give me the copy of the marriage document. But he jumped me and we struggled; the gun went off. I couldn't believe it at first. He fell away from me, so slowly, to the floor. Then I thought, surely, the servants— someone—had heard the shot and would come bursting into the room. But no one came. And then all I could think of was to get rid of him. You can understand that—how I had to do what I did."

The gray eyes studied me anxiously, as if, I thought, shivering, he was waiting for my approval. Or was it forgiveness? It didn't matter. I had nothing to give him, this terrified shadow of a man. All I felt was a vague sense of relief that at least neither Kevin nor Patrick had learned what would have been, for Kevin, the ultimate betrayal. That Fiona had not only married Lord Michael but borne him a son; that it was his own half brother Kevin had killed.

I saw that Kevin was watching me, waiting. I knew I must say something, keep him talking until I had time to pull myself together, plan what I must do next. "How . . .

how did you manage the rest?" I asked, as if it mattered, as if any of it mattered now.

"It wasn't difficult, after all." Kevin's voice became a trifle smug. "There was the stained glass window and I simply pushed Patrick out onto the grass. I spilled the ink over the bloodstain on the rug, put the gun back in the drawer, and climbed out of the window myself, closing it behind me. Then I fetched Liam. It was his idea to take Sean's horse with Patrick's body on it down through the gully to the Abbey road, hoping that poachers or Moonlighters would be blamed for the shooting. It was a disappointment, of course, that we didn't find the marriage lines on Patrick's body, but I was sure he hadn't told anyone of his discovery. Until you showed up at Abbey Court and started asking questions. And nothing would stop you. You were like a terrier with a bone. Heaven knows, I tried to discourage you."

"It was you," I said slowly, "in my room, trying to frighten me away from Abbey Court."

"Not me, my dear child," Kevin said quickly. "Liam. It was very naughty of him but it was all his idea. I knew nothing about it until I returned to Abbey Court from London. Naturally I disapproved. I had already planned to marry you, you see. It was the ideal solution. I could certainly use the fortune your mother must have left you and I needed an heir. Once we were married, I was sure I could make you forget everything else."

I stared at him, dumb-struck. "You would have married me? You would have gone through with it?"

"Why not?" Kevin's smile was patronizing. "It isn't unknown, you know. I could name several important, perfectly respectable families in the peerage, in which the husband has his lover on the side. It's a bit of a strain, I admit, but one has one's duty and position to consider. The Earl of Abbeymore is expected to produce an heir. You're young and healthy. I imagine you can have babies as easily as one of the tenant women. We would have had as good a marriage as most."

He suddenly laughed, a pleased smirk on his face. "Unfortunately, Liam is insanely jealous. He took a most unreasonable dislike to you from the first. When he knew I had decided to marry you, he decided to pay a little visit to your room. I'm sure he only meant to frighten you, at first, but I gather he got carried away with his role the second time. Liam, at times, can be quite violent, I'm afraid. I had some harsh words with him about it. It was very foolish. He could so easily have been caught."

Kevin sighed. "Still, in the long run, it might have been better if he had succeeded. It would all be finished now."

I took a step backward. It wasn't menace I saw in Kevin's face. What I saw in his eyes was even more frightening—and final. It was sorrow, the way he would look at an animal caught in a trap and hate to see it killed; the way he must have looked, I thought suddenly, when he had been unable to see Rory destroyed. If I could appeal to that pity, I thought feverishly, if I could reach that part of Kevin that could still feel sorrow, compassion . . .

I spoke softly, coaxingly. "I never knew any of this, Kevin, you must believe me. I didn't know about Fiona's marriage and I never found any jewel case in the Abbey or anywhere else."

Kevin frowned impatiently. "It's no good, Meg. You're bluffing. Seamus tried that. But I knew he was lying. Why else was he so anxious to leave the country? He even thought he could frighten me into giving him money. But once I paid him, how could I trust him to keep quiet? It was much simpler sending him the note, using Sean's handwriting. Then Liam moved one of O'Toole's traps, hiding it across the path O'Toole was sure to take the next morning on his way to the office. If there were questions, well, it was Sean's note, and if not Sean, then the poachers, to take the blame."

"I swear to you, Kevin, I didn't know about the marriage. I'm not bluffing. I don't have any document." I heard my voice rising hysterically and Rory, investigating a fallen pillar a few feet away from me, lifted his head at the shrill tone of my voice. I forced myself to calmness. I would not convince Kevin by screaming at him. I must be quiet, rational. "Listen to me, Kevin. You can search me if you like."

"Oh, we've already done that," he said airily. "Last night Liam went through your room thoroughly."

"How could he?" I asked, bewildered. "I would have heard him."

Then I remembered how soundly Rose and I, and even Rory, had slept last night.

"Liam was one of the servants in the kitchen being questioned by the magistrate last evening," Kevin explained. "It wasn't difficult for him to slip a sleeping potion in the dinner Rose carried upstairs for you, and in the cup of tea Rose had in the kitchen with her meal. Even a little something in the dog's food." Kevin scowled petulantly. "Unfortunately Liam couldn't find the marriage lines so I know you must still have the document on you . . . or is it still buried here in the Abbey? That's why I had Mother send you the note, asking you to drop by the dower house this morning."

"Lady Margaret!" I said, shocked. "She knows?"

Kevin lifted a pained eyebrow. "Of course not. What do you take me for? It would destroy her if she had the slightest notion. But naturally I couldn't allow you to leave Abbey Court and take the marriage document to your solicitor in Dublin. I planned to meet you accidentally as you left the dower house and ask you to take a farewell stroll with me. But your leaving the dog tied up outside the house made everything easy. I know how fond you are of Rory. If you thought he was caught in a trap or hurt, you'd come looking for him."

"For God's sake, Kevin, listen to me! I don't have any marriage document. I don't know where the jewel case is."

Irritation twitched at the corners of Kevin's mouth; anger smoldered beneath the surface of his voice. "Stop lying, Meg. You made a mistake, you know, wearing the Abbeymore brooch. I saw it on your dress the morning I found Sean pawing you in the office. I recognized it at once from the drawings of the brooch Father had in his books in the tower. It was one of the jewels in the case Fiona buried that day. If you had possession of the brooch, you had to have the marriage lines too."

I felt such a wild sense of relief that I almost laughed aloud. "That's a reproduction, Kevin," I cried. "Mother had it made years ago in New York. That's not the original brooch."

"I told you not to lie," he said irritably, but I could see he was for the first time shaken, his manner, uncertain.

"I'm not lying. You can get my jewel case, look for yourself. You'll see at once the brooch is a reproduction."

A terrible emptiness filled his eyes. He lifted his hands, then let them fall helplessly to his side, murmuring sadly, "Then it's all . . . for nothing."

At first I didn't understand. And when I did it was too late, as if the steel jaws had finally, cruelly sprung upon me, I knew. Even if I didn't have the document that branded Kevin a bastard, I knew too much now. I couldn't be allowed to escape.

I took a careful step away from Kevin, keeping my voice low and cajoling. "You mustn't act foolishly, Kevin. Think a minute. If I were to die, it wouldn't be like Seamus or Patrick. You couldn't blame Moonlighters or poachers. There'd be a complete investigation of three deaths in a row here at Abbey Court. And one investigation would lead to another . . ."

I was emboldened by his stillness, his air of perplexity, as if he weren't sure what to do next. Another step back and I would turn and make a dash for the archway, I thought. I kept talking softly, reassuringly, as if to a frightened child. "I know you, Kevin. You wouldn't kill a woman. You couldn't hurt me."

"Kevin couldn't . . . but I could, Miss O'Brien."

I whirled, a scream rising in my throat. For what I was staring at was myself, clothed all in black, standing in the archway.

29

The woman in the archway, a mirror image of myself, wore my black half cape over a plain black traveling gown. She carried my black beaded reticule and the heavy mourning veil covering my black bonnet almost hid her face from view, except for a glimpse of bright red hair tucked demurely beneath the hat, her hair almost exactly the same shade as my own.

"I think I'll pass very nicely for you, don't you, Miss O'Brien?"

Even the voice was an eerie reproduction of mine, mimicked expertly. "Of course, I'm a wee bit taller, but I doubt if anyone will notice that, not from a distance. And Kevin will be with me in the carriage, escorting me to the station, and he won't allow anyone to get too close, will you, Kevin?"

The black kid-gloved hand lifted the gauze veil slowly and I looked into Liam Carmody's face, the blue eyes sparkling, amused, as if it were all a grand joke.

"My clothes," I blurted. "Where did you get them?"

"There now, did Kevin forget to mention it?" The voice dropped, became Liam's own, velvety soft. "While I was searching your luggage, in vain, last evening, I did manage to pick up a few things. Some of your clothes—and this." His right hand had been hidden beneath the cape. Now it came out and I saw Patrick's gun, the silver engraving gleaming in the sunlight. "Only the revolver's not empty any longer, Miss O'Brien. If you had looked in the desk drawer, you would have found that your brother always kept a few extra cartridges there." He frowned thoughtfully. "However, I'm a passably good shot. I shouldn't need more than one."

Fear was a pain squeezing my ribs just beneath my breastbone, like a vise, slowly tightening. And even worse than the fear was the knowledge taking hold of me that Liam was enjoying himself. He could have shot me as I stood there with my back to him, talking to Kevin, but he had wanted to see my face, savor the terror that must be clear in my eyes, watch me cringe as he raised the gun, leveled it at my head, and waited for me to beg for my life. Well, he was wrong, I thought, anger loosening, easing the vise a little. I wouldn't give him that satisfaction. An O'Brien didn't grovel . . . Jamie had taught me that. And his aim was bad, I thought almost absently, as if one part of my mind couldn't resist thinking normally, refusing to accept the unacceptable. I had fired Patrick's gun. It shot high.

I spoke quickly, stalling for time. Someone might come along the Abbey road, although I knew it was a remote chance. Still, I had to try to keep him talking. He was so filled with pride, fairly bursting with the vanity of his cleverness. And a vain man could make a slip. "Why go to all this trouble?" I asked. "Such an elaborate deception. Surely someone will suspect."

Liam shook his head, smiling faintly, as if he guessed what I was doing but decided to indulge me. "Why should anyone suspect? Kevin will ride in the carriage with me to the station where he'll put Miss O'Brien on the train. She'll arrive in Dublin, check into the Shelbourne Hotel, and that's the last we'll ever hear of poor Miss O'Brien. She'll simply disappear. There'll be a search, of course, after a week or two, or perhaps longer, but the search won't be here at Abbey Court. You were right about that. Abbey Court can't afford another unexplained death. The search will be in Dublin, the police looking for a wealthy young woman foolish enough to travel alone. Terrible things do happen to them, you know. It's unfortunate you won't tell the truth about where you've hidden the jewel case but it's not important. With you gone, the case and its contents will stay hidden forever."

"I tell you I never found any jewels or any marriage document! Kevin, you believe me!" I turned imploringly toward the slim, tall figure standing motionless, the column above him throwing a shadow like a black bar across his body. Kevin was not looking at me. His glance was riveted abjectly on Liam with a fixed intensity, as if he could not pull his eyes away. I had always thought that it was Kevin who was master over Liam—the lord of the manor and his faithful, obedient servant. Now suddenly I saw it was reversed. It was Liam who dominated the scene and Kevin who stood in the shadows. Whatever relationship lay between the two, it was Liam who made the plans and pulled the strings, not Kevin. Kevin, alone, would never have had the courage or temperament to kill a man, much less a woman.

"Kevin, please . . ." Despite my intentions, I could hear myself begging. "You can't let him do this. Help me!"

Just for a moment I thought I saw something move, come alive, in the blank gray eyes. Kevin's gaze shifted, uncomfortably toward me. Something of my own horror was reflected in his still face. Then I heard a sound that was like a burst of thunder in my ears but was only the hammer of the Colt being pulled back and cocked, before the trigger could be pulled.

Kevin heard it too. His glance swung wildly back to his lover, and he cried, "No! Wait till I leave . . . I don't want to see!"

Then three things happened almost simultaneously. There was an explosion of sound richocheting against the broken walls of the ruins, and from every niche and cranny hundreds of rooks flew upward in a wild, noisy confusion. Above their high, lamenting cries, the flapping of their wings within inches of my head, I saw Kevin fling up his hands to protect his face against the rooks.

"Keep them away from me," he screamed in terror, and scrambled up the scree of the wall in a blind panic to escape.

What happened next seemed to occur in slow motion. The stones under Kevin's feet began loosening, sliding downward, the grumbling noise becoming a roar as the larger rocks gathered speed and dragged bits of stone and gravel with them. Dust and mortar flew in a gray choking cloud around me as the whole wall slid slowly, inexorably forward. I screamed a warning to Kevin and then something struck me hard in the forehead, like a pebble flung from a sling shot. I stumbled backward and the ground was all at once gone from under me and I felt myself falling . . . falling into darkness.

I don't know how long I lay unconscious. When I finally drifted back to semiconsciousness, it was only for a few seconds. My thoughts were confused, disjointed. At first I thought I was dead. Only death could be a void so dark and cold and filled with pain. How strange it was. Not at all peaceful the way I had imagined death to be, I thought before oblivion like a shroud wrapped around me again. When finally the pain once more drove me to full consciousness, I stared around me, groping through a fog of memory.

I wasn't dead, and after that first certainty I realized how unfortunate that was. I would have been much better off dead. The darkness wasn't as black as I had first thought and, as my eyes adjusted to the dimness, I could see where I was. The rock that had hit me in the forehead—not a bullet or I would surely have been dead now—had thrown me backward into the stair well. And the rock slide had done the rest.

Still half dazed, I studied my surroundings. What appeared to be a stone lintel was braced a good two feet above me, fallen across the staircase, braced against the well itself. However it had got there, it had stopped most of the stones from sliding down on top of me and crushing me completely. How high the rocks were piled above the lintel, though, I had no way of knowing. Cautiously, I discovered I could move my arms, and my fingers traced a path over the stone cage around and over me. I was having no difficulty breathing. Air, as well as speckles of light, must be reaching through the tiny cracks in the fallen pile of rocks. Carefully I avoided touching the lintel above my face and upper body for fear that its position might be precarious. A shift could bring the full weight of rocks down on top of me.

After I finished the inventory of my surroundings, I began an even more cautious inspection of myself. The top and back of my head throbbed, and blood was caked, dry now, in my hair, but I found I could lift my head a little. When I tried, however, waves of nauseating dizziness engulfed me.

My hands and arms were cut and bruised but apparently no bones were broken. When I tried to move my legs, though, they would not budge.

Whimpering with the pain the effort brought me, I forced my body high enough to see that my legs from my thighs down were pinned fast beneath a load of rock. One stone, larger than the others, had wedged so that the rocks could move no farther forward. Oddly enough I felt no pain in the lower portion of my body. I felt nothing at all, as if, beneath the rocks hiding them, my legs no longer existed.

I sank back again, and this time it was horror, not dizziness, that swept over me and I began to scream—over and over again like a trapped wild thing until the inside of my throat felt as if the skin were scraped raw. Then I was exhausted. The hysteria passed and, no matter how hard I tried, only tremulous, weak moans came from my mouth.

It was no use, I thought, closing my eyes, no longer caring, only wishing that it would be over quickly. No one would hear me. Kevin and Liam had wanted me dead. They had probably planned to bury my body somewhere near the Abbey but the rock slide had taken care of my burial for them. Even if my screams could be heard through the barrier of rock above me, how many people ever used the old Abbey road? How many more, if they did hear strange sounds coming from the ruins, would hurry along without a backward glance, frightened half out of their wits for fear of seeing the ghostly abbot on his eternal vigilance for the dead martyrs?

As for Meg O'Brien, by now she must have been seen leaving Abbey Court in the carriage, saying a decorous good-by to Lord Fletcher at the station, and boarding the train with her mourning veil pulled securely down over her face. How long would it be, I wondered vaguely, before someone began checking into my whereabouts? Perhaps only Mr. Corcoran might become concerned. And Sean . . when he received no word from Dublin about an investigation into Patrick's death, would he begin to wonder? Or would he assume that my solicitor had sensibly decided to disregard my story too? Thinking of Sean, though, brought a pain more agonizing than the pounding from my bruised head. I began to cry soundlessly, hopelessly, as if I could bear the idea of dying but not endure the thought of never seeing Sean again, never being able to tell him how wrong I had been, how stupid and blind. For by the time anyone began looking for Meg O'Brien, scouring the back streets and alleyways of Dublin, it would already be too late for me.

At last I slept, drifting between consciousness and unconsciousness, never fully asleep, never completely awake. The icy, numbing cold crept over my body, as if the flow of my blood was slowing, freezing in my veins, and then even more tormenting, came the thirst. When I felt with my fingers a few drops of water trickling down the side of the wall beside my head, I reached out and licked the stone with my tongue. The drops slid like soothing balm down my throat. I thought of calling for help again but realized with the darkness crowding around me, it must be night. There was no use wasting my breath until morning came.

Hours . . . days passed, it seemed, as I shifted my stiffly aching body time and time again as much as I could, trying to find a more comfortable position, before the darkness in my stone tomb turned paler, grayer in shade. I guessed it must be daylight and began to call again, pacing myself, crying for help for several minutes, then resting for several minutes. Once I thought I heard a dog barking in the distance and I thought of Rory with a new pang of misery; had he escaped or had the rock slide caught and buried him too? Then the barking stopped and I wondered if I had imagined the sound. No other noise came filtering down to me, but surely, I thought, clinging to any hope no matter how frail, if I had heard a dog, then my cries for help could be heard too.

I tried to reckon how long I had been buried—two days, three? How long could I survive without food and only a few drops of water? And I remembered years ago, in one of the mining camps in which we had lived, four men trapped in a mine cave-in. The miners had been recovered after six days without food and only a little water, still alive. "The will to survive," Maggie," Jamie had said solemnly. "That's the important thing."

But as the icy cold deepened its hold on me, I could feel my will lessening, my voice growing progressively weaker. It was useless . . . crying . . . listening . . . screaming again . . . just let go . . . like the torture of clinging to the edge of a cliff with your fingertips . . . straining, pulling, when it's so much simpler just to drop.

One more time. I commanded myself, and it was not Meg O'Brien but someone else urging me on, disgusted at my weakness, prodding me, refusing to let me stop. It was no longer a loud cry for help, but more like a sob and when I heard a faint answering sound above me I thought at first it was my imagination. There was an odd, scrabbling noise that I didn't recognize immediately, until I heard the eager, frantic barking accompanying it—the most beautiful sound I'd ever heard.

"Rory!" It was a whisper, not a scream. But at least I knew it wasn't my imagination. There were other sounds, human voices, fading, coming nearer, one man's voice, finally, louder than the rest, "Here, over here."

More light came pouring into the stair well as I could hear stone being moved, and Sean's voice, closer now, "Meg, can you hear me? You'll have to help us. Tell us if the rock starts to shift."

"Yes." I was laughing and crying at once. "Yes, I can hear you. Hurry, please hurry."

Then finally the darkness was gone and I stared, awestruck, up into a blue sky, as if it were too beautiful to believe, dust motes glinting like silver in the sunlight. The rubble over the lower part of my body was being removed and arms eagerly reached down to me. Sean's hands tightened around my shoulders. When he started to lift me gently, the muscles and nerves in my legs I had thought completely numb came, like searing flames, painfully alive. I screamed for the last time and remembered nothing more.

Later, I learned that I had been trapped beneath the rock slide for almost forty-eight hours and that it was Rory who saved my life. The dog kept returning to the Abbey ruins, whining and digging obsessively at the rock tumbled above me. When carried away forcibly and tied in the stable, he bit through the rope and returned to the ruins to continue his futile digging and scratching. Finally, when for the third time Rose came to fetch him away, as she bent to take the unwilling, struggling dog in her arms she thought she heard a muffled cry from deep beneath the rock slide.

"My hair stood on end, it did," she exclaimed, her round face flushed with excitement as she told me about it, almost a week later, when the doctors finally said I could have visitors. I lay once more in my bedroom at Abbey Court, my legs bound in splints and heavily bandaged. For the first time in days, though, the drug the doctors had been giving me for the pain had worn away. My mind, no longer befogged, was reaching for answers. One answer, in particular, to a question I was afraid to ask . . . something the doctors had spoken of when they thought I was unconscious.

"I was that afeared I couldn't run," Rose continued, as she gently brushed my hair. "Sure and I thought it was those poor lost souls burned to death, buried there in the Abbey, may the saints have mercy on them, but then I thought I should tell someone and I found Mr. Sean, and . . ."

Her hand flew to her mouth, aghast. "It's forgetting I am. Himself is waiting to see you with his lordship."

Kevin! But I couldn't face him, I thought, all the terror I had felt in the Abbey ruins returning in a cold sweat. What could I possibly say to him? "Rose, wait!" It was too late. She had already opened the bedroom door.

I shrank back among the pillows, wishing I could make myself invisible. To my surprise, Cormac Fletcher wheeled into the room with Sean behind him, pushing the chair.

Sean came immediately to the bed. There were lines cut in his face I hadn't seen before, his heavy-lidded eyes were red-rimmed and haggard, as if he hadn't slept in days. "The doctor said it was all right for you to have visitors, but if you're not feeling strong enough . . ."

Bewildered, I looked from Sean to his father. "Where is Kevin?"

Then I saw my answer in Cormac's bleak gaze and knew why Rose had called Cormac Lord Fletcher. "We thought you knew, lass," he said quietly. "Kevin was caught in the same rock slide that buried you."

"We would never have found him so quickly," Sean explained, "but I'd sent several groomsmen out looking for Regan when she didn't return from her ride, and her horse finally came back to the stable without her."

At my look of concern, he shook his head grimly. "No, she's not hurt. We had a wire from her the next day. She and Flaherty ran off together to Dublin where we can only hopefully assume they are now married."

"And a bad bargain Flaherty will get from that one," Cormac growled. "Only this time I'll not be wasting my time chasing after her."

"Kevin?" I had to know. "Was he alive when the groomsmen found him?"

Cormac shook his head. "Kevin must have been killed instantly, the doctors say; a pillar fell across his head. Of course, we had no way of knowing that you had been caught in the slide too." He frowned at me, puzzled. "And why should we? Didn't I see you myself go off in the carriage in a great hurry several hours before they carried Kevin back to the house? The coachman swore he saw you leave on the noon train for Dublin."

So Liam had made his escape after all, dressed as me, I thought, not sure whether I was relieved or dismayed. But not Kevin. I remembered with a shudder his mindless, desperate screams of fear as the rooks had swarmed around him. I wondered if Kevin heard, for a moment, as I had, in the frenzied cries of the birds, those tortured souls trapped and burned alive in the Abbey by Kevin's ancestor, at last exacting their own terrible vengeance.

Sean drew up a chair beside the bed and asked slowly, "It was Liam Carmody, wasn't it, who left in the carriage?"

"How . . . how did you know?"

He shrugged. "Liam's hair, it's almost your shade. And Carmody always had a flair for the dramatic." His mouth tightened and I saw, deep in his eyes, the banked anger. "But why the charade? What were you and Kevin doing in the Abbey ruins?"

I hesitated, uncertain, wondering how much of the story I should tell. With Kevin and Liam both gone, it was finished. What would be the good of dredging up the past now?

Sean's eyes searched my face as if he guessed what I was thinking. Sternly, he shook his head. "It's gone too far, *alannah*. And I'll not have you bear the burden of memory alone for the rest of your life."

And so I told them, not well, I'm afraid, stopping and starting haltingly; what I had pieced together on my own, what I had learned from Kevin those terrible moments in the Abbey before the rock slide.

When I finished, Cormac's massive head was slumped down on his chest, his voice harsh and broken. "I can believe there was no other way Michael could have had Fiona except through marriage. She would never have given herself to any man otherwise. Didn't I try every way I knew to twist the heart out of her? If I had not been such a young fool, I would have offered her marriage myself. There was no other woman I loved as much. It would have been a fine match, too, the two of us." He lifted his head and glared at me, as if daring me to disagree.

"But you said . . ." I fell silent, remembering those moments in his room when had boasted of his conquest.

Cormac's face burned a brick red, his voice was sheepish. "An old man's lies. I suppose I knew Michael always stood between us. I told myself I shipped Fiona off to America because it wasn't safe for her here in Ireland, but it was pride, not love, that sent her away."

"You saved her life. Seamus might not have failed a second time."

Cormac nodded dourly. "O'Toole made a good confession to Father Vincent before he died. He admitted Michael had paid him to get rid of Fiona. All these years, the money I've handed that blackhearted weasel faithfully, never knowing it was blackmail to keep him quiet, only knowing it was Michael's last wish." Cormac sighed gustily. "It's a sin to speak ill of the dead, and O'Toole did a good turn by dying anyway. At least, he cleared Fiona's name in the end. She was never the informer and he knew it. Oh, she warned Michael of the attack well enough, but she never gave names to the soldiers. It was O'Toole's brother Cullen, the poor sod caught and beaten until he was ready to tell the soldiers anything. He confessed the names of every man in the group before he died. But the shame of it kept Seamus from ever telling the truth about his brother, and he hated Fiona enough so that he willingly put the black name of informer on her."

"The people of Abbeymore," I said eagerly, "you'll tell them the truth?"

"That I will," the old man said gruffly. "They'll hear the truth. I'll swear to that. About the rest, the marriage of your mother to Michael and Patrick's murder, how much and how many will know of that . . ." He shook his head sadly. "I'd not pass the sorrow and shame of it on to Lady Margaret, but it's your decision, not mine, to make."

"Of course she mustn't know," I said, appalled at the thought. In any case, I didn't have the marriage lines and unless I intended to dig up the whole Abbey, I doubted if the document, or the jewels would ever be found. Then, remembering with a dull thrust of pain what I had overheard the doctors say, it didn't seem likely I would be doing any digging anyway, even if I wanted to.

Cormac's voice gentled as he looked at me. "You don't have Fiona's beauty, lass, but you have her loving heart." Then, as if ashamed of exposing any sign of weakness in himself, he scowled up at his son. "Well, why are you standing there like a great stone face? Are you as helpless as a boyeen? Must I do your courting for you too?"

A spark of amusement appeared in Sean's face, but his voice, as always, was properly respectful. "If there's any courting to be done, Father, it can wait until Miss O'Brien has recovered." He wheeled his father to the door where Cormac's manservant stood in the hall, waiting. "And don't you think you should be sending a message to the authorities in Dublin to be on the lookout for Liam Carmody? For all we know he may still be living in the lap of luxury at the Shelbourne Hotel as the wealthy Miss O'Brien.

"Sean . . . wait." There was something I had to ask him, not before his father, but alone.

He closed the door and returned at once to my bedside. The exhaustion was still there webbed across his face, but there was a wariness, too, his eyes guarded as he looked at me. I knew then it was true, what I had overheard the doctors say about my legs. I lost my courage and asked instead, "If they find Liam, won't he tell them about Kevin and the marriage? Suppose Lady Margaret should hear."

"There's few who'd believe such a story coming from a thief and a murderer," he said grimly, "especially with no evidence to back up his story. And you mustn't worry about my aunt. She isn't at Abbey Court any longer. As soon as Kevin was buried, she made arrangements to stay at the nunnery of the Poor Clares at Mallow. It's what she's always wanted."

I sank back, relieved. "At least then she'll never learn about Kevin and . . ." I broke off, finding it impossible even now to put the relationship between Kevin and Liam into words.

A shadow moved across Sean's face. He spoke thoughtfully. "Sometimes I think she suspected the truth, although, of course, it was never mentioned. And always before, Kevin had had the good sense to keep his . . . liaisons in Dublin or London, away from Abbey Court. Until Liam. I guessed what was happening between them but there was nothing I could do to stop it. I thought tumbling the Carmody cottage would end it, but I was wrong. God help us, Father and I were wrong about Patrick too. We thought . . ." He flushed and shrugged helplessly. "Patrick spent so much time with Kevin at the tower, and it was obvious he and Regan weren't getting along. When you came to Abbey Court and started looking into your brother's death, we were afraid you would find out about Patrick and Kevin. I didn't want you to be hurt that way."

Perhaps not completely wrong about Patrick, I thought, surprised that I could think it, even more surprised how little it mattered. For how unlike Patrick to strike out viciously at Kevin that way in the office. Had he been furious with Kevin, I wondered, or with himself for what he suspected about his own feelings? Well, none of it was important now nor altered in the slightest my love for Patrick, as if anything ever could.

Sean smiled wryly. "Since apologies seem to be in order, perhaps I should make one for Father and myself. Tact has never been Cormac's long suit, nor mine either, I'm afraid. If it's any defense, it's not uncommon, you know, in Ireland for a father to try to arrange a good marriage for his children. It's still done, all the time, and the larger the dowry, the more sought after the bride."

"I'm not a wealthy heiress," I blurted. "I don't have a mountain of silver. All I have is what Patrick left me and the house and Mother's jewels in Boston." Then, looking into Sean's face, at the utter lack of surprise in his expression, I said accusingly, "You knew that, didn't you?"

He nodded indifferently. "Patrick told me your mother had left you mostly stock in the Silver Lady Mine. Unlike Father, I keep up with the economic news in the United States. I happen to know that American silver stocks are depressed, practically valueless."

"And you didn't tell Cormac?" I said, shocked.

Sean grinned, drawling in the soft mocking brogue. "Sure and it's an obedient son I've always been. If Cormac wanted me to marry you, I'd not be the one to say no, even if my reasons for wanting you as my wife were not his own," he added softly.

He reached for my hand, his glance lingering on my face, centering on my lips, then leaned purposely downward. The delicious warmth I remembered so well flowed through me at his touch, until, remembering, I pulled myself free. My heart slammed in long, slow beats in my chest. "No," I said.

Sean straightened, scowling darkly. "I've been a thick-headed fool, Meg O'Brien, I'll not deny it. But if you'll not have me, I'll not come begging on my hands and knees."

I shook my head helplessly. "You don't understand. I can't . . . I heard the doctors talking . . . they said the bones in my legs would heal but the nerves . . . the nerves are permanently damaged. I'll not walk again."

The anger that flashed then in Sean's eyes was something to behold, like a great storm breaking over me with all its fury. His hands tightened on mine till I winced with the pain. "The doctors are grand fools, all of them!" His voice was a roar, pounding at me. "You'll walk again, Meg O'Brien. As proud as you please, you'll come walking down that church aisle to me, I promise you. And never again do I want to hear you say otherwise."

This time when Sean's arms closed fiercely around me I didn't pull away. Perhaps because, cowardly enough, I wanted so much to believe. Or perhaps because I knew the stubborn, ruthless tenacity that was part of the very bone and sinew and heart of the man.

During the pain-filled, exhausting months that followed, I learned to rely on that strength. The love woven daily ever stronger between us was a life line I clung to, as if to life itself. Never once in all that time did Sean relent or weaken in his determination that I would walk again. And never once did he allow me to falter or wallow in self-pity.

As soon as the bones in my legs had knit sufficiently so that the splints could be removed, he took me to Bath and carried me himself from my hotel room to the hot-water springs. When we returned to Abbey Court he imported a doctor from Sweden who was noted for his health-giving massages. Every day Sean insisted that I exercise my legs and try to force my muscles to respond, though months went by without the slightest reward for all my efforts, my legs with as little feeling in them as two slabs of wood.

Sean coaxed and cajoled me to continue the exercises and massage when the pain of frustration brought tears of rage to my eyes. He badgered and threatened me when, discouraged, I wanted to give up. One day when he found me sulking in my room, refusing to try again, he jeered at me for a quitter, "not worthy of the name O'Brien," and ducked handily when I flung a book at him and swore furiously in a way that would have made even Mother blush. But that was the day I finally managed to move my big toe, a grand triumph to be celebrated.

Through it all, Rory stayed, a golden shadow, by my side, a never ending source of quiet, loving encouragement. When I tried and failed, his tongue would lick gently at my hand in sympathy. And when I would like awake at night, unable to sleep, the rhythmic thumping of his tail on the floor beneath the bed would let me know he was there if I needed him.

The word brought from Dublin in November that Liam Carmody had been found in one of the seamier boardinghouses in Dublin, stabbed to death by the man he had been living with, brought no respite in my unending schedule of massage and exercise.

Sean even decided I should start working again on the

account books. We still fought about how the estate should be handled and we both managed to win some victories. I finally convinced Sean that the estate rents should be lowered, and as Cormac, every day growing more feeble, withdrew almost completely from running the estate, Sean was free to try his experiments, to increase the yield of the harvests, to plant more trees and buy more dairy and beef cattle. The suffering brought about by generations of greed and 'ignorance and indifference still lay over much of Ireland, but little by little at Abbey Court the oppressive hand had begun to lift.

Christmas was celebrated quietly at Abbey Court because we were still in mourning for Kevin and Patrick, and then on St. Stephen's Day, I took my first faltering, triumphant steps alone across the library into Sean's arms. Laughing, he swept me up and carried me to a chair in the front hall where the young men and women carrying holly and ivy, had gathered for the caroling. The courting couples, with Rose and her intended, stood among them.

As we listened to the carols, Sean's eyes met mine and I knew that in our hearts we were quietly pledging our own troth to each other, without any need of words. Then Sean insisted we must join in the merry singing of the young couples before they left, their pockets filled with coins, and for one night at least, old hatreds and hurts were forgotten at Abbey Court.

I whispered to Rose to stay behind a few minutes. I wanted to show her how I could take a few steps on my own. Sean watching me, the pride and love plain on his face for the whole world to see. Rose's eyes were bright with tears as she crossed herself happily and said, "It's a blessed miracle, that's what it is."

And perhaps, after all, she was right. For isn't love the greatest, most wonderful, miracle of them all?